This book is to be returned on or before the last date stamped below.

0 2 JAN 2013

LEES
NOV 18

A3 387 113 1

"I don't have much time," she said before he could speak.

"That's why I came to Silver Creek today. And that's why I'll need your answer right away. I know, this isn't fair, but if you say no, I'll have to try to find someone else...though I'm not sure I can." She didn't stop long enough to draw breath, and her words ran together. "Still, I'll understand if you want to say no, but, Grayson, I'm praying you won't—"

"What are you talking about?" he finally said, speaking right over her.

"Perhaps you should sit down for this."

"I'd rather stand," he let her know.

"No. Trust me on this. You need to be sitting."

That took him several steps beyond just being curious, and Grayson sank into the chair across from her. Eve sat as well, facing him. Staring at him. And nibbling on her lip.

"I'm not sure how to say this," she continued, "so I'm just going to put it out there." She paused. "Grayson," she finally said and looked him straight in the eyes. "I need you to get me pregnant. Today."

GRAYSON

BY
DELORES FOSSEN

MILLS & BOON

All the characters in this book have no existence outside the imagination of the author, and have no relation whatsoever to anyone bearing the same name or names. They are not even distantly inspired by any individual known or unknown to the author, and all the incidents are pure invention.

All Rights Reserved including the right of reproduction in whole or in part in any form. This edition is published by arrangement with Harlequin Enterprises II B.V./S.à.r.l. The text of this publication or any part thereof may not be reproduced or transmitted in any form or by any means, electronic or mechanical, including photocopying, recording, storage in an information retrieval system, or otherwise, without the written permission of the publisher.

This book is sold subject to the condition that it shall not, by way of trade or otherwise, be lent, resold, hired out or otherwise circulated without the prior consent of the publisher in any form of binding or cover other than that in which it is published and without a similar condition including this condition being imposed on the subsequent purchaser.

® and ™ are trademarks owned and used by the trademark owner and/or its licensee. Trademarks marked with ® are registered with the United Kingdom Patent Office and/or the Office for Harmonisation in the Internal Market and in other countries.

First published in Great Britain 2013
by Mills & Boon, an imprint of Harlequin (UK) Limited,
Eton House, 18-24 Paradise Road, Richmond, Surrey TW9 1SR

© Delores Fossen 2011

ISBN: 978 0 263 90340 9
ebook ISBN: 978 1 472 00685 1

46-0113

Harlequin (UK) policy is to use papers that are natural, renewable and recyclable products and made from wood grown in sustainable forests. The logging and manufacturing processes conform to the legal environmental regulations of the country of origin.

Printed and bound in Spain
by Blackprint CPI, Barcelona

Imagine a family tree that includes Texas cowboys, Choctaw and Cherokee Indians, a Louisiana pirate and a Scottish rebel who battled side by side with William Wallace. With ancestors like that, it's easy to understand why Texas author and former air force captain **Delores Fossen** feels as if she were genetically predisposed to writing romances. Along the way to fulfilling her DNA destiny, Delores married an air force top gun who just happens to be of Viking descent. With all those romantic bases covered, she doesn't have to look too far for inspiration.

OLDHAM METRO LIBRARY SERVICE	
A33871131	
Bertrams	07/12/2012
ROM	£5.49

Chapter One

Silver Creek, Texas

Sheriff Grayson Ryland couldn't shake the feeling that
someone was watching him.

He slid his hand over the Smith & Wesson in his
leather shoulder holster and stepped from his patrol
truck. He lifted his head, listening, and glanced around
the thick woods that were practically smothering the
yellow cottage. The front door and curtains were closed.

No sign of the cottage's owner, Eve Warren.

No sign of anyone for that matter, but just twenty
minutes earlier Eve had called his office to report that
she had seen someone *suspicious* in the area.

Grayson knew this part of the county like the back
of his hand. Along with his brothers, he had fished in
the creek at the bottom of the hill. He'd camped these
woods. There were a lot of places to duck out of sight….

Plenty of memories, too.

That required a deep breath, and he cursed himself
for having to take it.

The front door opened, and he spotted Eve. She was a

five-foot-six-inch memory of a different kind. She'd obviously known he was there. Maybe that was the reason his brain was firing warnings on all cylinders.

"Grayson," she said, her tongue flickering over her bottom lip. "You came."

That nervous little tongue flicker and the too-hopeful look in her misty blue eyes riled him. "You called the sheriff's office and asked for me," he reminded her. "You said you thought you saw someone."

"Of course." She nodded, swallowed hard. "But I wasn't sure you'd come."

Neither was he, especially since he was neck-deep in a murder investigation, but when he'd gotten her message, he'd decided not to send a deputy, that he would be the one to personally respond.

Well, respond to the call anyway.

Not to the woman.

Not ever again.

It'd been over sixteen years since he'd last seen Eve. She'd been standing in a doorway then, too. Her blond hair had been well past her shoulders back in those days, but it was short now and fashionably rumpled. The last decade and a half had settled nicely on her curvy body.

Something he decided not to notice.

Since his eyes and body seemed to have a different idea about that not-noticing part, Grayson got down to business.

"You reported someone suspicious?" he prompted.

"I did." She scrubbed her hands down the sides of her pearl-gray dress. The cold December wind caught the hem, making it flutter around the tops of her knees. "I was about to call you anyway…about something else… and then I saw him. A man. He was down by the creek."

Grayson lifted his shoulder and wondered why the heck she'd intended to call him, but he didn't ask. "Could have been a neighbor." Even though there weren't any close ones to the Warren cottage.

"I don't think it was a neighbor," Eve insisted. "I got a bad feeling when I spotted him."

Yeah. Grayson knew all about bad feelings. The one he had about this situation was getting worse with each passing moment.

"I didn't want to take any chances," she continued. "What with the murder you had here a few days ago. How are you handling that, by the way?"

She probably hadn't meant to irritate him with that question, but she did. Hell, no matter what she said, she would irritate him. But Grayson didn't want anyone, including Eve, questioning his ability to handle a murder investigation, even if it was only the third one in his twelve years as sheriff of Silver Creek.

"I heard you haven't identified the body, or the killer," she added.

"Not yet." And Grayson got back on target. "You have any idea who this person was you saw?"

Eve shook her head. "No. But for the past couple of days I've been getting hang-up calls at my condo in San Antonio. And there's been a time or two when I thought someone was following me. Nothing specific. Just a feeling. It was one of the reasons I decided to come out to the cottage. So I could get away."

Well, that explained that. Eve had inherited the cottage from her grandmother eighteen months ago, but to the best of Grayson's knowledge, this was her first visit to the place. And she hadn't just come to relax. She'd planned on calling him.

Why?

Again, he didn't ask. He kept this conversation focused on the job he'd been called out to do.

"Any reason you know of why someone would follow you or make those hang-up calls?" he asked.

Another head shake. "I've been under a lot of stress lately," she admitted. "The job. And some personal stuff. Until I saw the man, I kept telling myself that it was all in my head. But he was real, Grayson."

He mentally groaned at the way she said his name. It was intimate, the way she used to murmur it after one of their scalding hot kissing sessions.

He glanced at the woods, then the creek. "I'll have a look around," Grayson let her know. "But if you're worried, you probably shouldn't be staying out here alone."

He turned to have that look around.

"Wait," Eve called out. "Don't go. I wanted to ask about your family. How are your brothers?"

He had four living brothers. Four sets of news, updates and troubles. Since it would take the better part of an hour to catch her up on everything, Grayson settled for saying, "They're all fine."

Grayson turned again, but again Eve stopped him.

"Even Nate?" she questioned. "I heard his wife was killed a few months ago."

Yeah. That was all part of the troubles. The worst of them. "Nate's coping." But Grayson knew that wasn't true. If Nate didn't have his baby daughter to care for, his brother wouldn't make it out of bed each morning. Grayson was still trying to figure out how to take care of that.

"And the ranch?" Eve continued. "I read somewhere that the ranch won a big award for your quarter horses."

Fed up with the small talk, Grayson decided to put an end to this. Chitchat was an insult at this stage of the game. However, when he looked back at her, he saw that she had her hands clenched around the door frame. Her knuckles were turning white.

Grayson cursed under his breath. "Okay. What's wrong?" But he didn't just ask. He went closer so he could see inside the cottage to make sure someone wasn't standing behind her, holding her at gunpoint. Because Eve wasn't the white-knuckle type. He had never known anything to scare her.

The place was small so he was able to take in most of it with one sweeping glance. There was no one in the living and eating area, and the loft/bedroom was empty, too.

Grayson looked her straight in the eyes. "Eve, are you all right?"

She hesitated and nibbled some more on her lip. "I really did see someone about a half hour ago, I swear, and he ran away when he spotted me."

Since that sounded like the beginning of an explanation that might clarify the real reason for her call,
Grayson just stood there and waited for the rest of it.

"Could you come in?" Eve finally said. "I need to
talk to you."

Oh, hell. This couldn't be good. "Talk?" he challenged.

He was about to remind her that it was long over
between them, that they had no past issues to discuss,
but she kept motioning for him to come in.

"Eve," he warned.

"Please." Her voice was all breath and no sound.

Grayson cursed that *please* and the look in her eyes.
He knew that look. He'd seen it when she was thirteen
and had learned her mother was dying from bone cancer.
He'd seen it again sixteen years ago when on her twenty-
first birthday she'd stood in the doorway of the ranch
and demanded a commitment from him or else.

Because he'd had no choice, Grayson had answered
or else.

And Eve had walked out.

Now, Grayson walked in. She stepped back so he
could enter the cottage, and she shut the door behind
him. He didn't take off his Stetson or his jacket because
he hoped he wouldn't be here that long.

It was warm inside, thanks to the electric heater she
had going near the fireplace. No fire, though. And it
would have been a perfect day for it since the outside
temp was barely forty degrees.

With a closer look, Grayson could see the place was

in perfect order. Definitely no signs of any kind of struggle or hostage situation. There was no suitcase that he could spot, but Eve's purse was on the coffee table, and her camera and equipment bag were on the small kitchen counter. Several photographs were spread out around the bag. Since Eve was a newspaper photographer, that wasn't out of the ordinary, either.

"The pictures," she mumbled following his gaze. "I was trying to work while I waited for you."

Trying. And likely failing from the way they were scattered around. "Are you in some kind of trouble?"

"Yes," she readily admitted.

Surprised, and more worried than he wanted to be, he turned around to face her. "Trouble with the law?"

"I wish," Eve mumbled. She groaned softly and threaded her fingers through both sides of her hair. That stretched her dress over her breasts and gave Grayson a reminder he didn't want or need.

He'd been attracted to Eve for as long as he could remember. But he refused to let that attraction play into whatever the hell this was.

"Trouble at work?" he tried next.

She lifted her shoulder but answered, "No."

He glanced at the photos on the table again.

"I took those at a charity fundraising rodeo in San Antonio," she explained.

So, they were work, but judging from the casual way she'd mentioned them, they weren't the source of the worry in her eyes. "Look, I could play twenty questions and ask about a stalker, an ex or whatever. But let's save ourselves some time and you just tell me what you have to say."

She nodded, paused, nodded again. "It's personal. And it has to do with you. I need to ask you something."

Grayson braced himself for some kind of rehashing of the past. After all, he was thirty-eight now, and Eve was thirty-seven. Hardly kids. And since neither of them had ever married, maybe this was her trip back down memory lane.

Well, he didn't want to take this trip with her.

"I've been having some medical problems," she continued. But then paused again.

That latest pause caused Grayson to come up with some pretty bad conclusions. Conclusions he didn't want to say aloud, but his first thought was cancer or some other terminal disease. Hell.

Had Eve come home to die?

"What's wrong?" he settled for repeating.

She shook her head, maybe after seeing the alarm in his eyes. "No. Not that kind of medical problem."

Grayson silently released the breath he'd been holding.

"I'm, uh, going through, well, menopause," she volunteered.

Of all the things Grayson had expected her to say, that wasn't one of them. "Aren't you too young for that?"

"Yes. Premature menopause." She swallowed hard again. "There's no way to stop it."

Well, it wasn't a cancer death sentence like her mother's, but Grayson could understand her concern.

"So, is that why you're here, to try to come to terms with it?"

He'd asked the question in earnest, but he checked his watch. Talking with him wouldn't help Eve come to terms with anything, and he had work to do. That included a look around the place and then he had to convince her to head back to San Antonio. It was obvious she was too spooked and worried to be out in the woods all alone.

"I don't have much time," she said before he could speak. "That's why I came to Silver Creek today. And that's why I'll need your answer right away. I know this isn't fair, but if you say no, I'll have to try to find someone else…though I'm not sure I can." She didn't stop long enough to draw breath, and her words bled together. "Still, I'll understand if you want to say no, but Grayson, I'm praying you won't—"

"What are you talking about?" he finally said, speaking right over her.

Now, Eve stopped and caught on to the back of the chair. "Perhaps you should sit down for this."

The rushed frantic pace was gone, but her eyes told him this particular storm was far from being over.

"I'd rather stand," he let her know.

"No. Trust me on this. You need to be sitting."

That took him several steps beyond just being curious, and Grayson sank into the chair across from her. Eve sat as well, facing him. Staring at him. And nibbling on her lip.

"I'm not sure how to say this," she continued, "so I'm just going to put it out there."

But she still didn't do that. Eve opened her mouth, closed it and stared at him.

"Grayson," she finally said and looked him straight in the eyes. "I need you to get me pregnant. *Today.*"

Chapter Two

Eve had tried to brace herself for Grayson's reaction.

She'd anticipated that he might just walk out. Or curse. Or even ask her if she'd lost her mind. He might still do those things, but at the moment he just sat there while his jaw practically hit his knees.

Other than his slack-jaw reaction, there was no sign of the storm that she must have stirred up inside him. Not that Eve had expected him to show any major signs of what he was feeling.

Grayson was Grayson.

Calm, reliable, levelheaded, responsible.

Hot.

In those well-worn Wranglers, black Stetson, black shirt and buckskin jacket, he looked like a model for some Western ad in a glossy magazine.

A comparison he would have hated if he had known what she was thinking.

Even though he had that scarred silver badge clipped to his rawhide rodeo belt, Grayson was first and foremost a cowboy and, along with his brothers, owner of one of the most successful ranches in central Texas. That success was due in large part to Grayson.

There was nothing glossy about him.

Eve forced herself away from that mental summary of Grayson's attributes. His hot cowboy looks and ranching success weren't relevant here. It had been the calm, reliable, levelheaded and responsible aspects of his personality that had caused her to want him to father her child.

Maybe it was her desperation, but Eve had hoped that Grayson would also be cooperative. That slack jaw gave her some doubts about that though.

"When I was at my doctor's office this morning, I found out I'm ovulating," she continued. That seemed way too personal to be sharing with anyone except maybe a spouse or best friend, but she didn't have time for modesty here.

Time was literally ticking away.

"The fact that I'm ovulating is nothing short of a miracle," she continued. "The doctor didn't think it would happen, and it almost certainly won't happen again."

Grayson just kept staring.

She wished he would curse or yell, but no, not Grayson. Those silver-gray eyes drilled right into her, challenging her to give him an explanation that he could wrap his logical mind around.

There wouldn't be anything logical about this. Well, not on his part anyway. To Eve, it was pure logic.

"I desperately want a child, and I'm begging you to help me," she clarified in case the gist had gotten lost in all her babbling. "I don't have time to find anyone else. I've got twenty-four hours, maybe less."

Grayson dropped the stare, blew out a long breath and leaned back in the chair. He was probably glad that she had insisted on the being seated part.

He flexed his eyebrows. "How can you possibly ask me to do this?"

"You're the first person I thought of," she admitted.

Actually, he was the *only* person. Those Ryland genes were prime stuff, and all the Ryland males were able-bodied, smart as whips and drop-dead gorgeous with their midnight-black hair and crystal-gray eyes. Again, the looks were just icing.

Grayson wasn't just her first choice for this. He was her *only* choice.

"Don't say no," Eve blurted out when she was certain Grayson was about to do exactly that.

Now, he cursed. This time it wasn't under his breath. "No," he stated simply, but it had not been simply said. There was a flash of emotion in all those swirls of gray in his eyes. "You already know I don't want to be a father."

It was an argument that Eve had anticipated, and she had a counterargument for it. "Yes, because you had to raise your younger brothers after your father walked out and your mother died."

Now, *she* cursed. She should have rehearsed this. Bringing up Grayson's reckless father was not the way to earn points here even though it'd happened over twenty years ago when Grayson was barely eighteen. A lifetime wouldn't be long enough to forget or forgive that kind of hurt, and it had shaped Grayson to the very core of who he was now.

Yes, he'd been a father figure to his five younger siblings. Head of the ranch and the family. And he'd sacrificed so much for both that by the time Eve had been looking to settle down and have a family with him, Grayson no longer had anything to give anyone.

Including her.

Still, she wanted him for this massive favor.

"I'm not asking you to be a father." Eve tried and failed to keep the emotion out of her argument, but her voice broke. "I only need you to get me pregnant, Grayson. Nothing else. In fact, I would insist on nothing else."

She hated to put him into a corner as she'd done all those years ago. That had been a massive mistake. But she did need an immediate answer.

Grayson shook his head again and eased to the edge of the chair so they were closer. And eye to eye.

"I can't." He held up his hand when she started to interrupt him. "I know the difference between fathering a child and being a father. I can't say yes to either."

Oh, mercy. He wasn't even giving it any thought or consideration. He had doled out an automatic refusal. Eve had thought she had prepared herself for this, but she obviously hadn't. That sent her desperation to a whole new level. Everything inside her started to race and spin as if she were on the verge of a panic attack.

She immediately tried to come up with other ways

she could persuade him. First and foremost, she could try to use their past. Their connection. They'd been close once. Once, they'd been in love.

Well, she had been in love with him anyway.

Grayson never quite let himself take that leap of the heart, and he'd certainly never said the words.

She had hoped the close-to-love feelings that he had once had for her would be a trump card she could use here to convince him. Heck, she wasn't too proud to beg.

But she shook her head.

Begging might work. *Might.* However, this was Grayson, and because in the past she had loved him, Eve owed him more than that. She reined in her feelings and tried to say something that made sense. Something that would make him see that she wasn't crazy, just desperate.

"I'm sorry," she somehow managed to say. Her breath suddenly felt too thick to push out of her lungs, and she understood that whole cliché about having a heavy heart. Hers weighed a ton right now. "When the doctor told me I was ovulating and that I probably had a day or two at most, I thought of you. I jumped right in my car and drove straight to Silver Creek."

"I'm flattered. I think." The corner of his mouth lifted a fraction.

Ah, there it was. The biggest weapon in the Grayson Ryland arsenal. That half smile. Even now, after his refusal, it made her feel all warm and golden inside.

Since he'd attempted some levity, Eve did, too, but she doubted the smile made it to her eyes. God, this hurt. She wanted this baby more than her own life, and it was slipping away as the seconds ticked off.

"You can find someone else?" Grayson asked.

"I hope." But that was being overly optimistic. She'd lost a lot of time by driving out to Silver Creek, but then she'd had no choice. She very well couldn't have explained this with a phone call. Plus, she had prayed that she would be able to convince him once they were face-to-face.

She'd obviously been wrong.

Eve felt the raw blush on her cheeks and got to her feet. "I need to hurry back into San Antonio."

Grayson stood, as well. "Maybe you can use a sperm bank or fertility clinic?"

"No." She tried to blink back the tears, but failed at that, too. "Not enough time. The doctor said it takes days, even weeks to go through the screening and get an appointment. Plus, many of the clinics are closed because Christmas is only three days away."

He acknowledged that with a shrug. "A friend then?"

The drive had given her time to consider that, as well. It was sad but true that she was seriously lacking male companionship. Heck, she hadn't had a real date in nearly a year, and her last boyfriend was married now. As for male friends and coworkers, none had fit the bill as well as Grayson Ryland.

She shook her head and hurried to the kitchen where she crammed the photos back into her bag. The pictures were yet another kettle of fish, but they would have to wait. Eve wasn't ready to give up her baby mission just yet, even if she'd failed with Grayson.

She put on her red wool coat and hoisted both her purse and equipment bag onto her shoulder. Moving as fast as she could, she shut off the heater, unplugged it and turned back around to face Grayson. Even after his refusal, she couldn't help feeling that jolt of attraction when she looked at him.

Drop-dead gorgeous was right.

And for several brief moments Eve considered tossing the little bit of pride she had left. She could just throw herself at him and try to seduce him.

But she rethought that.

Grayson would resist. He had already shown her that he had a mountain of willpower and discipline to go along with those looks.

"What will you do?" he asked.

Because she felt the tears start to burn in her eyes, Eve dodged his gaze and grabbed her keys. "Maybe I can hire a friend of a friend."

She could make some calls the second she was back in her car, but she had no idea where to start.

"Hire someone?" Grayson questioned. He stepped outside the cottage with her.

Eve nodded. She closed and locked the door before she headed for her car. It wasn't below freezing, but the icy wind sliced right through her.

"You'd hire someone?" Grayson repeated when she didn't answer. He caught on to her arm and whirled her around to face him. "Eve, listen to yourself. Yes, I know you're desperate, and this baby must be important to you or you wouldn't have come here, but you can't just hire someone to sleep with you."

"To provide semen so I can be inseminated," she corrected, maneuvering herself out of his grip. She couldn't look at him and didn't want him to look at her. Eve hurried across the yard. "I have no intentions of sleeping with anyone to get pregnant. I was serious about not having a biological father in the picture. I'll make some calls, find a donor, pay him for his sperm, and, if necessary, I'll do the insemination at home."

Grayson made a sound of relief, or something. Probably because he'd thought she was indeed crazy enough to jump into bed with the first guy she ran across on the drive home. Eve's biological clock was screaming for her to do that, but she wanted a healthy baby and body.

"I want to raise a baby on my own," she continued. "And if I find someone, he'll have to agree to giving up his paternal rights."

No need to rehash the emotional baggage that had brought her to that conclusion. Besides, Grayson knew about her absentee father and the abusive stepfather that she'd had as a kid. He didn't know about the three failed relationships she'd had since leaving Silver Creek, and that included one episode of her being an honest-to-goodness runaway bride.

It was just as well he didn't know that.

Best not to spell it out that she considered Grayson and only Grayson for a life partner. He was literally the only man she trusted, even if he had crushed her heart all those years ago. And now he'd managed to do it again.

Frustrated with herself and her situation, Eve threw open the back door of her car so she could dump her bag and equipment onto the seat. She hesitated for just a moment because she knew Grayson was right behind her. If she turned around, she'd have to face him once more.

"I'm sorry I bothered you," Eve mumbled.

She turned and, still dodging his gaze, she tried to sidestep around Grayson.

He sidestepped, too, and blocked her path. She hadn't thought it possible, but he looked more uncomfortable than she felt.

"I can call the Silver Creek Hospital," Grayson suggested. "Doc Hancock might be able to pull some strings and speed up things with a sperm bank. Or I could talk to my brothers. They might know—"

"Don't involve your brothers," Eve interrupted.

Anything but that. Just talking about this would be hard enough for Grayson, especially telling them that he had turned her down. Eve didn't want to be the subject of conversation at the Ryland dinner table.

"Best not to involve anyone from Silver Creek," she added. "I'll go to a hospital in San Antonio and, well, beg." And she would. This pregnancy was going to happen, even if she didn't have a clue how she would manage it.

She stepped around him and hurried to the driver's

side of the car. Since she wasn't looking at Grayson, that was probably the reason she saw the movement.

In the cluster of trees about fifty yards from her car.

"What?" Grayson asked when she froze.

Eve looked around the trees, trying to figure out what had caught her attention.

There.

She saw the man.

Dressed in a dark shirt and pants, he had a black baseball cap sitting low on his head so that it obstructed his face. He quickly ducked out of sight, but from just that quick glimpse, Eve recognized him.

"That's the same man I saw earlier, by the creek," she told Grayson.

Grayson drew his gun from the shoulder holster beneath his jacket. The metal whispered against the leather, and he moved in front of her. "Any idea who he is?"

"No." But she knew that he was hiding, and that couldn't be good.

Did this have anything to do with the hang-up calls she'd been getting? Or could it be her imagination working overtime? Everything suddenly seemed to be going against her.

"I'm Sheriff Grayson Ryland," Grayson called out. "Identify yourself."

Eve stood there and held her breath, waiting. But the man said nothing.

"You think it's a local kid playing a prank?" she whispered, praying that was all there was to this.

Grayson fastened his attention to those trees. "No. A local kid would have answered me."

True. Grayson commanded, and got, respect in Silver Creek. And that caused her heart to pound against her chest. After all, there was a killer on the loose. Eve almost hoped this was connected to the hang-up calls. Better that than having a killer just yards away.

Grayson lifted his gun, and he took aim. "Well?" he prompted, his voice loud enough that the person hiding wouldn't have any trouble hearing him. "Come out so I can see who you are."

Still nothing.

"Get in your car," Grayson instructed from over his shoulder. "I'll get a closer look."

Eve wanted to latch onto him, to stop him from walking toward those trees, but this was his job. Plus, Grayson wouldn't stop. Not for her. Not for anyone.

"Just be careful," she whispered, her voice cracking a little. Eve eased open her car door and ducked down to get inside.

The sound stopped her.

It was a loud blast, and it shook the ground beneath them. Her stomach went to her knees, and her breath stalled in her throat. For a split second she thought someone had shot at them.

But this was much louder than a gunshot.

"Get down!" Grayson shouted.

He didn't give her a chance to do that on her own. He hooked his arm around her waist and pulled her behind her car door and to the ground.

Eve glanced behind her, at the cottage, and she saw what had caused that nightmarish sound.

An explosion.

Her grandmother's cottage was on fire.

Chapter Three

What the hell was going on?

That was Grayson's first thought, quickly followed by the realization that if Eve and he had stayed inside the house just a few more minutes, they would have both been blown to bits.

Behind them, the cottage had orangey flames shooting from it, and there was debris plunging to the ground. Maybe a propane tank had exploded or something, but Grayson wasn't sure it was an accident.

After all, there was a guy hiding in the trees.

Grayson figured it was too much to hope that the two things weren't related.

Had this person somehow rigged the explosion? If so, that meant the man would have had to have gotten close enough to the cottage to tamper with the tank that was just outside the kitchen window, but Grayson hadn't heard him. Of course, he'd been so involved with Eve's baby bombshell that he might not have noticed a tornado bearing down on them. He would berate himself for that later.

Now, he had to do something to protect Eve.

Grayson took cover in front of her and behind the car door, and he re-aimed his gun in the direction of the person he'd seen just moments before the explosion.

"Get out here!" he shouted to the person.

After hearing no response to his last demand, Grayson didn't expect the guy to comply this time. And he didn't.

No answer.

No sign of him.

Grayson kept watch behind them to make sure no one was coming at them from that direction. Other than the falling debris, the fire and black smoke smearing against the sky, there was nothing.

Except Eve, of course.

Her eyes were wide with fear, and he could feel her breath whipping against his back and neck. "We could have died," she mumbled.

Yeah. They'd been damn lucky. A few minutes wasn't much of a window between life and death, and her storming out had literally saved them.

Because she looked to be on the verge of panicking, Grayson wanted to reassure her that all would be fine, but he had no idea if that was true. The one thing he did know was that it wasn't a good idea for them to be in the open like this. There could be a secondary explosion, and he needed to get Eve someplace safe so he could try to figure out what had just happened.

He glanced at his truck, but it was a good thirty feet away. Too far. He didn't want Eve to be out in the open that long. There wasn't just the worry of a second explosion but of their tree-hiding *friend* and what he might try to do.

"Get inside your car," he told Eve, "and slide into the passenger's seat so I can drive."

"Oh, God," he heard her say.

And Grayson silently repeated it. He didn't know just how bad this situation could get, and he didn't want to find out with Eve in tow.

"Put the keys in the ignition," Grayson added when he felt her scramble to get into the car. "And stay down. Get on the floor."

No *Oh, God* this time, but he heard her breath shiver as it rushed past her lips. He wasn't exactly an old pro at facing potentially lethal situations, but he had the training and some experience during his time as sheriff. This had to be a first for Eve.

Not too many people had ever come this close to dying.

Grayson glanced behind him to make sure she had followed his orders. She had. Eve had squeezed herself in between the passenger's seat and the dashboard. It was safer than sitting upright, but Grayson knew a car wouldn't be much protection if anything was about to happen. A secondary explosion could send fiery debris slamming right into them.

He tried to keep watch all around them while he eased into the driver's seat and adjusted it so he'd fit. He needed to put some distance between the cottage, woods and them, and then he would call for assistance. Someone could take Eve to the sheriff's office, and

Grayson could figure out why all of this didn't feel like an accident.

While keeping a firm grip on his gun, he shut the car door and started the engine. He took out his phone and handed it to Eve. "Call the fire department."

She did but without taking her stunned gaze off the flames that were eating their way through what was left of the cottage. It had to break her heart to see the damage, and later the full loss would hit her.

As if she hadn't had enough to deal with for one day.

Even now, with the chaos of the moment, he still had her request going through his head.

I need you to get me pregnant.

He'd made it clear that wasn't going to happen, so the situation was over for him. But not for Eve. He had seen that determination in her eyes, and one way or another, she was going to get this dream baby. Hell, this near-death experience might even make her more determined.

"Hang on," Grayson warned her as he drove away— fast. He didn't exactly gun the engine, but he didn't dawdle, either.

The narrow road was dirt, gravel and mud since it had rained hard just that morning. With the sinkholes poxing the surface, it was impossible to have a smooth ride. But a smooth ride was an insignificant concern. Right now, he just wanted Eve out of there so he could deal with this situation on his own terms.

In other words, *alone*.

"The gas was turned off," Eve murmured. "It's been turned off for months. So, what caused the explosion?"

"Maybe a leak in the gas line." And if so, that would be easy to prove.

"Call the first number on my contact list," Grayson instructed. It was for the emergency dispatcher in the sheriff's building. "I want at least one deputy out here with the fire department. Have them meet me at the end of the road."

Once help arrived, he could hand off Eve to whichever deputy responded, and Grayson could escort the fire department and others to the scene. He didn't want anyone walking into a potential ambush.

Eve made the call, and he heard her relay his instructions to the emergency dispatcher. Just ahead, Grayson spotted the first curve of the snaky road. He touched the brakes.

And nothing happened.

Nothing!

The car continued to barrel toward the curve. So, Grayson cursed and tried again, but this time he added a lot more pressure.

Still nothing.

Hell.

"What's wrong?" Eve asked.

Grayson dropped his gun onto the console between them so he could use both hands to steer. "I think someone cut the brake line."

Eve put her hand against her chest. "W-hat?"

She sounded terrified and probably was, but Grayson

couldn't take the time to reassure her that he was going to try to get them out of this without them being hurt. The curve was just seconds away, and the road surface was as slick as spit. But his biggest concern was the trees. The road was lined with them, and if he crashed into one of them, Eve and he could both be killed on impact.

"Get in the seat and put on your seat belt," he told her, fastening his attention on the curve.

She scrambled to do just that, but he figured there wasn't enough time. To buy them a little more of that precious time, Grayson lifted the emergency brake lever, even though it wouldn't help much. The emergency brake would only work on the rear brake, and it wouldn't slow them down enough. Still, he had to try anything to reduce the speed.

"Hold on," he warned her.

Eve was still fumbling with the seat belt when the car went into the curve. Grayson had no choice but to try to keep the vehicle on the road since the trees were just yards away.

The right tires caught the gravel-filled shoulder, kicking up rocks against the metal undercarriage. The sound was nearly deafening, and it blended with his own heartbeat, which was pounding in his ears.

Eve's car went into a slide, the back end fishtailing. Grayson steered into the slide. Or rather that's what he tried to do, but he soon learned he had zero control. He saw the trees getting closer and closer, and there wasn't a damn thing he could do about it.

For just a split second, he made eye contact with Eve. Her gaze was frozen on him while her hands worked frantically to fasten the seat belt. Her eyes said it all.

She thought they were going to die, and she was silently saying goodbye.

Grayson didn't say goodbye back because he had no intention of dying today.

He heard the click of her seat belt, finally. And Grayson jerked the steering wheel to the left. The car careened in that direction, but not before the back end smashed into a live oak tree. The jolt rattled the entire vehicle and tossed them around like rag dolls.

Thank God they were wearing their seat belts.

He also thanked God that he was able to hang on to the steering wheel. They'd dodged a head-on collision, and the impact with the tree had slowed them down some, but they literally weren't out of the woods yet.

The car went into a skid in the opposite direction.

More trees.

Grayson didn't even bother to curse. He just focused all his energy on trying to control an out-of-control car.

And it was a battle he was losing.

There was a trio of hackberry trees directly in front of them. If he managed to miss one, he would no doubt just plow into the others, or one of their low-hanging limbs.

He fought with the wheel, trying to make it turn away, but they were in another skid, the mud and rocks helping to propel them in a direction he didn't want to go.

"There's the man we saw earlier," Eve said, her voice filled with fear.

She pointed to Grayson's right, but he didn't look in that direction. Not because he doubted her. No. The hiding man probably was there, but Grayson had to give it one last-ditch effort to get the car into the best position for what would almost certainly be a collision.

"Cover your face," Grayson managed to warn her. Because the limbs would probably break the glass.

His life didn't exactly flash before his eyes, but Grayson did think of his family. His brothers. His little niece, Kimmie.

And Eve.

She was there, right smack-dab in the middle of all of his memories.

He watched the front end of the car slide toward the middle tree, but at the last second, the vehicle shifted. No longer head-on. But the driver's side—his side—careened right into the hackberry.

Grayson felt the air bags slam into his face and side. The double impact combined with the collision rammed him into Eve and her air bag. There were the sounds of broken glass and the metal crunching against the tree trunk. The radiator spewed steam.

"We're alive," he heard Eve say.

Grayson did a quick assessment. Yeah, they were alive all right, and the car was wrapped around the hackberry.

"Are you hurt?" he asked Eve, trying to assess if he had any injuries of his own. His shoulder hurt like hell, but he was hoping it was just from the air-bag punch and that it hadn't been dislocated. He would need that shoulder to try to get them out of this crumpled heap of a car.

When Eve didn't answer, Grayson's stomach knotted, and he whipped his head in her direction. Her hands were on the air bag that she was trying to bat down, but her attention was fixed on the side window.

Grayson soon saw why.

The man, the one who'd hidden in the trees, was running straight toward them.

Chapter Four

The man was armed, a pistol in his right hand.

Eve heard Grayson yell for her to get down, but she didn't have time to react. Grayson pushed her down, her face and body colliding with the partially inflated air bag.

"My gun," he snarled.

Grayson cursed and punched at the air bags. He was obviously trying to find his weapon. When Eve had last seen it, Grayson had put it on the console, but the crash had probably sent it flying.

Oh, mercy.

That meant they were sitting ducks, unarmed, with a gunman bearing down on them. She couldn't get out of the car, not with the man so close and on her side of the vehicle. They couldn't get out on the driver's side because it was literally crunched around a tree. Thank God for the air bags, or Grayson would have been seriously injured or killed.

Eve glanced up at the approaching man. The person who was likely responsible for the explosion that had destroyed her grandmother's cottage. The fear raced through her.

Still, she felt anger, too.

This idiot had endangered them and was continuing to do so. She wouldn't just stand by and let him shoot Grayson and her. Neither would Grayson.

They both grappled around the interior of her car, and Eve remembered her own gun in the glove compartment. It took some doing to get the air bag out of the way, but she finally managed it. She threw open the glove box door, latched onto the gun and handed it to Grayson.

He immediately took aim.

The man must have seen him do that because he ducked behind a tree. She wasn't sure if that was a good or bad thing. If the man had stayed out in the open, Grayson would have had a clean shot. This way, they were still trapped.

"One of the deputies will be here soon," Grayson reminded her.

Probably one of his brothers. Both Dade and Mason were Silver Creek deputy sheriffs, and since Grayson had requested backup, they would no doubt get there as soon as humanly possible.

But that might not be soon enough.

Using his left hand Grayson continued to bat away the air bag, but he kept his attention pinned to the tree where the man had ducked out of sight. Eve kept watch as well, but there were other trees near that one, and it wouldn't take much for the man to move behind one of those closer trees and sneak right up on them.

"Who is he?" Eve meant to ask herself that question, but she said it aloud.

"I don't know," Grayson answered. "But he could be the killer we're after."

Yes. Eve was aware that there was an unidentified killer on the loose.

Thanks to the newspaper coverage, she was also aware that just a few days ago a young woman's body had been found in the creek. The woman had been fully clothed, no signs of sexual assault, but her fingerprints and face had been obliterated. That's the term the press had used, *obliterated,* and Eve had assumed the killer had done that to prevent her from being identified.

It had worked.

So, why would this killer come after Grayson and her now?

Until the body was identified, and that might never happen, it wasn't likely that Grayson would be able to come up with a list of suspects.

But Eve had a sickening thought.

Perhaps the man had killed the woman in or near the cottage. Maybe he was destroying any potential physical evidence that would link him to the crime. And here she'd walked in with so much on her mind that she hadn't even considered a trip home could be danger-ous. This in spite of her knowing about the murder that possibly happened just a stone's throw away from the cottage.

That oversight could be deadly.

She choked back a sob. Only minutes earlier her main worry had been getting pregnant, but for that to happen Grayson and she had to survive this. If something went wrong and he got hurt, it would be her fault because he wouldn't have been out here in these woods if she hadn't called him.

"I'll get you out of here," she heard Grayson say.

It sounded like a promise. But Eve knew backup was still a few minutes away. A lot could happen in those few short minutes.

Because she had her attention pinned to that tree, she saw the man lean out. Or rather she saw his gun.

"Get down!" she warned Grayson.

Just as the shot slammed through the window directly above Eve's head. The sound was deafening, and the bullet tore through the safety glass.

Grayson moved forward, his body and forearm pushing her deeper onto the floor so that she could no longer see what was going on.

And Grayson fired.

Eve automatically put her hands over her ears, but the blast was so loud that it seemed to shake the entire car. What was left of the safety glass in the window came tumbling down on top of her.

Grayson elbowed the chunk of glass aside and fired another shot. All Eve could do was pray, and her prayers were quickly answered. Even with the roaring in her ears from the shots, she heard a welcome sound.

A siren.

Maybe the fire department. Maybe a deputy. She didn't care which. She just wanted Grayson to have backup. Her gun was fully loaded, but Eve didn't have any other ammunition with her, and she didn't want to risk a gun battle with the man who had a better position behind the tree.

"The SOB's getting away," Grayson growled.

Eve hadn't thought this situation could get more frightening, but that did it. If he managed to escape, he might try to come after her again.

She didn't need this, and neither did Grayson.

Grayson obviously agreed because he climbed over her and caught on to the door handle. He turned it, but it didn't budge. Eve didn't relish the idea of Grayson running after a possible killer, but the alternative was worse. Besides, the gunman had quit shooting.

For now, anyway.

Eve rammed her weight against the door to help Grayson open it. It took several hard pushes, but with their combined effort the door finally flew open.

"Be careful," she warned him.

"You, too," Grayson warned back. "Stay put and try to find my gun. I figure he's trying to get as far away from that siren as he can, but if this guy is stupid and doubles back, shoot him."

That didn't help with her ragged nerves, but as Grayson sprang from the car, Eve made a frantic search for the gun. She also kept watch, blindly running her hands over the floor and seats.

The sirens got closer, and she saw the flashes of blue lights at the end of the road. Backup was just seconds away, but Grayson was already running past the tree that the gunman had hidden behind.

Her fingers brushed over the cold gunmetal, finally, and Eve snatched up Grayson's Smith & Wesson. Her hands were shaking like crazy, but she positioned the gun so it would be easier for her to take aim. But she was hoping that might not be necessary.

A Silver Creek cruiser came to a screeching stop next to her wrecked car, and she recognized the man who jumped out. It was Dade, Grayson's brother. Like Grayson, he wore jeans and a badge clipped to his belt, and he had his gun ready. He was lankier than Grayson, but Eve didn't doubt Dade's capabilities. From everything she'd heard, he was a good lawman.

"Eve?" he asked. Dade was clearly surprised to see her in Silver Creek. Then his gaze flashed to the cottage. Or rather what remained of it. It was still on fire, but there wasn't much left to burn.

Soon, very soon, it would be just a pile of ashes.

"Someone blew up the cottage. And then he fired a shot at us," she explained. "He might be the killer you're looking for." Mercy, her voice was shaking as badly as her hands, and she tried to rein in her fear so she could point toward the tree. "Grayson went after him."

Concern flashed through Dade's eyes, and he snapped his attention in the direction where she'd pointed. "Stay here," Dade said, repeating Grayson's earlier order. "The fire crew is right behind me. And keep that gun ready, just in case."

She watched him run toward the spot where she'd last seen Grayson, and Eve added another prayer for Dade's safety, too. Like all the Rylands, she'd known Dade her entire life, and even though he was only two years younger than she was, she had always thought of him as her kid brother. That probably had something to do with all the meals she'd helped cook for Dade and the others after their mother committed suicide.

"The dark ages," she mumbled.

That's how she'd always thought of that time twenty years ago when Grayson and his brothers had basically become orphans. During the years that followed, Eve had gotten close with all of Grayson's brothers, closer than she had been with her own family.

She blinked back the tears. And here she'd endangered yet another *family* member. Heck, Mason was probably on the way, too. Before the hour was up, she might have put all three of them at risk.

Eve heard a second set of sirens and knew that the fire department was close by. She stayed in the car, as both Grayson and Dade had warned her to do, but she moved to the edge of the seat, closer to the open door, so she could try to pick through the woods and see Grayson.

She still had sight of Dade, but Grayson was nowhere to be seen.

She glanced behind her at the fire engine as it made the final turn from the farm road onto the gravel drive that led to the cottage. The driver turned off the sirens, and everything suddenly went silent.

Eve could hear the wind assaulting the trees. She could hear her own heartbeat in her ears.

She also heard Dade shout, "Get down!"

And the sound of a gun going off ripped through the silence.

Chapter Five

Grayson cursed and dove to the ground.

He'd already had enough surprises today, and he didn't need this SOB firing any more shots at him. Besides, Eve wasn't that far away, and he darn sure didn't want a stray bullet traveling in her direction.

"You okay?" Dade called out. His brother had dropped to the ground, too, but was crawling toward Grayson.

"Yeah. I'm just fine and dandy," Grayson barked. "You see him?"

Dade didn't answer right away, giving Grayson some hope, but that hope went south when his brother finally said, "No."

Grayson lifted his head and examined the woods. Since it was the dead of winter, a lot of the foliage was gone, but that didn't mean there weren't plenty of places to hide.

And then Grayson heard something he didn't want to hear.

The sound of water.

Hell. This guy was in the creek, and that meant he was getting away.

Dade apparently heard it, too, because he cursed and got to his feet. So did Grayson, and they started to run toward the sound of that splashing. Of course, the splashing was long gone before they arrived on the creek bank.

And there was no sign of the gunman.

Dade and Grayson stood there, looking hard, but there was no way to tell which direction he went. If the guy was smart, he could have just floated downstream and out of sight. Of course, he could have scrambled over the outcropping of rocks on the other side of the creek bed and then disappeared into the dense woods.

"We need a tracking dog," Dade mumbled.

Yeah. And they needed their brother, Mason, out here on horseback. Mason was a better tracker than any dog or any of the local Texas Rangers, but Grayson intended to ask for their help, too. He wanted this gunman caught *now,* and he would use any resource available.

"I got a good look at his face," Grayson let Dade know. "If he's in the system, I think I can pick out his photo."

Though that would take time. Maybe lots of time. Something Grayson wasn't sure he had.

This guy would be back.

The question was why? Grayson was sure if he could figure that out, then he would have a better chance of identifying him and stopping another attack.

"Why don't you get Eve away from here? She's pretty

shaken up," Dade suggested. He took out his cell phone. "I'll start making calls."

Grayson started to say no, that he wanted to stay. If they got lucky with the search, he wanted to be the one to put the cuffs on this piece of slime, but Dade was right. Eve didn't need to be here. Neither did he. His brothers could handle it and handle it well. So he turned and headed back toward Eve and her car.

He spotted her the moment he came out of the thick cluster of trees. She was out of the wrecked car, talking to Dusty Bullock, the fire chief. She looked calm enough, but Grayson knew that underneath her nerves had to be raw since to the best of his knowledge this was the first time she'd experienced anyone trying to kill her.

And there was no doubt that the killing attempt had been aimed at Eve.

When she saw Grayson, Eve ran toward him, but he quickly closed the distance between them because he didn't want her out in the open.

"Did you catch him?" she asked.

Grayson shook his head and watched her expression go from shock to fear. Yeah. She understood how important it was for them to find this gunman *today*.

Since she looked ready to launch herself into his arms, or cry, he took his gun from her, reholstered it and handed Eve her handgun. She slipped it into her coat pocket. And Grayson caught on to her shoulder so he could lead her in the direction of his truck.

"I need to get you back to my office," he grumbled.

Grayson hated the gruffness in his voice. Hated even more that he couldn't comfort her at a time when she needed comforting, but after the conversation they'd had in the cottage, it was best if he kept his distance.

"But what about the gunman?" she challenged. "He's still out there."

"Dade's looking for him, and we'll bring in help." Grayson stopped next to the fire chief. "Call me the minute you know what caused the explosion in the cottage."

"You're thinking it was foul play?" Dusty asked, his craggy face bunched up with concern.

"Yeah," Grayson answered honestly, though he knew that would cause Eve more panic. "I want the brake line on Eve's car checked, too, because I'm sure someone cut it."

"Oh, God," Eve mumbled.

He got her moving again, but she stopped first to retrieve her purse and equipment bag from her car. Since she looked ready to fall apart, Grayson decided to use the drive to his office to get her to concentrate on how they could bring this nightmarish day to a good conclusion.

A conclusion that would end with an arrest.

"Did you see the gunman's face?" Grayson asked. He drove away from her cottage, which would soon be taped off and processed as a crime scene.

"Not really." When she couldn't get her seat belt on after two tries, Grayson reached over and helped her. His hand brushed against hers, and he quickly pulled back. With the energy between them already on edge, it was best to avoid touching her.

And *thinking* about touching her.

Something he didn't quite accomplish.

Grayson huffed and continued. "The gunman had brownish-red hair. About six-two. Around a hundred and seventy pounds. Ring any bells?"

She shook her head. "Should it?"

"Maybe. I figure you've crossed paths with him. Why else would he want to come after you that way?"

Eve mumbled another "Oh, God," and plowed her fingers through the sides of her hair. "I don't recognize him." She pressed hard against her temples and head. "What could I have done to make him want to kill me?"

That was the million-dollar question, and Grayson had to explore all possibilities. "An old boyfriend, maybe? Maybe he altered his appearance so that you didn't easily recognize him?"

Her hands slipped from her hair and dropped into her lap. She stared at him. "You're the only boyfriend I have who's riled at me."

"I'm not riled," Grayson protested.

She huffed. "You're riled all right."

He huffed, too. "Just because I turned down your offer to make a baby doesn't mean I'm pissed off." But when he heard his tone, he realized he was. Grayson cursed. "I just wasn't expecting you to ask anything like that, okay? You surprised the hell out of me."

"Yes, I figured that out. But you can't blame me for trying. I just thought… Well, I just thought *wrong*."

She was right about that. So, why did Grayson feel so blasted guilty for turning her down? Since that was something he didn't want to think or talk about, he went back to the investigation. They were still fifteen minutes out from his office, and he wanted to put that time to good use instead of adding to that guilt trip.

"I heard you were engaged but broke things off," Grayson tossed out there. "Could your ex be holding a grudge?"

She mumbled something he didn't catch. "No. It's true, I called things off the day of the wedding, but he's moved on and already married to someone else."

Maybe her ex-fiancé had indeed moved on, but Grayson wanted to verify that was true. Love and love-scorned were motives for a lot of crimes.

And a lot of questions.

He wanted to ask Eve why she'd waited until her wedding day to end things, but it was none of his business.

"How about a member of your ex's family?" he pressed. "Sometimes family members or friends think they need to avenge a broken heart."

She sat quietly a moment. And she didn't deny that broken heart part. "Why wait over a year to get revenge?" She shook her head again. "I was thinking maybe what happened today has to do with the killer. Maybe he was trying to destroy evidence by destroying the cottage?"

Yes. That was the next theory on Grayson's list. Perhaps the killer had left some kind of forensic evidence in or near the cottage. That was a solid reason to destroy it.

"But then why would he want to kill you?" Grayson pressed. He turned off the ranch road and onto the highway that would take him back into town. "Is it possible you know something about the murder?"

"How could I? I wasn't in Silver Creek when it happened. I was in San Antonio."

"The murder might not have happened in Silver Creek," he reminded her. "In fact, I suspect it didn't. I think the body was just dumped there."

She gave him a flat look. "Trust me, I would have remembered if I'd witnessed someone being murdered."

True. But there had to be a reason this guy was after her. Grayson really needed to get an ID on that body because he couldn't shake the feeling that the dead woman and this attack were connected.

"We don't have an identity on the dead woman, but she was five-six and was in her early twenties." Grayson hoped that would spur Eve to remember something.

Eve nodded. "I read that in the paper. Her face and fingerprints had been obliterated." She paused. "What does that mean exactly?"

"You don't want to know." But Grayson would never forget the sight of what was left of the woman. Someone had literally bashed in her face so that none of her features had been recognizable, and then cut off the pads of her fingertips. He'd also broken off her teeth, probably so that dental records couldn't be used to identify her. "But the killer didn't obliterate her hair, and it's unique.

Three colors—red, black and blond. Remember seeing anyone with hair like that?"

She shrugged. "It's possible. That type of hair isn't so rare in a city the size of San Antonio."

True. But it was the only thing he had to go on. Now it was time to grasp at a few straws. "When did you start getting hang-up calls?" Grayson pressed.

"Four days ago," she answered without hesitation.

Four days. According to the ME, that was an estimate of when the woman had been killed.

He was about to continue his questions when Grayson spotted the familiar rust-scabbed red truck barreling down the highway. It was his brother, Mason, responding to the scene. Grayson didn't slow down. Neither did Mason. They exchanged a glance, and in that split-second glance, Grayson saw exactly what he wanted to see: Mason's determination to find the man who'd taken shots at Eve and him.

Sometimes keeping Mason's intense moods under control was like trying to keep a leash on a rogue bull. But it was that intensity that made Mason a good cop. Mason wasn't the sort of man Grayson would go to with his personal problems—he wouldn't get much empathy there—but for everything else Mason was the brother he knew he could rely on the most.

Grayson stopped in the parking lot of his office and turned to Eve. "I need to get your statement about what just happened and ask you a few more questions about those hang-up calls. Then I can take you to the ranch. You can stay there until we catch this guy."

She was already shaking her head before he finished. "I can't go to your ranch."

No. He didn't have time for this argument. "Look, I know it might be a little uncomfortable for you there, what with Dade and Mason around—"

"It's not that. I'm comfortable with your family. Always have been."

Grayson couldn't argue with that. Heck, his brothers had, and probably always would, consider Eve a sister. His youngest brother, Kade, often said that Eve was more like a mother to him than his own mother had been.

So what was Eve's issue?

She stared at him. "I need to get back to San Antonio, and I intend to do that as soon as I can arrange for transportation. Your reports will have to wait. I have to find a place where I can be inseminated *today*."

Grayson was sure he looked at her as if she'd lost her mind. "Eve, someone tried to kill you," he reminded her, though he was positive she hadn't forgotten that.

Her hand was still shaking when she touched her fingers to her lips. She paused a moment, still trembling, and her gaze came back to his. "If I don't do the insemination today, I'll never have a baby. And yes, I know there's a killer out there. And yes, that killer might have been the one to take shots at us today. But I don't have time to wait for him to be caught."

Grayson broke his no-touching rule and caught on to her shoulders. He wanted to make this very clear. But for a moment he lost his train of thought when he saw the nicks and scrapes on her face. From the air bag, no doubt. But even with the superficial damage, Eve was still the most beautiful woman he'd ever seen.

He pushed that thought aside with all the rest of the carnal things that came to mind whenever he looked at Eve. She had, and always would have, his number.

Grayson met her eye to eye. "The killer could come after you in San Antonio."

She blinked, swallowed hard. "So, I'll hire a bodyguard as soon as I call the rental car company to come and get me. I want to be on the road within the next thirty minutes."

He didn't know whether to curse or try to shake some sense into her. "Eve, is this baby worth your life?"

Her breath rattled in her throat. Tears sprang to her eyes. "Yes," she whispered.

And with that, she grabbed her equipment bag and purse and got out of his truck. The bag went on one shoulder. Her purse on the other.

Well, he'd asked the question, and even though it hadn't been the answer he wanted to hear, Grayson knew it was Eve's final answer. She wasn't going to budge on this.

Hell.

That meant he had to drive back into San Antonio with her. Or else send Dade or Mason. Now Grayson cursed because he sure didn't have time for this.

He got out, slammed the truck door with far more force than necessary and followed her into the back entrance of the law enforcement building. It wasn't a huge place—especially considering how much time he spent there. It had a reception area, four offices, two interrogation rooms and a holding cell on the bottom floor. There was an apartment-style break room on the top floor where there'd once been jail cells before a new facility had been built on the edge of town.

Grayson stepped inside and heard the day shift dispatcher, Tina Fox, talking from her desk in the reception area. An area roped off with twinkling Christmas lights and a miniature tree that played annoying tinny carols when anyone walked past it. Mason had already kicked it once. Grayson was considering the same. As far as he was concerned, this was a bah-humbug kind of Christmas, and this attempt to kill Eve wasn't doing much to change his opinion about that.

Tina looked back at him and waved. From the sound of it, she was getting an update from Dade. Soon Grayson would want that update as well, but first he had to deal with the most hardheaded woman in Texas.

Ahead of him, Eve made her way to his office while she fished for something in her purse. She finally pulled out her cell phone when she came to a quick stop. Her hand and phone had been moving toward her ear, but that stopped, as well. She stood there frozen, her gaze fixed on something in his office.

Grayson cursed and hurried to pull her aside because he knew what had shocked her. The crime board in his office had photos of the dead woman. Or rather what was left of her. To put it mildly, they weren't pretty.

"Sorry about that," he mumbled. And he crossed the

room to turn the board around so that the gruesome pictures would be facing the wall.

"Wait!" Eve insisted.

She walked closer, her attention nailed to the grisliest of the photos. It was a close-up view of the dead woman's bashed-in face and had been taken several hours after her body had been fished out of the creek.

"There's no need for you to see these," Grayson assured her. When he tried to turn the board again, she caught on to his arm to stop them.

She moved even closer, until her face was just inches from the photo. Eve mumbled something and then dropped her equipment bag onto his desk. Frantically, she began to rummage through it, pulling out the pictures that Grayson had seen earlier on the counter at the cottage.

"What is it?" he asked.

"I've seen her before." Her voice was all breath now. "Well, I've seen that hair anyway."

Grayson glanced back at the dead woman's hair, though the image was already embedded into his mind. He wasn't sure he'd ever be able to forget it. But the hair was certainly distinctive. Three colors. Red, blond, black, and the black was only on the ends of her choppily cut hair.

Eve continued to pull photos from her bag, glancing at each and then tossing them aside on the tops of folders and reports that Grayson had spread out on his desk. She plucked another from the bag and froze again.

Grayson looked at the shot from over her shoulder.

He recognized the location—it had been taken at the indoor rodeo arena in San Antonio. There were at least a dozen people standing at the railings, their eyes fixed on the bull rider who had just been tossed into the air.

Then he saw the woman.

And her hair.

"When did you take this?" Grayson couldn't ask the question fast enough. He grabbed the picture from her so he could study it.

"Four days ago at the fundraiser rodeo. I had these printed because I wanted to take a better look at them to see which to include in the story. But I didn't use this one." She paused. "It's her, isn't it?"

Grayson paused too, but not because he wasn't sure. He was.

The image of the dead woman stared back at him.

Chapter Six

Eve hadn't realized she was holding her breath until her lungs began to ache. "Is that the murdered woman?" she asked Grayson.

"Yeah," he finally said, his attention still glued to that photo. "Any idea who she is?"

"No, I took dozens of random shots that day. She was just someone in the crowd."

"Yes. But if the medical examiner is right, this is also the day she was murdered." He tipped his head to her bag. "I need to look at all the pictures."

She gave a shaky nod, and while she was doing that, Grayson peeled off his jacket and tossed it over the back of his chair. Then he put the photo on his fax machine. "I'm sending it to the Ranger crime lab in Austin with a request for immediate processing."

Good. Soon, he might have a name to go with that face.

Eve continued to dump pictures onto his desk, but with each one she mumbled a no. She huffed. "That's it. The only one I have of her."

"Then I'll have to get what I can from it."

He made several more copies of the picture, one that he pinned on to the corkboard with the other photos. The others, he put in his in-basket so he'd have them for other law enforcement agencies. Then, he sat at his desk, placing the original picture right next to him, and he fired off that request message to the Ranger crime lab.

While he did that, Eve took herself back to that photo session. It had been routine, something she'd done dozens of times.

"Four days ago," she said softly. "That's when my hang-up calls started."

That got Grayson's attention. He stood and stared at her, and Eve knew what he was thinking. Was there something in the photo that had caused the hang-up calls, the fire at the cottage and the shooting?

Was the killer in the photo?

Eve rifled through her equipment bag and came up with a small magnifying glass. She handed it to Grayson, and he used it to zoom in. She hurried beside him so she could take a look, as well.

Unlike the rest of the spectators, the woman wasn't looking at the bull rider. She had her attention on the man wearing a baseball cap on her left. Her face was tight, as if she was angry. *Very* angry. And the man had his hand gripped on to her arm.

"I'm pretty sure that's the guy who shot at us today," Grayson mumbled, tapping his finger to the guy in the baseball cap.

Eve sucked in her breath. She hadn't gotten a good

look at him, but the build was right. So was that baseball cap.

Grayson turned back to his keyboard. "I'll ask the
lab to put the entire picture into the facial recognition
program. It's the fastest way for us to get an ID."

Good. Eve wanted that. But she also wanted to get out
of there and on the road. It was already past noon, and
time was running out. She took out her cell to call for a
car rental, but before she could make the call, Grayson's
phone rang.

"Sheriff Ryland," he answered, and she knew from
his expression that whoever was on the other end of the
line was telling him something important. Was it possible the Rangers had already managed to ID the dead
woman? Eve prayed they had. Because the sooner that
happened, the sooner Grayson could proceed with the
investigation.

"Yeah. I'll let Eve know," Grayson mumbled several
seconds later. "What about the search? Any sign of the
gunman?" He paused. "Keep looking."

"What happened?" she asked the moment he hung
up.

"That was the fire chief." Grayson pulled in a long
breath. "He said he's positive someone tampered with
both your brakes and the gas line that led to the cottage.
Plus, there was a tracking device on your car."

Eve had tried to brace herself for bad news. After
all, it was a logical conclusion about the brakes and gas
line, but it still sent an icy chill through her. So did the
fact that someone had tracked her out to the cottage.

God, did someone really want her dead because she'd taken a photo?

"Do you park your car in a garage in San Antonio?" Grayson asked.

"No. I use the lot adjacent to my condo."

In other words, her vehicle had been out in the open. Not just there but at her downtown office, as well. Obviously, someone could have planted that tracking device at any time in the past four days. And during those four days, the person had no doubt watched her, plotting the best way to get the picture and eliminate her.

She held on to Grayson's desk to steady herself.

Grayson cursed, moved out of his chair, grabbed her arm and forced her to sit down. "I hope now you realize that going back to San Antonio is a bad idea."

Yes. She did. But that wouldn't stop her. "Then I'll go to Austin. I'm sure they have fertility clinics there."

Grayson didn't curse again, but the look he gave her showed the profanity he was choking back.

"I don't expect you to understand." She got to her feet and squared her shoulders. She looked him straight in the eye. "You're burned out with the whole idea of fatherhood so how could you understand that for me having a baby, *my* baby, is the most important thing in my life?"

Grayson looked her straight in the eyes, too. "Eve, what I understand is this killer knows you took his picture, and he'll do anything to get it back. I can keep you safe here in Silver Creek until we can get the picture printed in tomorrow's paper. That way, the killer won't have a reason to come after you because thousands of people will have seen his face, along with the woman he probably murdered."

She tried to shrug. Eve wasn't immune to the fear, but she wasn't giving in to it, either. "Then print the photo, and tomorrow I can celebrate both my insemination and my safety."

He didn't answer that and just kept glaring as if searching for the right argument to change her mind. There wasn't an argument that could do that.

Eve adjusted her cell again, ready to make her call. "I'll get a car rental, and on the drive to Austin, I'll phone clinics and start begging. One way or another, I'm getting pregnant today."

Now, he cursed and shook his head. "Give me a few minutes, and I'll drive you to Austin myself."

Eve hadn't thought the day could have any more surprises, but that was a big one, and she knew just how massive a concession that was for Grayson.

"You can't," she argued. "You have too much to do to babysit me."

"Save your breath," he growled. He grabbed his coat and put it on as if he taking his anger out on the garment. He also snatched the rodeo photo of the dead woman. "You're not the only hardheaded person in this room. And if you can make calls on the drive over, then so can I. If I have to, I'll run this investigation from my truck."

He brushed past her and headed for his door, and she heard him tell the dispatcher that he had to leave. Eve didn't want to think of what kind of complications this might cause for Grayson, but she knew it would. She also knew this was another huge compromise for him. Maybe Dade and Mason could find this gunman today so this would all be over.

She gathered up the pictures and stuffed them into the equipment bag. Her hand knocked against another photo. The only framed one on Grayson's desk. It was of his maternal grandfather, Sheriff Chet McLaurin.

Despite her own horrible circumstances, she smiled when she saw the man's face. Eve had known him well, and he'd become like her own grandfather. When he'd been murdered twenty years ago, Eve had grieved right along with the Ryland clan.

She wondered if Grayson and his brothers realized that the man in the photo was the reason they'd all gotten into law enforcement. An unsolved murder could do that. It was a wound that would not heal.

Eve spotted another wound.

The silver concho hooked on to the top of the frame. She recognized it, as well. Grayson's father had given all six of his sons a concho with the double *R* symbol of their family's ranch. He'd done that, and then less than a week later, he'd left Silver Creek and abandoned the very family that he claimed to have loved.

No wonder Grayson didn't want kids of his own.

He'd witnessed firsthand that parenthood could cut to the core. Eve swore she would never do that to her child.

"Ready?" Grayson said from the doorway.

She'd been so caught up in the picture of his grandfather and the concho that she hadn't noticed Grayson was there. He had also noticed what had caught her attention.

"Yeah," he mumbled as if he'd known exactly what she'd been thinking.

Eve silently cursed the legacy that Grayson's father had left him, and she stuffed the rest of her things into the equipment bag.

"You kept the concho he gave you," she commented as they went to his truck.

He didn't answer until they were both inside the cab of his truck. "Sometimes, it helps to remember how much I hate my father."

She stared at him. "How could that possibly help?"

"It's a reminder that sometimes the easy way out can hurt a lot of people."

He didn't look at her when he said that, and if Eve hadn't known him so well she might have thought that was a jab at her decision to go through with this insemination. But since she did know him, she figured he was talking about his family duties. For Grayson, family came first, and that hadn't always been easy for him.

"Mason put a bullet in his concho," Grayson said under his breath. He drove out of the parking lot and onto the road that would take them out of town and to the highway. "Then he nailed it to the wall directly in front of his bed so he could curse it every morning when he woke up."

Eve sighed. So much hurt caused by one man. Their

father, Boone Ryland. "I remember Dade told me that he threw his away."

"Yeah." And for a moment, Grayson seemed lost in those bad memories. The dark ages. However, his cell rang, and he morphed from the wounded son to steely sheriff.

"Sheriff Ryland," he answered. He put the phone on speaker and slipped it into a stand that was mounted to the dashboard. He also kept watch around them as they passed the last of the town shops.

"It's me, Dade. I just got off the phone with the Ranger lab. They got a match on the photo."

"Already?" Grayson questioned.

"It wasn't that hard. Her name is Nina Manning, age twenty-two, from Houston, and she had a record for drug possession and prostitution. There's also a year-old missing person's report complete with pictures."

"Nina Manning," Eve repeated. It didn't ring any bells.

"Is Eve still with you?" Dade asked.

Eve looked at Grayson and waited for him to answer. "Yeah. I have to drive her, uh, somewhere. But I want to know everything that's happening with the case. Any sign of the gunman?"

"No. But Mason's out here. If the guy's still in the area, Mason will find him."

Eve doubted the gunman was still around. Heck, he'd probably parked his car on one of the ranch trails and was now probably long gone. Or maybe he was looking for her. Despite the importance of Dade's call, that caused her to look in the rearview mirror. No one was following them. The rural road behind them was empty.

"Were the Rangers able to identify the other man in the picture who had hold of Nina's arm?" Grayson asked.

"There was no immediate match."

Grayson shook his head. "I think he's the guy who tried to kill us today so we need an ID."

"The Rangers are still trying," Dade assured him. "But they did get a match on the man to the woman's right. His name is Sebastian Collier."

Now, that rang some bells. Eve had seen the surname many times in the newspaper, mainly in the business and society sections. "He's related to Claude Collier, the San Antonio real estate tycoon?" Eve asked.

"Sebastian is his son," Dade answered. "And sonny-boy has a record, too, for a DWI and resisting arrest. Guess his millionaire daddy didn't teach him to call the family chauffeur when he's had too much to drink."

Eve picked up the photo that Grayson had brought along, and she zoomed in on the man to Nina Manning's right. Sebastian Collier looked like a preppy college student in his collared cream-colored shirt and dark pants. It certainly didn't seem as if he was with the woman with multicolored hair.

But then Eve looked closer.

Sebastian's attention was certainly on Nina. His eyes were angled in her direction, or rather in the direction of the grip the other man had on Nina's arm. Sebastian looked uncomfortable with the encounter.

"Keep pushing the Rangers," she heard Grayson tell

his brother. "I want that other man identified. I also want someone out to question this Sebastian Collier." He looked at his watch, mumbled something in disgust. "I'll try to get to San Antonio myself as soon as I'm sure Eve will be safe."

Dade assured Grayson he would do everything to get a name to go with that face in the photo, and he ended the call.

Eve hadn't missed Grayson's mumble of disgust, and she was positive she was the cause. He wanted to be in the heat of this investigation, but here he was driving her to Austin instead. She turned to face him, to tell him that he could just drop her off in Austin and leave. Not that it would do any good—he would insist on staying. But she had to try. This investigation was important to both of them.

However, before she could launch into another argument, she heard the sound.

It was a thick, hard blast.

At first she thought maybe they'd had a blowout. But the second sound was identical.

"Get down!" Grayson shouted.

Just as a third blast ripped through the truck window.

Chapter Seven

Grayson slammed his foot onto the accelerator to get Eve and him out of there, but it was already too late.

He heard the fourth shot, and he also heard Eve repeat his shouted command of *get down.* But he couldn't duck out of sight. He had to fight to keep them alive. He pushed Eve down onto the seat so that she wouldn't be hit with the bullet or the broken glass.

But the bullet didn't crash through the glass.

It hit the tire.

Grayson's stomach knotted, and he felt his truck jerk to the right. He fought with the steering wheel and tried to stay on the road, but it was impossible. The now-flat tire and metal rim scraped against the gravel shoulder.

"Hang on," he warned Eve.

They were going to crash.

He couldn't avoid that. However, the crash was the least of Grayson's worries. Someone had shot out the tire, and that someone was no doubt waiting for them. That meant Eve was in danger all over again, and Grayson cursed the bastard responsible for that.

There were no trees near the road, thank God, but

there were clusters about a hundred yards off the road. That's probably where the gunman was hiding. And then there was the creek directly in front of them. He didn't want to go there because there were some deep spots in the water that could swallow them up.

"We have to jump," Grayson told her, and he pumped the brakes to slow the truck as much as he could. However, he didn't have much control of the vehicle.

Jumping was a risk, but the greater risk would be to remain inside so the gunman would have an easier chance of killing them. Besides, there was that potential for drowning.

Eve didn't answer, but she nodded and caught on to the door handle.

"When you jump out, run toward the trees to the right," he added. "And grab my cell phone."

Grayson took out his gun. Eve grabbed the phone.

"Now!" He barreled out at the same time as Eve, and he hit the soggy ground ready to fire. The truck gave Eve some cover for just a few seconds, until it plunged nose-first into the creek.

The gunman fired, the shot kicking up mud and a clump of grass several yards in front of Grayson. Grayson returned fire, a single shot, praying it would buy Eve enough time. He could hear her running, but he had to do everything to keep the gunman's attention on him.

Grayson spotted the gunman, or rather the sleeve of his jacket. He spotted Eve, too. She had ducked behind an oak and had taken out her own gun from her coat pocket. She leaned out and took aim at the gunman.

What the hell was she doing?

That knot in his stomach twisted even harder. She had purposely left cover, the very thing he didn't want her to do. Grayson frantically motioned for her to get back. But she didn't. She fired. Her shot slammed into the tree where the gunman was hiding. The bullet didn't hit him, but it caused the man to jump back.

Even though Eve's diversion could have been deadly, it was exactly what Grayson needed because he scrambled toward Eve and dove behind the tree. He also caught on to her and pulled her deeper into the woods. He damn sure didn't want her to get hurt trying to protect him.

"Stay back," Grayson warned her in a rough whisper. But he soon realized that staying back might be just as dangerous as staying put. That's because the gunman was on the move. He dropped back into the thick patch of trees. The SOB was trying to circle behind them.

Grayson had faced danger alone and had even faced it with other lawmen, but being under fire with a civilian was a first. And to make matters worse, that civilian was Eve. He wished he could go back in time and save her from this.

He repositioned Eve behind him and went deeper into the woods as well, but not toward the gunman. They needed to get into a better position, so with Eve in tow, he started moving, going at a right angle. He tried to keep his steps light so that it wouldn't give them away, but that wasn't easy with the dead limbs and leaves littering the grounds.

Eve and he ran, until he lost sight of the road and truck, and he didn't stop until he reached a small clearing.

Another shot came at them.

It wasn't close, at least twenty feet away, but the gunman had sent it in their direction. However, Grayson now knew the gunman's direction, too.

He moved Eve to the right, and they followed the thick woods until they reached the other side of the clearing. Grayson glanced back at Eve to make sure she was okay.

Her breath was gusting now, she was pale, but she didn't appear to be on the verge of panicking. There was some fear there in her eyes, but there was also determination to get out of this alive.

Eve motioned across the clearing, and Grayson saw the gunman duck behind another tree. He caught just a glimpse of the man's face, but Grayson was more convinced than ever that this was the same person in the photo with the dead woman. Grayson hadn't had many doubts left that this was connected to the photograph Eve had taken, and he certainly didn't doubt it now.

The gunman continued to work his way to his right, and Grayson did the same. It was a risk taking Eve deeper and deeper into the woods, but he had to figure out a way to stop this guy. Preferably alive. But he was more than willing to take him out if it meant Eve and he could get out of there.

When they'd made it all the way to a new section of the creek, Grayson stopped and waited.

He didn't have to wait long.

Grayson spotted the gunman just as the man spotted them.

The gunman lifted his weapon, but Grayson was already braced for the attack. He shoved Eve back, took aim and fired before the gunman could. It was a sickening sound of the bullet slamming into human flesh.

A deadly thud.

Clutching his chest, the man flew backward and landed among the dense underbrush.

"Is he...dead?" Eve whispered.

"Maybe." The moments crawled by, and Grayson waited. Watching. He looked for any movement, but he didn't see it. "Stay here."

Eve caught on to his arm and looked ready to launch into an argument about why he should stay put, but her gaze dropped to his badge. Resignation went through her eyes as a worried sigh left her mouth. "Be careful."

"That's the plan," he mumbled, and he headed in the direction of the fallen gunman.

He kept watch on Eve and tried to push aside all the other things that crept into his mind, but Grayson knew once this threat was over, he had a dozen other things to deal with—especially Eve.

Grayson reached the spot he'd last seen the gunman, and he cursed. The gunman was still there, in the exact place where he'd taken his last breath. His gun had dropped from his hand.

"He's dead," Grayson relayed to Eve.

She started toward him, practically running. "You're sure?"

Grayson leaned down and checked for a pulse, but that was just to keep everything straight for the reports he'd have to write up later. "Yeah."

Eve was nearly out of breath by the time she made it to him. She took one look at the man's ash-white face, and she shivered and leaned against Grayson.

He'd seen death before, maybe Eve had, too, but it was different seeing it like this. She was trembling hard now, and there were tears in her eyes, so he took her arm and led her away. There was no need for her to see any more of this.

"Why did he try to kill us?" she whispered, her voice clogged with emotion.

Grayson didn't know for sure, but he figured it had something to do with the dead woman in the photos. Maybe this gunman had killed her. "I'll find out," he promised Eve.

Since she looked ready to collapse, Grayson pulled her into his arms. She didn't put up a fight, probably because there was no fight left in her. This had taken, and would continue to take, a lot out of her. Grayson regretted that, but he didn't regret that this guy was dead.

Or that he was able to give some small comfort to Eve.

She was still trembling, but her breathing started to level. What she didn't do was move away, and Grayson was thankful for it. He hated to admit it, but the shooting had shaken him, and being this close to Eve was giving him as much comfort as he was hopefully giving her.

Even now, under the worst of circumstances, he couldn't help but notice how nicely Eve still fit in his arms. Her body practically molded against his.

"We're not bad people," she mumbled. "This shouldn't happen to us."

Yeah. But Grayson knew that neither good nor bad had anything to do with this. The dead man was likely trying to cover up a murder, and in his experience people would do anything and everything to avoid jail.

She pulled back and stared up at him. Their gazes connected, and that *fit,* too. He could read her so well and knew the tears were about to spill again. She had a good reason to cry, and later he would lend her his shoulder, but for now, he had things to do.

"This guy might not be the one who killed Nina Manning. He could be just a triggerman," Grayson explained, trying to keep his voice void of emotion so that she would stay calm.

He failed.

Despite her leveled breathing, Eve still looked anything but calm. So, to soothe himself and her, he brushed a kiss on her temple and then eased back so that she was no longer in his embrace.

"The only way we make this better," Grayson whispered to her, "is to end it. I have to find out why this man came after us."

Eve's bottom lip trembled, and she nodded. Seconds later, she nodded again. "I'm not weak," she assured him. Something he already knew.

"You just saw me kill a man. There's nothing weak

about your reaction. Truth is, I'm shaking inside." And that was the truth. Killing didn't come easy to him, and he hoped like hell that it never did.

Another nod. Eve blinked back tears and reached out to him, but neither of her hands was free. She had her gun in her right hand. The cell phone in the other.

He took the cell from her and motioned for her to move even farther away from the body. "I'll call Dade," he let her know. And he tried. But the signal was so low that the call wouldn't go through. Grayson sent him a text instead and gave Dade their location.

Eve slipped her gun into her pocket and pulled her coat tightly against her. It wasn't freezing, but it wasn't warm, either. Besides, she was battling adrenaline and nerves, and that was no doubt contributing to the trembling.

"What now?" she asked.

Grayson took a deep breath before he answered. "We wait."

She blinked. "For how long?"

He heard the unasked questions, and he knew she wouldn't like the answers to any of them. "The text will eventually get through to Dade, and he'll come after us."

"Good." Her face relaxed a little. "Then we should walk back to the road to meet him."

Grayson glanced back at the body. "The coyotes won't leave a fresh kill alone for long. I need to preserve the crime scene as much as possible because I need an ID on this guy."

Eve started shaking her head. "But I need to get to Austin."

He nodded and settled for saying, "I know."

"No. You don't know." She huffed and blinked back more tears.

Hell.

Well, at least she wasn't shaking so hard, but this was about to get ugly.

"You don't know," she repeated, and she just kept on repeating it until the words and the tears got the best of her. She sagged against a tree.

"Eve," he said reaching out to her, but she just moved away.

Her breath broke on a sob. "I've made some terrible mistakes in my life. First, giving you that ultimatum. And then I promised my heart and life to a man I didn't love. I'm the Typhoid Mary of relationships, Grayson, but I know I'm meant to be a mother."

She was. Grayson didn't doubt that. Heck, she'd practically been a mother to his youngest brother. Grayson, however, didn't have a good track record. And he tried one last time to convince Eve of that.

"I'm not the man you want to father your baby," he insisted.

She opened her mouth to say something, but Grayson didn't want her to tell him something along the lines of his being the only man she wanted for that job. He couldn't hear that. Not now. Not with Eve falling apart like this.

"I sucked as a father," he continued, trying to snag her

gaze. Eye contact might help her see the determination. "My brother, Gage, is dead."

"Gage died doing a job he loved," she clarified. "You couldn't and wouldn't have stopped him from joining the Justice Department any more than he could have stopped you from being sheriff of Silver Creek."

Maybe. But that didn't change things. Besides, Gage was just one of his failures.

"Dade has got so much rage inside him. Nate's just one bad day away from needing professional help. And Mason? Hell, I wouldn't be surprised if he hunted our father down just so he could kill him in cold blood." Grayson paused because he had to. "That's the kind of family I raised."

Now she made eye contact, and the jolt was like a head-on collision. Grayson had hoped she would see his emotion, and maybe she did, but he saw hers in complete vivid detail. The pain. The need.

The hopelessness of her situation.

"If I helped you," he managed to say, "I'd just screw things up again."

She swiped away the tears and stared at him. "If you don't help me, I'll never know what it's like to be a mother. I'll never have a part of my life that I want more than my next breath." She walked closer. "Grayson, you would have no responsibility in this, other than having sex with me. I swear, *no responsibility.*"

He had to say no. Had to. And Grayson just kept repeating that.

But he knew the reality here.

Even if Dade got the text and responded right away, it would be an hour or more before they could get this body out of the woods. Grayson would need another vehicle since his truck was in the creek. It would be nightfall or later before he could get Eve to a clinic in Austin. Since it was just three days before Christmas, it was likely the clinics had already closed for the day. Maybe for the rest of the holiday week.

Still, Grayson had to say no.

Didn't he?

"Don't think too much," she whispered, walking closer.

The cold air mixed with her breath and created a misty fog around her face. It seemed unreal. Like a dream. And Grayson had had so many dreams about her that he nearly got lost in the moment.

Oh, man.

She could still make him burn.

Eve stopped, directly in front of him. So close he could take in her scent. She leaned in and put her mouth to his ear. She didn't touch him. Didn't have to touch him. Her scent was enough. He fought to hang on to the denial he intended to give her, but it was a battle that Grayson knew he was losing.

Worse, he *wanted* to lose.

"Just consider this a big favor for an old friend," she whispered.

A friend? Eve was plenty of things, but she wasn't a friend. Whatever she was, she was pulling him closer. And closer.

"Please," she said. Just that one word. Her warm breath brushed against his mouth like a kiss.

He looked into her eyes and didn't look beyond that. Yeah. He could say no. He could turn and walk away.

But that wasn't what Grayson was going to do.

What he did was exactly as Eve had said. He didn't think too much. He didn't look beyond this moment and the bad mistake he was about to make.

Grayson cursed and pulled her to him.

Chapter Eight

Eve was too afraid to ask Grayson if he was sure about this. She was too afraid to delay even a second because she couldn't risk that he would change his mind.

This had to happen, and it had to happen now.

Grayson was obviously with her on the *now* part. He slid down, his back against the tree, and he pulled her down with him.

Eve's breath was racing already. Her heart pounded against her ribs so hard that it felt her bones would break. She was trembling, scared and cold, but she pushed all those uncomfortable things aside and pressed her mouth to his.

Big mistake.

She felt him stiffen, and the air between them changed. He'd agreed to the sex, to the making a baby part, but that stiff mouth told her that he wasn't ready or willing to go back to where they'd been.

"All right," she mumbled, hoping the sound of her own voice would steady her nerves.

It didn't, but Eve didn't let raw nerves or Grayson's steely look get to her. She worked fast, sliding up her dress and moving onto his lap in the same motion. She didn't meet his gaze. Didn't want to. This was already difficult enough without seeing the proof of what he was thinking.

And he was no doubt thinking this was a big mistake.

Eve didn't let him voice that. She knew what she had to do. She'd had years of experience making out with Grayson. After all, they'd had their first kiss when she was fifteen, and they had spent years driving each other crazy.

She knew how to make him crazy.

Eve didn't kiss him again, but she put her mouth right next to his ear. He liked the breath and heat. He liked the pressure and the touch of her tongue there. Well, at least that's what used to fire him up. She had another moment of panic when she realized that her mouth might not have the same effect on him as it had back then. He might push her—

Grayson made a slight, familiar sound.

If she'd been any other woman, she might not have even heard the catch in his chest, the small burst of breath that he tried to choke back. But Eve heard those things, and she knew exactly what they meant. This was still a fire spot for him. So were her hands on his chest. Since his shirt was already partially unbuttoned, she ran her fingers through his chest hair. And lower.

Grayson liked lower.

Still did, apparently.

Because by the time she trailed her fingers from his

stomach and to the front of his jeans, she found him already huge and hard. She pressed her sex against his.

Eve suddenly didn't feel so cold.

A thought flashed through her head—this was like riding a bicycle. Well, better actually. Her body knew exactly what Grayson could do to her, how he could make her soar. And fall. That wouldn't happen now. It couldn't. She had to keep this as clinical as possible. He was merely a sperm donor here and not her lover.

Eve fumbled with his zipper and finally managed to lower it. No thanks to her hands. She was trembling. So was her mouth, but that didn't seem to affect the kisses she lowered to his neck.

She reached to take off her panties, but Grayson latched onto her hand. His grip was as hard as the part of him she was pressed against.

Her gaze snapped to his, and again Eve was terrified that he was stopping this. But Grayson didn't look her in the eyes. He made another of those sounds, a growl from deep within his throat, and he grabbed her with his other hand. He turned her, shoving her back against the tree. The impact and her surprise nearly knocked the breath out of her.

Grayson seemed to have no trouble breathing. He yanked off her panties and pushed his hips between her legs. He was on his knees now, and the weight of him pinned her to the tree.

For just a moment, she registered the rough bark against her back and bottom. His raw grip. The harsh profanity he was mumbling. Then, he thrust into her.

One long stroke that was nearly as rough as the hold he had on her wrists.

Her body gave way to his sex. Welcoming him. Yes, he was rough, and the thrusts inside her didn't become gentle, either. Of course, he knew her body as well as she knew his. And Grayson knew her. Gentle didn't work for *her*. She had always been in such a hurry to have him that she had begged for hard and fast.

Exactly what he was giving her now.

The man knew what he was doing, that was for sure. He'd learned to make love with her. He knew how to bring her to climax within seconds. Normally, Eve would have gladly surrendered to that climax. She would have surrendered to Grayson, but she instinctively knew that would make the aftermath even worse than it already would be.

And it would be *bad*.

This would cut her off from Grayson forever. Once he'd had time to apply his logical no-shades-of-gray mind to this, he would feel that she'd manipulated him. And she had. Later, Eve would deal with it, too. But for now, she pressed her mouth to the spot just below his ear. She whispered his name.

"Grayson."

The trigger, he had once called it. To finish him off, all she had to do was say his name. It had just the effect she knew it would.

He thrust into her one last time and said her name, too. *Almost.*

"Damn you, Eve," Grayson cursed.

And he finished what he'd started.

Chapter Nine

Grayson got up as soon as he could move. He fixed his clothes and then put some distance between Eve and him. He couldn't go far, but even a few yards would help.

He hoped.

Behind him, he could hear Eve milling around. She was also mumbling. Grayson didn't want to figure out what she was saying. He didn't want to figure out anything except why he'd snapped and done the very thing he'd sworn he wouldn't do.

"If you're waiting for me to say I'm sorry, then you'll be waiting a long time," Eve let him know. "Because I'm not sorry, and I hope you're not, either."

Oh, he was. Sorry and stupid. But that wouldn't change what had happened. There was no way he could justify having sex with Eve. Yes, she might get pregnant. She might finally get that baby she wanted, but that put him right in a position he didn't want to be.

He didn't want to be a father.

Of course, the odds were against Eve having conceived. Grayson had no idea of the stats, but even with her at the prime time of the month, this had to be a long shot.

Hell.

That bothered him, too.

He wanted Eve to have this chance at motherhood, but Grayson wanted what he wanted, as well. Too bad he couldn't quite put a finger on what he did want. Nor did he have time to figure it out. His phone beeped, and he glanced down at the message as it came onto the screen.

"Is it Dade?" Eve asked, hurrying to his side. She was still fixing her clothes, and she smelled like sex. Looked like it, too, Grayson noticed when he risked glancing at her. He looked away as fast as he could.

"Yeah." Grayson worked his way through the abbreviations Dade had used in the message and gave her a summary. "He used my cell phone to pinpoint our location and will be here soon."

She made a sound of relief. So different from the sound she'd made just minutes ago when he'd taken her against the tree. The memory of it flashed through his head, and Grayson knew that memory would give him no peace.

His phone beeped again, and there was a new message from Dade. "He wants me to take a picture of the body," Grayson relayed to Eve. "As soon as we have a better signal, I can send it to the Rangers and they can feed it through the facial recognition program."

Something that Grayson should have already thought of, but then he'd had sex with Eve on his mind.

He cursed himself again.

"Wait here," he ordered, and Grayson walked across the woods to the body. Even the mini break from Eve might help because right now his stomach was knotted even harder than it had been in the middle of the attack.

The dead man was still there, of course, sprawled out among the clumps of dried leaves and fallen tree limbs. Grayson snapped a couple of pictures and checked the signal. Still too weak to send the photos, but he made a mental note to keep checking. He made another mental note not to do any more looking at Eve. No thinking about Eve. No more need for her that was generated below the belt.

Hard to do with her standing there in that body-hugging dress.

"Thank you," she whispered when he went back to her.

He didn't want to hear this. "Don't," Grayson warned. "Don't say anything." He wasn't a man who dwelled on regrets, but by God he could make an exception.

She stepped in front of him and forced eye contact. "Thank you," Eve repeated, and she leaned in pressed a chaste kiss on his cheek.

His cheek!

Here his body was still burning for her, and she had risked giving him a brotherly kiss like that. The woman really was playing with fire.

Grayson stepped back and fastened his attention on the area where the dead man was. "Did I hurt you?" he growled.

"No." Eve answered it so quickly that she'd probably

anticipated the question. Which meant he'd been too rough. Grayson shot her an over-the-shoulder glance to let her know that.

She shrugged. "I don't mind a little rough. But you're aware of that."

Yeah, he was. He knew every inch of her body and could have gotten her off with just a touch. But Grayson had tried to keep the pleasure factor out of this. For him that was impossible. His body was humming, and well satisfied, even though his brain was confused as hell.

"How long before you know if this worked?" he asked.

"I'm not sure. I'll have to ask my doctor." She hesitated. "I figured I wouldn't call you or anything with the results. I thought it would be easier that way. Is that okay?"

Was it? Grayson didn't have a clue what was okay. His brain was a mess right now. "Yeah," he settled for saying.

She pulled her coat around her and shivered. Eve was obviously cold, but Grayson intended to do nothing about that. He'd already done enough for the day.

"I don't want you to tell your family about this," she insisted. "As soon as we're out of here, I'll leave so you won't have to see me."

He gave her another look that was probably more scowl than anything else.

She huffed. "Grayson, I'm not stupid. I know what's going on in your head, and you'll want to put as much distance between us as possible."

True. But distance was going to be a problem until he figured out why the man had wanted her dead. Grayson was about to remind her of that when he heard Dade call out to them.

"Over here!" Grayson answered. With Eve right behind him, he went in the direction of his brother's voice.

Eve raked her hand through her hair, trying to fix it, and she brushed off the bits of leaves and twigs from her coat. Grayson tried to do the same.

He soon spotted Dade, and he wasn't alone. Deputy Melissa Garza was with him. Mel, as she liked to be called. And Grayson was thankful Dade had brought her along.

"You okay?" Dade asked when he was still a good twenty yards away.

Grayson nodded, but he was far from okay. He tipped his head to the body. "Single gunshot wound to the chest, and he bled out. It's the man we chased into the woods behind Eve's cottage."

Mel began to trudge her way through to the dead man, but Dade stayed on the path that led directly toward Grayson. As his brother walked closer, he glanced at both Eve and him. Not an ordinary glance but a suspicious one.

"I have the photos," Grayson said showing Dade his cell. Best to get Dade's suspicious mind back where it belonged—on the investigation. "Is the medical examiner on the way?"

"Yeah. He and his crew are right behind us." Dade volleyed more glances between the two of them.

"Good. Mel can stay with the body, and you can get Eve and me out of here," Grayson instructed. "I want to get the photos to the Rangers."

Dade called out Grayson's instructions to Mel, and the deputy nodded.

"Are you really okay?" Dade asked Eve as the three of them headed back toward the road.

"You mean other than the raw nerves, the tear-stained cheeks and adrenaline crash?" The corner of her mouth lifted. "Yes, I'm okay."

Dade hooked his arm around her shoulders. "I wish you could have had a better homecoming." He shifted his attention to Grayson but didn't say anything. Dade's left eyebrow lifted.

Grayson ignored him and kept on walking. Thankfully, they soon reached a spot where the cell signal was stronger, and he fired off the photos. If the dead man had a police record, then it wouldn't take the Rangers long to come up with an ID.

It took a good ten minutes for them to get back to the road where Dade had a cruiser waiting. Dade helped Eve into the front passenger's seat, closed the door and turned back around to stare at Grayson.

"Don't ask," Grayson growled in a whisper.

Dade lifted his shoulder. "Hey, you got my vote if you're getting back together with Eve."

"It's not a vote." Grayson cursed. "And what part of 'don't ask' didn't you understand?"

"The *don't* part." Dade smirked as only a younger brother could manage to do.

Grayson cursed some more. "Look, I'm in a bad mood. The kind of mood where I'd love to beat someone senseless. My advice? Stay out of my way, or that someone will be you." He threw open the door and climbed into the driver's seat.

As soon as Dade got in, Grayson sped back toward town. His mood improved a little when he saw the ME's van approaching from the opposite direction. That meant Mel wouldn't have to stay out there very long, and that was good. He needed all his deputies back at the station so he could figure out what the heck was going on.

"Any idea how the dead man tracked you down?" Dade asked from the backseat.

Grayson was about to say no, but then he groaned. "Probably a tracking device. He put one on Eve's car, we know that, and I'm guessing he put one on the truck, too."

Eve made a small gasping sound of surprise.

"I'll have someone check when they fish your truck from the creek," Dade assured him. But Grayson heard the hesitation in his brother's voice. Dade was no doubt wondering why Grayson hadn't thought of the possibility of a tracking device before he'd driven the truck away from his office.

Grayson didn't need another reason to put some distance between Eve and him, but there it was. He was thinking like a rookie, and the stakes were too high for him to make another mistake.

This mistake could have gotten Eve killed.

He wouldn't forget that.

Since Eve was shivering, Grayson decided to turn up the heat, though the adrenaline was probably more responsible than the chilly temperature. Eve apparently had the same idea because she reached at the same time he did. Their hands collided. And she pulled back as if he'd scalded her. Ironic, since just a half hour earlier he'd been deep inside her. Still, it was good they were in agreement about this no-touching thing.

"Uh, I'm guessing Eve's in protective custody?" Dade wanted to know. It sounded like a loaded question.

Eve turned in the seat to look at Dade, and Grayson nodded. "She can stay at the ranch."

"At the ranch?" She shook her head. "That's probably not a good idea."

Yeah. He was in agreement with that, too. The sex against the tree had only created more tension and friction between them, but there couldn't be any more mistakes.

"You might not have to be there long," Grayson explained. "We just need to tie up some loose ends on this case." He looked in the rearview mirror so he could see Dade. "Any more news on our DB, Nina Manning?"

"Still waiting on the preliminaries. Once we have the next of kin identified, we can talk to them, as well."

Grayson shook his head. "You said there was a missing person's report filed on her a year ago. Who filed that?"

"Her mother, Theresa Manning. She was a single

parent, no record of the father, and Theresa died about a month ago. Yeah," Dade added when Grayson glanced at him in the mirror. "Theresa was diabetic and died from an insulin overdose. Could have been an accident, but I asked the Houston cops to look into it."

Yes, because the timing was suspicious.

Grayson's phone buzzed, and he saw the caller was from the Texas Ranger lab. "Sheriff Ryland," he answered and put the call on speaker so Dade could hear.

"Ranger Egan Caldwell," the man identified himself. "I have a match on the photos of the dead man."

Grayson released the breath he'd been holding. "Who is he?"

"Leon Ames. He has a record, obviously. Seven years ago for assault with a deadly weapon. He spent two years in a Bexar county jail and is still on probation."

Well, prison hadn't rehabilitated him, that's for sure. "He tried to kill me twice today, and he's in the photograph with the dead woman, Nina Manning. Is there a connection?"

"Nothing obvious, but he's got a history with the other man in the photo, Sebastian Collier."

"How?" Dade and Grayson asked in unison. Eve leaned closer to the phone and listened.

"Leon Ames works...worked for Sebastian's father, Claude. He was a handyman at their San Antonio estate."

Handyman. That was an interesting word, considering the photograph with the dead woman and the attempts to kill Eve and him.

"I'm faxing you the rest of the report," the ranger

continued. "For what it's worth, I don't think Leon Ames was working alone. From everything I can see, he was nothing more than a lackey."

"What makes you think that?" Grayson asked.

"A large sum of money deposited into his bank account the day after the murder. Twenty thousand dollars. We can't trace the money because he made the deposit in cash. My guess is that money was a payoff for services rendered."

Grayson suspected as much. "So, who hired Leon—Claude or Sebastian?"

"Either is possible," the ranger answered. "But I think all roads in this investigation lead to the Colliers, and that you'll find a killer at the estate."

Chapter Ten

Eve needed a friendly face, and she saw one the moment Grayson pulled to a stop in front of the Collier estate. His brother, Lieutenant Nate Ryland, was there waiting for them on the sidewalk in front of the towering black-iron fence that fronted the equally towering Collier estate.

Nate smiled, his dimples flashing, and the moment she stepped from the car, he pulled her into his arms. "Even under these circumstances, it's good to see you," Nate whispered.

"It's good to see you, too." And Eve meant it. She'd never felt more at home than in the arms of a Ryland, and Nate was no exception.

She inched back to meet his gaze and return the smile. The Ryland DNA was there all right, etched over his perfectly chiseled face, black hair and storm-gray eyes. But Nate was smooth around the cowboy-edges in his dark blue suit, which was a job requirement for San Antonio P.D. Like the rest of the Ryland clan, he was more at home in Wranglers and on the back of a horse.

Would her baby be the same?

Her baby, she mentally repeated. And she felt her smile deepen. Yes, a pregnancy was a long shot, but it was possible that she was well on her way to getting the child she'd always wanted.

"Eve?" Nate said, drawing her out of her daydream. "You okay?"

"Of course. I was just distracted for a moment." Eve stared at him, and her smile faded when she remembered what Nate had gone through. "I'm sorry about your wife's death," she whispered.

Eve was even sorrier that she hadn't gone to the funeral or spoken to him about it before now. Nate had always felt like a brother to her, and she'd let him down at a time when he no doubt needed all of his friends. "How are you handling things?"

His smile faded, too. "It's, uh, complicated," he mumbled. Nate's gaze swung in Grayson's direction, an indication to her that this conversation was over. "Are you ready to do battle with the Colliers?"

"Considering their hired gun tried to kill us, yeah, I'm ready."

Nate gave a crisp nod. As a lieutenant, he'd no doubt done his share of interrogations. He was also a cop with some clout when it came to handling an investigation.

And Grayson.

If Nate hadn't had some influence, Eve wouldn't have been allowed to tag along. As it was, she'd practically had to beg Grayson to let her come. He'd wanted to tuck her safely away at the ranch. Eve wanted to be safe, but she didn't want that at the expense of learning the truth.

She had taken the incriminating photo, and she wanted to confront the person responsible for what was going on.

"Anything I should know before we go inside?" Grayson asked his brother.

"Well, they haven't lawyered up. But I doubt that means you'll get a lot of cooperation, especially when you link the dead woman to their now dead employee."

Eve hoped Nate was wrong. She wanted answers today so she could start distancing herself from Grayson. She couldn't keep leaning on these Ryland shoulders.

"So, Claude and Sebastian know that Leon was killed?" she clarified.

"They do. And when I spoke to them over the phone, I also told them that Leon tried to murder both of you." Nate walked toward the gate and flashed his badge at the monitor. Seconds later, the gate creaked open.

"I'd like to handle the interview myself," Grayson insisted.

"Figured you would. But if we learn anything we can use to hold either one of them, I need to make the arrest since we're not sure where this murder occurred."

An arrest. Eve hoped that would happen, and then things could finally get back to normal. Well, maybe. If she was indeed pregnant, then nothing would be *normal* again.

Nate shot her a glance. "And I hoped you would say as little as possible. I want them to see you, so they'll know that the picture you took is no longer a reason to come after you. That's the only reason I'm allowing you in the middle of a murder investigation."

She nodded, mumbled a thanks.

"Eve knows the rules," Grayson said, and it sounded like a warning. He walked ahead of them toward the porch that stretched the entire width of the three-story house. There were dozens of white columns, each of them ringed with fresh holly, and a five-foot-tall vertical wreath hung on the door.

Nate fell in step alongside her. "Did something happen between you two?" he asked.

What—did she have a big sign stuck to her back proclaiming that she'd had sex with Grayson? Of course, *sex* was a very loose term for what had happened between them. It had seemed more like a biology experiment.

And that, she reminded herself, was exactly what she'd asked of Grayson.

No strings attached. No emotion. No discussion.

Well, she'd gotten all of that. He had hardly said two words to her when they'd gone back to the sheriff's office to change his clothes. Or on the drive from Silver Creek to her San Antonio condo so she could get a change of clothes, as well. Ditto for more of his silence on the drive to the Collier estate.

And that was just as well.

He was making it easier for her to walk away.

"Nothing happened," she lied.

Nate made a sound that could have meant anything and joined Grayson on the porch as he rang the doorbell. Eve stayed just behind them. A maid wearing a uniform opened the door, and without saying a word, she ushered them through the marble-floored foyer and into a sitting room where two men waited for them.

The room was decorated in varying shades of white and cream. A stark contrast to the floor-to-ceiling Christmas tree that was practically smothered in shiny blood-red ornaments. After the real blood she'd seen today, the sight of those ornaments twisted her stomach a little.

Eve recognized both men in the room—Claude from his photos in the newspapers and Sebastian from the picture she'd taken of him at the rodeo. Both men were dressed in suits. Claude's was black. His son's, a dark gray. Both men were sipping something from cut-crystal glasses that looked and smelled expensive.

"Sheriff Grayson Ryland," he said, stepping ahead of Nate and her. "This is my brother, Lt. Nate Ryland from SAPD, and Eve Warren."

"Ah, Ms. Warren, the woman who took the photo in question," Sebastian quickly supplied. He crossed the room and shook all of their hands. His expression and greeting were friendly enough, but Eve wondered just how long that would last.

The friendly demeanor didn't extend to the other Collier in the room. Claude was a carbon copy of his son, but he was at least twenty pounds thinner and his scowl bunched up his otherwise classic features. His navy blue eyes were narrowed, and he watched them as if they were thieves about to run off with the family silver. He also didn't ask them to sit, probably because he hoped this would be a short visit. Or maybe he was just naturally rude.

"Yes, I took the picture," Eve answered when Sebastian continued to stare at her. "How did you know about that?"

That question earned her scolding looks from Nate and Grayson, who obviously didn't want her involved in this questioning, but Sebastian only flashed that thousand-watt smile. A smile that probably worked wonders on his business associates, but to her it felt slimy.

Just like the man himself.

"A journalist friend told me," Sebastian volunteered. "I understand it was going to be printed in tomorrow's newspaper. But then you managed to ID the unfortunate victim."

"Yes," Grayson verified. He kept his gaze pinned to Sebastian. "Mind explaining what you and your *handyman* were doing in the photo with Nina Manning?"

Sebastian opened his mouth to answer, but his father's voice boomed through the room. "Leon Ames is not my handyman. I fired him three days ago."

Grayson and Nate exchanged glances. "Why?" Grayson demanded.

Claude shrugged as if the answer wasn't important. He responded only after Grayson continued to stare at him. "Erratic behavior," Claude finally supplied. The man couldn't have sounded snootier if he'd tried. "I expect impeccable behavior from my employees, and Leon didn't live up to that."

"How so?" Grayson pressed.

Claude blew out an irritated breath. "If you must know, he used one of the family cars to run a personal errand. I questioned him, he lied about it and I dismissed him. End of story."

Grayson matched the irritated breath response. "No. It's not the end of it. Because the day before you fired him, Leon and your son were photographed with a woman who was murdered."

"I can explain that," Sebastian offered, still sounding very cooperative. "I went to the charity rodeo, and I ran into Leon and the woman. I believe they were lovers."

"Lovers?" Grayson again. "Leon was twice her age."

Claude flexed his eyebrows. "Then, maybe *lover* isn't the right term. I think the woman was a pro. She was hitting up Leon for cash."

Since Nina did indeed have a record for prostitution, that could be true, but Eve wasn't about to believe him. Sebastian almost certainly wouldn't admit if he'd been the one who hired Nina for her *services*.

"Tell me everything you remember about the meeting," Grayson demanded, looking directly at Sebastian.

Sebastian took a sip of his drink and gave another nonchalant lift of his shoulder. "As I said, I went to the charity rodeo so I could make a donation and ran into Leon. The woman was with him, and they seemed to be, well, cozy."

"In the picture they appeared to be angry," Grayson fired back.

"That came later." Sebastian didn't hesitate. "The

woman's attitude became less friendly when Leon refused to give her money."

Grayson stepped closer to Sebastian. "Did she say what the money was for?"

Sebastian shook his head. "I didn't listen to their conversation, Sheriff. The woman was obviously low-rent. Probably high on drugs. Once I realized that, I moved away and let them finish their discussion. I didn't want to be seen in that kind of company."

"Did it seem as if Leon knew Nina before this meeting?" Nate asked.

"I'm not sure." Sebastian finished his drink in one gulp.

"You should be talking to Leon's friends about that," Claude interrupted. "I won't have my family's good name dragged through the mud for the likes of Leon Ames."

Grayson gave him a flat look. "I don't suppose you have the names of Leon's friends?"

Claude's mouth twisted as if he'd tasted something bitter. "I do not make it a habit of delving into the personal lives of my employees." He slapped his glass onto the table. "And that's the end of this interview. Anything else goes through our family attorneys."

Sebastian gave an embarrassed smile. "I've already told you everything I know."

"Not quite." Despite Claude's rude dismissal, Grayson stayed put. "When's the last time you saw Leon and the dead woman?"

"Probably just a few minutes after Miss Warren here

snapped the photo. I left, and I have no idea where they went." Sebastian checked his watch. "Now, if you'll excuse me, I need to get ready for our guests. We're having a small Christmas gathering here tonight."

"If you remember anything else about the encounter with Nina and Leon," Grayson said to Sebastian, "I want you to call me." He extracted a business card from his jacket pocket and dropped it on the glass end table. "I'll also need you to go to SAPD and give a written statement."

Sebastian groaned softly. "Please tell me that can wait until after the holidays. Christmas is only three days away."

"And SAPD will be open all day," Grayson fired back. "A woman is dead, and she deserves justice. I need that statement and anything else you can remember about Leon's friends."

"Of course," Sebastian finally agreed, but he was no longer so cordial. His mouth tightened.

Both father and son turned to walk out, but they stopped when the sound of a woman's high heels echoed through the room. They all turned in the direction of the sound, and Eve spotted a curvy blonde in a plunging liquid-silver dress, who was making her way toward them. She, too, had a drink in a crystal highball glass, and she was teetering on five-inch red heels that were the exact color of the Christmas ornaments.

"Claude, you didn't tell me that we had guests." She clucked her tongue and smiled first at Grayson. Then, Nate. She didn't even spare Eve a glance.

"They're not guests," Claude snapped. "They're cops. And they were just leaving."

"Leaving?" The woman gave a quick fake pout. "Well, let me introduce myself. I'm Annabel Collier, Claude's wife." Her cherry-lacquered smile went south when she glanced at Sebastian. "And I'm his step-mother."

Eve hadn't studied the background info on Annabel, but she was betting that stepmother and son were close to the same age. Annabel was clearly a trophy wife.

A drunk one.

"The maid was about to show them out," Claude re-iterated, and just like that, the maid appeared in the doorway of the sitting room.

"I can do that," Annabel volunteered. She hooked her arm through Grayson's, and Eve didn't think it was her imagination that the woman pressed the side of her double Ds against Grayson's chest.

"Isn't the estate beautiful this time of year?" Annabel babbled on. Some of her drink sloshed onto the floor and the toes of those red stilettos. "I love all the sparkles and the presents. Claude is very generous with presents, you know. I peeked, and all I can say is five carats, platinum setting." She punctuated that with a drunken giggle.

Behind them, Eve heard Claude mumble something, but both Sebastian and he stayed put as Annabel es-corted Grayson to the door. Nate and Eve followed, and Eve wondered if she could trip the bimbo who was hang-ing all over Grayson. Since Grayson and she weren't together, it didn't make sense to be jealous, but Eve felt it anyway.

Annabel threw open the door, and the cold December wind poured into the foyer and rustled the shimmering gold wreath. Despite her strapless dress she stepped onto the porch with them. She glanced over her shoulder, and when her gaze returned to them, she was a changed woman. No bimbo smile, and her sapphire-blue eyes were suddenly intense.

Eve was too dumbfounded to do anything but watch, which was probably a good thing.

Annabel plucked something from her cleavage and pressed it into Grayson's hand, which she pretended to shake. "The Colliers have secrets," she whispered, her bottom lip trembling. "Deadly ones."

Annabel giggled again, sliding right back into the persona of the drunken trophy wife. "Happy Holidays," she told them as she stepped back inside. She gave Grayson one last pleading look, and then shut the door.

"What was that all about?" Nate mumbled.

But Grayson didn't answer. He hurried off the porch and toward the car. So did Nate and Eve. He waited until they were outside the gates and away from the security cameras that dotted the fence.

Then Grayson opened his hand so that Nate and Eve could see what Annabel had given him.

Eve stared it and shook her head.

What the heck was going on, and why had Annabel given them *this?*

Chapter Eleven

Grayson was several steps beyond exhaustion, but he kept his eyes on the road. It was nearly dark, and the temperature had dropped, and the last thing he needed was to wreck another car today.

"Anything?" he asked Eve again.

It was a question he'd asked her several times since they'd left San Antonio nearly a half hour earlier. Most of that time, Eve had been using the laptop that she'd picked up from her condo so she could view the pictures.

Pictures on the tiny memory card that Annabel had given them.

Grayson had already emailed a copy of the card's contents to the crime lab in Austin, but he wanted to have a closer look for himself as to what Annabel had considered important enough to pass along to a sheriff who was investigating her husband and stepson.

Eve shifted the laptop to a position so that Grayson could see. He glanced at the screen and saw the thumbnails of the photographs. There were dozens of them.

"Annabel obviously likes to take pictures, but I think I finally have them sorted," Eve mumbled. She tapped the ones in the first row. "These are shots taken in what appears to be Claude's office. My guess is Annabel took them with a hidden camera mounted somewhere in the room because the angle never changes."

"Anything incriminating?" Grayson asked.

"Hard to tell. Claude's obviously having a discussion with this dark-haired woman, but there's nothing sexual going on. I think they're arguing."

Grayson agreed. Everything about their body language conveyed anger, not romance. "I need to find out who that woman is." And the crime lab could maybe help with that.

"Well, I think we can rule her out as a mistress. Claude seems to prefer women half his age, and this woman looks to be about fifty." Eve enlarged the photos on the next row, and she made a sound of surprise.

"What?" Grayson asked. He didn't want to fully take his eyes off the road, but Eve's reaction grabbed his attention.

"There are a dozen or more shots taken in a hotel lobby. An expensive hotel, judging from the decor. And there's Nina." She pointed to the next series of pictures. "Nina's not alone, either. Both Claude and Sebastian are there with her."

Eve met his gaze. "That means Sebastian lied about never having seen Nina."

Yeah. Annabel had been right about family secrets. Was this what she'd meant?

"Is a lie enough to arrest Sebastian?" Eve asked.

"No. With his money and connections, we need more.

We need a motive." Grayson turned off the highway and onto the ranch road that would take him home.

She huffed and pushed her hair from her face. Eve was obviously exhausted, too. Even with the watery light from the laptop screen, he could see the dark circles beneath her eyes. He could also see how damn attractive she was, and he wondered if there was ever a time he wouldn't look at her and think just that.

"Maybe Sebastian and Nina were lovers?" Eve tossed out there. She was obviously unaware that he was sneaking glimpses of not just the photographs but of her. "Maybe Sebastian snapped when he found out his lover also had a romantic interest in his father?"

Grayson shook his head. "That doesn't look like a lover's encounter. Even though it's possible that one or both had sex with her, and Nina was trying to blackmail them. After all, Claude did say he wouldn't have his family's good name dragged through the mud. Maybe this was his way of making sure that didn't happen."

And Claude could have hired Leon to kill a blackmailing Nina.

But then why was Sebastian in the picture?

Better yet, why had Annabel given him this incriminating evidence?

Grayson wasn't sure, but he intended to find out. He'd already requested a more detailed background check on Nina and all the Colliers, including Annabel.

"There are some pictures taken at the charity rodeo," Eve let him know. "Not mine. These are ones that Annabel or someone else shot. High angle, zoom lens. She was probably in the top seats of the stadium."

Maybe so that the men wouldn't notice her, which meant that Annabel probably knew she was snapping pictures of something incriminating.

"Did she photograph the encounter with Leon, Nina and Sebastian?" Grayson asked.

He took the last turn to the ranch and could see the lights of the sprawling two-story house just ahead. Sometimes, he took home for granted. But not tonight. It was a welcome sight.

"Not that I can readily see," Eve answered, her attention still nailed to the computer screen. "I need to enlarge the photos and study them."

"Later." The pictures were important, perhaps even critical, but he wanted to get her settled into the guestroom first. He'd already called the housekeeper, Bessie Watkins, to let her know they were on the way so that she could prepare the guestroom.

Eve looked up as if surprised to see they were already at the ranch. "Wow," she mumbled.

That reaction was no doubt for the Christmas lights. There were hundreds of them lining the fence that led all the way to the main house. Even the shrubs had been decked with twinkling lights, and there were two fully decorated Christmas trees on each end of the porch.

"Bessie did this," Grayson explained. "For Nate's daughter, Kimmie. It's her first Christmas."

Grayson felt a tightness in his chest. Because it was a Christmas that his niece wouldn't be able to spend with her mother. It made him even more determined to keep Eve safe. And he'd taken measures to make sure that happened.

The ranch was huge, over three thousand acres, but it was equipped with a full security system that monitored all parts of the house and property. There were also at least a dozen ranch hands in quarters on the grounds.

Then, there were his brothers.

Mason and Dade were still at work in town, but soon they would return for the night. Nate, too, even though Kimmie and he lived in a separate wing of the ranch house. The youngest, Kade, was at his apartment in Austin where he worked for the FBI, but he could be at the ranch in an hour if necessary.

Grayson hoped it wouldn't be necessary.

He stopped the car in the circular drive and looked around. It was pitch-dark now, but there were enough security and Christmas lights for him to see that no one was lurking around, ready to strike. Still, he didn't want to dawdle. Grayson grabbed the suitcase that Eve had taken from her place in San Antonio. She latched onto the laptop, and they hurried up the flagstone porch steps.

Other than the Christmas lights, there was no glitz here like at the Collier estate. The porch was painted white, and the rocking chairs weren't just for show. They used them often.

"You're finally here," Bessie said the moment she threw open the door. And despite the laptop between them, Bessie hugged Eve. "Girl, you are a sight for sore eyes."

"It's great to see you too, Bessie," Eve answered.

"I got a room all made up for you." Bessie caught on to Eve's arm and led her across the foyer. Not marble, but Texas hardwood.

The furnishings here and in the rest of the house leaned more toward a Western theme with pine tables and oil paintings of the various show horses and live-stock they'd had over the years. One of Dade's girl-friends had joked that it was cowboy chic.

Eve glanced around and took a deep breath. She was probably thinking things hadn't changed much since she'd last been here. Grayson's thoughts went in a differ-ent direction. As always, she looked as if she belonged there.

Under different circumstances, she would have.

But it hadn't been different circumstances since his father had walked out on his family twenty years ago. Since then Grayson hadn't wanted a wife or a family. Of course, that hadn't stopped him from having sex with Eve in the woods.

Later, he'd have to figure out how to deal with that.

Bessie directed Eve toward the stairs to the right of the entry. "I can run you a bath. And then you can have something to eat. I made chili and pecan pie, your fa-vorites."

Eve looked back at Grayson as if she expected him to rescue her. "I need to go over these pictures," she insisted.

Grayson took the laptop from her, balancing it in his left hand since he had her suitcase in his right. "The pictures can wait a few minutes. Besides, I'm starving. Take your bath so we can eat."

That wasn't exactly true. Eve and he had grabbed some fast food on the way out to the Collier estate, but Grayson knew he could get Eve's cooperation if she thought the dinner and bath breaks were for him and not her.

It worked. Eve didn't argue.

While Bessie chattered away about the Christmas dinner plans, she led Eve into the bathroom of the guest suite. Grayson deposited Eve's suitcase in the bedroom and went to his suite directly across the hall so he, too, could grab a quick shower.

Grayson tossed his clothes and Stetson onto the bed and hurried because he wanted to get back to the pictures. He also needed to find out the status of the background checks on Annabel, Claude, Sebastian and Nina. However, he wasn't nearly as quick as Eve because he had barely dried off and put on a pair of clean jeans when there was a knock at the door.

"It's me," Eve said, but she didn't wait. She threw open the door just as Grayson was zipping his jeans.

"Oh, sorry," she mumbled. Her hair was wet, no makeup, and she was wearing a dark green sweater top and pants. She wasn't wearing shoes but rather a pair of socks.

She fluttered her fingers behind her as if indicating that she was about to return to her room so he could finish dressing. But she stayed put with her gaze pinned to his bare chest and stomach.

She pulled in her breath and held it for a second. "You have a scar," she whispered.

For a moment Grayson had thought that breathless reaction was for his half-naked body. It's a good thing it wasn't.

And he was pretty sure he believed that.

She walked toward him, slowly, leaned down and touched the six-inch scar that started at his chest and ended on his right side. "How did it happen?"

"I broke up a fight at the cantina on the edge of town. Didn't see the switchblade until it was too late."

Another deep breath. "You could have been killed." Her voice was suddenly clogged with emotion.

Yeah. But Grayson kept that to himself. He also caught her hand to move it off his stomach, but somehow their fingers ended up laced together.

And neither of them pulled away.

Their eyes met. She was so familiar to him, but those eyes always held a surprise or two. Sometimes they were a misty blue. Other times, the color of a spring Texas sky.

Grayson cursed that last analogy.

He was a cowboy, and the last thing he should be doing was thinking poetic thoughts about the color of Eve's eyes.

His thoughts weren't so poetic when it came to the rest of her.

Grayson knew exactly how she looked beneath those winter clothes. He knew how much she liked it when he kissed her belly. And the inside of her thighs. He knew the way she smelled. The way she tasted. The sounds that she made when he was driving her hot and crazy. And it was because he knew all those things that he had to back away.

But he didn't.

They stood there, gazes locked, as if paralysis had set in and neither could move. Eve's breath became thin. Her face flushed. She glanced at his bed, and Grayson knew exactly what she was thinking.

He'd made love to her in that bed.

Things had been different then. Ten years ago they'd remodeled the house and turned all the bedrooms into suites. But the black lacquered wrought-iron bed was the same. It'd been his grandfather's, and Grayson had staked claim to it twenty years ago after his grandfather had been killed. He'd gone through several mattresses in those twenty years, but the bed itself had remained unchanged.

No telling how many times Grayson had sneaked Eve up to his room. To this very bed.

In the beginning, neither had had a clue what they were doing. They had followed their instincts. Did the things that felt good. And plenty of those times, he'd had to kiss her hard and deep to muffle the sounds she made when she climaxed.

Grayson could hear those sounds now echoing through his head.

He couldn't help but respond to those memories. To the touch of her fingers linked with his.

Part of him, the part straining against the zipper of

his jeans, started to rationalize that he could put her on that bed again. He knew how to get those sounds from her. Knew the delicious heat of her body.

"Mercy," she mumbled, but it didn't have any sound. She shook her head. Moistened her lips.

He wanted to hear her voice. Those sounds. But most of all, he just wanted to kiss her.

"It would be a mistake," Grayson said more to himself than her.

"Oh, yeah. A big one." But she inched closer. So close that he tasted her breath on his mouth. That taste went straight through him.

Something inside him snapped, and he latched onto the back of her neck and hauled her to him. Their mouths met, and he heard the sound all right. A little bit of whimper mixed with a boatload of relief.

Grayson knew exactly how she felt.

Helpless. Stupid.

And hot.

"Should I close the door and give you time alone?" someone snarled from the doorway. It was his brother, Mason.

Eve and Grayson flew apart as if they'd just been caught doing something wrong. Which was true. They couldn't lust after each other. Sex against the tree to make a baby was one thing. But real sex would turn their status from *it's complicated* to *it's damn impossible.*

"Well?" Mason prompted in that surly noninterested way that only Mason could manage. "You need time to do something about that kiss or what?"

"Did you want something?" Grayson fired back at his brother.

Mason lifted the papers he had in his hand and dropped them onto the table near the door. "Background reports on the Colliers and the dead girl. You should read them. There's some interesting stuff in there." He tipped his head to the laptop. "Anything with the photos?"

"Not yet," Eve and Grayson said in unison.

If that frustrated Mason, he didn't show it. He turned but then stopped. "Good to see you, Eve." From Mason, that was a warm, fuzzy welcome.

"It's good to see you, too." Eve's was considerably warmer. Strange, most people steered clear of Mason, but Eve went to him and planted a kiss on his cheek.

Now Mason looked uncomfortable. "Yell if you need me." And with that mumbled offer, he strolled away.

Both Eve and he hurried to the reports that Mason had dropped on the table, and Grayson snatched them up. There were at least thirty pages, and with Eve right at his shoulder, they started to skim through them. It didn't take long for Grayson to see what Mason had considered *interesting stuff.*

There was a photo of Claude's first wife, Cicely, and it was the same woman in the photos taken in his office. So that was one thing cleared up. Claude's ex had visited him. Nothing suspicious about that. Since she was the mother of his son, they would always have a connection.

That required Grayson to take a deep breath because he couldn't help but think that one day, soon, Eve and he might have that same connection.

"Cicely had twins," Eve read, touching her finger to that part of the background. "Sebastian and Sophia."

This was the first Grayson had heard of it, but then he'd only had a preliminary report of Sebastian before the interview at the Collier estate.

Grayson read on. "When Sophia was six months old, the nanny, Helen Bolton, disappeared with her, and even though Helen turned up dead three months later, Sophia was never found."

On the same page of the report, there was a photo of baby Sophia that had obviously been taken right before she went missing.

"You have a scanner in the house?" Eve asked, her attention nailed to the picture of the baby.

"Sure. In my office."

Eve grabbed the laptop and headed up the hall. She practically raced ahead of him, and the moment they were inside, she fed the picture into the scanner and loaded it onto the laptop with the other photos they'd gotten from Annabel.

"What are you doing?" Grayson wanted to know.

While she typed frantically on the keyboard, Eve sank down in the leather chair behind his desk. "I have age progression software. It's not a hundred percent accurate, but it might work."

Grayson watched Eve manipulate the copied image of the baby, and soon it began to take shape. The adult version of Sophia Collier appeared on the screen.

Grayson cursed under his breath. The hair was different, but there were enough similarities.

"Oh, God," Eve mumbled. She leaned away from the laptop and touched her fingers to her mouth. "Do you see it?" she asked.

"Yeah." Grayson saw it all right.

And it meant this investigation had just taken a crazy twist.

Because the dead woman, Nina Manning, hadn't been Claude's mistress as they'd originally thought. She was Sophia Collier, Claude's missing daughter.

Chapter Twelve

"I wished you'd stayed at the ranch," Grayson mumbled again. He kept his attention pinned to the San Antonio downtown street that was clogged with holiday shoppers and traffic.

Eve ignored him. She'd already explained her reasons for tagging along for this visit to Cicely Collier. She wanted the truth about the dead woman, and when that happened, the danger would be over. She could go home and, well, wait until she could take a pregnancy test.

It had been less than twenty-four hours since Grayson had agreed to have sex with her, but she'd read enough of the pregnancy books to know that conception could have already happened.

She could be pregnant.

Despite everything else going on, Eve smiled and slid her hand over her stomach. Even though it was a long shot, she wanted to hang on to the possibility as long as she could.

Even if she couldn't hang on to Grayson.

That kiss in his bedroom had felt so much like old times, and as stupid as it sounded, it had felt more intimate than the sex. It had been real, not some gesture that she'd had to talk Grayson into doing.

And that's why it couldn't happen again.

She could coax him into kissing her again. Maybe even talk him into coming to her bed. But he would soon feel trapped, and he would blame himself—and her—for feeling that way. She cared for him too much to make him go through that. Grayson already had enough duty forced on him in his life without making him feel even a shred of obligation to her. More kissing would make him feel obligated.

"You okay?" Grayson asked.

She glanced at him and realized he'd seen her hand on her stomach. "I'm fine."

He seemed suspicious of her answer, but he didn't press it. Nor would he. A discussion about the baby was off-limits for both of them, and Eve was thankful for it. Conversation wasn't going to help with this matter. No. The only thing that would help was to put some distance between them.

The voice on the GPS directed them toward another turn, and Grayson drove into the upscale San Antonio neighborhood. Of course, she hadn't expected Cicely to live in a shack, but it was obvious the woman had done well in the divorce settlement.

Grayson parked in the driveway of the two-story Victorian-style home. It was painted a soft buttery yellow with white trim, and despite the fact that it was the dead of winter, the lawn was as pristine as the house.

"I have a warrant for Cicely's DNA," Grayson explained, grabbing the large padded envelope that earlier he'd put on the backseat. "I can compare it to Nina's. If it's a match, we'll have proof that Nina is really Sophia Collier."

"What about Claude's DNA?" Eve asked.

"There's a warrant for that, too. Nate's over there now collecting it."

Poor Nate. She doubted Claude would make the process easy. For that matter, maybe Cicely wouldn't either, especially when they told her that her long-lost daughter was likely dead. Murdered, at that.

Eve was bracing herself for the worst.

Grayson and she got out of the car and went to the door. Unlike at the Collier estate, Cicely already had the door open and was waiting for them.

Cicely looked exactly as she had in the photographs that Annabel had taken of her in Claude's office. Her short, dark brown hair was perfect, not a strand out of place, and she wore a simple olive-green wool suit. She was nothing like Annabel, her curvy young replacement, but it was easy to see that Cicely had once been stunningly beautiful.

"Sheriff Ryland," Cicely greeted. Her nerves were there in her voice and the worry etched on her face.

"Mrs. Collier. This is Eve Warren. She's helping with the investigation."

"Yes." She stared at Eve and repeated it. "Sebastian called and told me that Ms. Warren had taken a picture that you have some questions about."

Cicely stepped back, motioning for them to enter. She

didn't say anything else until she led them into a cozy room off the back of the foyer. The painting over the stone fireplace immediately caught Eve's eye. It was an oil painting of two babies. One was definitely Sophia, and she guessed the other one was Sebastian.

"My children," Cicely explained, following Eve's gaze. "Won't you please have a seat?" She motioned toward the pair of chairs.

There was a gleaming silver tray with a teapot and cookies on the coffee table. Cicely sat on a floral sofa and began to serve them. Eve sat across from her.

"Sebastian dropped by earlier, and we had a long chat." Cicely's hands were trembling when she passed Eve the tea that she'd poured in a delicate cup painted with yellow roses. "He's worried. And so am I. You think Sebastian had something to do with Nina Manning's death."

"Did he?" Grayson asked. He waved off the tea when Cicely offered it to him and sat in the chair next to Eve.

"No." Cicely's pale green eyes came to Eve's. "But of course, that means nothing. I would say that because he's my son."

Eve was more than a little surprised that a mother would admit that. Of course, despite her comment about *being worried,* maybe Cicely and Sebastian weren't that close.

Grayson took out the warrant and the DNA kit from the envelope and handed them to Cicely. "I need a sample of your DNA."

Cicely's forehead bunched up, and for a moment Eve

thought she would refuse, but she only refused the warrant. She pushed it aside, took the swab and without questions, she used it on the inside of her mouth.

"It's not necessary, you know," she said, handing the kit back to Grayson.

Yes, it was, and Eve figured Grayson was about to tell her why. Eve held her breath.

"Mrs. Collier—" But that was as far as Grayson got.

"Yes," Cicely interrupted. "I know that Nina Manning is…was my daughter."

Eve didn't know who looked more surprised—Grayson or her.

Cicely took a sip of tea, but her hand was trembling so much that some of it sloshed into the saucer. "I've already done the DNA test, and I can provide a copy of the results if you need them."

Grayson stayed quiet a moment. "How long have you known that she was your daughter?"

Cicely dodged his gaze. "About a month."

"A month?" Grayson mumbled something under his breath. "And you didn't think you should tell the police that your kidnapped daughter had returned?"

"I considered many things but not that." Cicely let the vague comment hang in the air for several seconds. "About a month ago, Nina showed up here and claimed to be Sophia. She said that as a baby she'd been abandoned at a church and had been raised in foster care. I didn't believe her, of course. Not until I got back the results from the DNA test."

Cicely blinked back tears. "I thought my daughter was dead."

After twenty-two years, that was reasonable, but Eve knew if she'd been in Cicely's shoes, she would have never stopped looking. *Never.*

"What happened when you found out Nina was telling the truth?" Grayson asked.

Balancing her cup on her lap, she picked at a nonexistent piece of lint on her jacket. "I begged her to come home. It was obvious that she needed help. Rehab. Counseling. Did you know that she'd been selling her body to support her drug habit?"

Grayson nodded. "She had a record."

Cicely pulled in her breath as if it were physically painful to hear her suspicions confirmed. "She refused my help. She only wanted money, and I didn't want to hand over cash because I knew she'd just use it for drugs. So, I called Claude to see if he would help me convince her to go to rehab."

Grayson and Eve exchanged a glance.

"Claude knew that Nina was your daughter?" Grayson asked.

"Of course," Cicely said without hesitation. "What? Did he deny it?"

"He did," Grayson confirmed.

Her mouth tightened. "Well, apparently he wasn't just a weasel of a husband, he's also a weasel of a father." She practically dumped her teacup onto the table and got up. She folded her arms over her chest and paced. "Did you meet his new tart of a wife?"

"Yes, we met Annabel." Grayson didn't say a word about the photos Annabel had provided. Without them, it might have taken a lot longer to make the connection between Nina and Sophia. However, Eve wasn't sure that had been Annabel's intention.

"Annabel," Cicely repeated the name like it was a profanity. "You can put her at the top of the list of suspects as my daughter's killer. She probably hired her lapdog, Leon Ames, to murder my baby in cold blood."

Eve set her tea aside also. This conversation was definitely loaded with bombshells. "Why would Annabel do that?" Eve wanted to know.

Cicely rubbed her fingers together. "Money, plain and simple. Claude's dying, you know?"

Grayson shook his head. "You're sure?"

"Positive. Sebastian told me all about it. Claude has a malignant nonoperable brain tumor. Probably has less than two months to live. And when they put Claude in the ground, the tart will inherit half of his estate. If Sophia had lived, the split would have been three ways. Apparently, that wasn't enough money for her."

Mercy. If that was true, then Cicely had not only just given Annabel a motive but Sebastian, as well. After all, Sebastian certainly hadn't volunteered anything about the dead woman being his sister. In fact, he'd lied to Grayson from the very start.

"I need to re-interview Claude and Sebastian," Grayson said, standing.

"Annabel, too," Cicely insisted. "She's the one who

had my baby killed, and I'm going to prove it. I want her surgically perfected butt tossed in jail."

Cicely wasn't so shaky now. She looked like a woman on a mission of revenge.

"You need to stay out of the investigation," Grayson reminded her. "If Annabel is guilty, I'll figure out a way to prove it."

Cicely didn't respond, and Eve wondered just how much trouble the woman would be. She wasn't just going to drop this.

"You can see yourselves out," Cicely said with ice in her voice. She'd apparently worked herself into a frenzy and was no longer in the hostess mode.

Grayson and Eve did just that. They saw themselves out, but Eve was reeling from what they'd just learned. Reeling and frustrated.

"I thought by now we'd have just one suspect," Eve whispered to Grayson on the way to the door. "Instead we have two—Annabel and Sebastian."

"We have four," Grayson whispered back, and he didn't say more until they were outside. "Claude might not have been so happy to see his drug-addicted, prostitute daughter return to the family fold."

True. He had a thing about keeping mud off his good name. "And the fourth suspect?"

Grayson opened the car door for her, and she got inside. "Cicely."

Eve shook her head. "You think she would kill her own daughter?"

"I don't know, but I'm going to find out." He shut her

door, got in behind the wheel and drove away. He took a deep breath. "I could drop you off at SAPD headquarters while I re-interview the Colliers."

Eve gave him a flat look. "I'm going with you."

Grayson matched her look and added a raised eyebrow. "There could be a killer in the house."

She wasn't immune to the fear, mainly because Eve believed that one of the Colliers was indeed a killer. But she was stuck on this investigation treadmill until Grayson made an arrest. Eve wanted to confront the danger head-on, and the sooner that happened, the better.

Grayson mumbled something about her being stubborn and grabbed his phone. "Then I'll have Nate bring the Colliers into the police station."

Eve didn't have to guess how this would play out. "They aren't going to like that."

"Good. Because I don't like the lies they've told us. Plus, I'd like to see how Claude reacts when I show him the memory card his wife gave us."

Eve almost felt sorry for Annabel. *Almost.* But then, Annabel did have a strong motive for murder—her soon-to-be-dead husband's money. And it was as if Annabel was trying to put the blame on either Claude or her stepson with those pictures she'd taken.

Grayson made the call to Nate, and while he was arranging the follow-up interview with the Colliers, Eve grabbed her laptop because she wanted to continue studying the photos. Before she could do that, however, she noticed the email from her doctor, Alan Stephenson.

The message was simple. "I've been trying to reach you. Call me."

Eve automatically reached for her cell, only to remember she didn't have one. It was in Grayson's truck, which had gone into the creek. She hadn't checked her answering machine at the condo either, mainly because Grayson had been in such a hurry to get her out of there.

"I need to use your phone," she told Grayson the moment he ended his call with Nate.

"Anything wrong?" he asked.

"I'm not sure." Eve took the cell and frantically pressed in the phone number at the bottom of the email. A dozen things went through her mind, most of them bad. Had the doctor been wrong about her ovulating? Had she put Grayson through all of this for nothing? Her heart broke at the thought of her being too late to have a child of her own.

She got the doctor's answering service first, but Dr. Stephenson had left word to put her call through to him. Moments later, the doctor picked up.

"Eve," he greeted, but she could hear something in his voice. This was not good news.

"I got your email. You've been trying to call me?"

"Most of yesterday afternoon. I found a private sperm donor, but as you probably already know, it's already too late. I'm sorry."

Her lungs were aching so she released the breath she'd been holding. "I found a donor." She didn't look at Grayson, but she sensed he was looking at her.

"That's wonderful." The doctor sounded both surprised and relieved. "Did you use artificial insemination?"

The image of Grayson in the woods flashed through her mind. "No. There wasn't time."

The doctor cleared his throat. "Well, the old-fashioned way works, too."

And was a lot more pleasurable. But Eve kept that to herself. "I know it's probably a long shot."

"Maybe not. Having sex when you're ovulating substantially increases the odds. Come in next week, and I'll run a test. We should be able to tell if you're pregnant."

Everything inside Eve began to spin. "Next week? That soon?"

"That soon," the doctor assured her. "Call the office and make an appointment. I'll see you then."

The doctor ended the call, and Eve just sat there and stared at the phone. It was exactly the news she wanted. The doctor was hopeful that she had conceived, and she wouldn't have to wait long. Seven days. That was it. And she would know if Grayson and she had made a baby.

But she immediately shook her head. She couldn't think of this as Grayson's baby.

Only hers.

"My doctor can do the pregnancy test next week," she relayed to Grayson, though he was looking at everything but her now.

He didn't respond. Which was just as well. Best not to mention pregnancy tests or the baby again because if this interview with the Colliers went well, maybe

Grayson could make an arrest. Then, they would go their separate ways.

That stung.

But it was necessary. A baby had to be enough. She couldn't go weaving a fantasy life with Grayson when the last thing he wanted was to raise another child.

Eve cursed the tears that sprang to her eyes, and then she cursed Grayson for being able to detach so easily. She glanced at him to see if he'd had any reaction whatsoever to the test news, but he was volleying his attention between the street ahead and the rearview mirror.

That wasn't a detached look on his face.

"What's wrong?" she asked, turning in her seat to follow his gaze.

He reached inside his jacket and drew his gun. "Someone's following us."

Chapter Thirteen

Next week.

The timing of Eve's pregnancy results should have been the last thing on Grayson's mind, but he was having a hard time pushing it aside.

"That dark blue car is the one following us?" Eve asked. She apparently wasn't thinking baby tests, either. She had her attention on the vehicle behind them.

"Yeah." It wasn't right on their tail, but the blue car had stayed several vehicles back and had made the last three turns that Grayson had taken.

"Can you see the driver?" she asked.

"No." The noon sun was catching the tint of the windows at the wrong angle, and Grayson couldn't even tell how many people there were in the car. Heck, he wasn't positive they were even being followed.

So, Grayson did a test of his own.

Without signaling, he took a right turn so quickly that the driver behind him honked. But Grayson got his answer. The blue car made the same turn.

"What now?" There was a tremble in Eve's voice, and

it had been that way since she'd spoken to her doctor. But now it was heavy with concern.

"We drive to SAPD headquarters as planned." Grayson only hoped the car followed them into the parking lot so he could confront this moron. Of course, he didn't want to do that with Eve around, but maybe he could get her inside the headquarters building first.

Grayson made his way through the side streets and spotted the SAPD parking lot just ahead. He pulled in, heading straight toward the drop-off that would put Eve just a few yards from the front door.

"The driver didn't turn," Eve relayed.

A glance in the rearview mirror verified that. Maybe this idiot hadn't wanted to risk arrest, but that didn't mean he wouldn't follow them when they left. Grayson would have to take extra precautions. He damn sure didn't want someone trying to shoot out their tires again.

"I'll park and be inside in a minute," Grayson told Eve and was thankful she didn't argue with him about that. The instant he came to a stop, Eve hurried inside the building.

Nate was there, just inside the door waiting for her, and Grayson caught a glimpse of Nate pulling her into his arms for a hug. It was ironic. His brothers had always loved Eve, had always thought of her as part of the family. How would they react if it turned out that she was indeed pregnant with his child?

Grayson groaned.

Maybe the better question was, how would *he* react? Well, next week he'd know. By then, he'd hopefully have Nina Manning's killer behind bars and would be able to have some time to think this all through.

He parked and went inside to join Eve and Nate who were waiting for him in the reception area.

"Eve said someone was following you?" Nate asked.

"Yeah. But he apparently got cold feet. I got a description but not the plates."

Nate's forehead bunched up. "When you get ready to take Eve back to the ranch, I'll have one of the cruisers accompany you. That should deter anyone from following or launching another attack."

You'd think, but this investigation was twisting and turning too much for Grayson's liking. He just wanted it to end so that Eve could be safe.

"Sebastian Collier is already here," Nate announced, leading them through the headquarters toward the interview rooms. "Claude and Annabel are on the way."

"Did they give you any hassle about coming?" Eve asked.

The flat look Nate gave her indicated they had. "Claude says he'll sue us for harassment."

Grayson figured the man would use that threat, but if the DNA proved that Nina was his biological child, then that might get SAPD authorization for a search warrant to start going through not just the Collier estate, but Claude and Sebastian's financials. After all, someone had paid off Leon Ames, and Grayson was betting it was a Collier. Unfortunately, if they used cash, then the financial records might be a dead end.

"Eve and I can watch through the two-way mirror in

the adjacent room," Nate suggested. Both Grayson and he looked at Eve, and she opened her mouth, probably to argue.

"Give yourself a break from the stress," Grayson told her, and he dropped his gaze to her stomach.

Her eyes widened and just like that, she nodded. Yeah, it was a dirty trick considering she might not even be pregnant, but there was no reason for her to go a second round with this pack of jackals. Just being in the same room with them spiked his blood pressure.

Nate maneuvered them through the maze of halls until they reached the interview room, and he took Eve next door. Sebastian was seated, but he didn't offer the smile and warm welcome that he had earlier.

"I'm assuming this is important?" Sebastian asked. Everything about his body language revealed his impatience and annoyance. His face was tight, and his breath was coming out in short bursts.

"It's important," Grayson assured him. He didn't sit. He wanted to stand so he could violate Sebastian's personal space and make him even more uncomfortable. "Did you have someone follow me a few minutes ago?"

"Please." Sebastian stretched out the syllables. "I have better things to do, like last-minute shopping. Tomorrow's Christmas Eve." He stared at them, and then he mumbled a profanity under his breath. "Look, I don't know why I'm suddenly a suspect, but I did nothing wrong."

"You lied to me."

The staring match continued, and Sebastian was the

first to look away. More profanity came. "About two weeks ago Nina Manning called me and asked to meet her. She claimed she was my long-lost sister. The timing was suspicious because her call came less than twenty-four hours after my father found out he was dying."

Grayson reserved judgment on the suspicious part. "Did you meet with her?"

"Yes. At a hotel in downtown San Antonio. I didn't believe her. I thought she was running a scam, but because I didn't want her upsetting my father, I was prepared to pay her off. Then, my father showed up, and after they argued, Nina ran out."

Well, that explained Annabel's pictures. "How did your father know about the meeting?"

"Nina called him, too. I guess she figured if she couldn't get the money from me, then she'd get it from my father."

Something about this didn't sound right. "If Nina wanted money, why did she run off after the so-called argument?"

"Because she was a drug-addicted, lying little witch," someone said from the doorway. It was Claude, and Annabel was by his side. Both looked about as thrilled to be there as Sebastian was.

Sebastian got to his feet. "You should sit, Father."

"I don't intend to be here that long," Claude fired back. "My attorney is on the way, and I've already put a call in to the mayor. I will not be treated like a common criminal." He aimed that remark and an accompanying glare at Grayson.

"Besides, Claude isn't well enough for this," Annabel added. The words were right, but the emotion didn't quite make it to her eyes. No glare for her, but she did look uncomfortable.

"A woman is dead," Grayson stated, looking at Claude. "She was last seen alive with your son and former employee. That employee tried to kill me and the woman who photographed Nina Manning." He paused. "Or maybe I should call the dead woman Sophia Collier."

"Never!" Claude's voice boomed through the hall, and with his index finger pointed at Grayson, he stepped into the room. "That piece of trash has no blood of mine in her."

Grayson shrugged. "Your ex-wife thought differently. She believed Nina was Sophia."

Annabel huffed. Now, there was real emotion. "Of course Cicely would believe that. She's mentally unstable, you know."

"She is," Sebastian agreed.

Grayson glanced at Claude to see if he had a comment about his ex, but Claude's jaw was so tight that Grayson figured he wasn't capable of speaking. Grayson made a mental note to do some digging to see if Cicely was indeed suffering from any form of mental illness.

"Since Nina's paternity is in question, we needed the DNA sample from you," Grayson told Claude.

"Which I gave," Claude spat out. "But there's no test that will convince me that she was my Sophia."

"Your son must have thought it was at least possible,"

Grayson disputed, "because he met with her again at the charity rodeo."

"I didn't meet with her," Sebastian insisted. "I already told you she was there with Leon. I simply ran into them."

Grayson just looked at them, waiting for an explanation he could actually believe—because he didn't buy the running into them story. His stony look didn't stop with just Sebastian, either. When Grayson let his intense stare stay on Annabel, her breath began to tremble, and she actually dropped back a step, probably because she thought she was about to be outed about the memory disk she'd given him. And Grayson considered it, but if either Sebastian or Claude was the killer, then that might make Annabel the next victim.

There was a soft knock, and since the door was still open, Grayson didn't have any trouble seeing who'd made the sound.

Cicely.

She was holding her leather purse in front of her like a shield, and she looked at them as if trying to figure out what was going on. Grayson knew how she felt.

"By any chance were you the one who followed Ms. Warren and me?" Grayson asked.

"Yes." And Cicely didn't hesitate, either. "I wanted to see if you'd run to Claude and tell him everything I said to you." She gave a smug nod. "But instead you ordered him to come here. Did he deny it?" Cicely asked, sliding her venomous gaze at Claude.

Claude had some venom of his own. The veins on his

forehead and neck started to bulge. "If you're talking about that woman claiming to be Sophia, of course I denied it. She wasn't our daughter."

"I told you that I did a DNA test," Cicely said between clenched teeth.

"A test that could have been faked," Sebastian interrupted. "You're so eager to find your long-lost daughter that you're willing to believe anything."

"I faked nothing, and neither did Sophia." Cicely was so angry now that she was shaking, and she opened her purse and snatched something from it. Something encased in a plastic zip bag. She slapped it onto the table.

Grayson walked closer to see what it was. He'd expected a photo or something else that might shed light on this.

But it was a diamond bracelet.

Grayson frowned. "Is this connected to the investigation?"

"It is." Cicely pointed to Annabel. "She gave the bracelet to Sophia as a bribe to get her to leave."

Annabel, Sebastian and Claude all disagreed, and they weren't quiet about it, either. "I've never seen that bracelet before," Annabel insisted. She reached for the bag, but Cicely snagged her wrist.

"Sophia said you gave it to her and demanded that she sell it and use the money to get out of town. I sealed it up because I'm betting the police can find your DNA on it."

Maybe. But that wouldn't prove anything other than

perhaps Annabel had told him another lie. It didn't mean she was a killer.

"How did you get the bracelet?" Grayson asked Cicely.

And with that one simple question, the room fell silent, and all eyes were on Cicely.

Cicely lifted her chin as if insulted by the implication of the question. "When Sophia came to my house, she had the bracelet with her and said it was a bribe from Annabel. She also said she was scared, that she thought Annabel would kill her if she didn't leave town and not try to stake a claim to her rightful inheritance."

"It's only a rightful claim if she was my sister," Sebastian tossed at her. "And she wasn't."

That started up another round of accusations, and Cicely was loud and liberal with the name calling—especially the names she called Annabel.

"Shut up!" Grayson practically yelled. And he turned back to Cicely. "Why would Sophia leave the bracelet with you?"

Cicely didn't jump to answer that. In fact, she swallowed hard. "She didn't say, exactly, but I think she knew something bad was going to happen to her. I think she wanted me to have it so I could prove that Annabel was her killer."

Annabel gasped and caught on to Grayson's arm. "I didn't kill her. I…" But she didn't finish, and the grip she had on his arm melted away. "I didn't kill her," she repeated.

Sebastian moved closer as if checking to make sure

Annabel was okay. When his attention came back to Cicely, his eyes were narrowed. "Mother, why don't you tell the sheriff about your association with Leon Ames?"

"Association?" Cicely pulled back her shoulders. "I don't know what you mean."

"Really?" Sebastian challenged. He walked toward his mother. Slow, calculated steps. "Leon visited you often. In fact, he visited you in the past week."

Cicely didn't deny it, and when she tried to look away, Grayson got right in her face. "Is it true?"

The woman finally nodded, prompting an I-told-you-so huff from Sebastian. Neither Annabel nor Claude seemed surprised with Cicely's admission, which meant they had likely known.

"Leon was my friend." Cicely's voice was practically a whisper.

Friend. That was an interesting relationship, especially considering Leon worked for Claude. Of course, that didn't mean he hadn't been secretly working for Cicely, as well. Since Grayson believed that Leon had likely killed Nina, now he had to figure out who had given the man orders to kill.

"Leon was your lover and would have done anything for you," Sebastian accused. He was smirking when he looked at Grayson. "My mother has an affinity for associating with lowlifes. That's probably why she was so eager to believe that woman when she claimed she was Sophia."

That put some fire back into Cicely, and she opened

her mouth, probably to verbally blast her son into the next county.

But a sound stopped her.

A gasp.

Not just any ordinary gasp, either. It was as if all the air swooshed out of Claude's lungs.

"Sebastian," Claude managed to say. A split second before he clamped his hands to the sides of his head and dropped to the floor.

Chapter Fourteen

Eve got out of Grayson's car and made her way up the steps of the ranch house. Despite the fact that someone had tried to kill them twice today, her nerves were no longer firing on all cylinders.

Thank God.

The bone-weary fatigue was no doubt responsible for that. The Christmas lights helped, too. Hard to think of murders and attacks when there were hundreds of multicolored lights twinkling around her. And then she stepped inside and knew this was the main source of her calmer nerves.

For reasons she didn't want to explore, the Ryland ranch always had and always would feel like home to her. So many memories, and they flooded through her, easing away the rest of the tension.

Grayson walked in right behind her. He had his phone sandwiched between his ear and shoulder, a place it'd been during most of their drive from San Antonio back to the ranch. Along the way, he'd gotten several updates on the investigation.

And Claude.

Judging from the part of this particular conversation, Grayson was talking with Claude's doctor.

When the man had first collapsed at the SAPD precinct, Eve had thought he was faking it so he could put a quick end to the interview. But after he'd been rushed to the hospital in an ambulance, the doctors had informed Grayson that Claude's condition was critical. So, no more interviews until the man was stable. Whenever that would be.

"Claude is still touch and go," Grayson relayed to her when he ended the call. "He might not make it through the night." He slapped his phone shut and pulled in a long, weary breath.

Eve understood that weariness. She wasn't fond of Claude, but if he died, he might take his secrets to the grave. Especially one secret.

Had he been the one responsible for Nina's death?

Or did that guilt lie with Sebastian, Annabel or even Cicely?

"What about the DNA results?" Eve wanted to know because she'd heard Grayson's phone conversation with Nate about that, as well.

Grayson shook his head. "Nothing yet, but we should have preliminary results in an hour or two." He used the keypad on the wall to arm the security system. "Nate's also checking to see if anyone else, including Cicely, ran a DNA test on Nina."

She thought about that for a moment. "But Cicely said she'd done the test. Why would she lie about something like this?"

"Who knows? I'm still working that out, but I'm not ready to believe anything a Collier says."

Eve agreed. All of them seemed to have something to hide, but the DNA results might be a start toward learning the truth. If Nina was indeed Sophia, then that only strengthened Sebastian and Annabel's motives for murder. They might not have wanted to split Claude's estate three ways.

Still, there were some things Eve hadn't been able to grasp. "I understand why Claude might have had Nina killed," she commented. "With his elitist attitude, he would never admit to having a drug addict daughter. But what about Cicely? She seems more than willing to admit that Nina was hers. So, why would she kill her?"

"*Seems*," Grayson emphasized. "That's why I want to see when and if Cicely ran the DNA test."

Ah, Eve got it then. Because the test could have been a cover-up. Nina could have confronted or even attempted to blackmail Cicely, and Cicely could have refused to believe this was her long-lost daughter. Cicely could have had Nina killed out of anger. However, the woman wouldn't look like a major murder suspect if she told everyone that she knew Nina was truly Sophia.

If Cicely had done that, it was a smart move.

"Anyone home?" Grayson called out. When no one answered, he headed for the kitchen, and Eve followed.

She immediately spotted the note from Bessie on the double-door stainless-steel fridge. "Mason called. He and Dade are staying in town to work on the case," Grayson read aloud. "Nate and the baby won't be home, either. Haven't heard a peep from Kade. Dinner's in the fridge and I'm headed out for girls' night at my sister's place in Saddle Springs. Give Eve a good-night kiss for me." Bessie had added a smiley face.

The woman's attempt at humor didn't cause either Grayson or Eve to smile. But it did give Eve an uneasy feeling because she realized that Grayson and she were alone in the house. She glanced at Grayson, and his quick look away convinced her that he was aware of it, as well.

"You'll need to eat," he reminded her.

"You, too," she reminded him right back.

But neither of them moved. They both stood there, staring at Bessie's note, while the air zinged around them. For a moment Eve wondered if Grayson might act on that good-night kiss after all, but he mumbled something about being hungry and pulled open the fridge door.

There was a large baking dish with lasagna on the center shelf. She was suddenly starving. She knew from experience that Bessie was an amazing cook, but Eve decided both Grayson and she could use a little space to clear their heads. After all, in the past twenty-four hours, they'd nearly been killed and had then gotten embroiled in a murder investigation.

They'd also had sex.

Even the fatigue couldn't erase the too-familiar tingling she still felt. And that was another huge reason for a little head-clearing space.

"I think I'll take a shower before I eat," Eve told him.

Grayson didn't have time to respond because his cell phone rang. Eve waited just a few seconds to make sure it wasn't critical, but when she realized it was the youngest Ryland, Kade, calling for an update about the investigation, she excused herself and went to the guest suite.

Eve intended to head straight for the shower, but she saw the photo album on the guest bed. The leather cover had probably once been white but had aged to a rich cream color, and it was thick, at least three inches.

"Here's your Christmas present. Thought you'd like copies of some old memories," was written on the sticky note attached. "Love, Bessie."

She was reasonably sure she didn't need any more memories or copies of memories, but Eve sat on the edge of the bed and opened it. The first picture was of Boone and Marcie Ryland, Grayson's parents, on their wedding day. They were both smiling, and there were no hints of the troubles to come nineteen years later when Boone would walk out on Marcie and his six sons. A few months after that, Marcie would take her own life.

What a waste. So many lives had been changed because of Boone's departure. Especially Grayson's. If he hadn't had to raise his brothers, he might have wanted a family of his own. But it hurt Eve too much to dwell on that particular *if*.

Eve turned the page to Grayson's baby picture—probably taken when he was no more than a day or two old. She smiled. If she was indeed pregnant, then this was a glimpse of how her baby could look.

She flipped through the pages, each of them snapshots of time. Grayson's first horseback ride—barely a toddler in the saddle. His first day of school.

And then Eve was in the picture—literally.

Nearly all the subsequent pages had photos of her with the Ryland family. Christmas. Easter. Birthdays. She'd been a part of them. Always engulfed in those strong arms that had always given her so much love.

She ached to be part of that again but knew it was lost forever. The ultimatum she'd given Grayson all those years ago had sealed her fate and separated her from him, and his family, forever.

Or had it?

Her mind began to spin with the possibility of her baby being part of this. Not permanently part of the family but maybe visits so the baby would know his or her bloodline.

But she forced herself to stop.

She'd made the deal with Grayson—if he got her pregnant, that would be it. No strings attached. So, her fate was sealed. Her baby's fate, too. One way or another, she would leave as soon as it was safe.

Eve blinked back tears, but more followed. She was still swiping them away when the house phone rang. She glanced at the caller ID screen and saw that it was Annabel Collier. Since this could be important, she lay the album aside and hurried downstairs.

Grayson was in the kitchen where he was already talking to Annabel, and he had put the call on speaker. "I'm listening," he said to Annabel.

Annabel didn't say anything for several seconds. "I'm not sure how to say this."

Grayson huffed. "Try," he insisted. He looked at Eve then, and his right eyebrow slid up, questioning her about something. When she shook her head, Grayson went to her and touched her cheek. Or so she thought. But not a real touch. He wiped away a stray tear.

"You okay?" he mouthed.

Eve moved away from him, and thankfully didn't have to explain anything because Annabel continued.

"I lied to you," the woman confessed.

Grayson didn't huff this time, but he looked as if he wanted to do just that. "Which lie would that be?"

"About the diamond bracelet. It was mine. I figured you would discover that when you had it tested so I decided to come clean. I gave it to Nina, hoping it would convince her to leave."

Now Eve was the one to huff. The Colliers were certainly free with their lies, and she didn't think it was a coincidence that the lies seemed to be attempts to prevent them from being charged with murder.

"Then Cicely was right." Grayson took out a plate of heated lasagna from the microwave and handed it to Eve.

"Cicely was trying to make me sound guilty. That's the only reason she had the bracelet. She wants to incriminate me."

Eve got them both out some silverware and paper napkins and sat at the counter. Grayson got out two longneck beers and his plate. He looked at her. Studied her. Maybe trying to figure out what had caused those tears.

"The question you should be asking yourself is how Cicely got that bracelet in the first place," Annabel went on. "Because I seriously doubt Nina freely gave it to her. That bracelet was worth thousands, and a druggie like Nina wouldn't have handed it over without a fight."

"Are you saying Cicely killed Nina and took the bracelet?" Grayson didn't wait. He sat and started to eat.

"Yes, that's exactly what I'm saying." But then Annabel paused. "Or maybe Sebastian killed her and gave the bracelet to his mother. He could have done it to try to incriminate me, too."

"Sebastian," Grayson repeated. "I wondered when this conversation would turn to him."

"What do you mean?" Annabel accused.

He had a gulp of beer first. And another look at Eve. "I mean your husband is dying. By tomorrow morning, you could be a wealthy widow—thanks to your huge inheritance. If Sebastian were out of the picture, you'd have double the wealth and no pesky stepchildren around to cash in on their daddy's will."

Annabel made a sound of outrage. "I didn't kill anyone!" she practically shouted.

"Maybe. Can you say the same for your husband?" Grayson challenged.

Silence. The moments crawled by, and Grayson continued to sip his beer. The glances at her continued, too. What didn't happen was a denial from Annabel about her husband's innocence.

"If Claude recovers, you'll have to ask him that." Annabel's voice was no longer hot with anger. It was ice-cold and impatient.

"I will," Grayson assured her. "Now, tell me why you gave me the memory card with the photos."

She paused again. "Because I knew something wasn't right when Nina showed up. Claude and Sebastian were having secret conversations. And Cicely kept calling. I didn't know Nina was going to die, but I thought I might need proof."

"Proof of what?" Grayson pressed.

"That I didn't have anything to do with her, her life or her death."

"Well, the pictures don't prove that." Of course, they did prove that all their suspects had had close contact with a woman who was murdered. Even if Annabel hadn't taken the pictures herself, she had certainly been aware of them.

"I didn't kill her," Annabel insisted. "Now that I've told you about the bracelet, we have nothing further to discuss." And she hung up.

Without taking his attention off Eve, he leaned over and pressed the end button on the phone. Since his stare was making her uncomfortable, Eve focused on the square of lasagna in front of her.

"Why are you looking at me like that?" she finally asked.

Grayson opened his mouth. Closed it. And the staring continued.

Eve decided she'd just spill it. "I was crying because

I'd been looking at a photo album that Bessie gave me for Christmas. Old memories," she settled for saying.

"Oh." And judging from his tone, that was not the answer he'd expected. "I thought maybe…well, I thought you'd learned you weren't pregnant."

Now, it was her turn to say "Oh." He'd seen the tears and assumed the worst. Or maybe in his case, the best—that maybe she'd gotten her period. However, that wouldn't be just bad news. It would break her heart.

"No." Since the lasagna suddenly wasn't settling well in her stomach, Eve got up so she could put it back in the fridge. "I won't know until next week."

"Okay." He nodded, repeated it.

She could feel his regret. His doubts. And Eve was just too tired to go there. She whirled back around to remind him that from here on out he wasn't part of her life.

But Grayson stood and whirled around at the same time, and they practically smacked right into each other. Eve started to move back, way back, but Grayson caught on to her arm, anchoring her in place. She could have shaken off his grip, of course, but she didn't.

"I can't do this," she managed to say.

His eyebrow came up again, and he was obviously waiting for an explanation of what specifically she couldn't do, but Eve hesitated one second too long, and in that second she got caught up in Grayson's eyes. His scent.

His touch.

She'd never been able to resist him, never, and apparently tonight was no different.

"I can't, either," he answered. Though she had no idea what he meant by that.

She soon learned though.

Grayson leaned in and put his mouth on hers. It was just a touch, barely qualifying as a kiss, but this was Grayson. He could make her melt with a simple brush of his mouth and she'd forget all the arguments she had going through her head about why she couldn't do this. Kissing would only lead to more complications.

Still, Eve moved closer.

She hooked her arm around the back of his neck and eased him down to her. His mouth pressed harder, and that barely-a-kiss became a real one.

He snapped her to him, body to body, and took her mouth the way he always had. He was clever and thorough, and any thought of resisting him flew right out of her mind.

In fact, she did the opposite of resisting.

Eve got even closer, sliding her hands down his back and adjusting their positions so that the kiss turned to full body contact. Yes, there were clothes between them, but she knew his body so well that she had no trouble filling in the blanks of how it would feel to have him naked against her.

"You still can't?" he mumbled against his mouth.

She couldn't answer because the kiss turned French and scalding hot. If she'd had breath left to speak, she wouldn't have used it to state the obvious because clearly she *could*.

Couldn't she?

This wouldn't be lab sex for the purpose of getting her pregnant. This would be like old times. And then what?

Eve forced herself to consider *then what*.

Grayson cursed, and for a moment she thought he had reached the same *then what?* roadblock that she had. It took her a moment to realize he was cursing because his phone was ringing. She hadn't heard it over the roar in her head.

"It's Nate," Grayson let her know after he glanced down at the screen. He flipped the cell open and jabbed the speaker button. He also leaned against the kitchen counter and tried to level his breathing.

Eve did the same, though it would take more than some deep breaths to get back to normal.

"Please tell me you have good news," he greeted Nate.

"Well, it's news," Nate explained. "I'll let you decide if it's good or not. Just got the preliminary DNA results, and Nina Manning was indeed Sophia Collier."

So, there it was—the proof that at least some of the Colliers weren't going to like because that proof was also motive.

"I did a statewide search of labs that had tested Sophia's DNA," Nate continued, "and I couldn't find any record that Cicely had requested a test."

Another lie, and Eve was betting that Cicely would just lie again when Grayson questioned her about it.

Eve huffed. Would they ever learn the truth so that Sophia's killer could be brought to justice and so that she could finally get on with her life?

She looked at Grayson and felt his kiss still burning her mouth. Maybe getting on with her life wasn't even possible. That kiss had proven that she would never get Grayson out of her blood and out of her system.

Never.

"But someone else did request a test on Sophia's DNA," Nate added. That caught Eve's attention. "That happened just three days before Sophia was murdered."

"Who?" Grayson and Eve asked in unison.

"Sebastian," Nate answered.

Eve saw the surprise in Grayson's eyes. Sebastian had denied that Nina was his sister, but yet he obviously knew the truth because he'd had her DNA tested.

"You're positive about this?" Grayson pressed.

"Positive, and I have proof. Sebastian tried to cover up the payment for the test by using cash, but the lab has 24/7 surveillance. We have footage of him going into the lab and then picking up the results."

"What kind of a timeline are we looking at for this? Did Sebastian have the DNA results before Nina was murdered?" Grayson wanted to know.

"Oh, yeah," Nate assured him. "He had them all right. Less than twenty-four hours after he got the results that confirmed Nina was his sister, someone killed her."

Grayson shook his head, mumbled something. "Then as far as I'm concerned, that makes Sebastian Collier our number-one suspect."

Eve agreed, and judging from the sound he made, apparently so did Nate.

"So, what do you want me to do?" Nate asked Grayson.

Grayson didn't even hesitate. "Pick up Sebastian and put him in a holding cell. I'll be at SAPD first thing in the morning to read him his rights and arrest him."

Chapter Fifteen

Grayson downed the shot of whiskey. It was strong stuff, Mason's private stash, and it burned his eyes and throat. What it didn't do was clear his head.

But then, that was asking a lot from a shot of whiskey.

The details of the case kept running through his head. Thoughts of Eve kept running through his body. Neither would give him much peace tonight, even though the house was whisper-quiet and would likely stay that way because it was going on midnight.

"Midnight," he mumbled.

Since he had an early-morning trip to SAPD to question and arrest Sebastian, he should be sleeping. Heck, Eve probably was. She'd called it a night well over an hour ago.

Good thing, too, because before her good-night Grayson had been on the verge of resuming the make-out session that Nate's call had interrupted.

He shouldn't have touched her.

And he damn sure shouldn't have kissed her.

He should have just walked away and let fate sort out the details of what was to come in the next week or so. But the sight of those tears in her eyes had shaken him. Grayson considered himself a strong man, but he wasn't strong enough to keep her at arm's length when she'd been crying.

He poured himself another shot and took it in one gulp. Still no relief. So he gave up on the whiskey and headed out of the den and to his bathroom for a shower. He stripped along the way, dropping his clothes on the bedroom floor, and he kept the water ice-cold.

That didn't work, either.

There was a furnace of heat in his body, and there was only one cure for what he felt.

Eve.

Damn her. Damn *him*.

Grayson knew that pretty much any woman could satisfy his body, but there was only one woman who could satisfy *him*. And that was Eve.

For most of his life, she'd been what had fired him up and cooled him down—sometimes in the same minute. She'd been the one woman he couldn't get out of his head. And no amount of whiskey or cold water was going to cure that. No. There was only one cure, and she was right across the hall.

Grayson cursed and put on his jeans. No sense trying to talk himself out of jumping off this Texas-size cliff. He was going to jump all right, and this could be a fall that would hurt for the rest of his life.

He didn't knock on the guestroom door. Didn't want anything to slow him down and stop him. Well, that was the plan anyway, but his mouth went dry when he spotted her. Not asleep as he'd thought she would be. No. Eve was wide-awake, lying in bed, the ice-white covers draped loosely over her breasts and the rest of her.

Grayson shut the door. And went to her.

"The right thing would be for me to go back to my room," he told her.

Her mouth trembled slightly and turned into the hint of a smile. "Grayson, for once in your life, don't do the right thing, okay?"

She caught on to his hand, pulled him closer. Grayson obliged and leaned down for a kiss. He'd kissed her a thousand times, maybe more, but each time always felt like the first. That punch hit him hard in the chest and then below the belt.

How could he want anyone this much?

And worse, why would he want her this much even after he'd had her?

Grayson kept the kiss simple, though his body was revved up way past the kissing stage. Still, he needed this. The feel of her mouth against his. The sweet silk of her lips. Her taste. He needed it all, and apparently Eve did, too, because she kept inching him closer.

The covers shifted, and the sheet slipped off her breasts. No bra. Just Eve's bare breasts. He met her gaze and saw the little spark there.

Grayson used just the tip of his index finger to draw the covers down. He got an interesting show as he revealed every inch of her. Bare stomach. Bare hips. He heard himself choke back a groan.

No panties.

"I like to sleep naked," she whispered.

"I like that you like to sleep naked." He tried to chuckle. Failed at that, too.

"No." Eve tightened the grip on his hand. "Don't you dare have any doubts about this."

Oh. He had doubts, but he wasn't going to do anything about them. Grayson did what he did best. He took control of the situation. He raked back the rest of the covers, exposing every bit of Eve's naked body.

Yeah, she was beautiful.

He hadn't had to see her naked to remember that, but this trip down memory lane was a good one.

Grayson put his knee on the bed, the feather mattress giving way to his weight. He let himself ease into a fall and kissed her on the way down until his body was pressed hard against hers. The fit was right. Perfect. And it created pressure in all the right places.

"Jeans," she mumbled and fumbled for his zipper.

Grayson let her deal with that so he could make some headway with what he'd started. And what he'd started was a full-body kiss.

He trailed the kisses down her throat to her breasts. Yeah. That taste hadn't changed. He took her nipple into his mouth, and the zipper fumbling stopped, just as he figured it would. Eve moaned, arched her back and shoved her fingers into his hair to pull him closer.

"Yes." She repeated it and wrapped her legs around him.

His jeans were still between them, but Eve got the

position and the pressure just right for this to go to the next level.

"Make me crazy, Grayson," she whispered and then laughed, low and husky.

He was too involved in the kissing to laugh, but he smiled when he slid his body through her leg lock and kissed her where she really wanted to be kissed. Right in the center of all that wet heat.

But Eve didn't stay on just the receiving end. She ran her hands over his shoulder and into his hair. Her legs caressed his back...and lower.

She knew exactly how to drive him crazy, too. And how to pleasure him. After all, they'd spent their teen years making out in his truck. Kisses only, at first. Lots of kisses.

Then, the touches.

He'd given Eve her first climax with his hand in her panties. They'd lost their virginity on her seventeenth birthday. They'd both been clumsy and awkward. But they'd both learned a lot over the years.

"Too crazy," she let him know when she was close to climaxing.

She caught on to him, pulling him back up so she could go after his zipper again. She wasn't playing this time. She was hot and ready so Grayson helped her, and she used her feet and hands to work the jeans off his hips.

"Commando," she said when she noticed he wasn't wearing his usual boxers. She smiled when she looked down between their bodies and no doubt saw that he was hard as stone. "That's my Grayson."

She froze and got that deer-in-the-headlights look. As if she'd crossed some line and tried to take them back to a place they could never go again. And maybe she had with that *my Grayson*. But he didn't care a flying fig about lines. He'd crossed the biggest line of all just by coming into her room.

He pinned her hands to the bed. Pinned her body, too. She would want his full weight on her so Grayson obliged, and he pushed himself inside her.

Mercy.

The pleasure was blinding.

It was like coming home for Christmas.

Eve arched her back and pressed her head against the pillow. She rocked her hips into his, causing him to go deep and hard into her. He was probably too rough. That thought was just a flash, and soon he couldn't think at all.

He moved inside her. Faster. Harder. Deeper. Until she was so close to climax. Until everything was a blur.

Everything except Eve.

Everything inside him pinpointed on her. Just her. The primal ache clawed away at him. This need as old as man. The need to take and claim.

But there were other needs, too.

And it was that need that sent Grayson in search of a kiss. He wanted the taste of her in his mouth when he lost all reason. When she slipped over the edge.

Eve came in a flash, when Grayson was deep inside her, when his mouth took hers.

Grayson said her name. It came from a place deeper than the primal need that had brought them to this point.

Somewhere in his brain, it registered that this was going to complicate the hell out of things. But that was only a split-second thought. Eve's legs tightened around him. She pulled him closer, and her climax brought on his.

Grayson felt his body surrender. Felt that slam of pleasure that was beyond anything he ever deserved to feel. Something so perfect. So amazing.

So Eve.

Chapter Sixteen

"You did what?" Grayson snapped to the person on the other end of the phone.

Eve thought the caller might be Nate, but she wasn't sure, and she couldn't tell from the conversation what Grayson was snapping about now. But there was no doubt, he was snapping.

Eve stared out the car window, sipped her coffee and debated—again—what she should say to Grayson once he had finished this call. Or if she should say anything. After all, he certainly hadn't volunteered much about coming to her bed for one of the most amazing nights of her life.

In fact, he had avoided the subject.

Of course, he'd been on the phone most of the morning and during the entire drive from the ranch to San Antonio. So that was his excuse, but she had to wonder, if it hadn't been for the calls, would he have come up with another reason for them not to talk?

"You're positive this isn't some kind of ruse so Sebastian can escape?" Grayson demanded.

Mercy, that didn't sound good, and she didn't think

it was a good sign when Grayson turned off the interstate two exits before the one for SAPD headquarters. Grayson had been on his way to arrest Sebastian, but there had obviously been a change of plans.

"No," Grayson continued. Except that wasn't a bark or a snarl. He mumbled it. "Eve's with me. There wasn't anyone at the ranch to stay with her. The ranch hands have already left for their Christmas break."

Even though he practically mumbled that part, too, she heard the frustration. Grayson hadn't wanted her to come along when he questioned Sebastian. He'd wanted her tucked safely away at the ranch, but both Dade and Mason were still in town working the details of Nina's murder. Or rather Sophia Collier's murder. And with Bessie and the ranch hands off the grounds, Grayson had reluctantly brought her along to arrest and interrogate Sebastian.

Not the ideal way to spend Christmas Eve.

Of course, the danger was almost certainly over for her now that the photos she'd taken were in the hands of the authorities. Sebastian had no reason to kill her. Well, unless he was hell-bent on getting some kind of revenge because she'd inadvertently incriminated him, and now that he was in police custody, even that wasn't possible.

She hoped.

This could all be over soon, especially if Grayson managed to get a confession from Sebastian. Or if something hadn't gone wrong with his arrest. Judging from

Grayson's sour expression and change of direction, that wasn't just possible but likely.

Grayson slapped his phone shut and took the turn for San Antonio Memorial Hospital.

Her heart dropped.

"Is someone hurt?" she asked and then held her breath.

He shook his head. "Claude's doctor doesn't think he'll last much longer so he requested the family's presence at Claude's bedside. That includes Sebastian."

Since Claude was critical, the doctor's request was reasonable, or at least it would have been if Sebastian weren't a murder suspect.

"An SAPD officer is escorting Sebastian," Grayson let her know. "They should arrive at the hospital any minute now."

And that explained why Grayson took the final turn toward San Antonio Memorial. It wasn't a large hospital but was in one of the more affluent neighborhoods of the city. No surprise about that, considering Claude was a millionaire many times over.

"Did Nate say if Claude was talking?" Eve asked.

"He's lucid." Grayson paused. "And he wants to see me."

Strange. Claude certainly hadn't wanted to see Grayson when he'd been ordered to SAPD headquarters. "Do you think he'll make a deathbed confession?"

Grayson's scowl deepened. "Maybe. But if he does, it'll probably be for one reason—not to tell the truth, but to save his son."

Of course. With Claude dying, it wouldn't matter if he confessed to a murder he didn't commit. But then, it was possible that he had indeed killed Sophia since there was no tangible proof that Claude knew she was his biological daughter. And even if he had known, he could have killed her when he realized she wasn't the darling little girl he wanted in his family.

There was no street parking, just a multilevel parking garage so Grayson drove in and looked for a spot. He took the first one available, at the back of the second level.

Grayson glanced around. So did Eve. And somewhere amid the glancing, their gazes collided.

There.

Eve saw it in his eyes then—the conversation he'd been avoiding all morning.

"Do I need to apologize?" Grayson tossed out there like a gauntlet.

She thought about her answer. "No. Do I?" She tossed that proverbial gauntlet right back at him.

He cursed, looked away and scrubbed his hand over his face. "I'm the one who went to your bed."

"And I could have said no," Eve reminded him.

But that was a lie. She'd never been able to say no to Grayson, and she wouldn't have started last night. Still, this had caused more tension between them, and that's the last thing they needed when they were within minutes of facing the Colliers.

And facing a possible pregnancy.

Eve certainly hadn't been thinking about getting

pregnant when Grayson had climbed into bed with her. She'd been thinking about making love with him, but now that it was the morning after, she knew that last night had increased her chances of getting the baby she'd always wanted.

However, it hadn't helped her *relationship* with Grayson.

She could feel his uneasiness, and she had to do something to diffuse it.

"What happened between us doesn't have to mean anything," she settled for saying, but those words hurt. Because it sure as heck had meant something to her. It meant that Grayson had still wanted her enough to risk plenty by coming to her like that.

He looked at her, as if he might dispute her not-mean-anything offer, but he only shook his head. "We'll talk about this later."

Eve caught on to his arm when he started to bolt. "No need." That hurt, too, but she had to give Grayson an out. He'd done her a huge favor by having sex with her, and she didn't want him to feel guilty or tormented.

She leaned over and brushed a chaste kiss on his cheek. "I already know how you feel about fatherhood, about a lot of things." Eve had to take a deep breath before continuing. "And I know when this investigation is over, your life can get back to normal."

Something flashed through his metal-gray eyes, and his face tightened. For a moment she thought they might have that blowup they'd been skirting around all morning. But he didn't toss out any more gauntlets or launch into an argument. He eased her hand off his arm and stepped from the car.

Eve could only sigh and do the same.

The garage wasn't just dank, it was cold, and Eve pulled her coat tighter against her. She had no scarf or gloves. She'd forgotten to pick those up when they'd been at her condo the day before, and women's clothing was in short supply at the Ryland ranch. Eve had made do with the gray pants and sweater that she'd packed, but she had been forced to wear the same red coat that had survived their trek through the woods.

Ahead of her, Grayson pulled the sides of his buckskin jacket together, as well. No festive red for him. He was wearing his usual jeans and dark shirt. Practically a uniform for him. He'd also worn his badge and shoulder holster, of course, which meant because he was armed, they would have to go through security inside.

She fell in step alongside Grayson as they walked to the elevator that would take them into the hospital, but they didn't get far before Grayson stopped. He lifted his head and looked around, just as he'd done when he had first parked. She looked, too, but only saw the sea of cars in the dimly lit space.

"Is something wrong?" Eve asked.

Grayson didn't answer. He glanced around again and caught on to her to get her moving to the elevator. It was clear he was hurrying now, but Eve didn't know why.

"I got a bad feeling," Grayson mumbled.

That put her on full alert because she knew from experience that Grayson's instincts were usually right.

And they were.

The sound zinged through the garage. It wasn't a blast. Eve wasn't sure what it was until the window shattered on the car next to them. Then she knew.

Oh, God.

Someone had fired at them.

GRAYSON CURSED AND SHOVED Eve to the side between two parked cars. He followed, moving directly in front of her, and in the same motion, he drew his gun.

What the hell was happening now?

The danger to Eve should be over. Finished. She was no longer a threat to Sophia's killer since her photos had gone public. Obviously, the shooter wasn't aware of that.

Because another shot came right at them.

Not a loud blast but more like a swish. That meant the gunman was using a weapon rigged with a silencer.

This had to be connected to Sophia's murder. They couldn't be that unlucky to now be the victims of a random attack. Maybe someone didn't want them hearing whatever deathbed confession Claude was likely to make. If so, then it was even more vital that Grayson speak to the dying man.

Grayson pushed Eve flat on the concrete floor and tried to pinpoint the origin of those two shots. He also tried to spot the gunman. There was no sign of anyone, but he thought maybe the shots had come from a black van on the other side of the parking lot. It wasn't a huge space, only about fifty feet across, but with the vehicles jammed together, there were plenty of places for a would-be killer to hide.

"Call Nate and tell him we need backup," Grayson told Eve. Without taking his attention off that black van, he grabbed his phone from his jacket pocket and handed it to her.

Another shot.

This one smacked into the headlight of the car right next to them. The glass shattered, flying through the air, and Grayson had to duck down and shield his eyes.

Almost immediately, he heard footsteps.

Behind him, he also heard Eve call Nate and request assistance, but Grayson shut out what she was saying and concentrated on those footsteps. Someone was running, and he caught just a glimpse of that someone before they ducked out of sight.

The person was dressed head-to-toe in black and was wearing a black baseball cap that obstructed the shooter's face.

It could be anyone.

And that *anyone* ducked between two other vehicles—a white pickup truck and a red sports car.

"Nate's on the way," Eve relayed. "He said he'll seal off the exits to the garage and do a silent approach."

Good. He needed his brother because this situation could get more dangerous than it already was. If anyone came out of that elevator, the gunman would probably shoot to kill so there'd be no witnesses to this attack. Plus, someone driving into the garage could also become a target. Right now though Grayson's biggest concern was Eve, and getting her safely out of there.

He lifted his head a fraction and listened for any sound of movement or more footsteps. None on both counts. Just Eve's too-fast breathing, and she was mumbling something that sounded like a prayer. She was obviously terrified, and it didn't help that this was the third attempt to kill her. In fact, it was probably worse now because she might be pregnant.

But Grayson pushed that thought out of his mind.

He needed to focus, and he couldn't do that if he thought about the baby he'd possibly made with Eve.

The next shot got his full attention. It didn't slam into the car as the others had. This one was aimed at the ground, and it ripped through the concrete just a few feet in front of them. The shooter had obviously gotten himself in a better position to deliver a fatal shot.

Grayson needed to throw him off-kilter as much as he could. That wouldn't be easy since he only had his sidearm. There was extra ammunition in his car, but that was yards away and would be too dangerous to try to reach. That meant he had to make every shot count while maneuvering the gunman as far away from Eve as possible.

Grayson waited for the next shot, and he didn't have to wait long. It, too, tore into the floor and sent a cloud of debris and dangerous concrete bits right at them. He ducked out of cover for just a second and then fired in the direction of the shooter.

He hit the red sports car.

The shot bashed into the front end, and almost immediately the alarm went off. It was a piercing roar that was almost deafening. And worse. It blocked out any sound of the gunman's footsteps.

"Stay down!" Grayson warned Eve when he felt her move behind him.

He knew for a fact that she didn't have her gun with her because he'd talked her out of bringing it. Now, he wished he hadn't. He didn't want Eve up and returning fire, but it would have been nice to have the extra ammunition.

Even with the distraction of the car alarm, Grayson saw where the next shot landed. This one hadn't been aimed at them but rather the overhead lights. The gunman took out the ones near the elevator and stairwell, plunging that area into total darkness.

That could be good or bad.

Good because Nate would likely make his approach using the stairs, and the darkness would help conceal him. But that same darkness could also conceal the shooter if he tried to escape. Grayson didn't want this SOB to get away. He wanted to end this now.

Two more shots came at Eve and him, one right behind the other.

The gunman had moved again. This time to the right. Hell. The gunman was moving toward those stairs. Not only would that give him an escape route, it would also give him a better angle to fire more of those lethal bullets.

"What's going on up there?" someone called out. "I'm the security guard for the hospital."

"Sheriff Grayson Ryland. We're under fire. Stay back!"

But the words had no sooner left Grayson's mouth when he saw something out of the corner of his eye. To his left. There was a man in a dark gray uniform. The security guard, no doubt. He had his weapon drawn and had ducked down a little, but he was still making his way toward them.

The gunman obviously saw him, too.

Because a shot went in that direction.

The guard dove to the ground, but he was literally out in the open and therefore an easy target. Grayson had to do something, so he came out of cover, estimated the position of the shooter, and sent a bullet his way.

Because of the blasted car alarm, he couldn't tell if the gunman even reacted. Maybe he'd managed to hit the bastard, or at the very least maybe he had gotten the guy to back off so the guard could scramble to safety.

"You need to get down!" Eve snarled, and she put her hand on his back to push Grayson to the ground again.

It wasn't a second too soon.

The next bullet that was fired would have slammed right into him if Eve hadn't pulled him down with her.

However, Grayson didn't have time to thank her because everything seemed to happen at once. Another shot went toward the security guard who was trying to scramble away.

And then there was the movement in the stairwell.

For one horrifying moment, Grayson thought it was the gunman getting away. But this person wasn't dressed all in black.

It was Nate.

His brother was sneaking up the stairs, trying to get a drop on the gunman. But it was dark, and Nate was out of position. Unlike the gunman, who was probably only a few feet away.

"Watch out!" Grayson yelled to his brother.

But it was already too late.

Grayson couldn't hear the shot that the gunman fired, but he saw the end result.

A bullet slammed right into Nate's chest.

Chapter Seventeen

Eve screamed, but the sound of her voice was drowned out by the blaring car alarm.

Her scream didn't warn Nate in time. Neither did Grayson's shouted warning to his brother. And because they'd failed, she watched in horror as the bullet hit Nate.

He flew backward from the impact.

"Oh, God." And Eve kept repeating it like a hysterical mantra.

Had he been killed?

She thought of his baby daughter, Kimmie, who would be an orphan if Nate died. And it would be partly her fault. If she just hadn't taken that damn picture then there would have been no attempts to kill her. All of this had started because of that.

Eve automatically bolted toward Nate so she could help him, but Grayson latched onto her and pulled her back to the ground. Good thing, too. Because the shots came at them again. This time, however, they were nonstop. Frenzied. They pelted into the cars on either side of them and the concrete floor in front of them.

Eve covered her head with her hands, but she couldn't

stay behind the shelter of the vehicles for long. "We have to help Nate," she shouted, though she was certain that Grayson already knew that.

Because Grayson was practically lying on top of her, she could feel the rock-hard muscles of his body, and his chest was pumping from the adrenaline. His gaze volleyed between the stairwell and the area where the gunman was likely hiding. He was primed and ready to fight, but he would also do whatever it took to save his brother.

Eve couldn't see Nate, nor could she hear him, but she prayed he'd somehow managed to survive the gunshot and the fall. Either could have been fatal.

She saw some movement at the other end of the parking lot and spotted another uniformed security guard on the stairwell. He had his gun ready, thank God, but he didn't seem to be in any better position than Grayson was to stop this. Still, he might be able to do some good if the shooter moved.

Finally, the shots stopped. Maybe because the gunman had to reload. Or, God forbid, maybe because he was escaping. The thought of that sickened Eve. She didn't want a killer to get away.

But right now, Nate was their first priority.

Grayson eased off her and inched toward the car to their right. He was probably thinking of making a run to the stairs, but she prayed he wouldn't do that. He could end up like Nate, or worse.

Since she still had Grayson's phone, she called nine-one-one to report an officer down, though someone was likely already aware of that. She doubted that Nate had come alone. But she immediately rethought that. Maybe that's exactly what Nate had done. Maybe he'd rushed to help his brother and her and hadn't considered the consequences.

She would have reacted the same way if it meant saving Grayson.

The moment she ended the call, Eve saw Grayson's gaze swing to the left. And she soon saw why. The first security guard was crawling toward them. She saw the blood on his shoulder and knew that he, too, had been shot. They had to get an ambulance up here right away, but that couldn't happen until the gunman had been stopped.

Grayson latched onto the guard and pulled him next to Eve. The man was clearly in pain, and even though he was clutching his gun, he had both it and his hand pressed to the wound. It didn't take medical training to know he'd already lost too much blood. Eve pushed aside his hand so she could apply some pressure.

"Wait here," Grayson ordered. "Use the gun if you have to." His eyes met hers, and she could see that it was indeed an order.

But, God, what was he going to do?

Please.

She didn't want him out there in the open, making himself an easy target. She wanted him to stay behind cover, even though cover didn't mean safety. Not with those bullets flying everywhere.

Her heart was pounding against her chest now, and

her breath was so thin that she felt light-headed. Despite the cold, there was a fine mist of clammy sweat on her face. She felt sick, but she tried to fight off the feeling of dread. They would survive this, somehow, because there was no other alternative. It couldn't end here for Grayson and Nate.

Grayson took the gun from the security guard and handed it to her. Eve latched onto it, but she was shaking her head. "You can't go out there."

He shook his head, too. "I don't have a choice. This has to stop."

That was it. No other explanation. Grayson maneuvered around her and the guard and went behind them. He disappeared when he ducked around the front of the car to her right.

Well, at least he wasn't going to charge out into the center of the garage. He was obviously trying to get to the stairwell, and maybe the security guard could provide some backup. However, that still meant Grayson was moving closer and closer to the gunman, and she was betting the gunman would be looking for them to do just that. Shooting Nate could have all been designed to draw Grayson and her out into the open.

If so, it had worked.

Eve couldn't hear what the security guard was mumbling, but he squirmed, his face tightening in pain. She pressed harder on the wound to try to stop the flow of blood, but she also kept watch of the area near the black van where the last shots had originated.

"This is Sergeant O'Malley, SAPD." The man's voice

boomed from a bullhorn. It sounded as if he was at street level. "Put down your weapon and surrender."

Backup. Thank God. But since there was no response from the shooter, Eve doubted he would just do as the sergeant had demanded.

By her calculations it'd been a minute, maybe more, and the gunman hadn't fired. Eve had no idea if that was good or bad, but it was certainly easier to think without those bullets bashing into the cement and other cars.

And because it was easier to think, tears sprang to her eyes.

Eve blinked them back. She couldn't give in to the worry and fear, but she was terrified for Grayson. For Nate. For this wounded security guard whom she didn't even know.

But who was out there doing this?

Sebastian? Maybe. But only if he'd managed to get away from his police escort. Of course, either Claude or Sebastian could have hired a gunman. It was possible Claude wasn't even in critical condition but instead had orchestrated this to get Grayson and her into a position so they could be killed.

That brought her back to why again.

If they could just figure out who'd fired shots at them, then knowing the *who* would tell them the *why*.

Eve finally spotted Grayson again. He was seven cars over to her right and was inching his way to the stairwell. She held her breath, waiting for another shot.

Nothing.

The seconds crawled by so slowly that she could

feel them ticking off in her head. Finally, she saw some movement in the stairwell.

Nate.

Thank God he was moving. However, he wasn't just moving. He had his gun aimed and ready and was making his way back up the stairs. Not easily. He, too, was wincing, and Eve soon realized why. His shirt was open, but there was no blood. Only a Kevlar vest.

Relieved, she let out her breath in a rush. Nate hadn't been shot. The impact of the bullet had probably knocked him down the stairs. He looked shaken up but very much alive.

So, that was one prayer that'd been answered.

The security guard moved again, the muscles in his body going stiff, and Eve looked down at him to see what had caused that reaction. His eyes were wide and not focused on her.

But rather behind her.

Oh, God.

That was the only thought that had time to form in her head because Eve felt a hand grip on to her shoulder. She didn't have time to move. There was no time to react.

Before someone pressed the barrel of a gun to her head.

GRAYSON'S HEART WENT to his knees.

This couldn't be happening.

He'd had just a split second of relief because his brother was alive, but that relief went south in a hurry when he saw Eve. She was no longer where Grayson had left her—crouched with the injured security guard between the two cars. She was standing now.

And she wasn't alone.

Someone was behind her, their arm curved around Eve's neck, and that someone had a gun pointed directly at Eve's head. The person had a second gun next to Eve's neck. Both weapons were positioned to deliver a fatal shot.

Grayson couldn't see the person's face, only the black baseball cap. But he could see Eve's. The color had drained from her cheeks, and she was looking around as if trying to figure out how to escape.

But Grayson didn't want her to move.

Not with that gun pressed to her head.

"Drop your weapon and surrender," Sergeant O'Malley called out again.

Grayson was thankful for the backup, but he didn't want the sergeant's demand to make this bad situation worse.

He took aim, and with his attention nailed to the gunman's hand, Grayson inched closer.

"There's no need to do this," Grayson shouted. "Let her go."

If the gunman responded, Grayson didn't hear it. He wished like the devil that the car alarm would stop. He had to try to negotiate Eve's release, and it was hard to do that when he couldn't hear what was going on.

"Eve is no threat to you," Grayson tried again, all the while moving closer.

He didn't have a clean shot, not with the gunman

using Eve as a human shield, but he needed to get as close as possible because it was likely this SOB was planning an escape. After all, Eve was still alive, and there had to be a reason for that. The gunman had taken her hostage.

But why?

Grayson was certain he would soon learn the answer, but he hoped he wouldn't learn it too late. Eve couldn't die. She just couldn't. Someway, somehow, he had to put himself in a position where he could save her.

He glanced over his shoulder at his brother. Nate wasn't following him but instead had crouched down and was making his way to the other side of the garage toward the black van and the red car with the blaring alarm.

Good move.

His brother might get a better angle on a shot that way, and Nate could also possibly block an attempted escape. The second security guard could help with that, too, since he was covering the other end of the garage. Grayson couldn't let the gunman get Eve out of there because once he no longer had any use for a hostage, the shooter would almost certainly kill her.

"The security guard needs medical attention," Grayson shouted to the gunman. Since the guy wasn't moving, he wanted to try a different approach. "Why don't you end this now so we can get an ambulance up here?"

Still nothing. But the guy was moving a little and looking around. Grayson didn't like the edgy movement because it proved the gunman was nervous and way out of his comfort zone.

Grayson stopped but kept his gun lifted and aimed. "Step out so I can see you." And he tried to make it sound like an order. Hard to do with that gun right at Eve's head.

"What should I do?" she mouthed.

But Grayson shook his head. He didn't want her to do anything. Not yet anyway. But if it came down to it, he hoped she could drop out of the way so that Nate or he would have a clean shot.

Grayson glanced around to see the best way to approach this, and while he was still studying the situation, just like that the car alarm stopped. Maybe the battery had given out or perhaps Nate had managed to disarm it. Either way, it was now deadly silent.

The gunman lifted his head, just a little, and even though Grayson still couldn't see his face, he didn't think it was his imagination that the guy wasn't pleased with the silenced alarm. But Grayson was certainly thankful for it. Maybe now he could hear this bozo's voice and figure out who he was dealing with. If it wasn't Sebastian, then maybe one of the Colliers had hired a triggerman.

"SAPD has the building surrounded," Grayson tossed out there. "You can't escape. But what you can do is let Eve go, and we can talk about a peaceful surrender."

No answer, but he hadn't expected one.

The guy finally moved. Well, he moved the gun away

from Eve's head anyway, and for a moment Grayson thought he might surrender. He didn't.

He lowered the gun, pointing it down to the floor, and he fired.

Hell.

Grayson couldn't see exactly what had happened, but judging from the look of sheer horror on Eve's face and from her scream, the gunman had shot the security guard at point-blank range.

Things had just gone from bad to worse.

The gunman moved again, quickly this time. He put the gun back against Eve's head and he pushed her forward. He followed with the front of his body pressed to Eve's back.

The gunman was heading for that black van.

Nate was there, somewhere. Hopefully, in a position to stop a getaway attempt.

"You won't be able to drive out of here," Grayson warned.

But he'd barely had time to issue that warning when the gunman shifted his weapon.

He fired at Grayson.

Grayson jumped to the side, just in time, and he landed hard against the concrete floor. His shoulder jammed, the pain shooting through him, but he ignored it and came up ready to fire.

The gunman fired first, and the shot pinned Grayson down behind the back of a small truck.

"I have to kill you, you know," the gunman said.

Or rather the gunwoman. Because that was a female voice. A familiar one.

"Cicely?" Grayson spat out. She was the last of the Colliers that he had suspected. "Why the hell are you doing this?"

"Because you all have to die." Cicely's voice was eerily calm, but there was nothing calm about her expression when she met his gaze over Eve's shoulder. "Step out and die like a man, Sheriff Ryland. The other one, too." She tossed a look in Nate's direction. "And that other security guard."

She was just going to kill them all?

Why?

"Your son is in custody for Sophia's murder," Grayson tossed out there. He was testing the waters, trying to get Cicely to talk. And he was also hoping to distract her.

What he didn't intend to do was surrender.

"That's a mistake. He didn't kill his sister." Cicely's voice broke on the last word. "I know because I did it."

Eve gasped, and that was pretty much Grayson's reaction. "You killed your own daughter?"

A hoarse sob tore from Cicely's mouth. "It was an accident, but I don't expect you to believe that."

"I do." And Grayson wasn't lying. He did believe her. "Why did you do it?"

With Eve still in a body lock against her, Cicely continued to inch toward the black van. "I'll tell you, but it won't save you. Nothing will."

Grayson would prove her wrong, somehow.

"I begged Sophia to come home to me, but she just laughed. She wanted money, you see. Claude's money and mine. She didn't want us. Didn't want to be family again."

"So you killed her?" Eve asked in disbelief.

Cicely jammed the gun harder against Eve's head. "I told you that was an accident," Cicely practically yelled. "Sophia said her foster mother confessed to her who she really was—a Collier. The foster mother wanted to try and get money out of us. But Sophia gave her an overdose of insulin to get her out of the way."

Grayson didn't think Sophia's motives were pure, that she did that in order to protect her biological parents. "Sophia did that so she wouldn't have to share the cash with her foster mother?" he asked.

Cicely nodded. "Then, when Sophia and I were arguing, I pushed her, and she fell and hit her head." Another sob. "I had Leon dispose of the body. But Leon remembered that someone at the rodeo had been taking pictures. Pictures that would link him to Sophia. And eventually link her back to me. Leon tried to get them back from Eve, and then you killed him."

"Because he tried to kill us," Grayson reminded her. "Eve did nothing wrong. She was only doing her job when she took the pictures."

"Yes, but I couldn't have the police thinking Sebastian had anything to do with this. He's innocent, you know." She pulled in a shaky breath. "Now, step out, Sheriff, and drop your gun so I can do what I have to do to protect my son."

"You mean so you can kill me," he answered flatly.

Eve frantically shook her head. "Stay put," she told Grayson.

Cicely fired at shot at him. "If you stay put or hold on to your gun, I'll make it painful for Eve. You're not the sort of man to cower behind a car while the woman you love is screaming in pain."

Grayson ignored that *woman you love* part and got ready to move. He would leave cover. There was no question about that. He wouldn't let this insane woman hurt Eve. But he couldn't just let Cicely kill him either, because he had to live so that he could rescue Eve. He wouldn't do her any good if he was dead.

"I'm coming out," Grayson let Cicely know. He glanced over at Nate who was ready to fire, as well.

Grayson slid out his gun first, not too far away. He needed to be able to reach for it. And then he stood.

At the exact moment that Eve shouted, "No!"

Eve rammed her elbow against Cicely and darted to the side. But Grayson didn't have time to get off a clean shot. Because Cicely darted to the side, too, and the woman didn't release the grip she had on Eve.

Grayson yelled for Eve to get out of the way, but the sound he heard turned his blood to ice.

The sound of the shot that Cicely fired.

Not at Grayson. Nor at Nate.

Grayson's world tipped on its axis when the bullet slammed into Eve.

Chapter Eighteen

Eve heard the shot.

She also heard Grayson call out to her.

But she couldn't answer. She couldn't do anything except slide to the floor.

The pain was instant, searing, and it sliced through her right side like a red-hot stiletto. She grabbed at the fire and felt the warm blood against her fingers.

She'd been shot.

That fact registered somewhere in her mind. It also registered that she needed to tell Grayson to get down so that he, too, wouldn't be shot. But Eve couldn't make herself speak.

Was she in shock?

Or worse, was she dying?

Ironically, she could deal with the thought of her death, but not of Grayson's. She didn't want his life to end here in this cold, dank garage.

Because she was in love with him.

Always had been. Always would be.

And that's why she had to save him. At least one of them had to make it out of here alive.

"Eve?" Grayson called out. "Are you all right?"

She tried to answer, but Cicely was still beside her, crouched down, with a gun in each hand. She jammed the gun to Eve's head again.

"Tell him to come to you," Cicely demanded.

Eve shook her head. She had to do something to buy a little time. "They'll put you in jail," she managed to say to the woman who'd just shot her. "They'll give you the death penalty. All of this will be for nothing."

"No," Cicely quickly disagreed. Her eyes were wild, her gaze firing between Grayson and Nate. "Annabel is tied up in that black van. When the Rylands and you are dead, I'll shoot her and make it look like a suicide. I've already forced her to write the note, and trust me, it'll be no hardship killing that bimbo witch. She stole my husband. And my life. She deserves to die a thousand deaths."

Oh, God. Cicely wasn't just crazy, she was smart. If Eve couldn't fight back and stop her, Cicely might just get away with this. Worse, Cicely was trying to maneuver herself into a better position to kill again.

Cicely tucked the gun she'd been holding in her left hand into the waist of her pants. That meant she could use that hand to put a tight grip around Eve's neck. Cicely wasn't choking her, exactly, but it was close. Eve was already light-headed enough, but it was obvious Cicely was going to do anything to force Eve to cooperate.

"Tell the sheriff to come to you," Cicely repeated. "And make sure he's unarmed."

She would die before she did that because Cicely intended to kill them all anyway. Eve wouldn't be the reason Grayson took a bullet.

"You're not just killing me," Eve whispered. "I'm pregnant. You're killing my child, too. Maybe a daughter. It would be like killing Sophia all over again."

Cicely blinked, and with that blink Eve saw the hesitation in the woman's eyes. Her gaze dropped to Eve's stomach and then to the blood on the side of Eve's gray sweater. It wasn't much more than a split second of time, but that brief lapse was all that Eve needed.

She latched onto Cicely's wrist.

It was risky, but at this point anything she did or didn't do was risky. All she knew was that every drop of blood she lost put Grayson, Nate, her possible pregnancy and herself in danger. Besides, Cicely had killed both Sophia and the security guard, and Eve knew she wouldn't hesitate to kill again.

Cicely made a feral sound, part scream and part groan, and she struggled to throw off Eve's grip. Eve held on and tried to wrench the gun from Cicely's right hand. Of course, the woman had a second gun that she could use, but Eve would deal with that later. For now, she needed a weapon so she could fight back.

"Eve?" Grayson called out.

The sound of the struggle must have alerted him because Eve heard his frantic footsteps. He was running to try and save her.

Or maybe running to his death.

Eve clamped onto Cicely's gun because she knew that Grayson's life depended on it.

Grayson cursed, and even though Eve couldn't see him from her position, he was close by. Cicely was aware of that, too, because she bashed the gun against Eve's head and then pointed the weapon at Grayson.

Cicely fired.

The fear and adrenaline slammed through Eve, and despite the blow Cicely had delivered to her head, she kept fighting.

"Grayson!" Nate called out.

Nate sounded terrified, and that spiked the fear inside Eve. Did that mean he'd just witnessed his brother being shot?

Oh, God.

Eve couldn't risk thinking about that now. She had to stay in the fight. Despite the pain and the fear, she had to keep fighting.

"Come closer and he dies," she heard Cicely say, and she let go of Eve.

Eve swiveled around and realized Cicely was talking to Nate as he approached them. He had obviously retrieved his weapon and now had it trained on Cicely.

But Cicely had her gun aimed at Grayson.

Another smart move because Nate wouldn't do anything to risk his brother being killed.

Nate froze, but he didn't lower his gun, and he glanced behind him at the stairwell. Hopefully, there were backup officers there and ready to respond.

And then there was Grayson.

He, too, was ready to respond, but he was no longer the calm, collected lawman. Grayson said her name.

Eve.

It was a hoarse whisper filled with concern. No doubt from the blood.

"I'm okay," Eve said to him, even though she had no idea if that was true. She might have lost the chance to be a mother, but worse, she might lose Grayson. "I'm so sorry," she managed to say.

He shook his head. "For what?"

Too many things for her to say here. Besides, there was nothing she could say that would allow them to go back and undo everything. This was their fate, and unfortunately it was in the hands of a crazy woman hellbent on covering up the murder of her own daughter.

"Eve needs a doctor," Grayson told Cicely. "End this now."

"It ends when you're all dead." But Cicely didn't sound as convinced of that as she had just moments earlier. She glanced at Eve. "I didn't know about your baby. If I had, I would have found a way to leave you out of this."

"Baby?" Nate mumbled. That obviously shocked him, but he didn't take his attention off Cicely.

Later, Eve would have to explain.

If there was a later.

The pain shot through her side again, and Eve felt the fresh trickle of warm blood. Grayson noticed it, too, because she saw his body tense. He was getting ready to have a shoot-out with Cicely. And he could no doubt kill her. But could he do that before she fired a lethal shot at him?

Eve couldn't take that risk. She had to do something, and she used her own body. She kicked at Cicely, and she put every ounce of her strength behind it. The heel of her shoe connected with the woman's shin, and Cicely howled in pain.

It wasn't much of an attack, but Grayson made the most of it.

He dove at Cicely, his muscled body ramming right into the woman, and he slammed her back into the adjacent car.

Cicely made a gasping sound, fighting for the air that Grayson had knocked from her, but that didn't stop her from trying to aim her gun at his head.

"Watch out!" Eve shouted.

Grayson latched onto both of Cicely's hands and bashed them against the car's body. Her gun clattered to the floor, and Grayson snatched the other weapon from the waist of her pants. He tossed it on the floor, as well.

Nate moved in and kicked both of Cicely's weapons away, but even unarmed, Cicely didn't give up. She continued to fight until Grayson turned her around and pushed her hard against the car's fender.

A sob racked through Cicely, and she went limp.

"Take Cicely," Grayson immediately told Nate. "I'm getting Eve to the E.R."

He kept his forearm on Cicely to hold her until Nate

switched places with him. Grayson didn't waste a second. He scooped Eve up in his arms.

"How bad?" he asked.

She wanted to lie. Eve wanted to tell him that everything would be all right, but the fight had taken the last of her breath. She opened her mouth, but no sound came out.

Grayson raced to the stairwell where the other officers were pouring up the steps. One of those officers latched onto Cicely, yanked her hands behind her back and cuffed her.

Grayson looked down at Eve as he ran toward the E.R. doors. He was so worried. And scared. She realized that was the first time she'd seen fear in Grayson's eyes.

Everything started to move in slow motion, and the edges of her vision turned gray. At first. Then, darker.

She fastened her gaze on Grayson and fought to keep her eyes open. But she failed at that, too.

Her eyelids fluttered down, and the last thing Eve saw was Grayson's face.

GRAYSON WAS AFRAID IF he stopped moving, he would explode.

So he turned and once again paced across the surgical waiting room of the San Antonio hospital. It didn't help his raw nerves, nor did it ease the massive knot in his stomach, but he couldn't sit and wait as his brothers were doing.

Nate and Dade were on the far side of the room. Nate was on the phone, but both Dade and he were staring at a TV where *It's a Wonderful Life* was playing. Grayson doubted they were actually watching the movie, but they were trying to maintain a calm, business-as-usual facade. For his sake no doubt.

They knew he was ready to explode.

Mason, being Mason, didn't even attempt a facade. He was in a chair on the opposite side of the room, and he was glaring at anything and everything—including Jimmy Stewart on the screen. He was especially glaring at the hall where a nurse had appeared earlier to tell them that Eve was finally being taken to surgery.

Two hours.

That's how long it'd been since Eve had been in the hospital. Grayson hadn't known that one hundred and twenty minutes could feel like a lifetime, but he damn sure knew it now. Every one of those minutes had crawled by.

"She'll be okay," Nate assured him.

Dade mumbled his agreement, but it didn't sound remotely convincing. Mason's glare deepened.

The glare wasn't for Eve. Mason wasn't fond of too many people, but he cared as much for Eve as Grayson's other brothers did. No, this glare was for Cicely, for what the woman had nearly done to Eve. But the good thing in all of this was that Cicely was locked away at the SAPD facility and couldn't come after any of them again.

"Claude Collier's condition has stabilized," Nate reported when he ended the call. "Annabel's still being checked out over in the E.R., but she's going to be okay.

Just some bruises and scratches from where Cicely attacked her and stuffed her in the van."

It was the wrong attitude for a lawman to have, but Grayson didn't give a flying fig about the Colliers. He only wanted good news about Eve.

At the sound of footsteps in the hall, his brothers stood, and Grayson turned to see Dr. Andrew Masters making his way toward him. Grayson had met the lanky no-nonsense doctor briefly when Eve had first been rushed into the E.R.

Grayson narrowed the distance between the doctor and him. "Is she okay?" he asked. But he wasn't sure he could take hearing any bad news.

The doctor nodded. "Eve should be fine."

"Should be?" Mason growled, taking the tone and the words right out of Grayson's mouth. "What the hell does that mean?"

The doctor gave a weary huff and looked at Grayson. "Physically, she'll be all right. The surgery didn't take long at all."

"Then what did?" That growl came from Dade. "It's been two hours."

"She had to be examined and prepped. The bullet entered her right side and made a clean exit. It didn't hit any vital organs, which makes her a very lucky woman."

Lucky. Yes, she was, but Grayson didn't feel so lucky. Eve had come damn close to dying.

"You said *physically* Eve will be all right?" Nate questioned.

Dr. Masters glanced at Grayson. A funny kind of glance. Had Eve told him about the possible pregnancy? No doubt.

She might not have actually mentioned that Grayson could be her baby's father, but the doctor wasn't an idiot. He had almost certainly put one and one together when he's seen Grayson's reaction to her being shot.

"Eve wants to see you," the doctor said to Grayson. "But don't stay long. I want her to get plenty of rest." Then, he turned that authoritative gaze on the rest of the Rylands. "You can all come back in the morning."

The trio looked as if they might argue, but Nate finally caught on to his brothers' arms. "Grayson will see to Eve," he reminded them.

Yeah. He'd done a stellar job of that in the past forty-eight hours, hadn't he? He'd had sex with her, twice, and had nearly gotten her killed.

Grayson took a deep breath and followed the doctor to the post-op room at the end of the hall. Everything in the room was watery white, including Eve. There wasn't a drop of color in her cheeks. Still, she managed a smile of sorts when she saw him.

"You've got five minutes," the doctor instructed, "and then I don't want her to have any more visitors until tomorrow. Don't worry. After what Eve's been through, she'll sleep during that time anyway."

Grayson prayed that was true, that she would sleep with no nightmares. He stood zero chance of that happening for him. Every time he closed his eyes, he would see the attack. It would torment him, and he would try to figure out what he could have done to prevent it. In his nightmares, he would stop Cicely's bullet from hitting Eve.

But saving her from that bullet was a day late and a dollar short.

"You look worried," she mumbled. Her words were slurred, and her eyes bleary.

"I am worried." Grayson walked closer. She looked too fragile to touch, but he skimmed his fingers down her arm, barely making contact with her skin. "The doctor said you were going to be okay."

"Yes." The half smile faded. "It's too early to know if that's true."

"The baby," he whispered.

She gave a shaky nod. "The trauma probably put an end to any pregnancy."

Of course. Her body had been through a lot. Too much. He didn't know much about the biology of conception, but the blood loss and the shock from the attack could have caused her body to shut down.

Being shot was hardly conducive to making a baby.

"Dr. Masters said I should brace myself for the worst," she added. "So, that's what I've done."

It made him ache to hear her say that, to see the resignation in her exhausted eyes.

"I'm sorry," Grayson said, because he didn't know what else to say.

She lifted her chin, though it was shaky, too. "I just wanted to thank you, for everything. That's why I asked to see you."

That hurt, as well. And it also riled him to the core. Grayson didn't want to be thanked for doing a half-assed job at protecting her. "Don't—"

"I know. You don't want to talk about it." She pulled in a slow breath and fought to keep her eyes open. "That's okay."

No. It wasn't *okay.* Far from it. He should tell her…

But tell her what, exactly?

Tell her that he wasn't sorry about sleeping with her? That was a moot point now that the gunshot wound had compromised her already slim chances of getting pregnant.

Maybe he should explain to her that he was sorry he hadn't stopped Cicely from shooting her? Or that the only thing he wanted was for her to be happy? She deserved happiness. She deserved a lot more than he could have ever given her.

But Grayson didn't say any of those things. He just stood there, looking at Eve, and knowing he couldn't do or say anything to make it better.

"Go home to your family." Her voice had no sound now. Even though her eyes drifted down, she smiled that sad half smile again. "Have a good life, Grayson."

The words went through him like ice. Like the dark cold he felt deep within his soul when he thought he'd lost Eve in that parking garage.

Because the words sounded like a goodbye.

And Grayson knew that's exactly what it was.

Well, he had his answer. Eve might have been groggy

from the surgical drugs, but he hadn't seen any doubt in her eyes, and she damn sure hadn't asked him to stay.

Have a good life, Grayson.

With those words slamming through his head, Grayson did as Eve wanted. He walked away.

Chapter Nineteen

The pain seared through her when she eased off the hospital bed and into the wheelchair, but Eve tried not to react visibly. She didn't want Dr. Masters to see the pain on her face because he would only give her more hassle about leaving. And there was no way she wanted to spend the rest of Christmas day in a hospital.

Besides, if she stayed, she would go stark-raving mad. Every moment she was in that bed, she thought of Grayson and of the life that she'd nearly gotten to have as a mother.

"You know how I feel about this," the doctor grumbled. It was a paraphrase of the grumble he'd been doling out since she'd insisted on going home.

So yes, she did know how the doctor felt. He wanted her to stay put one more day, even at the risk of her sanity. However, the moment he signed the release papers, Eve snatched them from his hand.

Dr. Masters gave her a flat look. "At least tell me you'll be with family or friends, that you aren't going home alone."

"I won't be alone," she lied.

His flat look intensified. "You told the nurse to tell the Rylands that you couldn't have any visitors, that you were in too much pain."

"I lied about that." And that was the truth.

She had told that lie not because of the pain. Well, not the physical pain anyway, but she couldn't bear the thought of saying goodbye to Grayson again. Once she was home and had recovered, she would email his brothers and thank them for, well, for being there when it counted most.

Dr. Masters scribbled something on another piece of paper and handed it to her. "A script for pain meds and antibiotics," he explained.

The antibiotics were a necessity but not the drug for pain. The pain was right there, stabbing through her, but she didn't want to put any more drugs in her body in case there was the minuscule chance that she might be pregnant.

Yes, it was a pipe dream, but Eve was going to hold on to it until a pregnancy test proved otherwise.

"I can't talk you out of this?" the doctor asked. He grabbed the back of her wheelchair when Eve tried to wheel herself toward the door.

"No. I've made up my mind."

He gave a heavy sigh, followed by a nod, and he stepped behind her so he could wheel her toward the door. With any luck, the taxi she'd called would be waiting and could take her to her condo. She'd also phoned the super because she didn't have her keys. He had promised to meet her there and let her in. Then she could get some cash to pay the taxi driver.

"What should I tell the Rylands when they show up?" Dr. Masters asked.

And they would show up. "Tell them I made a miraculous recovery and that I'm spending the holiday with friends."

The doctor made a sound of disapproval but wheeled her out anyway.

"The taxi is meeting me at the back of the building," she let him know.

Another sound of disapproval, but he went in that direction anyway. Eve looked over her shoulder. No sign of Grayson. And she tried to convince herself that was a good thing.

The tears came anyway.

She blinked them back and realized that the pain in her side was nothing compared to the piercing ache in her heart. Damn her. She had known not to get too close to Grayson, and she'd done it anyway.

Again.

The doors slid open as they approached, and the cold wind nearly robbed her of her breath. So did the man who stepped out onto the walkway. Not Grayson.

Dade.

He was there, right next to the taxi that was waiting for her. Dade smiled, flashing those killer dimples that had probably coaxed many women into his bed. The dimples had never worked on Eve because to her Dade would always be the brother she'd never had.

"I asked at the front desk," Dade explained, "and the nurse said you were checking out early. Since I didn't see you out front, I figured I'd check back here." He tipped his head to the taxi. "Going somewhere?" It was a friendly enough question, but there was concern in his voice.

"I need to get home." Eve kept it at that. She gave the doctor a nod of reassurance that all was well, and he went back inside.

"Right. You need to get home," Dade repeated. He blew out his breath as if resigned to the fact that they weren't going to have a real discussion here. "Want me to drive you?"

She shook her head. "It's Christmas and you should be with your family. The taxi will get me home just fine."

Another nod. He reached in his jeans' pocket, pulled out something and walked closer. "Your Christmas present," he announced. "Sorry, but I didn't have time to wrap it." Dade caught on to her hand and dropped something into her palm.

A silver concho.

Eve knew exactly what this was. One of the silver conchos that Boone Ryland had given to all six of his sons before he'd walked out on them and their mother.

She looked at Dade and shook her head. "I thought you threw yours in the creek."

Dade shrugged. "I had this one made for you a while back but never got around to giving it to you. I figured this was a good time."

Her mind slipped back to all those years ago, and she could see the hurt teenager whose father had run out on him. The concho was a reminder of both the pain from that loss and the family that Boone Ryland had made.

"Thank you," she managed to say despite the massive lump in her throat.

"I always thought you should have one," Dade added. "And if you decide to throw it in the creek, put a bullet in it or drape it around a picture frame, it's your right." He stooped down so he was eye level with her, and he caught on to her shoulders. "Eve, you're a Ryland, and you belong with Grayson."

The tears threatened again, and she hoped that Dade thought the cold wind was responsible. "I can't have Grayson," she said. She put the concho on her lap so her hands would be free to wheel the chair to the taxi door.

But Dade took over. "Because Grayson's too stubborn and proud."

"No. Because he's Grayson." She managed a smile when Dade helped her into the back of the taxi. She made sure she had hold of the concho, and then closed her hand around it.

Dade brushed a kiss on her forehead. "I can't do anything to change your mind?"

She didn't even have to think about this. "No."

Eve had seen Grayson's reaction the night before. He felt guilty for her injury and guilty that the bullet had almost certainly cost her a baby. That guilt would eat away at him, and he would come to her and try to make things right.

Eventually, they'd land in bed again.

And eventually the old feelings and wounds would resurface, and Grayson would resent her for forcing a relationship on him that he didn't want.

"I can tolerate a lot of things in life," she whispered to Dade. "But I refuse to be the person who brings Grayson Ryland to his knees. I love him too much for that."

Thankfully, Dade didn't argue. He didn't question her or her logic. He simply smiled, shut the taxi door and waved goodbye.

Eve pressed her hand and the concho to her heart, hoping it would ease the pain. But that was asking a lot from a little piece of silver, even if this piece of silver was one of the most precious gifts she'd ever received. She definitely wouldn't throw it in the creek or put a bullet in it. She would keep it close to her heart.

Eve waited until the driver was out of the parking lot before she broke down and cried.

Chapter Twenty

Grayson cursed. He'd actually punched a singing Christmas tree and rammed it into the trash can.

He'd thought it was a reasonable reaction at the time. The tree was stupid, sitting on the dispatcher's desk at the sheriff's office and bursting into that same tinny "Jingle Bell" tune every time anyone walked past it. Well, Grayson was tired of it. Plus, it was nearly two weeks past Christmas, and if he'd had any holiday spirit, it was long gone.

Still, he'd punched a Christmas tree.

And that's when he knew this had to end.

His mood was well past the surly stage, and even the usually even-tempered Nate had demanded that Grayson *do something*. Grayson hadn't needed to figure out what his brother meant. He knew.

He had to see Eve.

So he'd forced himself into his new truck and started driving.

However, now that he was parked in front of her condo in San Antonio, Grayson was rethinking his impulsiveness. He probably should have called or emailed first. Heck, he darn sure should have sorted out his feelings and what he wanted to say to her.

What if she told him to take a hike?

That wasn't the only worry on his mind. Still, he had to see for himself that she was okay, that she had recovered both physically and mentally from the shooting.

He was about to get out of his truck, when the front door to her condo opened, and Eve backed out. She had on jeans, a dark red sweater top, and she was dragging something.

A Christmas tree.

Not a fake singing one but a real one with dry, browning branches. No ornaments, but there were a few strands of silver tinsel that caught the cold January wind and the afternoon sun. Since she was struggling with it and since he was pretty sure she shouldn't be twisting and turning her body like that, Grayson hurried over to help her.

She must have heard his footsteps because she let go of the tree and whirled around as if she'd expected to be attacked.

Hell.

She'd been having those nightmares about the shooting.

But her expression quickly went from alarm to a smile. Not the weak half-assed smile that she'd given him in the hospital. This was a real one. An Eve smile that lit up her whole face. That smile caused him to freeze.

Oh, man. She was beautiful. Always had been, always

would be. And he would always feel as if it he'd been sucker-punched when he saw her.

"Grayson," she said on a rise of breath.

"Eve." His voice didn't sound any steadier than hers.

They stood there, staring, waiting. And because Grayson had to have something to do with his hands, he grabbed the trunk of the dead tree.

"Where do you want this to go?" he asked.

She motioned toward the Dumpster at the end of the parking lot where there were several other discarded Christmas trees. "The recycling truck is supposed to pick them up today," she let him know.

Grayson headed in that direction, and Eve followed along beside him. He looked for any signs of pain or limited movement, but there weren't any.

"I'm okay," she assured him as if reading his mind. "I had my post-op check up last week, and the doctor said I was healing nicely."

"Good." He cursed himself when he repeated it.

Grayson didn't hurry because he didn't want Eve to hurry to keep up with him, but he didn't dawdle, either. It was cold and blustery, and despite her *healing nicely* remark, he didn't want her outside any longer than necessary—especially since she wasn't wearing a coat. He tossed the tree next to the others and headed back.

"Would you like to come in?" she asked. The invitation was tentative, like her body language. She wasn't fidgeting exactly, but it was close.

"Yeah. I'd like to talk." And say what exactly, Grayson didn't know.

Well, except for asking her the results of the pregnancy test she'd taken. Of course, if by some miracle that result had been positive, she would have already told him.

Maybe.

And Grayson had to accept that maybe she had already written him out of her life. It seemed that way in the hospital.

Eve walked into the condo ahead of him and shut the door once he was inside, but didn't sit. She stuffed her hands into the back pockets of her jeans, causing her sweater to tighten across her breasts.

Something he shouldn't have noticed.

However, he also noticed her necklace. Not an ordinary one. It was a familiar concho with the double *R* brand of his family's ranch.

"Dade gave it to me for Christmas," she said, following his gaze. "He had it made years ago."

Funny, his brother hadn't mentioned a thing about seeing Eve or giving her a Christmas present. After Eve had left the goodbye note at the hospital, Grayson had thought all the Rylands had respected her wishes to be left alone.

Apparently not.

And he would take that up with Dade when he got home.

"The concho doesn't have bad memories for me like it does for you and your brothers," Eve explained. She shifted her weight, glanced away. "When I see it, I don't think of your father leaving. I think of all the memories of when he was there. When things were good."

Leave it to Eve to find the silver lining.

Grayson reached out and slid his fingers beneath the concho pendant. But it wasn't just the pendant he touched. His knuckles brushed against her breasts. She made a slight shivering sound and stepped back. Grayson let go of the concho and stepped back, too.

"Sorry," she mumbled. But then her chin came up. "I guess it's stupid to apologize for an involuntary response. I'm always going to feel an attraction for you, Grayson, and saying I'm sorry won't make it go away."

No. But admitting the attraction only reminded him that he felt the same about her. Not that he needed a reminder. Just seeing her had the heat sliding through him.

"Always?" he questioned. Oh, yeah. This was playing with fire all right.

She met his gaze head-on. "Always."

Their gazes held, and so many things passed between them. Questions. But very few answers, only the obvious one about this simmering heat. Yes, it would always be there.

"How are you, really?" he asked.

The corner of her mouth lifted. "Well, I'm not in any shape to haul you off to my bed, but I'm healing."

That didn't cool him down. Oh, man. He was stupid to keep at this, but Grayson had no choice. He needed to get to the bottom of this once and for all.

"Do you want to haul me off to your bed?" he asked.

He didn't quite get the reaction he'd hoped for. Eve huffed, and her hands came out of her pockets and went on her hips. "Yes. Happy now?" She didn't wait for his answer. Not that he had one. "What's this visit really about?"

He didn't have an answer for that, either. But he knew he sure as hell needed one. Grayson couldn't go back to kicking Christmas trees or to his nonstop surly mood. He had to resolve this situation once and for all.

"Well?" she prompted. She wasn't tapping her foot, but it was close.

Grayson tried to wrap his mind around his feelings, but Eve huffed again.

"I'm in love with you," she tossed out there like profanity. "I've tried not to be, but I can't make my feelings go away. So, there! Learn to deal with it." Another huff. "Would you like to know what I've been dreaming about for the past two weeks?"

Not the shooting. Grayson prayed it wasn't that.

"About *you*," she tossed out, as well.

Grayson was relieved. Sort of. "I've dreamed about you, too."

He had to gather his breath because he knew these next few minutes would be the most important of his life. Everything was about to change.

And it all hinged on Eve.

"I'm in love with you, too." He said the words fast, like pulling off a bandage, and he was surprised that it hadn't hurt one bit. Just the opposite.

Grayson felt relieved.

That relief didn't extend to Eve, however. Her eyes widened. Her mouth dropped open. "When did you realize that?" she asked.

"A long time ago. It just took me a while to get around to saying it." And because it'd taken him too long, he decided to repeat it. "I love you, Eve."

She didn't say a word. She just stood there, mouth open, and then the tears sprang to her eyes. Grayson moved first, but she was faster. Eve launched herself into his arms.

He took things from there.

Grayson kissed her, and for the first time in his life, he didn't hold anything back. He loved her, and he wanted her to know that. He must have succeeded because the kiss quickly turned fiery hot.

Eve coiled her arms around him, pulling him closer, but Grayson kept things gentle. Or at least he tried. Hard to stay gentle with the kiss going French and with Eve pressed against him. It wasn't easy, but Grayson pulled back to remind her of her injury.

"You're not in any condition for sex," he reminded her.

"Maybe not our normal version of sex." She put her mouth right against his ear because she was obviously a twisted woman who knew that would torture him in the best kind of way.

Grayson groaned and gladly gave in to the torture. He lifted his hands in surrender while she went after his neck.

Oh, yeah.

Eve knew every inch of his body, and within seconds had him rethinking that no-sex-right-now rule.

She pulled back slightly, met his gaze and gave him a nudge with her body that had his eyes crossing. "But remember, I'm in love with you," Eve confessed, "and we can find a way to make this happen."

He froze. And Eve noticed. She went stiff, too, and some panic raced through those jeweled blue eyes. "I was talking about sex when I said we can find a way."

"Were you?" he challenged.

More panic. She stepped back, as she'd always done in the past because she didn't want to put him in a corner. Well, Grayson was sure of two things—he was crazy in love with Eve, and he wanted to be in that *corner*.

He caught on to the silver concho pendant again, and because he wanted to hear that little shiver of arousal, he let his fingers trail over her right nipple.

He smiled when he heard the sound.

And then Grayson let go of the pendant and dropped to his knees.

Eve's sexy shiver turned to a gasp. "What are you doing?"

Grayson didn't even have to think about this. "I'm asking you to marry me."

The room was suddenly way too quiet. No more shivery sounds. No gasps. Eve just stared at him, and for one horrifying moment, he thought she would turn him down.

She certainly didn't say yes.

"Why are you asking me now?" she wanted to know.

Grayson had to release the breath he was holding so he could speak. "Uh, is that a trick question?"

"No." Eve was quick with that assurance but not with the answer to his proposal.

He shrugged. "I thought it was obvious. I'm asking because I love you. Because you're already part of the family, but I wanted to make it official. And because I want you in my bed every night."

She stared at him, as if waiting for more.

What?

That wasn't enough?

Grayson eased her down to her knees so they were face-to-face and so he could kiss her. She apparently needed a reminder of that love she'd professed for him just minutes earlier.

The kiss was long, satisfying and left them both breathless. "Say yes," he insisted.

But she didn't. She pulled back again. "Is this about the attempt to get me pregnant?"

"No." And he hoped she could see that was the honest to goodness truth. "This is about being in love with you. We can discuss the details of our future later, but for now I need an answer, and I need that answer to be yes. Because I can't imagine living the rest of my life without you."

Now, she made a sound. No shiver, but a melting sigh, and her smile returned. Eve slid her arms around him.

"Yes," she finally said. "Because I can't imagine living without you, either."

Grayson wasn't sure which he felt first—relief or happiness, but it was the happiness that filled every part of him.

Eve had said yes!

He wanted to whoop for joy and celebrate, but first he needed another kiss. Their mouths met, barely a touch at first, but in their case familiarity bred lust because this kiss quickly turned scalding hot.

Grayson wanted to tell his brothers about the engagement, but after a few more of those kisses, he knew his brothers would have to wait. Right now, he wanted to make love—gently—to his fiancée.

He got up, scooped Eve into his arms and headed for her bedroom. The kisses didn't stop. In fact, they got more heated as Eve pressed her mouth to his chin and then his throat.

"Wait!" she said the moment he eased her onto the bed.

Hell. That wasn't a word he wanted to hear. "You can't take back your yes," he let her know. "You're marrying me." And he hoped she didn't argue.

"I didn't mean wait about that. Of course, I want to marry you. I've wanted that since I was sixteen."

And that made Grayson smile.

He eased them onto the bed and then rolled her on top of him. "Then why did you say wait?" But his gaze dropped to her side. "Oh. Second thoughts about sex?"

"No." She made it sound as if he'd lost his mind. "I want sex. Trust me, I really want to have sex with you. But I have to tell you something first."

Her smile faded until she looked anything but happy.

Grayson froze again. In fact, he was reasonably sure that every muscle in his body locked up so he couldn't move. "What's wrong?"

"Uh..." And a moment later, she repeated it. She also licked her lips and bunched up her forehead. "The test was, well, it was positive."

It took a few seconds for that to sink in through the worry and the haze in his mind. "You're pregnant?" And that was something he thought he'd *never* hear himself ask Eve.

She nodded. Swallowed hard.

Eve eyed him as if he were a stick of dynamite about to go off. "I should have told you the minute you got on your knees, but I was so surprised. And happy. The only thing I could think of was saying yes. I didn't think that this baby could change everything."

He caught on to her arm. "Wait a minute." The thoughts and words were flying at him so fast that it took Grayson a moment to speak. "You think a baby could change the way I feel about you?"

She blinked back tears. "Does it?"

Oh, man. He had some explaining to do. Grayson decided to start that explanation with a kiss. He gently pulled her down to him and did just that.

"Yes, it changes how I feel about you," he admitted. He slid his hand over her stomach. "It makes me love you even more."

Her breath swooshed out and she snapped him to her.

Probably too hard. But Grayson couldn't make himself let go of her.

"But this messes up the plans you had for your life," she reminded him.

"Screw the plans." In fact, he was looking forward to a little chaos, especially the kind of chaotic love that a wife and a child would give him. He hadn't realized until now that having Eve and this child gave him something he'd never had—completion.

His life would be complete with them.

He wouldn't just have brothers. Wouldn't just be part of the Rylands. He would have his *own* family.

"So you're happy?" she asked.

Grayson wanted no room for doubt. "I'm the happiest man on earth." And he pulled her into his arms so he could hold her and kiss her.

He could have sworn he felt everything in the universe go into some kind of perfect cosmic alignment.

Or maybe that was just his heart.

Either way, this was right. No, it was better than that.

It was perfect.

And Grayson wanted to hold on to Eve and his baby like this forever.

* * * * *

"You've been good to me through all of this. I won't forget it."

Dade stared at her. "That sounds like some kind of goodbye."

She looked ready to say yes, it was. But Dade wasn't about to accept a goodbye, so he kissed her. It was ill-timed. But it was also what he needed. Hopefully it was what Kayla needed, too.

"Remember," he said against her mouth, "I'm the guy who makes you forget to breathe." He meant to make it sound light, but it sure didn't come out that way.

Her eyes met his again, but there was no humor, no teasing. "That's true. And if you don't think that scares me, think again."

He brushed his mouth against hers. "Fear is the last thing I want you to feel when it comes to me."

"Too late." And she kissed him in a way that made him melt.

Dade returned the favor. "Funny, you don't sound afraid." She sounded aroused, and looked it as well, with her heavy eyelids and flushed cheeks.

He felt her muscles go slack, and she slipped her hands around the back of his neck. "I'm only afraid you might stop," she whispered..

DADE

BY
DELORES FOSSEN

MILLS &
BOON

All the characters in this book have no existence outside the imagination of the author, and have no relation whatsoever to anyone bearing the same name or names. They are not even distantly inspired by any individual known or unknown to the author, and all the incidents are pure invention.

All Rights Reserved including the right of reproduction in whole or in part in any form. This edition is published by arrangement with Harlequin Enterprises II B.V./S.à.r.l. The text of this publication or any part thereof may not be reproduced or transmitted in any form or by any means, electronic or mechanical, including photocopying, recording, storage in an information retrieval system, or otherwise, without the written permission of the publisher.

This book is sold subject to the condition that it shall not, by way of trade or otherwise, be lent, resold, hired out or otherwise circulated without the prior consent of the publisher in any form of binding or cover other than that in which it is published and without a similar condition including this condition being imposed on the subsequent purchaser.

® and ™ are trademarks owned and used by the trademark owner and/or its licensee. Trademarks marked with ® are registered with the United Kingdom Patent Office and/or the Office for Harmonisation in the Internal Market and in other countries.

First published in Great Britain 2013
by Mills & Boon, an imprint of Harlequin (UK) Limited,
Eton House, 18-24 Paradise Road, Richmond, Surrey TW9 1SR

© Delores Fossen 2011

ISBN: 978 0 263 90340 9
ebook ISBN: 978 1 472 00686 8

46-0113

Harlequin (UK) policy is to use papers that are natural, renewable and recyclable products and made from wood grown in sustainable forests. The logging and manufacturing processes conform to the legal environmental regulations of the country of origin.

Printed and bound in Spain
by Blackprint CPI, Barcelona

Imagine a family tree that includes Texas cowboys, Choctaw and Cherokee Indians, a Louisiana pirate and a Scottish rebel who battled side by side with William Wallace. With ancestors like that, it's easy to understand why Texas author and former air force captain **Delores Fossen** feels as if she were genetically predisposed to writing romances. Along the way to fulfilling her DNA destiny, Delores married an air force top gun who just happens to be of Viking descent. With all those romantic bases covered, she doesn't have to look too far for inspiration.

Chapter One

Kayla Brennan sure didn't look like a killer.

That was Deputy Sheriff Dade Ryland's first thought when his glare landed on the blonde who was running down the staircase. His second thought went in a different direction.

A *bad* one.

More specifically to her dark purple dress that hugged every curve of her body. Real curves. Something that always got his attention even when it shouldn't.

Like now, for instance.

Sex and Kayla Brennan shouldn't be occupying the same side of his brain.

He'd seen her before, of course, from a distance. Just over a year ago at the Silver Creek sheriff's office where she was being questioned about her husband's suspicious fatal car accident. That day Dade watched her from the doorway of his office. But she'd been pregnant then and had hidden those spicy blue eyes behind a pair of designer sunglasses. She'd shown no emotion of any kind.

Unlike now.

He saw just a flash of fear before she closed down. That pretty face became a rock-hard wall.

Dade cleared his throat and kicked up his glare a notch, hoping both would give him an attitude adjustment. It did. But then it wasn't hard to remember that this curvy blonde might be partly responsible for the death of someone he loved.

"I heard the doorbell," Kayla announced. She paused on the bottom step when she spotted Dade in the doorway, and her attention flew in the direction of the other man in the foyer. "Who's he?" she demanded.

Because Kayla apparently didn't recognize him, Dade tapped the badge clipped to his rawhide belt. "*He* has a name, and it's Deputy Sheriff Dade Ryland." He nudged the other man aside and stepped into the foyer so he could close the door.

Her left eyebrow rose, and her gaze slipped back to Dade. "You're a deputy?" She didn't wait for him to answer. "You look more outlaw than lawman."

Yeah, he got that a lot, but Dade wasn't about to let Kayla get away with the observation. "You'd know all about outlaws, wouldn't you?"

She flinched a little. Just enough to make Dade wonder exactly how raw that nerve was he'd hit.

Her flinch quickly turned to a scalpel-sharp glare, and she was almost as good at that particular expression as he was. "What are you doing in my house?"

House. That was a loose term for what was actually the Texas-sized mansion on the outskirts of his hometown of Silver Creek. A mansion she'd inherited when her husband had been killed. Dade had been raised nearby in a big ranch house with sixteen rooms, but he was betting the Brennan place was double that size.

The same probably went for Kayla's pocketbook, although Dade had some one-upmanship on her in that particular department. His family had earned their money through hard, back-breaking, honest work on the ranch. Kayla had married her millions, and those millions were as dirty as she no doubt was.

"I'm here on official business," Dade informed her. He glanced at the bald, gorilla-sized man who moved a few steps away. Dade knew his name was Kenneth Mitchell.

Kayla's so-called bodyguard.

Probably more like a hired gun as dirty as the woman paying his salary, and that's why Dade kept his hand on his gun tucked in his shoulder holster.

"The deputy says you're in his protective custody," Kenneth relayed to Kayla. His bulky body strained against his black suit, just as the muscles in his face strained against his skin.

She studied Dade, her eyes narrowing. "How did you know I was here? I led everyone to believe that I'd be at my house in San Antonio."

Dade shrugged, figuring the answer was obvious. "The district attorney, Winston Calhoun, called the sheriff and told him."

The way she pulled in her breath let him know that the answer had not been so obvious to her after all. "Mr. Calhoun assured me that he would keep my whereabouts a secret."

Dade tipped his head to the badge again. "He didn't exactly announce it to the press. He told me because you're in my protective custody."

Her eyes narrowed even more. "Protective custody?" she repeated. "How do you figure that?"

Dade walked closer to her. "Easy. You're the state's material witness, and the D.A. wants you alive long enough to testify against your father-in-law."

There it was in a nutshell, but that didn't begin to cover what Dade wanted from this woman. Yes, he wanted her to testify against her late-husband's scummy father, Charles Brennan. He wanted her to take the stand and spill her guts about the extortion and murders that Brennan had committed. While she was at it, Dade wanted to know if Brennan had killed his own son—Kayla's husband.

But those were just the icing.

What Dade really wanted her to admit on the stand was that she'd had some part in another crime.

Ellie's murder.

Dade had to take a deep breath as those memories crashed through him.

Ellie hadn't been just his sister-in-law and his twin brother's wife. Dade had loved her as deeply as he did his blood family. Kayla Brennan and her scumbag father-in-law were going to pay for killing Ellie.

"Don't worry," Kayla said with a sappy sweetness that couldn't be genuine. "I didn't come out of hiding just to let someone silence me."

No, but Kayla had come out of hiding after nearly a year. So she could testify, she'd told the D.A. But Dade wondered if there was more to it than that. He knew the D.A. had been trying to contact her for months, and she hadn't responded.

Until three hours ago.

Then, Kayla had called D.A. Winston Calhoun and told him that she would testify against her father-in-law in an extortion and racketeering trial. A trial that could send Charles Brennan to jail for several decades.

Hardly the death sentence Dade wanted for him.

However, Dade was willing to bet that Brennan had no plans to spend one minute behind bars, much less a decade. And he probably wouldn't. From what Dade had read, the case was weak at best, and witnesses kept backing out or disappearing.

But now Kayla had arrived on the scene.

Dade couldn't believe Kayla had doing her civic duty in mind. No, this was probably some kind of revenge move to get back at her father-in-law. No honor among thieves in the Brennan clan.

"I wasn't worried about you," Dade corrected. "Just doing a job I was ordered to do." And he had indeed been ordered by not just the sheriff, who was his brother, but by the D.A. Kayla was a star witness in every sense of the word, and a lot of people wanted her alive.

She made a sound of sarcastic amusement and breezed past him to head toward the double front doors. "I'll stay alive so I can testify, and I don't need you or anyone else in your family to protect me. That's why I hired Kenneth."

Dade stared at her. Well, he stared at her backside

anyway because she was already walking away from him. Her low thin heels made delicate clicks on the veiny marble floor.

"I don't care how many guns you hire," Dade informed her. "You're still in my protective custody."

Kayla stopped and glanced at him from over her shoulder. The corner of her rose-tinged mouth lifted just a fraction, but it wasn't a smile on her face. "Protective custody, you say? Right. Those two words don't go together when it comes to you or any member of your family. The Rylands hate me."

Dade didn't deny it. "We have reason to hate you."

"No." She huffed, causing a wisp of her hair to move slightly. "You have reason to hate someone for your sister-in-law's murder, but I didn't have anything to do with it."

"Got proof of that?"

"Do you have proof to the contrary?" she fired right back at him.

He leaned in a little. "If I did, your butt would be in jail right now."

Another smirk. A short-lived one. She turned away so that he couldn't see her face. Her head lowered slightly. "Well, because I'm here and not in the Silver Creek jail, you obviously have no proof. So you can leave."

"I wish." Dade went closer while keeping an eye on Kayla's bodyguard. "Nothing would make me happier than to walk out that door and leave you to deal with the wolves, but I have my orders."

"You can take your orders and get out." She reached

for the doorknob, but Dade snagged her wrist with his left hand.

The wrist snag obviously didn't sit well with her bodyguard because he reached for his gun. Dade reached for his, too.

"Stop this!" Kayla practically yelled. She jerked her hand away from Dade and shook her head. "Please," she said. Her voice was softer now but edged with the nerves that were right beneath her skin. "Just leave."

Dade's nerves were too close to the surface, too, and touching Kayla certainly hadn't helped. He felt ornerier than usual, and that wasn't good because he was the king of ornery. Best to go ahead and lay down some ground rules.

Dade aimed his index finger at Kenneth. "You draw that gun and I'll shoot you where you stand. Got that?"

Oh, the man wanted to argue all right. Dade could see it in his eyes, but he knew what was in his own eyes—determination to finish this damn job so he could get the heck out of there.

When Kenneth finally eased his hand away from his weapon, Dade turned back to Kayla. "Where's your baby?"

She pulled back her shoulders. "That's none of your business."

He tapped his badge in case she'd forgotten. "This isn't personal, lady. I'm asking because I need to establish some security measures." He got closer, violating her personal space and then some.

Not the brightest idea he'd ever had. His chest

brushed against her breasts, and he got a fire-hot reminder that Kayla was a woman.

Dade held his ground and met her eye-to-eye. "Where's your son?" he repeated.

She didn't back down, either. "He's sleeping upstairs. Now tell me what this is all about."

Dade ignored her question. "Is your son away from the windows?"

She stepped back and her breath rattled in her throat. "Why?"

Dade gave her a flat look. "Because my protective custody extends to your son, Robert."

"Robbie," she corrected, although she looked as if she wanted to curse for giving him even that little bit of personal information about her child. A kid who was supposedly just eleven months old. A baby. And it was because of the baby that Dade had quit arguing about this assignment so he could drive out to the Brennan estate.

He didn't care a rat's you-know-what about Kayla, but he would do everything within his power to protect an innocent child.

Even her child.

"The deputy's trying to scare you," Kenneth interjected.

"Yeah, I am," Dade readily admitted. He looked at her again to make sure she got what he was saying. "And if you have any sense whatsoever, you'll be scared because you can't believe Brennan is going to let you get anywhere near that witness stand tomorrow morning."

Her bottom lip trembled a little, but she kept her chin up and her expression resolute.

"Your baby's safety is one of the main reasons for the protective custody," Dade informed her. "I have to take your son and you to a safe house. Sheriff's orders."

She started the head shaking again. "I've already had someone upgrade the security system, and I can hire more bodyguards." Kayla looked at him. "I wouldn't have come back here to Silver Creek if I hadn't thought I could keep my son safe."

Dade made sure they had eye contact again. "You thought wrong."

She glanced out the sidelight window. "I don't believe that. Charles wouldn't do anything that would risk hurting Robbie."

"That's a chance you're willing to take?"

She didn't answer that. "Besides, I don't trust you any more than I trust Charles."

Dade couldn't blame her. The Rylands hadn't exactly been friendly since Ellie's murder. Things would stay that way, too, but it wouldn't stop Dade from doing his job.

Kayla stepped closer to him. So close that he caught her scent. Not perfume but baby powder.

"I'll call my attorney," she said with her voice lowered. "But I'm certain you can't force protective custody on me."

She was right. Well, unless he thought she was going to run. But because she'd arrived voluntarily, he didn't exactly have reason to believe she would leave.

"Think about your son's safety," Dade reminded her.

"I am." And she turned and opened the door. "I can keep him safe without so-called help from the Rylands."

Fine. Dade had warned his brother and the D.A. that this wouldn't be an easy notion to sell, and both had told Dade that somehow he had to convince Kayla otherwise. Well, he'd failed, but he darn sure wasn't going to lose any sleep over it.

Dade was barely an inch out the door when Kayla slammed it so hard that he felt the gust of air wash over him. It mixed with the blast of chilly February wind that came right at him. He waited a second until he heard her engage the lock. He waited an extra second to see if she would change her mind, but when she didn't reopen the door, Dade cursed and headed off the porch and toward his truck.

Hell.

He really didn't want to go back to the sheriff's office and tell his brother, Grayson, that he'd failed. Not that Grayson was likely keeping count or anything, but Dade figured he already had too many failures on his records. Far more than the other deputies in Silver Creek. Still, he couldn't force a hardheaded woman to listen to reason.

Dade opened the door to his truck, moved to get inside and then stopped. He lifted his head, listened and looked around.

The area surrounding the circular drive and front of the estate was well lit so he had a good view of pretty much everything within thirty yards in any direction. But it wasn't the lit areas that troubled him. It was the thick clusters of trees and shrubs on the east and west sides of the estate.

He waited, trying to tamp down the bad feeling he had about all of this. But the bad feeling stayed right with him, settling hard and cold in his stomach.

Dade cursed, shoved his truck keys in his pocket and headed back for the estate. He didn't relish going a second round with the curvy Kayla, but he would for the sake of her son. Dade turned. Made it just one step.

And that's when the shot rang out.

Chapter Two

Kayla was halfway up the stairs, but the sound stopped her cold.

A sharp, piercing blast.

The sound tore through the house. And her.

She froze for just a second, but Kenneth certainly didn't. He drew his gun.

"Get down!" Kenneth shouted. "Someone just fired a shot."

Kayla's heart started to pound, and her breath began to race. She had no intentions of getting down. She had to get to her baby. She had to protect Robbie.

There was another shot, followed by someone banging on the front door.

"Let me in!" that someone shouted. It was Deputy Dade Ryland. He was cursing, and while he bashed his fist against the door, he continued to yell for them to let him inside before he got killed.

Her first thought was that Dade was responsible for the shots, but that didn't make sense. He'd come here to warn her of danger, and if he'd wanted to shoot at them, then he could have done it in the foyer at point-blank range. Still, that didn't mean she trusted the deputy.

"You need to get down," Kenneth warned her again, and he headed to the door to disengage the security system and let in the deputy.

Dade didn't wait for the door to be fully open. The moment Kenneth cracked it, he dived through nearly knocking down her bodyguard in the process. The deputy had his gun drawn and ready, and he reached over to slap off the lights. In the same motion, he kicked the door shut.

"Lock it and reset the security system," Dade ordered Kenneth. He took out his phone from his jeans pocket and called for backup.

Even though he'd turned off the lights in the foyer, Kayla had no trouble seeing Dade because the lamp in the adjacent living room was blazing. Dade's eyes were blazing, too, and he turned that hot glare on her.

"I heard your bodyguard tell you to get down. What part of that didn't you understand?" Dade barked.

"I have to get to my son," she barked right back, and Kayla continued up the stairs. Or rather that's what she tried to do, but the third shot wasn't just a loud blast. It ripped through the window in the living room, spewing glass everywhere. And worse, the bullet tore into the stair railing just a few yards below her.

She froze. Oh, mercy. Someone wasn't just shooting. The person was actually trying to kill her.

"Now will you get down?" Dade demanded.

Without warning, Dade aimed his gun into the living room and fired, the blast echoing through the foyer. He shot out the lamp, plunging them into darkness. It took a moment for her eyes to adjust.

Even over the blast still roaring in her ears, Kayla heard a sound that robbed her of what little breath she had left. Robbie started to cry. He wasn't alone. The nanny, Connie Mullins, was with him, but Kayla didn't want to count on the petite sixty-year-old woman when it came to a situation like this.

A situation that had turned deadly.

Kayla refused to think of the possibility this could end with her death. And that wouldn't even be a worst-case scenario. Worst case would be for Robbie to get hurt.

Dade pointed to the living room where he'd just shot out the light. "Can you see the SOB shooting at your boss?" he asked Kenneth.

Her bodyguard shook his head, and both men glanced up at her as she started to crawl toward the nursery.

Dade cursed. "Cover me," he said to Kenneth. The order barely made it out of his mouth when he came barreling up the stairs, his cowboy boots hitting against the hardwood steps.

But that wasn't the only sound.

More shots came. One right behind the other. Each of them ripped through the expensive carved-wood railing and sent splinters flying in every direction. That didn't stop Dade. He made it to her, crawling over her to shove her as low as she could get.

"Robbie," she managed to say.

Dade's gaze slashed to hers. "If you go to him, the bullets will follow you."

That was the only possible thing he could have said to make her stop.

Kayla froze, and the full impact of that warning slammed into her as hard as the bullets battering the foyer. Oh, no. She'd put her son in danger. This was the very thing she'd tried to avoid, the very reason she'd come out of hiding, and she had only made it worse.

Again.

The anger collided with the fear, and she wanted to hit her fists against the stairs. She wanted to scream out for the shooter to stop. But more than those things, she just wanted to protect her baby.

"Is your son with a nanny?" Dade asked.

Kayla managed a nod. She'd asked Connie to wait in the nursery when she heard Dade ring the doorbell. "In there," she said, pointing to the first door off the left hall.

"Are they near a bathroom with a tub?" he also wanted to know.

Another nod. "There's one adjoining the nursery." And Kayla hated that she hadn't thought of that herself. "Connie?" she shouted.

"What's going on, Kayla?" the woman shouted back.

"I'm not sure," Kayla lied. "Just take Robbie into the bathroom and get in the tub." The porcelain tub would be their shield against the bullets.

Robbie was still crying, and the sound of her son's wails let her know that Connie was on the move.

Robbie's voice became more and more faint until Kayla couldn't hear him at all.

That didn't help her nerves.

Hearing him had at least allowed her to know that he was all right. Still, she didn't want him out in the open in the nursery in case this attack continued.

As if to prove to her that it would, more bullets ripped through the foyer.

"How long before backup arrives?" Kenneth shouted.

"Too long," Dade answered. "At least fifteen minutes. This place isn't exactly in city limits."

Kenneth cursed and took cover behind a table. Kayla silently cursed as well. In fifteen minutes they could all be dead.

"I have to move you," Dade informed her. Other than a glance that had an I-told-you-this-could-happen snarl to it, his attention volleyed between the living room and the front door.

Kayla shook her head. "But you said I can't go near Robbie."

"You can't. But it's only a matter of time before the shooter changes positions." He tipped his head toward the front. "There are a lot of windows, and he'll have a clean shot once he moves."

Not *if* he moves but *once*.

"I'll roll to the side, just a little," Dade instructed. "And without standing up, I want you to get to the top of the stairs. Duck behind the first thing you see that can provide some cover."

Kayla managed to nod, and the moment that Dade

lifted his weight off her, she did as he'd ordered. She covered her head with her hands and scrambled up the stairs as fast as she could.

The shots didn't stop, and one plowed into the wall above her just as Kayla dived to the side of a table. She'd barely managed that when Dade came barreling toward her. He hooked his arm around her waist and dragged her away from the table, away from the wall.

But also away from the nursery.

He hauled her toward the right, the opposite side from where Robbie and the nanny were, and Kayla was thankful that Dade had given her son that extra cushion of security. However, there was no cushion for Dade and her. They were off the stairs, yes, but the bullets continued to come at them. Dade flattened her on the floor and crawled back over her.

Kayla was well aware of his body pressed hard against hers. His breathing, too, because it was gusting in her ear. But she also felt his corded muscles and the determination to keep her alive.

That didn't mean, however, he'd succeed.

And that both frightened and infuriated her.

Just like that, the shots stopped. Kayla held her breath, waiting and praying that this was over, but it was Dade's profanity that let her know it wasn't.

She glanced back at him, and her gaze collided with those steel grays. He barely looked at her, but in that glimpse he managed to convey his concern and his disgust.

He hated her.

All the Rylands hated her. And Kayla couldn't

blame them. Guilt by association. Her father-in-law had probably caused Ellie Ryland's death. And so far, he'd gotten off scot-free, thanks to a team of good lawyers and a technicality in some of the paperwork that had been used in his original arrest.

"What?" Dade snarled.

It took her a moment to realize he was talking to her, and she knew why. She was staring at him.

"Nothing," Kayla mumbled. And she forced her attention away from the one man who should disgust her as much as the shooter outside. But much to her dismay, what she felt wasn't total disgust.

Yet more proof that she was stupid.

She had noticed Dade Ryland's storm-black hair. It was a little too long, and his five o'clock stubble was a little too dark for her to think of him as handsome. No. It was worse than that. He wasn't handsome.

He was hot in that bad-boy, outlaw sort of way.

Well, she'd already been burned by one bad boy, and she wasn't looking for another. Not now. Not ever again.

Dade gave her another glance, and she could have sworn he smirked, as if he could read her mind.

"You see the shooter yet?" Dade called down to the bodyguard.

"No."

"The shooter's probably moving," Dade growled. He levered himself up just slightly and re-aimed his gun toward the front of the house.

Kayla could do nothing other than hope this would

end with her baby unharmed. She'd been a fool to come back, a fool to respond to Charles's latest threat.

But what else could she have done?

She had to get out from beneath the hold Charles had on her. She had to try to make a safe, normal life for her son. But instead, she'd gotten this.

"Someone told Charles I was here," she mumbled. "Probably the D.A. or a Ryland." She hadn't meant to say Dade's family name so loudly, but by God it was hard to tamp down the anger while bracing for another attack.

"No one in my family is responsible for this," Dade informed her. "Lady, you got into this mess all by yourself."

She wanted to argue, but the sound stopped her. In the distance she heard sirens. No doubt the backup that Dade had called. Even though she didn't like the idea of the place crawling with any more Rylands, it was better than the alternative.

She hoped.

Beneath them in the foyer, Kayla heard her bodyguard moving around. Maybe so he could try to spot the shooter. Dade moved, too. He used his forearm to push her face back to the carpet, and he maneuvered himself off her. This time not just an inch or two. He reared up and took aim at the front windows.

He fired.

The blast roared through her ears, and she had no time to recover before there was another shot. Not from Dade. This one came tearing through the foyer but from a different angle than before. This bullet took out one of the front windows and sent glass flying through the air.

Dade had been right. The shooter had moved. And now Dade and she were in his direct line of fire.

For a few moments at the beginning of the attack, Kayla had hoped the shots were meant as a warning. A way to get her to grab Robbie and go back into hiding. But this was no warning.

This was an assassination attempt.

Dade sent another shot the gunman's way, and she put her hands over her ears to shut out the painful noise. However, she could still hear them. And the siren. It grew closer and closer as the gunman's shots came faster and faster. He wasn't panicking, and he definitely wasn't running. He was trying to kill her before the sheriff arrived.

"Stay down," Dade warned her. He shifted his gun toward one of the other front windows and fired.

This time, Kayla heard another sound. A groan of some kind, following by a heavy thud. Had Dade managed to shoot the gunman? Maybe.

Kayla looked up and followed the direction of Dade's aim. There. Through the jagged shards of glass jutting from the window frame, she saw something.

A man.

He was dressed head to toe in black, and it was only because of the porch light that she could see his silhouette. She could also see his gun, and he took aim at Dade and her.

Kayla yelled for Dade to get down, and she latched

onto him to pull him back to the floor. But he threw off her grip and fired at the shadowy figure.

The man fired a shot as well and then clutched his shoulder. She couldn't be sure, but she thought this time maybe Dade had managed to shoot him.

Dade must have thought that too because he headed down the stairs, taking them two at a time while he kept his gun trained on the person on the porch. Kayla could only watch with her breath held and her heart pounding so hard that it might come out of her chest.

The man on the porch fired.

She yelled to warn Dade, but her warning was drowned out by another shot and the sounds of the approaching sirens. She heard Dade curse as if in pain, but what he didn't do was get down. He raced toward the door, threw it open and fired again.

But so did the gunman.

Oh, God.

She realized then that if this assassin managed to kill Dade that he would come after Robbie and her next. Of course, Kenneth was down there, somewhere, but if the gunman got past the bodyguard, then Kayla would have no way to defend her baby and herself.

Kayla cursed herself for not bringing some kind of weapon with her. But she wouldn't need a weapon if this goon tried to get to her baby. No. Pure raw adrenaline and the need to protect her child would give her the strength to fight whoever came through that door.

She stood, preparing herself for whatever she had to do, but instead she saw the blue swirls of the lights from a police cruiser. Red lights, too, maybe from an ambulance. The vehicles tore across the lawn and screamed to a halt. There were no more shots, just the noise of the men who scrambled from those vehicles.

Kayla waited, the seconds clicking off like gunshots in her head, and when the waiting became unbearable, she began to make her way down the stairs. The foyer was still dark, and the only illumination came from the jolts of red and blue lights from the responding vehicles.

"Kenneth?" she called out, her voice hardly more than a hoarse whisper. He didn't answer. "Deputy Ryland?" she tried.

No answer from Dade either.

Kayla inched down the steps, praying this ordeal was indeed over but also bracing herself for whatever she might see.

She didn't brace herself enough.

There was blood on the floor of the foyer. In the darkness it looked like a pool of liquid black, but she instinctively knew what it was.

And there, slumped in the doorway was Dade Ryland.

Chapter Three

Dade looked down at his left arm and cursed. This was not a good time to get shot.

Hell.

Using the doorjamb for support, he got to his feet and tried not to look as if his arm was on fire. He figured he'd failed big-time when he saw Kayla. Her eyes were wide, her face way too pale.

"You've been shot," she said, the words rushing out.

Was that concern he saw and heard? He had to be wrong about that. No, this was probably just a reaction to the blood. And there was no doubt about it, there was blood.

"Check on your bodyguard," Dade barked, and he pulled back his shoulders so he could face the responders who were coming right at him.

First, there was his brother, Sheriff Grayson Ryland. Tall and lanky like most of his five siblings, Grayson might not have been the biggest of the half-dozen people who came out of the cruisers and ambulance, but he was automatically the center of attention and the one in charge. Grayson commanded respect just by stepping onto the scene.

Another brother, Mason, stepped out from a vehicle, too—a weathered Ford truck that had been red once, maybe twenty years ago. Mason, like Dade, was also a deputy sheriff but worked only part-time because he also ran the family ranch.

Dressed in his usual black jeans, black shirt and equally black Stetson, Mason made his way toward the estate. Not with Grayson's speed, authority or concern. Mason always looked as if he were stalking something. Or headed to a funeral.

"You're hurt," Grayson said, and he used his head to motion to the medics so they'd hurry to Dade. Grayson also kept his gun trained on the man sprawled out on the porch.

The dead man.

Dade had managed to take the guy out, but not before the SOB had fired a shot into Dade's arm. Talk about a rookie mistake, and he hadn't been a rookie in fourteen years, not since he'd joined the Silver Creek sheriff's department on his twenty-first birthday. Considering that being a cop was his one-and-only desire in life, he always seemed to be screwing it up.

Like now, for instance.

The gunman who could have given them answers was as dead as a doornail. Added to that, Dade had nearly let Kayla Brennan be gunned down, her body-guard had been shot, or worse, and the jagged slice on his arm from the bullet graze was hurting like hell.

Grayson stooped down and put his fingers to the gunman's neck. "He's dead."

Yeah. No surprise there. "You need to check on Kayla's bodyguard," Dade let his brother know. He would do it himself, but he wanted a chance to catch his breath and get ahead of the pain.

"Kayla?" Grayson questioned, standing upright. He aimed a questioning glare at Dade, and Dade knew why. *Kayla* was way too personal to call someone who might be responsible for a family member's death.

Grayson was right, and Dade silently cursed that, too. He was a sucker for a damsel in distress, and while he wasn't sure about the damsel part, Kayla was definitely in distress.

And so was her baby.

With his glare morphing into a disgusted scowl, Grayson flipped on the lights and walked past him and into the foyer where Kayla was kneeling down next to Kenneth.

"He's still breathing," Kayla announced, and that sent two of the medics scurrying in the bodyguard's direction.

One medic, however, Carrie Collins, a leggy brunette in snug green scrubs made a beeline toward Dade.

"I'm okay," Dade tried to tell her, but she latched onto his arm to examine it.

"I'll decide if you're okay or not," Carrie answered.

Like Kayla, there was way too much concern in her voice and expression. In this case, though, Dade knew why. Carrie and he had once been lovers, but that wasn't just water under the bridge. The water had dried up nearly a year ago. Too bad Carrie didn't always remember that.

"You need stitches," Carrie mumbled, her forehead bunching up. "And probably a tetanus shot."

But Dade tuned her out and put his attention on Kayla, Grayson and the unconscious bodyguard. Grayson caught onto Kayla and moved her away from the man so the medics could get to work, but it was obvious Kayla had tried to help her employee. Her hands and dress were covered with blood.

Kayla looked down at her palms, which were shaking almost violently, and she shuddered. Now that the lights were back on, Dade also saw the tears well up in her eyes.

Dade's feet seemed to have a mind of their own because he started toward her. So did Mason. Mason grunted and glanced down at Dade's arm.

"You scratched yourself," Mason remarked with zero sympathy in his tone. "Don't expect me to do the paperwork for this goat rope."

It was just what Dade needed to hear. Sarcasm without sympathy. He knew his brother loved him. Well, Dade was pretty sure of that anyway. But Mason wasn't the sort to cut anyone any slack.

Unlike Kayla. Blinking back tears, she made her way toward Dade with her attention fixed on him. "I thought you'd been killed."

Dade was aware that both his brothers were watching and listening. "No. You didn't get lucky this time."

She flinched as if he'd slapped her, but quickly regained her composure. "Lucky?" she challenged.

"Right. Well, let's just say I'm grateful you did your job and put yourself in front of bullets for me." Her voice trailed off to a whisper. "Thank you, Dade."

Dade was one-hundred-percent positive that his brother hadn't missed the way his given name had just purred right off her sympathetic rose-tinged lips. Or maybe the purring and the sympathy were his imagination.

Oh, man.

Kayla was going to be trouble with a capital *T*.

"I have to check on my baby," she let them know.

Dade snagged her by the arm. "Have the nanny and Robbie stay in the bathroom, okay? This might not be over."

As expected, the fear returned to her eyes. She swallowed hard, nodded and raced up the stairs.

"I'll need to question you when you come back down," Grayson called out to her.

Without looking back, she gave another shaky nod.

Dade wanted to hit himself in his fire-burning arm just to get his mind off this asinine need to comfort and to play nice with the one woman he shouldn't want to comfort or play nice with.

The three of them watched her make her way up the stairs, and Dade waited for the lecture from his brothers. A lecture that would no doubt include a reminder to think with his brain and not with what was behind the zipper of his Wranglers. But the lecture didn't come.

Not verbally anyway.

Grayson stepped away to give the medics some instructions, and then he took out his phone to call the county medical examiner, something Dade should have already thought to do.

"Did the dead guy give you any warning before he started shooting?" Mason asked.

Dade shook his head. "Kayla..." He considered calling her Ms. Brennan, but heck, the damage had already been done. "She refused protective custody, and I was on my way back to town when I figured out something was wrong. The guy opened fire before I could get back inside."

Mason stayed quiet a moment, but his forehead bunched up. "She refused our help." It wasn't a question. Mason sort of growled it out in a disapproving way.

Dade shrugged and then winced when that sent another shot of fire through his arm. "Understandable. She doesn't trust us. Just like we don't trust her."

Mason made a sound, one of his grunts that could have meant anything. Or nothing at all. "I'll keep watch outside. We don't need any more of Charles Brennan's henchmen showing up here tonight."

No, they didn't. And it could happen all right. Dade figured there was no way Brennan was going to let Kayla get anywhere near a witness stand.

"I need to clean that wound," Carrie let him know.

"Later." Dade moved to the side so the medics could take the bodyguard out on the gurney. Grayson had finished with his call and Dade wanted an update. Thankfully, Carrie didn't follow him.

"The M.E.'s on the way," Grayson relayed. "And the

rest of the deputies. Once they arrive, we can get *Kayla* and her baby out of here."

Dade glanced at the pool of blood and the shards of glass on the glossy marble floor. Maybe that would convince her to accept protective custody and leave for someplace safer.

If a safe place actually existed.

"Did she say why she changed her mind about testifying and came back to Silver Creek?" Grayson asked.

Dade shook his head and looked in the direction of the footsteps he heard. Kayla was making her way back downstairs, and she was no longer wearing the blood-soaked dress. She'd put on black pants and a gray blouse. She'd also adjusted her attitude. No more threat of tears or sympathetic looks. She was sporting a first-class glare.

"How's your son?" Dade asked, pleased that he would have to deal with the real Kayla rather than the damsel.

"He's fine," she snapped and then turned her attention to Grayson. "Someone obviously leaked my location," she accused before she even reached them in the foyer.

"Seems that way," Grayson admitted. "I suppose you think it was one of us."

"I do."

Dade stepped in front of his brother so he could finish this fight. "We have better things to do than endanger a witness. So that means the leak came from your side. Who knew you were coming here?"

She folded her arms over her chest. "You mean besides the Rylands?"

"Yeah, besides the *cops*." Dade didn't budge an inch. He met her eye-to-eye and practically foot-to-foot. But when she glanced down, Dade looked as well and saw the drop of his blood that had spattered onto one of her high-priced shoes.

"You need stitches," Grayson grumbled.

"I need answers from Ms. Brennan," Dade grumbled right back. But he did step slightly away so he wouldn't bleed on her fancy clothes.

And speaking of clothes, she'd missed a button on the blouse. Why he noticed that now, he didn't know.

Wait, yeah, he did know.

His male brain was too alert to the fact that Kayla was a woman. A woman with a gap in her blouse that allowed him a peek of the top of her right breast.

Dade did a double take.

She had a tattoo, a little pink heart right there on the swell of her breast.

Kayla made a soft sound of outrage, obviously noticing what had caught his attention, and she quickly buttoned her blouse as if she'd declared war on it.

"Your son's nanny knew you were here," Dade reminded her. He rolled up his shirt sleeve to put some pressure against his grazed arm.

She gave him a flat look. "My nanny is not responsible for this. She was in just as much danger as we were."

Dade couldn't argue with that. "So who else knew?"

Kayla wearily touched her fingers to her forehead.

"My sister, Misty Wallace, but she wouldn't have told anyone."

Grayson and Dade exchanged glances, and Dade knew that Grayson would verify that as soon as he could.

Kayla noticed that glance and must have realized what it meant. "Don't waste your time with my sister. I trust her with my life, and she would die rather than tell Charles where I am. Instead, investigate the D.A.," she answered, her voice edged with anger.

"Winston Calhoun's not in the business of killing witnesses, either," Dade let her know, although he would check to make sure the D.A. hadn't accidentally said the wrong thing to the wrong person. "I've known Winston my whole life. We can trust him."

"Maybe not," Kayla disagreed. "Is he rich like you and your family?"

"No." And Dade didn't like where this was going. "But not everyone can be bribed."

"My former father-in-law has a knack for finding a person's weak spot and getting his way." There was no smugness in her statement, and a frustrated sigh left her mouth.

He couldn't argue with that, either. "What about your sister, then? Is Misty dirty rich like you?"

Oh, that got a rise out of her. The anger flashed through her eyes. "This isn't about Misty. It's about Charles and whomever he could have bribed."

"Maybe," Dade concluded. "Then I'll go back to my original question. Who knew you were coming here? A boyfriend? A lover?"

She shook her head and looked ready to slug him. "No, on both counts."

"Your driver, then." Dade tried again.

"I drove myself, and I didn't tell anyone else where I was going." She paused. She glanced around the foyer, her attention landing on Dade's bloody arm. "I came here because I thought Charles would believe this was the last place I'd be."

"Obviously you got that wrong," Dade grumbled.

"Obviously," she grumbled right back.

"Why did you change your mind about testifying?" Dade pressed when she added nothing else.

Kayla dodged his gaze. "You wouldn't believe me if I told you."

Because she was staring at the floor, Dade ducked down a little to make eye contact. "Try."

She lifted her shoulder, stepped away from him. "I wanted to do the right thing." Kayla paused. "This morning, I got a threatening email from my ex-father-in-law."

Dade and Grayson exchanged another glance. "You told the D.A. about this?" Grayson asked.

"No, what would have been the point? Charles's threats are nothing new and never specific enough to bring charges against him. But this time, something inside me…snapped." She paused. "Or maybe for the first time things got crystal clear." Her gaze came to Dade's again, and she blinked back tears. "After reading that email, I knew the only way I could get this to stop was to testify and make sure Charles is put away for the rest of his life."

Oh, hell. There it was again. Sympathy. It was burning as hot as the gash on his arm. Grayson obviously wasn't immune either because he gave a heavy sigh.

"And that's the reason I need you in protective custody," Grayson concluded. "I want to take you and your baby to a safe house so that Brennan can't get to either of you. Brennan is out of jail on bond, and we're trying to keep an eye on him. But you know better than anyone, he can hire guns to do his dirty work."

Kayla stared at Grayson. Then stared at Dade, too. "After what happened tonight, how can you possibly keep my baby safe?" she asked. Her voice broke on the last word.

Dade was about to assure her that he would do his best, but Grayson's phone rang. He glanced at the screen and mumbled some profanity before he stepped away to take the call.

"I still don't trust you," Kayla whispered to Dade.

He nodded. "Yeah, I get that." He pointed to the blood on the floor. "But you've got a very short list of people you can trust right now."

She must have known that was true, but she still didn't agree.

"That was one of the medics," Grayson relayed, putting his phone back in his pocket. He walked back across the foyer toward them, his attention nailed to Kayla. "Your bodyguard died on the way to the hospital."

That was all he said. Grayson didn't offer any details or reiterate that she could have been the one in that ambulance.

Kayla pulled in her breath, and what little color she had drained from her face. She gave one crisp nod and turned toward the stairs. "I'll let the nanny know that we're moving to a safe house tonight with Dade— Deputy Ryland," she corrected, her voice now chilled with that ice-queen tone.

Dade didn't exactly celebrate because it had taken way too long to convince her to do the right thing. Now, he only hoped it *was* the right thing. After all, she'd just put her son's and her lives right in his hands.

"I think we might have found our leak," Mason said, stepping into the doorway.

That got everyone's attention. Kayla stopped on the bottom step and turned to face him.

"I checked the dead gunman's phone." Mason held up the bagged cell for them to see. "About a half hour before this guy started shooting, he made three calls." He aimed his usual surly expression at Kayla. "First one was to some guy named Danny Flynn, a lowlife who likely works for your ex-father-in-law, Charles Brennan."

"He does," Kayla admitted. "I remember that name."

Well, that wasn't exactly a bombshell. Everyone knew how much Brennan wanted to stop Kayla. Of course, Brennan would deny any association with the employee who'd gotten the call, but the cops might be able to break the employee and get him to confess.

"You said you'd found the leak?" Dade prompted.

Mason glanced at the screen on the dead man's cell. "We got two possibilities. The next call the gunman made was to Misty Wallace."

The breath seemed to swoosh right out of Kayla. "My sister?"

"Your sister," Mason confirmed.

Kayla frantically shook her head. "But Misty wouldn't tell Charles or anyone else where I was going."

"Right," Mason grumbled. "That call to her says otherwise." He went to Grayson and handed him the phone so that his brother could also check out the screen.

From his angle Dade couldn't see what caused both his brothers' eyes to narrow.

Kayla had a white-knuckled grip on the stair railing. "Who's the third person he called?"

"What kind of game are you playing, Ms. Brennan?" Grayson demanded.

"What do you mean?" And her shock sure as heck sounded sincere.

But Dade didn't take her sincerity of the head shaking at face value. He leaned in so he could see the name of the last person the gunman had called.

Hell.

What was going on?

Chapter Four

Kayla was trembling, but that didn't stop her from marching across the foyer to see what had caused the Rylands to turn those accusing stares on her. And then she saw the cell phone screen.

No, it couldn't be. But it was.

It was her name and number.

"Why did the gunman call you?" Dade demanded.

"He didn't," Kayla answered as quickly as she could get out the words.

"The phone says otherwise," Mason Ryland growl.

"Then it was faked somehow." She hated the quiver in her voice. Hated even more that she cared one iota what these Rylands thought of her, but by God she'd had no part in this attack. "I wouldn't have hired someone to shoot into a house where my son was staying."

The trio exchanged glances. A united brotherly front against her. They didn't just look alike—they had the same scowls. And they were also waiting for more of an explanation. However, Kayla didn't have one.

"Where's your phone?" Dade asked after first giving an impatient huff.

She glanced around but didn't see it and remembered she hadn't seen it upstairs, either. Just moments before Dade's arrival, she'd been searching through her purse for it. "I must have left it in my car." She pointed to the side of the estate where she'd parked.

Even though none of the lawmen came right out and accused her of lying, it was clear from their deepening scowls they didn't believe her.

"I'll look for it," Mason insisted, and he strolled out, leaving her to face the remaining two.

"I didn't speak to the gunman," Kayla tried again. "And if he called me, it was to set me up."

"Why would he do that?" Grayson asked.

Kayla didn't have to think too hard to come up with an answer. "Maybe to try to discredit my testimony. Charles could have hired the gunman to do that because if he could prove I had an association with a killer, then it might make a jury less likely to believe anything I say."

Another exchange of glances before Grayson spoke again. "Or *you* could have hired the gunman to make Brennan look guilty of attempted murder. A crime that could put him away for life and not just the twenty years he'd get for the other charges."

Oh, mercy. As theories went, it wasn't a bad one, and Kayla had no idea how she would convince the Rylands that she was innocent.

"Maybe your sister is the one who did the hiring." Dade tossed that out there, not tentatively, but it wasn't a roaring declaration of Kayla's innocence, either.

But what had she expected?

Yes, Dade had saved her life. Had even been wounded in the process, but to him she was lower than dirt. Well, except for those heated looks that he hadn't quite been able to suppress. Kayla was too familiar with those looks. Her late-husband, Preston, had certainly given her enough of them, and she was painfully aware of where that had gotten her.

"I'll call my sister," Kayla mumbled and started for the house phone that was on a table in the foyer. Of course, to get to it, she would literally have to walk through her dead bodyguard's blood.

"Here," Dade offered, handing her his cell.

Kayla took it, her hand brushing against his. Not a gentle hand, either. It was rough. No doubt from the physical labor of ranch work.

The adrenaline was playing havoc with her body and memory so it took her a while to remember Misty's number. She began to press it in when she heard Robbie. Not crying, but he was making fussy sounds, and those sounds were getting closer. Kayla looked at the stairs and saw her nanny, Connie, making her way toward them. The petite brunette looked completely weighed down with Robbie in the crook of her left arm and a suitcase gripped in her right hand.

Kayla stopped the call so she could go help, but Dade motioned for her to finish it. Instead, he hurried to the stairs, took the suitcase himself and set it on the floor. Robbie was rubbing his eyes and fussing when his attention landed on Dade. The fussing stopped, and much to Kayla's surprise, her son mumbled something indistinguishable and reached for the lawman.

Her surprise grew to shock when Dade reached out as well and eased Robbie into his arm.

"I have two other suitcases upstairs," Connie let him know, and she looked at Kayla. The nanny's eyebrow lifted to verify if it was all right for Dade to have hold of her son.

It wasn't all right, and Kayla moved to do something about that.

Just as her call to Misty went straight to voice mail.

"I'll get the suitcases," Grayson offered. "Show me where they are," he directed to Connie, and the two started up the stairs.

"Misty," Kayla said when the voice mail instructed her to leave a message, "call me immediately. I have to talk to you. It's important. I need to know if you told anyone where I'd be staying."

And with that done, Kayla hurried to Dade and practically wrenched Robbie away from him. That didn't make her son or Dade happy. The baby immediately started to cry, and Dade winced when she bumped against his wounded arm.

"Sorry," she mumbled. Kayla eased Robbie's head against her shoulder and began to rock.

Dade gave her a flat look after he was done wincing. "I wasn't going to kidnap him."

"I know. It's just…" But she had no idea how to finish that explanation. At this point it would sound petty if she admitted that she didn't want her son in a Ryland's arms. "Misty didn't answer her phone, so I left a message."

Dade waited a moment, his stare drilling through

her, and she earned another of those impatient huffs. "You do realize I'll be around the baby and you while you're in my protective custody?"

Kayla was sure she blinked. "But you're injured. I thought someone else would guard us." Preferably someone who wasn't a Ryland.

"No...." He stretched out the word. "This isn't an injury. It's a scratch, and it won't affect my aim if I need to take out another gunman."

Another gunman. That sent an icy chill through her. Thankfully, it was a chill her son didn't seem to notice because he finally calmed down and started to go back to sleep. But Kayla knew there would be no sleep for her in the immediate future.

And she knew who to thank for that.

"I need to make another call," she told Dade, and she didn't wait for his permission to use his cell. Nor did she have to try to remember this particular number. She'd seen it countless times on her own phone.

Charles Brennan answered on the first ring.

"Dade Ryland?" Charles greeted, though he sounded more amused than concerned. "Why would the deputy sheriff be calling?"

"No, Charles. It's me," Kayla informed him.

Dade rolled his eyes and reached for the phone, but she moved away from him and held on tight to both Robbie and Dade's cell.

"Did you send someone to kill me tonight?" she demanded from Charles.

"I don't know what you mean."

She listened for any differences in his voice. Anything that would confirm that he was behind this attack. But he sounded like his normal arrogant self.

"Someone hired a gunman to come after me," Kayla clarified, even though she was certain he already knew what she meant.

"And where are you exactly?" Charles asked. Still no change in his inflection.

Even though she doubted Dade had actually heard Charles's question, he got right in her face, and his scowl intensified. Something she hadn't thought possible.

"I'm at a place where I won't be much longer," Kayla answered. "And I want you to stop this now. Robbie could have been killed tonight."

"What?" Charles barked, and it had a cold, dangerous undercurrent to it.

"You heard me. The idiot you hired could have killed us all. Call off your dogs, Charles, and take your punishment like a man."

"I wouldn't have sent an idiot after you." And there was the change of inflective. It sounded as if he were telling the truth.

Sounded.

But Kayla had learned the hard way that Charles was capable of deception in its purest form. He certainly hadn't denied that he'd hired a hitman.

"The gunman phoned one of your goons," Kayla informed him, even though Dade gave her a have-you-lost-your-mind look. "I want you to call whomever it takes to make this stop."

Charles didn't answer right away. "I'll get back to you." And he hung up.

Dade threw up his hands and winced again. "Did it occur to you to ask me before you made a call to our number-one suspect?"

"I thought I was your number-one suspect," she snarled and thrust his phone at him.

He opened his mouth, probably to confirm that she was, but he didn't. Dade just shook his head, snatched his phone from her hand and stuffed it into the front pocket of his jeans. "That call accomplished nothing."

"Well, it made me feel better," Kayla fired back. It didn't. Nothing would make that happen, not with her bodyguard dead and the body of a hired assassin on her front porch.

Dade mumbled some profanity. "Don't do anything else that might end up helping your father-in-law, understand?"

Oh, that stung. She would never help Charles. *Never.* "Look, I know you don't believe me, but we're on the same page when it comes to my late-husband's father. It's possible Charles was responsible for your sister-in-law's death. Likely, even. But you couldn't possibly want him in jail more than I do."

Dade met her eye-to-eye. "Wanna bet?"

Kayla didn't dodge him. She held her ground. "As long as Charles is free, I'm not. And neither is my son." Because she needed it, she brushed a kiss on Robbie's forehead. "It's not my fault that Charles isn't behind bars. If you want someone to blame, blame the cops who investigated Ellie Ryland's murder."

Dade didn't flinch, but it was close. Probably because his brother had been in on the investigation. Heck, all the Rylands had, even though it hadn't been their jurisdiction. In fact, the case had gone to the FBI when the lead investigator had uncovered some evidence of Charles's money laundering that was linked to a federal case.

"The FBI's search warrant was screwed up. It didn't include the storage facility at his estate," Dade reminded her. "And that meant all those files and records that were seized there couldn't be used to convict Brennan. To add insult to injury, there was no more proof to arrest him, much less get a conviction."

Kayla knew all of this by heart because she'd read the reports too many times to count. "Then blame the FBI. Blame Charles's team of lawyers who challenged the warrant in the first place. But know this—if I get the chance to put Charles away, I'm taking it. Not for you. Not for your late sister-in-law. But for my son. When are you going to believe me?"

The fit of temper and energy went as fast as it came, and Kayla felt beyond drained. Maybe that's why she hadn't heard Mason come back into the house. And he wasn't the only one to reappear. Grayson was at the top of the stairs, a suitcase in each hand, and all of them were staring at her again.

"Maybe we'll believe you when there's proof that you're innocent." That came from Mason—the dark and dangerous Ryland. The one who made her more nervous than even Dade. "Your phone wasn't in the car. I searched every inch of it."

Kayla wearily shook her head. "Then I must have lost it or left it at the condo where I was staying."

"Convenient," Mason mumbled.

"No, it's not," she argued, knowing it wouldn't do any good. "I wish I could produce the phone so you'd know I had no part in this."

"Call her cell," Grayson said, making his way down the stairs. "The number is there on the dead gunman's phone."

Kayla huffed and was about to tell any Ryland who would listen that calling her on the missing phone would be useless. She didn't have it with her in the house, and she honestly had no idea where it was. But she decided just to let them have their way.

Mason lifted the gunman's phone so he could see the numbers through the plastic bag, and he used his own cell to make the call.

Kayla's heart nearly stopped.

Because the moment that Mason finished pressing in the numbers, the sound shot through the foyer.

While the rest of them watched and while Kayla held her breath, Mason followed the sound.

He didn't have to go far.

Just a few feet away from her.

There, under the foyer table, at the edge of the pool of blood, her missing cell phone was ringing.

Chapter Five

Dade listened to Grayson's latest request and silently cursed.

Yeah.

This was going to be fun.

He snapped his phone shut, dropped it on the console between Kayla and himself and continued the drive to the safe house.

"We need your fingerprints so we can compare them to those on the cell we found in your foyer," Dade relayed to her. He whispered so he wouldn't wake Robbie.

Both the baby and the nanny, Connie, were asleep in the back seat of the SUV, and Dade wanted it to stay that way. They were less than ten minutes from the safe house, both clearly exhausted, and he'd have to wake them soon enough.

When Kayla didn't answer, Dade glanced at her. She was leaning against the window, her attention fastened to the side mirror. No doubt looking for another gunman who might try to follow them. Dade had done the same thing since he'd started the half-hour drive from her estate to the old Wellman ranch and had thankfully seen nothing but a coyote and a deer on the narrow country road.

"Fingerprints," she mumbled. "I have a juvenile record. You can probably get them from that."

"A juvenile record?" Dade hadn't meant to sound shocked, but he was.

"I was fifteen and stupid. I went for a joyride with a boy and didn't know he was driving a stolen car. When the cops stopped us, he told them we stole the car together."

All right. He had to think about that a moment. "I'm surprised a rich girl like you couldn't hire a good lawyer and get the charges thrown out." Dade hadn't meant it to sound so callous, but he had seen it happen too many times.

She gave him a look that could have frozen hell. "You know nothing about me. *Nothing*."

That was true. Until tonight Kayla had been the woman married to the mob. The daughter-in-law of a slimeball killer. And now she was Dade's responsibility.

Among other things.

She was also a woman, and he kept noticing that. Like now, for instance. Even though she was giving him that hell-freezing look, he could also see the fear and the weariness. Oh, and her hot body. He didn't want to think for one minute that it played into this, but he was afraid it did.

So did that little baby sleeping in the car seat behind him.

Dade might have been a bad boy with a badass reputation, but that kid had nearly turned him to mush when he'd reached for Dade in the foyer. The kid had something his mom didn't—complete trust that Dade would take care of him.

"My fingerprints will be on the phone," she reminded him. "Because it belongs to me."

"Yeah, but Kenneth's shouldn't be on it. Should they?"

"No." She paused a moment. "I'd been looking for my cell right before you arrived, and I'd just asked Kenneth if he'd seen it. He said no."

Well, that was a start. "So, if his prints are on it, then it could mean he was in on the attack."

Kayla shook her head before he even finished. "That doesn't make sense, either. If the gunman had called my cell and Kenneth had the phone on him, I think I would have heard it."

"Maybe it rang when you were upstairs with your son." And maybe Kenneth hadn't wanted her to hear it because he wanted to set Kayla up, to make her look guilty.

She shook her head. "If Kenneth and the gunman were both working for Charles, then why didn't Kenneth just kill me before you arrived? He had plenty of chances. And then why would the gunman have killed a fellow hired gun?"

Dade didn't have answers to her questions, but he hoped to remedy that soon. His laptop was in his bag, and he intended to spend most of the night working.

"The dead gunman's name is Raymond Salvetti," Dade told her. "Ring any bells?"

She sat up straighter in the seat and repeated it several times. "No. He has a record?"

"Oh, yeah. That's why Grayson was able to make such a quick ID."

Kayla blew out a long breath. "Did you connect him to Charles?"

"Not yet."

And maybe never.

Because Brennan would have known there was potential for the hired gun to be caught, he could have hidden the paper trail that would connect him to a possible killer. Still, that didn't mean they couldn't link Brennan to the dead bodyguard or to Danny Flynn, the other man the gunman had phoned. Flynn hadn't been at his residence when SAPD had checked, but his name and picture had been sent out to law-enforcement agencies throughout the state. Plus, Kayla could recognize the moron if he showed up.

Dade took the final turn down the ranch road and drove the last quarter of a mile to the house. He watched Kayla as she took in the place. It didn't take her long because there wasn't much to see—a simple wood frame house and two barns surrounded by acres of pasture and trees. There was no livestock, no other people, and there hadn't been since Pete Wellman died three years earlier. He'd had no heirs, so Grayson had bought the place as an investment.

"Wait here a second," Dade ordered. He brought the SUV to a stop directly in front of the porch and the front door. Mason had already been out to put things in order, but Dade wanted to be sure.

He got out, went to the front door and unlocked it. Dade was pleased to hear the security alarm kick on. He disarmed it temporarily and did a walk-through. A living-dining combination. A kitchen. Three bedrooms. Two baths.

Tight quarters.

Especially because Kayla had a unique way of reminding him that she was around.

When Dade was satisfied that the house was indeed safe, he went back to the SUV to grab the suitcases. There were five total, and by the time he'd gotten them all inside and in place, a drowsy-looking Connie had already taken Robbie to the room that Kayla and the baby would share. Dade's room was in the middle. Not by accident either. He wanted to be able to hear if anything went wrong.

Once they were all inside, Dade didn't waste any time resetting the security system. He was certain they hadn't been followed, but he didn't want any surprise visitors in the middle of the night. Just in case, he left on his shoulder holster and gun.

"Does the bandage on your arm need to be checked?" Kayla asked.

Dade was in the process of removing his jacket. And wincing. That's probably what had prompted her question. "No, it's fine."

He'd slathered the wound with antibiotic cream and bandaged it at the sheriff's office when they'd stopped to pick up the SUV and other equipment.

Kayla stared at him as if she might challenge him and then fluttered her fingers toward the bathroom. "I need to take a shower." And with that, she walked away.

Dade watched her.

In fact, he couldn't make himself look away. Well, until she glanced over her shoulder at him. Then, his attention flew to the bag he'd put next to the sofa. Time to get his mind on the investigation and off Kayla's backside. But man, the woman had some curves.

Dade grabbed a soda from the fridge that Mason had stocked, took out his laptop and sank onto the sofa. There were already emails and reports about the shooting. Of course, with two dead bodies there would be a lot more to follow.

He fired off an email to Grayson to let him know about Kayla's juvenile record and the possibility of getting fingerprints from that. Grayson answered almost immediately with a thanks.

Dade scanned through the rest of the reports until he got to an attachment with Kayla's name. It was the file with everything Grayson and the San Antonio police had gathered on her. Because Kayla and he would be joined at the hip for the next few days, Dade opened it so he could find out more about this woman who had his body zinging.

Kayla Wallace Brennan was thirty-one, four years younger than him. Born in Houston. Parents divorced when she was a kid. One sister, Misty. Kayla married Preston Brennan when she was barely twenty-four, and their marriage had lasted nearly six years. Six years was a long time to be under the influence of a mob family. A woman could pick up all kinds of nasty habits.

Dade scrolled down.

And his fingers froze on the keys.

There were pictures of Kayla. Not the cool, rich ice queen with a great butt. There were police photos taken three years ago. Her hair had been pulled back, no makeup, and the camera had gobbled up a dozen or more images of the bruises on her face and upper body. Her right eye was practically swollen shut. Her bottom lip, busted open.

Dade got a rock-hard knot in his stomach.

He skimmed through the report that followed the pictures, and that knot in his stomach tightened. Kayla hadn't been mugged. According to the report, her husband, Preston, had done this to her during a domestic dispute.

A day later, Kayla dropped the charges.

Hell's bells.

Dade had seen that happen before, but he hadn't thought this had gone on with Kayla.

That stomach knot quickly turned to raw anger. Preston had been a big guy, muscles on top of muscles, and he'd used his wife for a punching bag. Dade cursed some more and then nearly jumped out of his skin when he heard the sound.

A loud thump.

He came off the sofa, drew his gun and hurried in the direction of the sound. Dade braced himself to come face-to-face with a gunman or maybe even Charles Brennan.

But it was a naked Kayla against the wall.

Okay, she wasn't naked exactly. She had on a silky white bathrobe that had shimmied off her shoulder all the way to the top of her breast, and it was that naked part of her that grabbed his attention more than the clothed parts.

"I slipped," she mumbled and quickly righted the bathrobe. No more peeks at her breast and that tattoo. "My legs are like jelly."

Dade understood that. He suddenly felt a little wobbly, too. And aroused. Something he quickly pushed aside. But he did reholster his gun and catch onto her arm to steady her.

"It's the adrenaline crash," he let her know. "You should probably try to sleep it off."

She nodded, raked her hair from her face. "I just need a drink of water first."

Kayla eased out of his grip and stepped around him. At least she tried. But the hall was narrow, and they brushed against each other despite their efforts to avoid one another. Heck, she might as well have kissed him because that's the punch he felt in his body.

Dade put some distance between them and followed her. Best to get back to work. But he didn't succeed with that either because Kayla suddenly froze, her attention knifing right to the photos on his computer screen.

She made a sound, something small and helpless that came deep from within her throat. It was a split-second response before she steeled up again.

"Why are you looking at those?" she asked, but

her voice wasn't nearly as steely as she was trying to appear to be.

"I was going through your files." And Dade left it at that. It seemed a sick violation of her privacy, but those pictures told him more about Kayla than he'd ever wanted to know.

She swallowed hard and went to the fridge to get a bottle of water. She gulped some down as if her throat were parched. "Preston had a mean streak," she mumbled.

Yeah. And even though it was stupid, Dade wished the mean-streaked moron was still around so he could beat him to a pulp. "So why did you stay with him?" Dade asked before he could stop himself.

Her forehead bunched up, and the corner of her mouth lifted. A dry half smile. "What you really want to know is why I let him do that to me." She drew in her breath. "Because at first I loved him. I thought he would change. And then I began to believe I deserved to be hurt."

Even though it pulled at his arm wound, Dade put his hands on his hips. "You thought you deserved *that?*" He didn't wait for her to answer. "Because you didn't. No woman deserves it."

She nodded. Hesitated and then nodded again. "I figured that out eventually and was in the process of filing for a divorce when he was killed in the car accident."

Again, Dade had to adjust everything he knew about this woman. Here she'd been a battered wife, pregnant, and yet she'd planned to divorce a man who would have likely tried to kill her.

"I'm sorry he did that to you. Real sorry," Dade mumbled.

She tried to shrug and then blinked hard. The tears were right there, threatening to spill. He debated if he should do anything, but his feet started toward her before the debate even had a chance.

Kayla whispered a soft "no" when Dade reached out. But she didn't step back, and that made it easy for him to ease his good arm around her and inch her to him. She went board stiff but still didn't move to stop him.

"This isn't a good idea," she reminded him, even though she was sniffing back tears.

"Yeah. I don't always lean toward the *good idea* approach. I'm more of a go-with-your-gut kind of guy." And with that, he pulled her to him.

"I don't want your sympathy," Kayla insisted, still sniffing.

"Okay, because I'm also not good with that. This is just a little human kindness, that's all. You've been to hell and back, and I'm guessing that started a long time before today. Before those pictures were taken."

"That sounds like sympathy to me," she complained.

Dade didn't argue and he didn't let go of her. "Then we'll strike a deal. We can still dislike each other. Heck, it can border on hate. I won't give you any sympathy, but we'll call a truce."

She made a sound of disagreement and eased back so they made eye contact. "A truce that involves hugs." Now, she stepped back, but that didn't seem to make her any happier. "I'm very vulnerable right now. I'm scared, and I have a horrible knack for allying myself with the worst person possible."

Dade cocked his head to the side. "You talking about Preston now or me?"

She froze a moment. "You. Preston can't hurt me anymore, but you, well, you can."

And he instinctively knew she wasn't talking about physical violence. He had never hit a woman, and if he got his hands on Kayla, the last thing he'd want to do is hit her.

"*I* would be a mistake," he said, but he didn't say it under his breath as he'd intended. It was plenty loud enough for her to hear.

The corner of her mouth lifted just a fraction and then lowered just as quickly. "The worst kind."

Yeah. He was in trouble the size of Texas here. Because now they weren't indirectly talking about something beyond truces and protective custody. They were talking about this damn attraction.

And sex.

Dade cursed. "I wish to hell I hadn't seen your tattoo."

Or those pictures on the computer. And while he was at it, he wished her scent would stop sliding through him. She smelled like a fairy princess, all flowery and soft.

A smile barely touched her lips. "The tattoo is a relic from my youth. And I wish you hadn't seen it, either."

That was what she was saying, but her eyes were

warm now. Not that riled spicy blue. This was more like the color of the sky. Calmer. Welcoming.

She opened her mouth, closed it and then motioned toward the hall. "Good night, Dade."

He didn't argue. He'd already said enough stupid things, and if she stayed, there would only be a greater opportunity for more stupidity. However, she only made it one step before Dade's phone buzzed.

"It's Grayson," he said, glancing at the screen. Dade answered it and hoped like the devil this call was good news. Any good news would do.

"Thanks for the email about Mrs. Brennan's juvenile record," Grayson started. "Her prints were there, and we were able to do a quick comparison. It's her prints on the cell, and the account is in her name."

It was exactly as they'd expected, and it certainly didn't make her guilty of anything other than owning a cell phone. "Any other prints?" Dade didn't exactly pray that there would be, but he considered it.

"Just smudges," Grayson let him know. "Nothing we can match."

Damn. Not good news because the phone was pretty much a dead end. If Kenneth had indeed had the cell when the gunman called, then that was a secret that Kenneth had taken to his grave.

Dade locked eyes with Kayla who was hanging on to his every word. "What about the dead gunman's cell? Anything on it that'll help?" he asked Grayson.

"No breaks there. We're still looking for Danny Flynn. But we did locate the other person the gunman called."

"Misty Wallace?" Dade questioned, and that drew Kayla's full attention. She walked closer, and Dade went ahead and put the call on speaker.

"Yeah. San Antonio PD picked Misty up about twenty minutes ago," Grayson let Dade know.

SAPD. That meant his twin, Nate, had likely been involved in that pickup. Dade hated that Nate had to be part of this, but of course, he would be. Brennan was possibly the man who'd murdered Nate's wife. There was no way his brother would step back from this investigation.

"Nate will bring Misty here tomorrow morning so we can question her," Grayson added.

Kayla's fingers were trembling when she touched them to her mouth.

"Is Misty talking?" Dade immediately asked.

"Not to SAPD, but she says she'll talk to us. And she has a message for her sister. Misty wants you to tell her that she's sorry."

"Sorry about what?" Kayla said under her breath. It wasn't very loud but apparently loud enough for Grayson to hear.

Grayson grumbled something under his breath, too. "She wouldn't say, but I intend to find out."

Chapter Six

Kayla heard the sound, and her eyes flew open. It wasn't the sounds of bullets like those in her nightmares. This was laughter. And it was coming from the other side of the house.

"Robbie?" she called out and then remembered Connie had come and gotten him when he woke up earlier. The nanny had told Kayla to get a little more rest, and apparently she had.

She threw back the covers and spotted the sunlight speckling across the room from the tiny gaps in the blinds. She checked the clock on the nightstand—already seven-thirty. Not late by many people's standards, but she'd overslept.

How the heck could that have happened?

Here they were in the middle of a dangerous situation, and she'd slept in like the diva Dade already thought she was.

Kayla changed out of her gown and put on the dark blue pants and top that she practically ripped from her suitcase. She used the hall bathroom to finish dressing and raced toward the laughter. She soon found the source.

Her son.

Dade was at the kitchen table, Robbie in his lap, and her son was giggling because Dade was playing airplane with the spoon of oatmeal. Her son devoured the oatmeal the moment it made it to his mouth.

Kayla made eye contact with Connie who was near the stove pouring herself a cup of coffee. The nanny, who looked as if she had also dressed in a hurry, simply shrugged.

"Mommy's up," Dade announced, and he sent another spoonful of oatmeal Robbie's way. Another giggle. And her son lapped it up.

"I'm sorry," Kayla told Dade. "I should have been up to feed him."

Dade just shrugged as well. "I have a niece, Kimmie, who's just a little bit older than Robbie, and I feed her a lot of mornings."

So that explained why the bad-boy cowboy looked perfectly natural with flecks of oatmeal on his jeans and chest-hugging black T-shirt. Robbie hadn't escaped, either. He had oatmeal smeared into his blond hair.

"I can take over," Kayla insisted. But when she looked in the bowl, she realized that Robbie had finished.

"Da-da-da," Robbie babbled, and he slapped his hands on the highchair tray.

Kayla was mortified and was about to launch into an apology for that, as well.

"He's trying to say Dade," Connie quickly explained.

Dade lifted his shoulder again. "That seems a little easier to say than Deputy Ryland."

Maybe, but it was downright unnerving to hear those sounds come from her son's mouth. More unnerving to see the big grin that Robbie doled out to Dade.

"Let me get him washed up," Connie insisted.

"I can do it," Kayla offered.

But Connie glanced at Dade. "I think the deputy and you have some things to discuss."

Yes, they did. Misty, for one, because her sister had been brought in for questioning and had issued that vague *I'm sorry*. Kayla had tried to call her sister more than a dozen times before she went to bed, but Misty hadn't answered.

Connie eased Robbie out of the highchair and brought him over to Kayla so she could get a morning kiss. She got one all right, complete with oatmeal smears and a smile that could have lit up the night. Kayla had no choice but to smile back.

"I love you," she whispered to her son, and Robbie babbled back a string of sounds that could have meant anything. But Kayla knew he was telling her that he loved her, too.

"He's a fun kid," Dade said, and he got to his feet.

"Yes, but he's usually shy around strangers." Probably because Robbie hadn't been exposed to many, but he'd taken to Dade as if he'd known him his whole life.

Dade looked at her, as if waiting for more, but she didn't want to talk about how good he was with her son. Kayla also didn't want to stare. She failed at that. She stared. And wondered how anyone could look that good with flecks of oatmeal on them.

She reached up and plucked a piece of it from Dade's hair. "Robbie's a messy eater."

"Not as bad as Kimmie. Once she crammed a handful of strained peaches in my ear. Couldn't hear for hours." With that, he smiled.

Oh, mercy.

He was hot with his usual bad-boy scowl, but that smile made her weak at the knees. Kayla stepped back, cleared her throat and changed the subject. "When will Grayson question Misty?"

Dade's smile faded as fast as it'd come, and he checked the wall clock over the table. "Soon. They're setting up things now so we can watch. My laptop is already on, and I've connected to Grayson's computer at his office."

She glanced at his computer screen to verify that it was indeed on, and there on the screen was what appeared to be an office. An empty one.

"Watch?" she challenged. "But I thought I'd be able to see Misty in person."

"Not a chance," Dade informed her. "We aren't leaving this safe house unless it's an emergency."

Of course. That made sense for security reasons. But Kayla had wanted to see her sister and not through a computer screen.

"We'll be able to hear and see them," Dade verified. "They can hear and see us, as well." He grabbed a cup of black coffee from the counter and headed to the sofa.

Kayla poured herself some coffee, but when she joined him, she immediately saw the dilemma. The sofa wasn't that large, and with his computer perched on the coffee table, the only way she would see the screen was to sit right next to Dade. So, that's what she did, and Kayla tried not to react when her arm brushed his.

He reacted, though.

Dade winced. And that's when her attention shot down to the bandage. "I should check that."

She didn't wait for him to agree because he wouldn't have. Kayla eased back the bandage, afraid of what she might see. The gash was an angry red color and the area around it was swollen.

"I'm taking antibiotics," Dade reminded her.

He tipped his head to the prescription bottle on the end of the coffee table. It was sitting on top of a first-aid kit. Kayla dug through the kit and came up with a tube of antibiotic cream.

"This isn't necessary," he complained.

"It is," she complained right back. "You wouldn't have been shot if you hadn't been protecting me."

That was true, and Kayla didn't regret her decision to tend his wound. But what she hadn't considered was that touching Dade posed some problems of their own.

His arm was rock-hard, and even though he wasn't heavily muscled, he was still lean and solid. A cowboy. And for some strange reason that made her smile.

"What?" Dade questioned. He dipped his head so his eyes could meet hers.

Not a good idea, either.

Because it put them breath to breath and nearly mouth to mouth.

Everything seemed to freeze. Except her heartbeat. It jolted like crazy, a reaction she quickly tried to get under control.

Dade didn't tear his attention from her. Kayla didn't move either. She just sat there, her fingers smeared with cream and poised over his arm. And in that moment, she had a terrible thought.

What would it feel like to kiss Dade?

A glimmer went through his cool gray eyes that let her know he was thinking the same thing.

"Is there a problem?" someone asked.

Kayla jerked back so fast that her neck popped.

There, on the screen, was Lieutenant Nate Ryland. She recognized him from the investigation and from his picture in the newspaper. This was Dade's fraternal twin brother. A brother who no doubt hated her to the core. And God knows what he must have seen in Dade's and her eyes.

"Kayla was checking my arm," Dade volunteered. "How much longer until the interview?"

Nate didn't answer right away. He kept his attention on Kayla. Was it disgust she saw? Or worse, was it that painful for him to look at her?

"A few more minutes," Nate finally said. "I was just checking to make sure we'd be able to see and hear you. We can," he mumbled. "By the way, Grayson had to give your location to the D.A."

"Why?" Kayla and Dade asked together.

"Winston said he had to talk to her about the trial."

Dade didn't like the idea of anyone knowing their location. Judging from Kayla's expression, neither did she. "Can't it wait?"

"Not according to Winston," Nate answered. "He has to file some papers in court today or it could jeopardize the case."

Well, Dade didn't want that, but he also didn't want to put Kayla at further risk. "Warn Winston to be careful," Dade insisted.

"I will," Nate assured him. "For now, though, I'll get Ms. Wallace in here."

"Wait," Kayla blurted out. But then she fumbled with what to say. "I'm sorry about your wife," she finally got out.

Nate stood there, his jaw muscles working against each other. It felt like an eternity. Finally, he nodded. "Thank you." And he walked out of camera range.

Kayla held her breath, wondering if Dade was going to blast her for daring to bring up the topic of Nate's dead wife. But he merely pressed the bandage back in place, reached over and muted the sound on his computer. He also handed her a tissue so she could wipe the ointment from her fingers.

"I'm very protective of my brother," Dade threw out like a warning.

"I understand." And she did. Kayla often felt that way about Misty. "But Nate doesn't appear to be a man who needs protecting."

"Not now."

She shook her head, wondering if they were still talking about Ellie's murder.

"Things were different when we were kids," he mumbled. Dade huffed, paused, huffed again. "Something happened when Mom was pregnant with us, and Nate was born with a lot of medical problems."

Ah. She understood that, too. "So you fought his battles for him?"

"Yeah. Sometimes literally." He stared down at his hands and scraped his thumbnail over one of his knuckles. "The kids used to rag on him at school. But Nate, he was smart. A lot smarter than the kids who tried to bully him, so he could usually talk his way out of a butt whipping. Still can." Now, Dade looked at her. "He's the youngest cop in SAPD ever promoted to lieutenant. He's a big gun there."

"He's a survivor," Kayla mumbled.

Dade shrugged. "Losing Ellie nearly killed him."

And therefore it had nearly killed Dade. Kayla could see how much Dade loved his twin brother, and whether he realized it or not, he was still fighting Nate's battles. Still making sure that she wasn't a threat.

Kayla was about to assure him that she was no threat, but Dade spoke first. "Last night I did some digging into your sister's recent—"

He stopped when there was movement on the laptop screen, and Dade turned up the volume. Kayla wanted to know what Dade had been about to tell her, but she knew it would have to wait when she saw Grayson lead Misty into his office. Her sister dropped down into the chair directly in front of the webcam.

Misty did not look like a happy camper.

That was reasonable, because she was essentially in police custody and had been the entire night. Her short blond hair looked as if it hadn't been combed, and her sister wore no makeup. A rarity. It made her look much younger than twenty-seven. She looked more like a schoolgirl waiting out detention.

Misty's eyes zoomed right in on Kayla. "I can't believe you let them bring me in like this."

Kayla felt as if Misty had slapped her. All that anger in her voice, and she was glaring not at Dade or Grayson but at Kayla.

"Kayla was nearly killed," Dade responded before she could find her breath.

"Well, I didn't have anything to do with that," Misty fired back. But when she looked at Kayla again, her glare softened a little. "I'm sorry if you were almost hurt, but I'm not responsible for it."

"Not almost hurt," Dade again. "She was almost *killed* by a man named Raymond Salvetti who phoned you just a half hour before the attack."

Misty gasped. Hopefully because she was surprised by that revelation. It had to be that. Because Kayla couldn't believe that her sister would betray her. Their relationship wasn't perfect, but her sister loved her.

Kayla hoped.

Frantically shaking her head, Misty looked up at Grayson. "Someone did call me last night, and I didn't recognize the number so I let it go to voice mail. I swear, I don't know any gunmen."

"Maybe you do," Dade countered. "Think hard. Did you know Raymond Salvetti?"

Misty didn't hesitate even a second. "I don't have to think hard. I don't know anyone like that. Charles set this up. He would do anything to get to Kayla, and he probably hired this Salvetti guy."

"Yes," Kayla agreed. "But for him to do that, he had to know where I was staying. Salvetti came to the estate, Misty. He knew I was there."

Misty did more of that frantic head shaking. Kayla wanted to hold on to each one of them as the truth. "I didn't tell anyone where you were staying. You told me to keep it a secret, and I did. I swear, I did."

"How did you let Misty know that you'd be at the estate?" Grayson interrupted. He looked at Kayla. "In person? Phone? Email?"

"Phone," Kayla and Misty answered in unison. It was Kayla who continued. "Where were you when we had that conversation?" she asked Misty.

"At a bar on St. Mary's. But no one heard our conversation."

"You're sure?" Grayson pressed.

"Positive." Misty shoved her hands through her hair and groaned in frustration. "If you want to point the finger at someone other than Charles, you need to look in your own backyard. That Silver Creek D.A., Winston Calhoun, and his assistant, Alan Bowers, have been bugging me for months. Both have been trying to find Kayla. Well, I'm betting both of them knew she'd be at the estate."

It was true. Both men did know. And Kayla hadn't ruled either or both out as the leak that had led the gunman to her. Like Dade had apparently done last night, she needed to do some digging because the Rylands might not think of friends and neighbors as potential felons. But Kayla knew for a fact that Charles could be very persuasive. He had a knack for finding people's weak spots.

"Why would you think for one minute I would put Kayla in danger?" Misty demanded. She volleyed a glare between Dade and Grayson.

"Money," Dade volunteered, and he gave Kayla an *I'm-sorry* glance. "I dug into your financials last night, and I found you've recently come into some money. Ten thousand dollars to be exact."

Kayla heard the sound of shock escape from her throat. So that was what Dade had been about to tell her. Oh, God. Misty and she hadn't come from money, and even though Kayla gave her sister a monthly allowance to cover living expenses, Misty went through it as quickly as she got it. And Misty hadn't always spent the money wisely. Sometimes, she'd even used it to buy drugs. That's why Kayla hadn't just doled out more.

Ten grand was a huge sum for her sister, and Misty had to have an explanation. She just had to, and Kayla waited with her breath held.

Misty huffed. "I'm an artist," she snarled at Dade. "And I sold some paintings. That's all there is to it."

"You've got receipts for the sales, of course?" Dade remarked.

Her sister's eyes widened, and she lowered her head until she was staring down at her lap. "No, not exactly. It was a private sale. A cash deal."

Kayla's heart dropped, as well. Her sister had never

made that much money from her paintings, and a sale like that should have caused Misty to call her immediately.

"I need the name and contact info for the buyer," Grayson insisted. He grabbed a notepad and pen and slid them Misty's way.

Misty's attention stayed fixed to her lap. "I don't have it, but I can get it, I suppose."

"You suppose?" Kayla questioned. She tried very hard not to get angry about such a casual comment. "Misty, someone tried to kill me and maybe Robbie, too. You have to cooperate with the police. I need answers so I can keep Robbie safe."

That got Misty's attention aimed back at the webcam. "I don't have answers!" she shouted. "The person who bought the art didn't contact me directly. He went through a friend of a friend and said he wanted the deal to be secret, that he didn't want his soon-to-be ex-wife to know he was draining their accounts." She moved closer to the screen. "Can't you see, Kayla? Someone's trying to set me up."

"Then, prove it," Dade fired back before Kayla could say anything. "Get the name of the art buyer from your friend of a friend."

Misty's forehead bunched up and she mumbled something Kayla didn't catch. "Give me twenty-four hours," she bargained. She began to chew on her thumbnail. "And I think it's time I called a lawyer."

Dade and his brother exchanged a glance. "Twenty-four hours," Grayson confirmed. "If I don't hear from you, I'm hauling you right back here, and it won't be just for questioning. I'll arrest you for obstruction of justice and any other charge I can tack on."

"Thanks a lot, Kayla," Misty snarled, and she jumped to her feet. She practically ran out of the office.

Grayson leaned closer to the screen. "I'll call you if I find out anything."

A few seconds later, the screen went blank. Kayla's mind, however, didn't. It started to spin with plausible explanations, none of which she hoped would point to her sister's guilt.

"Charles could have set up that art deal to incriminate Misty," Kayla tossed out there. "He knows she's the only person I trust, and he might want to take that from me."

She expected Dade to counter her theory with a reminder that Misty had looked guilty of something. Or that her sister hadn't mentioned this art deal before now.

But he didn't say any of that.

Dade simply slipped his arm around her shoulder and eased her closer to him. Kayla thought about his shoulder. That this might be painful for him, but she couldn't refuse the comfort he was offering her. She'd had to stay strong for so long. All on her own. And it felt good to have a semi-ally.

"Grayson is a good cop," Dade reminded her. "He'll get to the bottom of this."

Yes. Dade was a good cop, too, and she was afraid that *bottom* would incriminate her sister. "I feel the same way about Misty as you do about Nate. I've always protected her."

Dade stayed quiet a moment and gently rubbed his fingertips on her arm. "You're positive she didn't sell you out to Brennan?"

Kayla wanted to be angry that he would even ask. After all, she'd had no trouble feeling that anger during Misty's interview. But it wasn't anger she felt this time.

It was fear for what Misty could have done.

"Charles could have manipulated her," Kayla suggested. "He could have made her believe that telling him my whereabouts would be the only way to keep me alive."

"But wouldn't she have admitted that to you, especially after I told her that you'd nearly been killed?"

Kayla hoped that would be true, but she had to shake her head. "She might be too afraid to tell me."

She braced herself for Dade to huff or roll his eyes, but he didn't. Maybe because he had five siblings, he understood the sometimes-delicate dynamics of family.

"Misty doesn't know how bad things were with Preston and Charles," Kayla continued. "She knows I witnessed some illegal activity. That I overheard conversations about money laundering and such. But Misty believes those were rare occurrences. They weren't."

Dade stayed quiet a moment. "Exactly how much did you witness?"

"Too much," she mumbled. "I overheard and saw enough to convict Charles of dozens of felonies."

"Good thing, too, because I doubt there's any physical evidence to nail him."

"There used to be," Kayla admitted. "He had files at his office and heaven knows what stashed in safe-deposit boxes under fake names." She had to take a deep breath because that was a reminder of just how dangerous her former father-in-law was and continued to be.

Dade turned slightly so they were directly facing each other. "Protecting Robbie and you comes first. I can't put Misty or anyone else ahead of that, understand?"

"Yes." It's exactly what she wanted Dade to do—to protect her son at all cost.

And Dade would. She didn't have to second-guess that.

Mercy.

How much her life had changed in these short hours. Just yesterday, she thought of Dade and all the Rylands as the enemy, but she no longer felt that way about Dade.

That could be a major mistake.

"Yeah," she heard him say and realized he was studying her eyes as if he knew exactly what she was thinking. Maybe he did because he looked away, cursed and mumbled something.

"What?" she asked.

He cursed again. "This," he answered.

This was bad. Because Dade turned back to her, leaned in and touched his mouth to hers. It was quick. And dirty. It packed a punch of a full-fledged French kiss.

"Hell," he mumbled. "If I'm breaking the rules, I might as well break 'em hard."

And he did.

His hand went around the back of her neck and he dragged her to him. Not just the lip contact but some body-to-body contact as well. Her breasts landed against his toned chest muscles.

Oh, he was good. Too good. His mouth blazed against her and sent a jolt of fire through all the wrong parts of her body.

She'd been right about Dade. He could melt chrome with that mouth and seduce her straight to his bed. Something that couldn't happen.

Kayla repeated that to herself. Several times.

Finally, she managed to pull back. Or maybe she was successful only because Dade pulled back as well.

"There are about a hundred reasons why that can't happen again," he insisted. And he inched away from her so they were no longer touching.

Kayla couldn't argue with that, and she could even add some reasons of her own. "I can't get involved because my last relationship nearly destroyed me. Besides, when you look at me, you'll always think of Nate's dead wife."

He made a sound of agreement.

And then Kayla heard another sound.

One that she hadn't expected to hear. Apparently, neither had Dade because he sprang from the sofa, and in the same motion, he drew his gun from his shoulder holster. He hurried to the window, and Kayla followed, but Dade only pushed her behind him.

"Hell," Dade mumbled. "We have a visitor."

Chapter Seven

Dade drew his gun and pushed Kayla behind him. No one should be here, but there was a black four-door sedan barreling up the dirt road toward the ranch house.

"Who is it?" Kayla asked. Her voice wasn't just trembling, it was downright shaking.

Dade kept his gun and his attention nailed to the car, and it didn't take him long to figure out who their *visitor* was. Or rather *visitors*. Because he instantly recognized the two men who exited the car when it came to a stop in front of the house.

"It's the D.A., Winston Calhoun, and the assistant D.A., Alan Bowers," he said.

She drew in a hard breath. "They're here already?"

"Is everything okay?" Connie called out to them.

"Yeah," Dade answered, but he had no idea if that was the truth. "Just stay put with Robbie."

When he started across the yard, Winston ducked his head down, probably because of the icy wind. He carried a leather briefcase and was dressed for work in an iron-gray business suit that matched the color of his hair and the winter sky. He was a good twenty years older than Dade, and Dade had known the man his entire life.

He couldn't say the same for Alan.

The thirty-something-year-old had moved to Silver Creek about a year and a half ago when he'd gotten the job at the D.A.'s office. He was lanky to the point of being wiry, with hair so blond that he looked more at home on the beach than he did in cowboy country. Like his boss, Alan wore a suit, so this obviously wasn't a social call.

When the men made it to the porch, Dade reholstered his gun, disengaged the security system and opened the door. "This had better be important," he snarled.

Winston spared him a glance, but his dark eyes went to Kayla. Yeah. Something was definitely wrong, but Winston didn't say a word until both Alan and he had stepped inside.

"Charles Brennan's lawyers just requested a trial delay," Winston announced.

Kayla didn't make a sound, but Dade could feel her reaction. Every muscle in her body tensed.

"Please tell me he won't get it," Dade insisted.

Alan lifted his bony shoulder, and Winston shook his head. Dade just cursed. Kayla and Robbie sure as hell didn't need this.

"You could have told us this over the phone," Dade pointed out. "Rather than risk someone following you."

Alan's mouth tightened. Probably because he was insulted that Dade had just slammed him for what Dade considered to be an unnecessary visit that could turn out to be a big-time security risk.

Winston, however, had no visible reaction. "This visit is important," he declared. "And for the record, no one followed us. We were careful."

Winston set his briefcase on the table near the door and extracted a manila file. "I need to get Kayla's signature on the statement she gave me over the phone two days ago." He handed her both the file and pen.

"Of course." Kayla's voice was still shaky and so was her hand. And Dade knew why. The statement and her signature would be needed if for some reason Kayla couldn't testify.

In other words, if Dade failed to do his job and Brennan killed her.

"I'd like to read through this first," Kayla said, her attention already on the first page. She sank onto the sofa.

"It's all there," Alan informed her. He made a nervous gesture toward the papers. "We just need your signature so we can leave."

Kayla lifted her eyes. Met his. "I'd still prefer to read it."

Dade was about to second that and even insist on it. Not because he didn't trust Winston but because this entire visit was well beyond making him feel uncomfortable. However, before Dade could say anything, Winston latched onto his arm and pulled him aside. Alan stayed near Kayla.

"We haven't been able to link the dead gunman, Salvetti, to Brennan," Winston whispered. "But we have been able to link Brennan to Danny Flynn, the guy the gunman called. Flynn did some handyman work at Brennan's estate."

None of this surprised Dade. "Any proof that Flynn orchestrated the attack last night?"

"No. But get this—Brennan says Flynn's trying to set him up because he fired him."

Of course Brennan would say that. He would say and do anything to cover his butt.

Dade heard Robbie make a sound. A squeal, followed by a fussy protest. And Kayla nearly jumped off the sofa.

"I'll check on him," Dade told her. Best for her to finish reading the statement so he could get Winston and Alan out of there.

Dade headed down the hall, and it didn't take him long to spot the baby. Connie had him in a snug protective grip, but Robbie clearly wanted to get down. Dade went closer, and when the baby reached out for him, Dade pulled him into his arms.

Without thinking, he brushed a kiss on Robbie's forehead.

That was something he often did to his niece, Kimmie, but he regretted it now. That kiss earned him a raised eyebrow from the nanny who clearly didn't trust him. Robbie, on the other hand, was loaded with trust. He babbled something to Dade and dropped his head on Dade's shoulder.

Heck.

Dade didn't want to feel the warmth of holding this

child in his arms. Because Kayla was still his family's enemy. There couldn't be anything between them.

Well, except for his feelings for her son.

And that kiss, of course.

But Dade was reasonably sure he'd be disgusted with himself about that later. Too bad the attraction he felt for her kept putting off that *later*.

Dade tried to hand Robbie back to the nanny, but when the baby fussed again, Dade kept hold of him and returned to the living room to check on Kayla. When she spotted them, Dade got another raised eyebrow. Dade looked at Robbie to see his reaction, and the little boy gave him a big toothy grin. Dade couldn't help but grin back.

"I'm finished." Kayla scrawled her signature on the last page of the statement and handed both the pages and the pen back to Winston. She didn't waste even a second taking Robbie from him.

Dade had expected those raised eyebrows from their guests, but he was a little miffed that Kayla would have that reaction, especially because they'd set fire to each other's lips just minutes earlier.

"I'll let you know if Brennan gets the trial delay," Winston assured them. He tipped his head in a farewell gesture, and the two attorneys headed to the door.

Dade followed them, closing the door behind them and resetting the security alarm. He turned to ask Kayla about that raised eyebrow reaction, but she spoke before he could.

"You trust both of those men?" she asked. It didn't

seem like an accusation exactly, but there was concern dripping from her voice.

"I trust Winston." But then he had to shrug. "I don't really know Alan. Why, did you get bad vibes from him?"

"From both of them," she corrected. "But then I'm getting bad vibes from almost everyone."

He stared at her. "Even from me? I noticed you didn't care for my holding your son."

She opened her mouth as if she might leap to dispute it, but then Kayla shook her head. "It's not that." And she repeated it. "Your brothers hate me, and I don't want to do anything that would hurt your relationship with them. I figured the D.A. would report back anything and everything he saw here."

Oh, he would. Maybe Alan, too. But Grayson had already seen the close contact between Kayla and him at the start of the interview with Misty. Grayson wasn't stupid, and he no doubt had already noticed what was simmering between Kayla and him.

"It might be too late to do that kind of damage control." Dade went closer, caught onto Robbie's foot and gave it a jiggle. He was rewarded with a grin.

"Is everything okay?" Connie asked from the hall.

"Yes," Kayla quickly answered. "I'll keep Robbie with me for a while and give you some time for reading."

The nanny made a sound of approval, but Dade doubted she'd get much quality reading time. The attack from the night before was too fresh on all their minds.

Kayla grabbed the diaper bag from the coffee table, took out several small stuffed animals and sank down onto the floor with Robbie so he could play. Dade checked out the window.

Nothing, thank God. Maybe it would stay that way.

He maneuvered himself so he could keep watch but sat on the floor along with them. Robbie seemed to approve because he handed Dade a blue horse and then laughed when Dade made a neighing sound.

"You're good with kids," Kayla said sounding more than a little surprised.

Dade shrugged and took out his wallet. He opened it to show her a picture of his thirteen-month-old niece, Kimmie. The picture was there all right, front and center, but something fell out.

A tarnished silver concho.

Kayla grabbed it before it could hit the floor and stared at it. The concho was a blast from the past that he didn't need, and Dade had forgotten it was even there.

"It's the symbol for the Ryland ranch." The double back-to-back Rs were prominently displayed. "My father gave me and each of my brothers one before... well, before he left."

One look in Kayla's suddenly sympathetic eyes, and he knew she'd already heard at least bits and pieces of this tragic story. Boone Ryland had run off and abandoned his six sons twenty years ago, and that had been just the beginning of things gone wrong for what was left of the Rylands.

"Twenty years," Dade mumbled, "and the gossip hasn't died down."

Kayla didn't deny she'd heard gossip. She reached out, touched his arm and rubbed gently. Her touch was warm and curled through him, but it was also a reminder that the events twenty years would always be a stab to his heart.

He took the concho from her, shoved it back into his wallet and put it away. Out of sight but never out of mind.

Kayla cleared her throat and eased Robbie back into her lap when he tried to crawl away. "Nate's child is your only niece or nephew?" she asked.

Dade was a hundred-percent thankful for the change in subject. "Yeah, but Grayson and his wife have one on the way." He kept his attention fastened to the window.

"Grayson looks as if he'd be a good father," she remarked. Her forehead bunched up. "Not your other brother, though."

He knew exactly which brother she meant. "Mason." And he couldn't disagree with her. "Mason is a hard man to figure out. Hard on himself. And others. After our dad left, Mason took his concho, shot it with a .38 and then nailed what was left of it to his bedroom wall. Said it was the first thing he wanted to see when he got up in the morning so he'd remember how much he hated the old man."

When Kayla didn't say anything, he glanced at her. Her mouth had dropped open a little. "That doesn't sound…healthy."

"Not much about our past was," he admitted. He

sure hadn't planned on spilling his guts this way, but he didn't stop, either. "Plain and simple, my father gave us those conchos to relieve his guilt, and then he destroyed us, especially our mom. She committed suicide on Grayson's eighteenth birthday and left a note begging him to keep the family together."

Kayla touched his arm again. Probably to give him another of those soothing rubs, but Dade moved away. "Grayson succeeded."

"Yeah, I guess. He's happy now anyway." One of six wasn't exactly a good track record, but before Grayson's wife, Eve, had come back into his life a few months earlier, the Rylands had been batting a thousand in the bad-relationship department.

Kayla stayed quiet a moment. "So what about you—have you always kept your concho in your wallet?"

This wasn't a story he was used to telling, not out loud anyway, although he remembered it like it was yesterday. "When we were fourteen, Nate and I threw ours in Silver Creek. But like a bad penny, mine turned up. Grayson's wife found it about a week ago when she was out taking some pictures for a newspaper article she's working on."

Kayla's mouth dropped open again. "She found it after all these years?"

He shook his head and waved her off. "Don't go there. This isn't some kind of cosmic sign for me to forgive my father." Dade bit back the profanity of what he really wanted to call Boone Ryland because Robbie was in the room. "It was just blind luck she found it, that's all. And first chance I get, I'll toss it right back in the creek. Heck, maybe the Gulf of Mexico. Doubt anyone would find it then."

The silence came. Of course it did. He'd just saddled a mountain of old baggage on Kayla. Right about now she was probably thinking he needed some big-time therapy, and she was no doubt regretting that kiss, too.

"Don't throw the concho away." Her voice was a whisper now. "Give it to me."

Dade was sure he looked at her as if she'd sprouted horns. "Why?"

She flashed him one of those half smiles, the ones that weren't of the happy variety. "So I have something to remember the man who saved my and my son's lives."

Good grief. That wasn't a good reason because it seemed intimate. Or something. It definitely didn't seem *right*.

"Plus," she continued. The smile was gone now, and her chin came up. Second-guessing her request, he figured. "If you want cosmic justice, what better way to get it than to give your enemy the guilt gift from a father you despise?"

Dade just stared at her, and she stared back. Robbie did, too, as if he was trying to figure out what was going on.

"Forget I said that," Kayla added. She tried to chuckle. Failed. "I won't need anything to remember you."

Yeah. Dade felt the same about her. Kayla would be in his dreams—hot, uncomfortable dreams—long after this assignment ended. It'd been a while since he'd wanted a woman as much as he wanted Kayla.

Dade could already feel his hands on her. Could taste her. Could hear the sounds she'd make when he was deep inside her. And that hard ache went through his body and begged him to kick this attraction up a notch.

But he couldn't. Because of her safety. And because of that cute little kid staring up at him.

Dade stood and took out his wallet. Then, the concho. He tossed it into Kayla's lap. Quick, like stripping off a bandage that had been in place way too long.

She picked up the silver-dollar-sized concho the way a person would handle fine crystal and closed her fingers around it when Robbie reached for it, as well. She gave her baby a kiss instead.

Yet another too-intimate moment that he shouldn't be experiencing with Kayla. He'd be thankful when this trial was over so he could put some distance between them.

And Dade was almost sure he believed that.

"A car," Kayla said at the same moment Dade heard the sound of the engine.

Hell. What now? Maybe Winston had driven back to tell them that Brennan had gotten the delay he'd requested. If so, Dade was going to give them instructions on how to use a phone to relay information.

Dade hurried to the window next to the door and looked out. He groaned, but inside his reaction was much worse.

Kayla latched onto Robbie and hugged him close to her body. "Who is it?"

"It's trouble," Dade let her know, and when he drew his gun he was afraid this time he might have to use it.

Chapter Eight

Kayla tried to brace herself for the worst, and the worst
would be Charles. However, he wasn't the person who
stepped from the car.

It was her sister, Misty.

Dade glanced back at her as if expecting an explanation, but Kayla didn't have one. "I didn't tell anyone
including Misty, where we were staying."

"Well, someone did, unless it's blind luck she found
her way out here," he snarled. "Go to the bedroom and
wait. Keep Robbie quiet if you can. Maybe she's just on
a fishing expedition and doesn't actually know you're
here."

Kayla was about to insist that Misty was no threat.
Old habits died hard, and she had a lifetime habit of
defending Misty. But the truth was their location had
likely been compromised. Now the question was how?

"Carrie Collins," Dade spat out like profanity.

It took Kayla a moment to realize why Dade had said
the woman's name, but then she spotted the tall brunette who got out of the driver's side of the car. It was

the paramedic who'd come to her estate right after the shooting.

"Your sister knows Carrie?" Dade asked, his attention fastened to the two women making their way to the porch.

"I don't think so." Yet, here they were together. What was going on?

Kayla shoved the concho into her pocket and hurried to the hall where Connie was waiting. The nanny had no doubt heard the car engine and was wondering if they were about to be attacked again.

She handed Robbie to Connie. "I'll be back after I talk to my sister."

And by God, Misty better have some answers.

By the time Kayla returned to the living room, Dade was talking on his cell. She didn't know who he had called, but he clearly wasn't happy. He had such a grip on the phone that she was surprised it didn't crush to powder, and his eyes were narrowed to slits.

"Who says I'm at the Wellman ranch?" Dade barked. He paused, then cursed. "How the hell did you manage to follow Winston?"

Kayla's stomach dropped. If her sister and this medic had followed the D.A., then Charles's hired guns could have done the same. Oh, mercy. This had just gone from bad to worse.

As if he'd declared war on it, Dade paused the security system and threw open the door. Carrie tried to push her way in, but Dade blocked her.

"I need to check your arm," Carrie insisted. "You could get an infection. Or worse."

"My arm is fine," Dade insisted right back, and he jerked away from Carrie when she tried to check the bandage that was visible just beneath the sleeve of his black T-shirt.

Carrie's eyes narrowed as well, and she shot Kayla a glare. Kayla ignored it and saved her glare for Misty, who was practically standing behind the much taller Carrie.

"Why did you come?" Kayla asked her sister.

"Why?" Misty stepped to Carrie's side. "Because you believe I tried to kill you. I had to see you, to convince you of the obvious. I would never take money from someone who wants to hurt you."

It certainly sounded convincing, and Kayla wanted to believe her, but there was the issue of the money that Misty had recently acquired. There was also her sister's mere presence.

"Why did you come here?" Kayla asked. Again, she had to dodge a glare from Carrie. "You must have realized that someone could have followed you."

"No one did," Carrie snapped, and she repeated it to Dade. "I'm not stupid, Dade. I know how to watch my back—and yours."

"Winston was certain no one had followed him, either," Dade informed them. "But you somehow managed it. How?"

Carrie huffed, and her glare softened. "I figured Winston or Alan would be out to see you sooner or later, so I kept an eye on the parking lot at the D.A.'s office. I got lucky and saw them leave."

"You did all that so you could check on my arm?"

Dade didn't sound happy about that. Or convinced that Carrie was telling the truth.

That put some fire back in her eyes. "I care about you," Carrie snarled under her breath. And then she put that snarl into the look she gave Kayla.

Oh, so that's what was going on. Carrie had a thing for Dade. That was, well, reasonable. After all, Dade was a hot guy and no doubt a prime catch. Still, it made Kayla uncomfortable, and she didn't want to explore why she didn't like Carrie going to extremes to check on Dade.

Kayla walked closer until she was side-by-side with Dade and snared her sister's attention. "Were you watching the D.A.'s parking lot, too?"

The seconds crawled by before Misty answered. "Yes, and when Carrie spotted me, we got to talking. I asked her to bring me out here with her."

"She demanded I bring her," Carrie clarified to Dade. "I agreed finally because I didn't want her to do something stupid by trying to follow me."

Kayla figured the *something stupid* had already happened.

"You put Robbie in danger by coming here," Kayla told Misty. Her sister opened her mouth, but Kayla spoke right over her. "We can talk about your innocence after the trial. After Robbie is safe. But for now, I need you just to back off and stay away from us."

Misty flinched, and her eyes actually watered. Because Kayla had never seen Misty cry anything but crocodile tears, she had to wonder if these were genuine. If so, Kayla would owe her a huge apology. Later. After the trial.

"You both need to leave," Dade said. And it wasn't a suggestion. It was an order. He started to close the door, but Carrie caught onto it.

However, the woman didn't look at Dade. She looked at Kayla. "You don't even remember me, do you?"

Kayla lifted her shoulder. "You were at the estate last night."

"Before that. I was with Preston the night you two met."

Kayla hadn't expected the woman to say that, and with so much already on her mind, it took her a few moments to remember that night.

"A charity fundraiser in San Antonio," Carrie added. "I was talking to Preston, and you interrupted us."

Yes, she remembered meeting them, and she vaguely recalled a woman next to Preston. Until now she'd had no idea it was Carrie. "A friend interrupted you," Kayla corrected, "so she could introduce me to Preston."

At the time, Kayla had thought it was one of the best moments of her life. And she continued to think that until she got to know the abusive man behind that million-dollar smile.

"Does this have anything to do with the trial or Kayla's safety?" Dade demanded. He clicked on his phone. "Because I have security arrangements to make."

"Yes, it does have something to do with the trial." Carrie had a death grip on the door to keep Dade from closing it. "Kayla was bad news then, and she's bad news now. She went to that fundraiser to meet a rich guy, and she succeeded. She didn't care that Preston and I were dating. She just moved right in on him."

Stunned by Carrie's accusation, Kayla pulled back her shoulders. "I wasn't aware you were seeing Preston. He didn't mention it."

"And I'm sure you didn't ask." Carrie paused and glanced away. "Preston ended things with me that night, and I figure you had plenty to do with that. I know your type, and I know you would have said and done anything to snag a man like him. All that money, all that power. You wanted it, and you didn't care who you pushed aside to get it."

Kayla could only shake her head. "You know nothing about me," she insisted.

"Kayla's right—you don't," Misty agreed. "And I didn't come out here so you could attack my sister."

Carrie ignored them and switched her attention to Dade. "Kayla could get you killed. You must know she had something to do with that attack last night. Why else would the gunman have called her?"

Because Kayla was right against Dade's back, she felt his muscles go stiff. "How did you know about that call?"

Carrie's eyes widened. For just a second. And then she shrugged. "I heard someone talking about it. Don't remember who." Her stare drilled into Dade. "How else would I have known? You're not accusing me of anything, are you?"

Dade cursed. "No, but I am telling you for the last

time to leave." And to make sure that happened, he slammed the door in their faces.

"I'm sorry," Kayla said at the exact moment Dade said it, too.

Kayla managed a frustrated groan. Dade skipped the groan and made a call. To his brother, no doubt. They had to get out of there fast, now that seemingly everyone in Silver Creek knew their location.

While Dade was on the phone, Kayla looked out the window to make sure their guests did indeed drive away. Her sister gave her one last glance before she got in the car. The glance was definitely one of disapproval. Maybe because Kayla hadn't welcomed her with open arms. Maybe because Misty thought Kayla should have defended her more.

It didn't matter which.

The bottom line was that she couldn't trust her sister. Coming here had been irresponsible at best and at worst, it had endangered Robbie.

Dade ended his call and looked out the window just as Carrie and Misty were driving away. "Get your things ready. Grayson will be out in a half hour to escort us to our ranch."

"Your ranch?" she questioned. "Your brothers aren't going to like that."

"My brothers are all lawmen, and they'd never put their personal feelings above the badge." But that troubled expression let her know that this would not be a laid-back visit. "It's only temporary, until we can make arrangements for another safe house."

Kayla turned to tell Connie the news, but she

stopped. So did Dade, and he shook his head. "Think back to last night," he told her. "Was the gunman's phone call mentioned while Carrie was still there?"

Kayla tried to pick through the details of that nightmare. "I don't think so." And that led her to her next question. "You suspect her of something?"

He shook his head. "Don't know yet. I don't like that she brought up her connection to your late-husband."

Neither did Kayla. "She seemed to think I was horning in on her possible relationship with Preston. And with you."

Dade didn't deny it, and the suddenly tight jaw muscles confirmed it. "Carrie and I were together, but things ended between us months ago."

Kayla didn't doubt that Dade had ended the relationship. Nor did she doubt Carrie still had feelings for Dade. She only hoped that Carrie wouldn't risk their safety all for the sake of getting Dade back into her life.

"I'll tell Connie we're leaving soon," Kayla let him know. But the nanny had obviously overheard the news because she was already packing their things.

Kayla started to help, but then she heard Dade's phone ring again. She hurried back to the living room to make sure nothing else had gone wrong.

"Kayla's not available," Dade said. His voice and his face were tense, and she walked closer, wondering who had caused this reaction.

"Do your slimy lawyers know you called me?" Dade asked whoever was on the other end of the line. "Brennan," he mouthed to her.

Oh, God. She'd already had enough for one day

without adding him to the mix. Why was the devil himself calling Dade?

Dade's mouth tightened even more. So did the grip he had on the tiny cell phone. "That sounds like a threat."

Threat. That word slammed through her like a heavyweight's fist. Charles was liberal with his threats, she had grown accustomed to them, but how dare he call now after nearly succeeding in killing her?

She marched across the room and held out her hand. "I need to talk to him."

Dade was shaking his head when she ripped the phone from his hand. "What do you want?" Kayla demanded from Charles.

"Kayla." Charles said her name in that sappy sweet way that only he could manage. "You're a hard woman to reach. I've been calling all around, trying to find you. Imagine my surprise to learn you're with one of the Ryland boys. My advice? Sleep with one eye open because the Rylands would love to slit your pretty little throat."

"What...do...you...want?" Kayla paused between each word because she was fighting to hold on to her composure. She wanted to scream. She wanted to reach through the phone and slap this vile man.

"I called to make sure Robbie was okay." The sappiness went down a notch.

"Well, he's not." She turned away from Dade when he tried to take the phone, but she did hold it so he could hear. "He's in danger because of you. Because of the assassins you hired to kill me."

"Kayla…" Silence, for a few seconds. "My differences with you would never extend to my grandson. Besides, I didn't hire any assassins."

She didn't believe him for a minute and judging from Dade's snarl, neither did he. "What kind of sick man endangers a baby just so he won't have to go to jail?"

Charles cursed. "I didn't endanger him, but I intend to find out who did." And with that, he ended the call, leaving Kayla to wonder what the heck had just happened.

"He's trying to trick me into believing he wasn't behind that attack last night," she mumbled.

Dade eased the phone from her hand and hit the end call button. He also turned so he could keep watch out the window. "Before that attack, had Brennan done anything to put Robbie at risk?"

Kayla didn't want to think of the past year or the months before that when she was pregnant, but she forced herself to go back. To the bad memories. To the beatings that Preston had delivered. To the verbal abuse from Charles.

"No," Kayla answered. "When Charles learned I was pregnant, he seemed happy. And he was even happier when he learned I was carrying a boy. He warned Preston not to hit me when I was pregnant because he didn't want to risk a miscarriage."

That confession cut through her because it was a reminder of the life she'd led. Trapped in hell. She was so ashamed of what she'd allowed to happen.

"Don't cry," she heard Dade say, and that's when she realized there were tears in her eyes.

Kayla cursed the tears. She was tired of crying and just as tired of breaking down in front of Dade.

"I'm not a wuss," she mumbled.

"Never thought you were." He huffed and pulled her into his arms. "Shh," he whispered, his breath brushing against her hair.

It felt so good to have him hold her like this. His arms were warm and safe, but she couldn't do this. Dade was nothing like Preston, but she had to stand on her own two feet.

And that's why Kayla stepped back.

Dade looked at her, frowned and hooked his arm around her waist. He snapped her right back to him. "I'm offering you a shoulder to cry on. That's it. No strings attached."

"Oh, there are strings." And she hadn't meant to say that aloud. Dade was looking out the window, keeping watch, but she waited until his eyes angled back to her. "This attraction has strings."

"Yeah," he admitted. He brushed his mouth over hers. "I wish I could do something about that, but I can't. I want you. You want me. You're scared of a relationship, and I don't want my brothers hating you any more than they already do."

Kayla took a deep breath. "So our decision should be easy. We keep our hands off each other."

He raised an eyebrow because his hands were already on her. And he wasn't backing away. Dade leaned down and put his mouth to hers again. It was just a touch, but it blazed right through her, leaving her breathless. Making her want more.

Kayla couldn't have more. Not now. Not ever.

She put her hands on his chest to push herself back. To put some much-needed distance between his hands and her body.

But a sound stopped her cold.

Chapter Nine

The blast ripped through the house.

Dade automatically drew his gun, but this wasn't another visitor. Nor were shots being fired.

This was an explosion.

"Go to Robbie," Dade told Kayla, but she was already heading in that direction.

Dade pressed the emergency response button on his phone to alert the dispatcher of a problem, and he hurried to the side of the window and looked out, not sure of what he might see. But what he saw sent his stomach to the floor.

His SUV was a fireball.

Dade knew this wasn't some kind of freak accident. No. Someone had put an explosive device in it. But Dade couldn't see that *someone*. He checked the yard and the pasture on both sides of the SUV.

No one.

It was too much to hope that the person had set the explosive and then left. In all probability, the bomber had moved to the back or sides of the house where he'd be out of sight.

And was ready to attack.

Dade did a quick check of the security system to make sure it was armed. It was. And he hurried to kitchen so he'd have a view of the backyard and the outbuildings.

"Take Robbie and Connie and get into the bathroom," he yelled out to Kayla.

Judging from the sound of the footsteps, Kayla was already doing that. Dade hoped it would be enough to keep them safe.

He peered around the window frame and into the backyard. He didn't spot anyone, but there were a lot of places to hide. Two barns, trees and even several old watering troughs in the corral area. Because the troughs were metal, that would make them an ideal place to hide and then launch an attack.

But what was this attack about?

Had Brennan sent someone to kill Kayla?

That didn't feel right. Because if he'd wanted her dead, he could have instructed the bomber to toss the explosive closer to the house. Of course, that would have endangered Robbie. So, maybe this was some kind of ruse to get them to run. The thought had no sooner crossed his mind when he caught the scent.

Smoke.

Dade couldn't see any flames, but he could certainly smell it, and threads of thin gray smoke started to seep through the tiny gaps around back door.

"The house is on fire!" Kayla yelled a split-second before the smoke detectors went off.

Their situation had just gone from bad to worse,

because Dade knew how this was going down. He had to get Kayla and the others out of the house. Outside. Where that bomber-arsonist was waiting for them.

Later, he would kick himself for allowing this to happen, but for now he needed to take some measures to keep them all alive.

With his gun ready, Dade hurried to the other side of the house where Kayla and Connie were waiting in the doorway of the bathroom. Kayla had Robbie in her arms, but the baby was kicking and fussing.

"The fire," Kayla said, pointing through the open doorway of the second bedroom.

Dade could see the flames now. Bright orangey red, and they were licking up the side of the house. There wasn't much time.

"We have to get out," he told them, although it was clear from their faces they already knew that. The trick was *how* to get them out.

He snatched a damp towel from a hanging bar and tossed it over Robbie. Maybe it would give him some protection. "Stay low and follow me. Hurry," Dade added.

There were two exits, front and back. Plus the windows, but he couldn't use those because it would take too long to get them all out. Speed was important now. They had to hit the ground running and get behind cover. Not easy to do with a baby in tow. Maybe they would get lucky, and Dade could hold off an assassin until backup arrived.

Thank God Grayson was already on the way.

Keeping watch, Dade led them back through the

living room, but he stopped to grab a backup hand-gun from his overnight bag. Unfortunately, they might need it.

"I can shoot," Kayla insisted, and she passed Robbie to the nanny so she could take the gun.

Dade wanted to say no, that he didn't want her to have to fend off an assassin, but right now he needed all the help he could get.

"We're going out front," Dade let them know.

It could be a wrong call. A gunman could be out there waiting, but his gut told him their attacker would be expecting them to leave through the back, as far away from that burning SUV as they could get.

Kayla's breath came even faster. Maybe because of the smoke that was drifting through the room. "What then?"

Another gamble. "I go first. Then Connie and the baby. We keep them between us." Protecting them from gunfire. He hoped. "Once we're off the porch, run out the gate to the right of what's left of the SUV and then drop down. There's a deep ditch out there, and we'll use it for cover."

Kayla gave a shaky nod, one that Connie repeated, but neither looked at all confident in his plan. Robbie peeked out at him, his head and body covered with the thick towel, and it nearly broke Dade's heart to think of the baby in danger. This wasn't right. No child should be in this position.

"It'll be okay, buddy," Dade whispered to the baby. He gave Kayla one last look. She was terrified, her hands shaking, but he saw the determination there, too.

She was a fighter, and that was exactly what he needed right now.

Dade hurried to the door and threw it open, not bothering to disarm the security system. Hopefully, the alarm would unnerve their attacker in some small way. He looked out, didn't see anyone waiting to attack, so he motioned for them to follow.

The blast of cold air came right at them the moment they stepped onto the porch. It was mixed with the stench of the fire, and the smoke from both the flames and the SUV. The SUV was already a goner, and it wouldn't be long before the wood frame house was reduced to ashes.

Dade moved quickly, maneuvering Connie and Robbie onto the porch and then the steps. Kayla was right behind them, not as close as he wanted but that's because she was keeping watch behind them. Good move. Because their attacker could come through the back of the house and ambush them.

"Hurry," Dade instructed Connie even though he doubted she could hear him over the clanging security alarms.

With Robbie in her arms, Connie stepped down into the ditch. Dade looked back to motion to Kayla to hurry as well, but she wasn't looking at him. Her body snapped to the right side of the house. So did her aim.

And she fired.

Everything happened fast. Dade got a split-second glimpse of the person dressed head to toe in black before Kayla's bullet sent the gunman ducking for cover on the opposite side of the house where the fire was blazing.

Kayla held her position. Her weapon raised and ready.

"Get down here!" Dade shouted to her.

He had already aimed at their attacker, and it didn't take long before the guy lifted his head again. He fired right at Dade.

Kayla yelled for him to get down. Dade did the same to her again, but she didn't move until a bullet came her way.

Hell.

She was out there in the open, too easy of a target. And she seemed to be frozen. Or maybe she was trying to use herself as a diversion so the gunman wouldn't send any bullets toward Robbie and Connie.

He didn't intend to let Kayla sacrifice herself.

Dade glanced at Connie to make sure she was deep in the ditch. She was. And she was using her own body to protect Robbie. They were away from the house fire and the SUV. The baby was as safe as he could be, so Dade did something about making sure Kayla didn't get killed.

He sprinted to her and hooked his arm around her waist. But he wasn't fast enough.

The bullets came flying right at them.

EVEN WITH THE DEAFENING noise of the security alarm, Kayla had no trouble hearing the shots. Or seeing their attacker as he leaned out and fired.

She returned fire just as Dade pulled her off the

porch and to the ground. He scrambled to get them to the side of the house. Opposite the gunman and so close to the fire that she could feel the heat from the flames.

But she was also yards away from her precious baby.

Kayla wanted to run to Connie and him. She needed to make sure they were all right, but if she stepped out, their attacker would kill her. She wasn't afraid for her own life, but if she got killed, she wouldn't be there to protect Robbie.

"Keep watch behind us," Dade shouted to her.

Oh, God.

She hadn't even considered that the gunman might run to the back of the house and shoot at them through the flames and smoke. If he did that, at least he wouldn't be near the ditch, but again she couldn't take the risk of Dade and her being gunned down. She turned, putting her back up against Dade's, and Kayla held her breath, waiting. And praying.

Somehow, she had to get her baby safely out of this.

She cursed herself for coming back to testify, but sooner or later it would have come down to this. A confrontation with Charles was inevitable, and she'd only delayed things when she went into hiding.

The winter wind shifted and sent the black smoke right at them, spreading it all around—not just the house but also the yard. The gunman could use it as a shield, but worse, the smoke burned her throat and lungs. Kayla started to cough. Not good. Because that would give away their position.

"We have to move," Dade insisted.

Kayla knew he was right, but there seemed no place

to go. The fire was directly behind them, and if they went into the front yard, the gunman would pick them off. That left the side. No fence. No buildings they could duck behind. However, there were some pecan trees about thirty feet away. If they could get to those, they could use the trees for protection and still be able to see the ditch.

"Stay low and move fast," Dade instructed, and he tipped his head to the trees.

Kayla nodded and prayed they could make it. Dade gave her one last glance, and he seemed to be trying to apologize to her. But Kayla was the one who'd gotten them into this mess. She hoped later she would have the chance to tell Dade how sorry she was for that.

"Now," Dade ordered. He, too, was coughing now, and she hoped the move would at least put them out of the smoke's path.

Each step was a victory, and she counted them off in her head while keeping watch over her shoulder. They only made it six steps before she saw the figure emerge from the smoke. She and Dade just kept running, but Kayla kept watch behind them.

At first their attacker seemed to be part of the smoke itself, but she realized that's because he wore black clothes. Only his face was visible. Definitely a man, tall and thin, and he had the cold, hard look of a killer.

The man took aim at them and fired. Just as Dade dragged her to the ground. The dirt was like ice, and the cold and adrenaline slammed through her. Her heart rate spiked when the bullet slammed into the ground just inches from her.

Dade pivoted and fired at the shooter. He didn't waste any time. He latched onto her wrist with his left hand and yanked her hard, shoving her behind the tree. Dade followed, readjusting his aim, but he didn't fire.

Kayla peered out from the pecan tree. She could no longer see the gunman, but thankfully the smoke wasn't obliterating her view of the ditch. Or the road—where she saw the approaching vehicle.

"There's a truck," she said to Dade.

His gaze whipped in that direction, but Kayla pinned her attention to the area where she'd last seen their attacker.

Where the heck was he?

As menacing as it was to see him step out of that wall of smoke, not knowing where he was chilled her to the bone. She kept her gun ready and tried to steady both her heart and her trembling hands.

"It's Grayson's truck," she heard Dade say.

Relief flooded through her, but it was short-lived. That's because a bullet slammed into the tree just inches from her. Kayla jumped back, bashing into Dade, but both of them somehow managed to keep hold of their guns.

Volleying glances between the direction of that last shot and the road, Kayla spotted the Silver Creek patrol truck that had come to a stop just twenty yards or so from the house. Grayson was behind the wheel and he was alone. She wished he'd brought the entire deputy force, but at the moment she would take whatever she could get.

"Keep watch," Dade ordered, and he took out his phone.

Because of the shrill security alarms, she couldn't hear much of what Dade was saying, but he'd no doubt called Grayson because she could see him on the phone, as well. She hoped they were figuring a way out of this nightmare.

There was movement just to the right of the smoke, and Kayla spotted the gunman again. He aimed and fired. The bullet flew past her, so close that she could have sworn she felt the heat from it.

Kayla reached out from the tree and fired back. With her shaky aim, she doubted she had hit anything other than the burning house, but she wanted to keep the shooter at bay. She didn't want to give him a chance to get closer to the ditch.

Dade slapped his phone shut and shoved it back into his jeans pocket. "We need to keep the gunman busy. Mason and the fire department are on the way, but Grayson's not going to wait for him. He'll go ahead and get Connie and Robbie away from here."

Kayla couldn't even manage a *thank God,* but she was beyond thankful that Grayson had put her baby first. She wanted Robbie far away from the bullets. Still, how did Grayson plan to get them into his truck?

"Stay here," Dade told her. That was it, all the warning she got before he dived out from cover and behind the adjacent tree.

The gunman fired at Dade.

Of course.

And she realized this was exactly what Dade wanted their attacker to do.

Dade moved again, jumping the narrow space between cover and the next tree. From the corner of her eye, she saw Grayson's truck speed forward.

The gunman saw it, too.

And he turned in that direction.

Kayla forced her hand to steady, and she fired a shot. The gunman jerked back as if he'd been shot and disappeared into the smoke again.

Grayson came to a stop, and the passenger's door flew open. Connie must have figured out quickly what was going on because it was only a few seconds before she came out of the ditch. With Robbie clutched close to her, she jumped into the truck. The moment the door was closed, Grayson sped away.

Kayla was so relieved that tears sprang to her eyes, but she blinked them back. Yes, her baby was safe, but now Dade and she had to finish this.

She glanced over at Dade when he motioned toward the backyard. At first Kayla didn't see the gunman, but she picked through the smoke and outbuildings and finally spotted him. He was crouched behind a large metal container in the corral area.

"You stay here," Dade mouthed. "I'll circle around behind him."

Kayla wanted to scream *no!*, that he should wait for backup, but Dade had already turned his back on her and was darting to another tree. He continued that way until he reached the last tree, and then he dropped to the ground.

When her lungs began to ache, Kayla forced herself to breathe, even though the air was clogged with smoke. She kept her wrist braced to help with the jitters, and she prayed her aim would be good enough to help Dade and keep him alive.

He was risking so much for Robbie and for her.

And the risks continued.

Kayla's heart started beating like crazy when she lost sight of Dade. The gunman was still there, lurking behind the container. He wasn't far enough out in the open to give her a clean shot, and she couldn't take one for fear of accidentally hitting Dade.

She spotted more movement. Not from the gunman, but from Dade. He was creeping along the side of the wooden corral fence. Because she could see him, she did something about creating a diversion. Kayla fired a shot just to the left of the container. It worked.

The gunman shifted in that direction.

It wasn't much, but it was enough. Dade vaulted over the fence and raced across the corral. Kayla was terrified and could only watch and wait. If necessary, she could fire another diversion shot.

It wasn't necessary.

Dade made it all the way to the container before the gunman whirled around. Too late. Dade knocked the gun from his hand and jammed his own weapon against the man's head.

Kayla broke into a run toward them, and she kept her gun aimed and ready. Dade made eye contact with her. Just a glance. Just enough to reassure her that this attack had come to an end.

Dade

But then she got a good look at the gunman's face. A face she recognized.

And Kayla realized this wasn't over. No. This was just the beginning.

Chapter Ten

Every muscle in Dade's body was primed for a fight. Yeah, Kayla and he had managed to capture the person who'd tried to kill them, but that person wasn't talking.

Danny Flynn, however, was smirking.

Despite the handcuffs and ankle shackles, the SOB *lounged* in the interview room while Carrie and another medic bandaged the graze wound on the top of his left shoulder. It wasn't a serious enough injury for him to go to the hospital. Besides, Dade didn't want this snake out of his sight.

"If this were the old days, I could beat a confession out of him," Mason mumbled. His brother was right behind Kayla and him, and all three of them were glaring at the hired gun who had refused to answer a single question, much less admit his guilt in nearly killing Kayla and Dade.

"I wish I could just slap that stupid smile right off his face," Kayla added, earning as close to an approving nod as Mason ever gave. "He put my baby in danger, and by God, he's going to pay for that."

Dade felt the same way. But Flynn had already lawyered up, and that meant Brennan would probably pay the bill for the attorney who was on his way from San Antonio. Somehow, they had to get Flynn to confess that Brennan had hired him to kill Kayla.

If that's what had really happened.

The pieces all seemed to point in that direction, but there was a niggling doubt in the back of Dade's mind. Maybe that had something to do with the way Carrie kept glancing back at him. Dade didn't trust her, and he was trusting her less and less with each passing second.

Kayla groaned again, and glanced first at Dade's phone, which he held in his hand. Then, she glanced at the dispatcher who was seated behind the front counter.

"Grayson will call as soon as he has Connie and Robbie settled," Dade reminded her.

That didn't soothe her. Nothing short of holding her son would, and Dade couldn't give that to her right now. Grayson hadn't wanted to bring Robbie and Connie back into town where they might be spotted by one of Brennan's cronies or someone who might inadvertently reveal their location. Instead, Grayson had decided to go ahead and establish a new safe house, somewhere, and Dade wouldn't know the location until everything was in place.

Kayla glanced up at him. There was no longer fear in her eyes. Just the anger fueled by what had to be a bad adrenaline crash. "I don't know how much more I can take of this," she whispered, leaning closer so that only Dade would hear.

"I know." And even though he knew it would earn him a glare from Mason, Dade slipped his arm around her and eased her out of the doorway and away from Flynn's line of sight.

But Mason didn't glare. Well, not at Kayla and him away. He glared at Flynn.

The medics finished and packed up their equipment. Tommy Watters came out first and nodded a farewell to them. Tommy was fresh out of his EMT training, and this was probably his first gunshot wound. He seemed in a hurry to get out of there.

Not Carrie, though.

She stopped, snared Dade's gaze. "How did this joker find you?" Carrie asked as if she hadn't already considered the possibilities.

"He followed you." And Dade didn't make it sound like a question. It was not only possible, it was likely that Flynn had followed either Carrie and Misty or Winston and Alan.

Carrie shook her head but not before sending a venomous glance at Kayla. Probably because Dade still had his arm around her.

"No one followed me," Carrie insisted. She looked around as if to see who was listening. "But her sister made some calls when we were driving out there. Why don't you ask her about it?" And with that toss under the bus, Carrie strolled away.

Dade cursed. He would ask Misty all right, but he hated the concern that created in Kayla's eyes. She had enough on her plate without suspecting her sister's involvement in these attacks.

"I'll find out where Kayla's sister is," Mason volunteered. "And I'll see if I can come up with something you can use for leverage to get this dirtbag to spill his guts."

The dirtbag was still smirking. If Flynn had any pain whatsoever from his injury, he certainly didn't show it. No fear, either. Probably because he thought his lawyers would be able to wrangle a deal, but there was only one thing that would make Dade deal with Flynn: for Flynn to hand them Brennan on a silver platter.

Kayla caught onto Dade's arm when he started to move around her and go into the interrogation room. "Can you call Grayson before you question Flynn?" she asked.

Dade didn't have to debate this, even though he knew Grayson was no doubt busy. Still, Kayla had to have some reassurance. It'd been nearly two hours since Grayson had driven off with Connie and Robbie.

Dade shut the door between Flynn and them and pressed in Grayson's number on his cell. His brother answered on the first ring, and Kayla moved closer so she could hear.

"Everything's okay," Grayson assured him before Dade could even speak. "I have Connie and the baby at a safe location."

"Where?" Kayla immediately asked.

But Grayson didn't give her an immediate answer. He hesitated big-time. "I'd rather not say. We obviously have some kind of breach in security. Maybe a leak in communication, and until I'm sure it's safe, I don't want to tell anyone where we are."

Tears sprang to Kayla's eyes. "But I need to see my baby."

"And you will," Grayson answered. "Just give me a few more hours to make sure I've made things as safe for Robbie as I can."

"How can you do that?" Kayla asked. Her voice was trembling now, and she was on the verge of a full-fledged cry.

"Nate is on his way there to the sheriff's building so he can run a bug sweep. I want to make sure Brennan or one of his henchman didn't plant some kind of listening or tracking device. Then, Nate will interview all four people who went to that safe house because one of them could have leaked your location."

So that meant Winston, Alan, Carrie and Misty would all be brought back in. Good. Dade was to the point where he didn't trust any of them.

"When I'm sure it's safe to do so, I'll arrange to have Dade bring you here. Okay?" Grayson asked.

It took her several seconds to agree. "Okay." It certainly wasn't the arrangement she wanted, but it would have to do. Robbie's safety came first.

"I'll have Nate call you when he's done," Dade told his brother, and he ended the call. He turned to Kayla. "Why don't you wait in my office while I talk to Flynn?"

Her breath rushed out with her words. "I don't want to. I want to hear what he has to say."

Dade couldn't have her in the interrogation room with Flynn. He had to follow the rules. Well, the basic ones anyway. Plus, Kayla was on the verge of losing it, and if she went after Flynn and tried to slap that smile off his face, she might get hurt.

"You can watch and listen in the room next door," Dade let her know. "There's a two-way mirror."

Kayla looked as if she might argue, but Dade brushed a kiss on her lips. "I won't be long." And he ushered her into the observation room.

Because the camera was already positioned near the two-way mirror to record Flynn's interview in the other room, Dade went ahead and turned it on to start the recording. He was about to go back to Flynn when he saw Mason making his way back toward him.

"I just got off the phone with Nate's contact at SAPD," Mason explained. "Flynn has a teenaged son that he calls Little Dan. Apparently, he's the apple of Flynn's wormy little eyes. The kid just turned sixteen and has a juvenile record. When he was in lockup last year, Little Dan lost it. Had some kind of panic attack because he's claustrophobic. My advice is play dirty with that bit of info and see where it gets you."

Dade would. Flynn certainly hadn't minded the dirty play when he fired those shots around Robbie and Kayla, so Dade would give him a little of his own medicine.

Flynn sat, waiting. Oh, yeah. He was a pro at this. Dade knew the man was thirty-six and had been arrested four times for assault and breaking-and-entering. However, there had been no arrests in the past two years since he'd been on Charles Brennan's payroll.

"You're wasting your time," Flynn volunteered the moment Dade stepped inside. His smile widened, revealing tobacco-stained, chipped teeth. With the yellowy gray in his dark hair, Flynn looked much older than his years. "I'm not saying anything to you."

Dade read him his rights. Then, he swiveled the empty metal chair around and sat in it so that he could casually drape his arms over the back. He wanted to look as laid-back as Flynn, even though inside him there was a bad storm brewing. Dade really wanted to beat this guy senseless for trying to kill Kayla.

"You don't need to say anything," Dade said. "I'll just keep you company until your lawyer arrives. Then we'll process you and put you in a holding cell." Dade forced a smile. "Look at you. So relaxed. Not bothered at all by any of this. Nothing like your son. He's really making a fuss over at SAPD."

Flynn's smirk evaporated. "What the hell does that mean?"

Dade shrugged. Paused long enough to get Flynn to squirm. "SAPD picked up Little Dan about a half hour ago."

Flynn would have come across the table if it hadn't been for the shackles tethering him to the chair. "You got no right to touch my boy."

"Oh, yeah? Well, SAPD disagrees. An eyewitness tied Little Dan to the shootings." Dade shook his head, feigning concern. "Accessory to attempted murder. And from what I hear from my brother over at SAPD, they're going to charge your *boy* as an adult."

Flynn made a feral sound and violently shook the chains. "I need to call him *now*."

Another headshake. "You got one phone call, and you made it to your lawyer."

"You can't do this." Flynn's jaw was iron stiff. "Little Dan can't stand to be penned up. He gets these fits, and he'll need his meds. He'll go crazy without 'em."

Dade made a sound of understanding. "Yeah, that probably explains why he tried to call you when he was picked up. But, of course, we have your phone in evidence, so his call went to voice mail. Too bad. I heard the officers had to get rough with him to put him in that cell."

Flynn opened his mouth again as if to make that animal sound, but then he squeezed his eyes shut and groaned. "He had nothing to do with this. Let him go."

"Can't do that. Attempted murder of a baby, a witness in protective custody and a deputy sheriff. Those charges aren't just going away."

Flynn's breath came out in short angry spurts, and the veins popped out on his forehead. The seconds crawled by, and Dade hoped Flynn would say something, anything, before the lawyer waltzed in and uncovered Dade's lie. The lie would hold up in court because cops were allowed to give false information during interrogation. However, the lawyer would no doubt advise Flynn to stay quiet.

"What do you want to hear?" Flynn growled.

"The truth, of course." And Dade waited and did some praying.

"My son had nothing to do with this," Flynn repeated. "So as soon as I've had my say, you'll make a call to get him released. Deal?"

Despite the time eating away at him, Dade pretended to think about that. "If you convince me that Little Dan is innocent, then I'll make that call."

Flynn's dirt-brown eyes narrowed. His mouth shook because his teeth were clenched so tight, but he finally nodded. "Charles Brennan hired me and Raymond Salvetti to scare his daughter-in-law. To do that, we had to find her, so we had someone watching her sister. I followed her out to the house where you and Kayla were hiding out."

Oh, that didn't help Dade's anger to hear it aloud, and he wondered how Kayla was doing with this. Maybe she would come bursting into the room.

"Scare?" Dade challenged. "You fired shots at her. You tried to kill her."

"No," Flynn quickly disagreed. "The orders were to scare her, but Salvetti got trigger-happy and fired into the estate. That was his doing, not mine. Hell, I could have blown up the house today with her in it, but those weren't my orders. I was just supposed to grab that baby and get out of there fast."

It took a moment for Dade to tamp down the emotion, the anger. Nope, it was rage. He hated this slimy piece of filth in front of him.

"Why take the baby?" Even though Dade was sure he already knew the answer, he wanted this on tape.

Flynn dragged in a weary breath. "For leverage. Brennan figured his daughter-in-law would do anything, including keeping her mouth shut, to get that kid back."

Yeah, that was what Dade had expected, but he hadn't expected for it to feel as if someone had slugged him. Robbie and Kayla could have been hurt or killed.

"Why did Salvetti call Kayla's cell?" Dade pressed.

"To make her look suspicious." Flynn cursed. "But Salvetti wasn't too bright because he wasn't supposed to call me."

Well, that explained that, and Dade believed the man was telling the truth. "What about Kayla's sister? Was that call to set her up, too?"

"I don't know." Another quick answer. "Salvetti was taking his orders directly from Brennan, not me. So, I don't know why he'd call anyone. Now, it's your turn. Phone your cop buddies and get my boy out of lockup."

Dade met him eye to eye. "If I do that, you'll just recant all of this later. What I want is proof that links you and Salvetti to Brennan."

Flynn looked up at the ceiling as if seeking divine intervention. Dade just waited him out, hoping the lawyer or Kayla wouldn't come barging in.

"There's something that ties Salvetti to a crime. If you dig hard enough, I'm betting you can connect the dots from Salvetti to Brennan. But if I tell you, you've got to promise witness protection for me and my boy."

"You know I can't make a promise like that, but I'll see what I can do." And Dade would. Because as much as Dade despised Flynn, he despised Brennan more and wanted to put him away for life. "What proof do you have?"

Flynn swallowed hard. "There's a wall safe in my house in San Antonio. Inside there's a gun with Salvetti's fingerprints. That gun was used in a murder."

Dade heard the voices in the front part of the building and figured the lawyer had arrived. "Connect the dots for me," Dade insisted. "What does this gun and murder have to do with Brennan?"

Flynn leaned closer. "Salvetti has worked for Brennan a long time. Longer than me. And he was working for Brennan when this murder happened. My advice? Dig into it. Now, *please* call SAPD."

Dade heard the hurried footsteps coming down the hall. Two sets. One belonged to Mason, he soon learned, and the others belonged to Darcy Burkhart, an attorney who had recently moved to Silver Creek. But Darcy was no stranger to Dade. No. She had been one of Brennan's attorneys during the initial investigation.

"This interview is over," the petite brunette said. She was a good foot shorter than Mason who loomed over her, but she still managed to have an air of authority. "I need to consult with my client."

Dade got to his feet. "Your client just confessed to an assortment of felonies."

Darcy stayed calm but fired a nasty glance at Flynn. "I need to speak to him *alone*."

Dade nodded and used the remote device on the wall to turn off the video recorder as he was required to do. Client-attorney privilege. But Dade thought he might already have what he needed without any additional statement from Flynn.

"Make that call," Flynn shouted out to him as Dade headed for the door.

"I will," Dade lied.

He stepped out into the hall with Mason. The lawyer went in, and Dade waited until she'd shut the door before he said anything.

"We'll need a search warrant for Flynn's safe," Dade instructed. "And we need Brennan back in custody."

"It's already in the works," Mason assured him. "SAPD will pick up Brennan, and they'll execute the search warrant the moment they have it in their hands. You think this will link us to Brennan?"

"I hope so." And Dade hated that he sounded so pessimistic, especially when he realized that Kayla was right behind Mason and hanging on his every word.

"Flynn did confess that Charles hired him," Kayla said.

"Yeah." And that would get Brennan back in custody. Temporarily anyway.

Because she looked ready to fall flat on her face, Dade caught onto her arm and led her down the hall toward his office. "This Darcy Burkhart is a tough attorney," Dade let Kayla know. "She could somehow get it all thrown out. That's why it's important for us to connect this so-called gun to a murder and then to Brennan. That's physical evidence and could be a helluva lot better than just a confession from a man with a criminal record."

"So-called?" she repeated. "You think Flynn lied about that?"

Oh, man. He hated to see her hopes smashed like this.

Dade took her into his office, made her sit in the chair across from his desk. He wished he could give her a shot of whiskey from the bottle he kept in his bottom drawer, but she would need a clear head because she still had to make a statement about the shooting. Instead, he handed her a bottle of water that he'd taken from the small fridge behind his desk.

"I'm sorry," Kayla mumbled. She drank the water as if it were a cure for what ailed her, gulping it down so fast that it watered her eyes. Or maybe that was just more tears on the way.

Dade wanted to pull her into his arms for a long hug. He wanted her to lean on him. But that would be a dangerous mix right now because of the attraction. He settled for skimming his fingers down her arm.

"Everything new we learn just seems to complicate things," she mumbled.

Yeah, it did. Dade would have preferred Flynn to give a clear, no-strings-attached confession, but instead he'd added this mystery gun to the mix. It might be critical, and it might be a smokescreen. But someone had to investigate it. That tied up manpower and resources when all those resources should be focused on picking up Brennan and canceling his bond.

Dade moved some things off the corner of his desk so he could sit. Not exactly touching Kayla but close enough. But Dade didn't watch where he was sliding a stack of folders, and they bumped into the framed photo, knocking it over.

Kayla reached out and picked it up. She started to put it back, but she froze, staring at the picture.

"It's my maternal grandfather, Sheriff Chet McLaurin." The shot had been taken outside a brand-spanking-new sheriff's office. Chet was smiling that good-ol'-boy half smile of his with his white Stetson slung low on his weathered face. "He was a legend around here before he was killed."

"Killed?" she said under her breath. Kayla continued to study the photo.

"Yeah. He was shot twenty years ago while investigating a robbery. His killer was never identified or caught." And after all these years, that sliced right through his heart. His brothers', too. In fact, it's the reason all the Rylands had gone into law enforcement. A case they couldn't solve.

A wound that couldn't be healed.

"I've seen this photo," she said, tapping it.

Surprised, Dade took it from her and had another look, even though he knew every detail. "There's one in Grayson's office."

She shook her head. "No, I saw it in Charles's office."

"What?" And Dade couldn't ask it fast enough. "What was Brennan doing with that picture?"

"I don't know." She had more water and licked her lips. "About eighteen months ago, I was sneaking around in his files. Looking for anything I could use to get Preston and him arrested. I knew that was the only way I could get out of…my situation. I'd just learned I was pregnant, and I was looking for a way to get out."

Dade felt it again. That jolt of hatred for the Brennan men who'd made Kayla's life hell.

"I remember the picture because it seemed out of place. I mean, there were other photos. Some mug shots. Some taken from a camera with a long-range lens. And then there was this one of the Silver Creek Sheriff's office. I looked at it a long time, trying to figure out why Charles had it."

Dade did the same now. He tried to see it with a fresh eye. His father was in the shot. His mother dressed in her Sunday best. Him, and all his brothers.

"Who's that?" Kayla asked, tapping the image of the person standing next to him.

"My brother Gage." Dade didn't want to feel the resentment for his younger sibling, but he did. "He left home not long after high school and didn't come back." Gage had run out on the family. Just like their father. "He joined the CIA and was killed on a deep-cover assignment."

"Oh, I'm so sorry," Kayla said softly.

Dade shrugged. "Thanks," he mumbled and got his mind off Gage and back on the picture taken all these years ago.

Next to Gage was Mel, the current deputy, who was then just starting her rookie year. Two deputies, long since retired. The then mayor, Ford Herrington, who was now a state senator. And then Dade's attention landed on the man at the far right of the happy group.

Winston Calhoun.

He was the assistant D.A. back then and had every right to be in the photo. After all, it was the grand opening of the Silver Creek law-enforcement facility. But because of Dade's recent suspicions about Winston, his presence in the photo seemed a little menacing.

"Where are the files that had this photo?" Dade asked.

"In the storage room off Charles's office. But it's no longer there," she quickly added. "I went back about a week later to see if I could find anything, and all the files were gone. I'm pretty sure Charles figured out I'd been snooping in there."

Dade didn't doubt it. Heck, Brennan probably had surveillance and knew what Kayla had done. It sickened him to think that the only reason Brennan had let her live was because she was carrying his grandchild.

The picture probably wasn't enough to get an additional search warrant for Brennan's place, but Dade would question the man about it when SAPD took him back into custody.

Which hopefully had already happened.

He reached for his phone to find out the status of that, but it buzzed before he could make the call.

"It's me," Mason greeted in his usual growl. "Brace yourself, little brother, because we got a problem. A big one. And the problem's name is none other than Misty Wallace."

Chapter Eleven

"What's wrong?" Kayla asked the second Dade got off the phone.

His mouth went tight, and he squeezed his eyes shut for a moment before he answered. "It's Misty," he finally said. "Grayson had flagged her bank account. It's routine when monitoring a suspect who might try to flee."

Kayla was about to argue that *suspect* label, but Dade's expression had her holding her tongue and waiting.

"About twenty minutes ago, Misty cleaned out her account. A detective at SAPD immediately tried to call her, but she didn't answer her cell. So, the detective called her apartment. Misty's roommate answered and told him that Misty had packed up and left." Dade paused. "Kayla, she stole her roommate's handgun."

Oh, mercy. Not this. Not now. What the heck was Misty thinking? This would only make her look guiltier. If that was possible.

"SAPD is looking for her," Dade added.

Of course they would, and then they would drag

her back in for questioning. Kayla didn't know which she feared most—that her sister was in danger or that Misty was running because she'd had some part in the two attacks.

Kayla's breath broke before she could choke back the sound, and just like that, Dade was there, gathering her into his arms.

"She's my sister," Kayla managed to say. And that seemed to be enough explanation because Dade only made a sympathetic sound of agreement. "I want her safe. I don't want her out there running around with a gun."

Dade nodded. "We'll find her."

The fear must have flashed through her eyes because Dade shook his head. "Don't go there," he insisted. "We'll find her and *talk* to her. That's all."

"Please," she begged. "Tell them not to shoot her."

"No need to tell them that because the cops know she's scared and on the run. They're trained to handle situations like this, Kayla."

His voice was so calm, so reassuring, and Kayla believed him because the alternative was too hard to accept.

"It'll be okay," he promised.

Dade brushed a kiss on her temple and pulled back so they were eye to eye. That was always a dangerous stance for them because it also meant they were close to being mouth to mouth.

"I can't believe this is happening," Kayla whispered. That included Misty, the attacks and, yes, even this bizarre attraction to Dade. "I'm terrified for my sister.

And I miss Robbie so much. It breaks my heart to know that he's in danger. He's just a baby."

"Yeah." He used the pad of his thumb to swipe a strand of hair away from her face.

Like everything else, the embrace, the temple kiss, the simple touch—all those things seemed far too intimate. Ditto for the way Dade dipped his head. Kayla braced herself for a bone-melting kiss, but with Dade's mouth and breath closing in on her, he only shook his head.

"Let me call Grayson and see how close he is to securing things with the new safe house." Dade took out his cell, pressed in some numbers and then put the call on Speaker. "Grayson, it's me," he said when his brother answered.

"Everything is okay," he immediately said. "I have two Texas Rangers en route, and once they're here, I can head out to pick up some supplies. Then we can make arrangements to bring Kayla out here."

She heard what Grayson said, but it was hard to concentrate because in the background she also heard her son. Robbie was laughing.

"I need to say hello to him," Kayla insisted.

Grayson didn't argue, and soon the sound of Robbie's laughter got closer and closer.

"Hi, Robbie. It's Mommy." Kayla tried to keep the fear out of her voice. Not easy to do. But she obviously succeeded because Robbie squealed with delight.

"He's being a really good boy," Connie let her know.

That put a lump in her throat. "Tell him I love him

and that I'll see him soon." Kayla moved away from the phone so that Robbie wouldn't hear her cry.

Dade talked with his brother a while longer, and judging from the conversation, they were working out how she would be transported from town and out to the new safe house. Of course, she would have to be back in Silver Creek to testify.

If Charles didn't get another trial delay, that is.

"You okay?" Dade asked when he ended the call. He slipped his phone in his pocket and pulled her into his arms.

"No." Kayla didn't even try to lie to Dade. Besides, he could see her tears. He kissed one of them off her cheek.

"Kids are tough," he told her. "Robbie probably thinks this is some kind of adventure. He's safe, and right now that's all that matters."

Dade was right. Thanks to Grayson and him, they had her son out of danger. And she, too, was safe in Dade's arms.

"I keep ending up here," she whispered.

The corner of his mouth lifted. "Yeah. Eventually, we'll have to do something about that." But it didn't sound as if he intended for that *something* to include staying away from her.

Just the opposite.

Dade lowered his head. Leaned in—

Just as there was a knock at the door. They flew apart, but not before their visitor got a good look at their near lip-lock.

"Nate," Dade greeted his twin.

Nate nodded, but there was no greeting in his eyes or the rest of his body. He obviously didn't approve of what he'd walked in on. And why would he? Nate still lumped her in the same category as Preston and Charles.

"We located Brennan," Nate explained, sounding all-cop. "A Texas Ranger is escorting him here."

Funny, when Kayla had seen Nate on the computer screen during Misty's interview, he'd looked calm and in charge, but in person she could see the nerves right there at the surface. Nate had that Ryland intensity in spades.

"His lawyer has filed a motion to throw out Flynn's confession," Nate added.

Dade cursed. "On what grounds?"

"Ms. Burkhart claims that Flynn isn't mentally stable, that he's had several stints in psychiatric facilities, and that when you interrogated him, he was in need of his medication. She also says you exacerbated Flynn's condition by lying to him about his son."

Kayla wanted to curse, as well. "Please tell me he's not going to walk," she begged. "The man tried to kill us, and he put my baby in grave danger."

Something went through Nate's ice-gray eyes. Sympathy maybe because he, too, was a parent. "I'll do everything humanly possible to keep him behind bars." Nate wearily scrubbed his hand over his face. A gesture that reminded her of Dade. They weren't identical, but they were alike in so many ways.

"What about the gun Flynn mentioned?" Dade asked. "Is the lawyer trying to kill the warrant?"

"She wasn't fast enough." Nate didn't smile exactly, but there was some relief in his expression. "SAPD already has it, and officers are headed over to Flynn's place now. The warrant allows them to search only the safe, though, so let's hope Flynn wasn't lying."

Yes, and while they were hoping, Kayla added that maybe the gun could be used to put Flynn and Charles behind bars for the rest of their lives.

"Is this lawyer working to keep Charles out on bond?" Kayla asked.

"Probably," Nate admitted. "But until the question of Flynn's sanity is decided, we can act in good faith and hold Brennan. Of course, with his connections he might be able to find a judge who'll speed through the sanity decision."

So, they might not have much time.

"I'd like to be there when you interrogate Charles," Kayla insisted. "Maybe I can rile him enough that he'll admit to something wrong."

Nate shook his head and moved back into the hall. "Can't do that. For one thing, Darcy Burkhart won't allow it." He said the attorney's name like the worst of profanity.

Dade stepped out, as well, and when Kayla looked into the hall, she saw why.

Charles was there.

"We have to follow the rules to a tee," Nate said to her, his voice a whisper now. "I don't want to give Brennan a chance at a free pass." But then Nate stepped aside. "However, there is no law against you speaking to your former father-in-law if you happened to run into him. Like now, for instance."

Kayla nodded. "Thank you." It was a concession that Nate didn't have to allow her. Now, she only hoped she could do something with it.

She maneuvered around Dade and Nate and started up the hall. There was a Texas Ranger on Charles's right side, and he stopped when Charles did. Charles had the gall to smile at her.

"Kayla, pretty as a picture," he purred.

"I was nearly a dead picture. Someone tried to kill me again." She didn't wait for him to deny it. Kayla got closer and leaned in. "You might think you hold the cards, but you don't. If you ever want to see your grandson again, then the hired guns stop now."

Of course, she never intended for Robbie to be in the same vicinity as his grandfather, but her son was the only leverage she had.

His smile faded. "I would never endanger my grandson. And I will see him, one way or another."

"Not if you're behind bars," she fired back. "Your hired gun rolled on you, Charles. Danny Flynn said you sent him to kill me."

The anger flashed across his face. Then, quickly left as the smile had done. "Flynn's a lunatic and a liar. I fired him, you know. Weeks ago. And this is all to get back at me."

She hated that the lies came so easily to him. And hated the sound of the woman's footsteps behind her. Kayla knew it was the attorney, and the woman would soon put an end to this.

"Who helped you put these attacks together?" Kayla demanded. And she prayed he didn't say her sister's name. "Was it Winston Calhoun?"

"This conversation is over," Ms. Burkhart said before she even reached them.

But Kayla didn't give up. "Who was it?" She latched hard onto Charles's arm. "Carrie Collins?"

Still no reaction, so Kayla tried again. "Alan Bowers?"

Now, there was a reaction.

Charles's smile returned.

"Alan," he mumbled. "Now, there's a man with secrets." He leaned in, put his mouth to her ear. "Ask him if he's had anything to drink lately. I think he prefers scotch on the rocks."

Kayla pulled back, shook her head. "What the heck does that mean?"

But Charles didn't get a chance to answer. His attorney wrenched him out of Kayla's grip and marched him down the hall toward the interrogation room. Nate and the Ranger were right behind them.

"What was that about?" Dade asked her.

Kayla had to shake her head again. "I'm not sure. Charles could be trying to put the blame on Alan."

Or maybe that's where the blame should be.

"I'll talk to Alan again," Dade assured her. And he phoned the other deputy, Melissa Garza. Mel, as Dade called her. He asked her to round up the available suspects for another interrogation.

Good, Kayla wanted them questioned again, but this could all be part of the game. No accomplice. Just

Charles and his two gunmen: Flynn and Salvetti. One of them dead, and the other was in custody. She wanted to believe that meant things were looking up, but they were dealing with Charles here.

Dade started down the hall, but first he grabbed the picture of his grandfather from his desk. "I'd like to try a little experiment," he explained.

He caught up with the others and ducked into the interrogation room where Mason and Nate were with Charles and his attorney. He handed the picture to Nate and then whispered something that Kayla couldn't hear.

"Let's watch." Dade caught onto her and led her into the room with the two-way mirror.

She watched as Nate set the photo in front of Charles. Nate didn't say a word, even when both Charles and Ms. Burkhart gave him questioning glances.

"What am I supposed to do with this?" Charles asked.

"Look at it," Nate explained. "See if you recognize anyone."

Nate suddenly looked calm and in control. Mason, on the other hand, looked like...himself. As if he preferred to beat a confession out of Charles. Kayla was in Mason's camp right now and wished that could happen.

Charles did pick up the picture, and a thin smile moved over his mouth. "Your grandfather," he said without hesitation. "A complex man."

Because her arm was next to Dade's, she felt him stiffen. Inside the interrogation room, Mason and Nate had similar reactions.

"You knew Chet McLaurin?" Nate asked.

"What does this have to do with my client's current situation?" Ms. Burkhart interrupted.

"Nothing," Charles assured her, and he pushed the photo away.

Dade cursed. "You said those files from his office were missing?"

Kayla nodded. "But I doubt he destroyed them. He probably has storage facilities somewhere."

"When things settle down here, I'll look and see what I can find."

That left Kayla with a sickening feeling. Everything Charles touched turned bad, and she hoped he hadn't had any kind of connection with Dade's grandfather. It was obvious Dade loved Chet McLaurin, and Charles shouldn't be able to hurt the few good childhood memories that Dade and his brothers had about the man.

She remembered the silver concho in her pocket and eased her hand over it. It was silly, but just having that piece of Dade so close to her made her feel better. But it was more than that. She was starting to feel protective of his family. As if she had some right to protect. Some need.

And she couldn't feel that way.

That was a sure path to a broken heart.

Charles's lawyer started the session with some legalese about the validity of Flynn's confession. Nate countered with some legalese of his own, and only then did Kayla remember that Nate had a law degree, as well. Kayla was trying to sort through what they were saying when Deputy Mel appeared in the doorway. She held out the phone for Dade.

"It's SAPD calling about that search warrant," the deputy explained. "I figured you'd want to talk to them."

Dade practically snatched the phone from her hand. "Deputy Dade Ryland."

Kayla moved closer, trying to hear the conversation, but the discussion being piped in from the interrogation room blocked out whatever was being said. Plus, Dade wasn't giving anything away. He was just listening.

"Do that ASAP," Dade instructed, and he ended the call.

"Did they find anything in the safe?" Kayla immediately asked.

"Yeah." Dade turned for the door. "Now, let's see if it's important to this investigation."

That's all Dade said before he turned the camera on and darted out and into the interrogation room next door. His entrance grabbed everyone's attention, and the lawyer was no doubt on the verge of objecting when Dade bracketed his hands on the interrogation table and got right in Charles's face.

"SAPD just executed the search warrant of Danny Flynn's safe." And he waited, the seconds crawling by.

"So?" the lawyer and Charles said in unison.

Dade glanced at his brothers first. "They found a gun. A .38 and a spent bullet."

Kayla couldn't believe it. Flynn had told the truth. Well, about that anyway.

"What do you know about the gun?" Dade demanded.

Charles pulled back his shoulders. His only reaction before he shrugged. "I know nothing about it. And when you test it, as I'm sure you will, you still won't be able to link it to me. Because I didn't have anything to do with that gun or anything else in Flynn's safe."

Dade didn't pull back. "That's because you're a coward. You hire people to do your killing."

The lawyer objected of course. Nate countered that objection, and while they were engaged in verbal banter, Dade and Charles just stared at each other. Except Charles's expression was more of a glare now.

Good.

Dade had managed to hit a nerve and that wasn't easy to do.

Kayla went closer to the tiny speaker mounted on the wall so she wouldn't miss any of the conversation.

"If the gun's not connected to you," Dade said to him, "then why would your disgruntled former employee lead us right to it?"

Charles's glare softened, and the cockiness returned. "Do you want me to guess why a nutjob would keep a gun and a shell casing in his safe?"

"Sure. Guess." Dade had some cockiness. too.

"I think Flynn was hiding a secret," Charles calmly provided.

"What kind of secret?" Dade demanded over the protest of the attorney.

Charles waved off his lawyer. Then smiled a smile that only he and Satan could have managed.

"Just guessing here, mind you," Charles said, his voice low and calculated, "but I think it's a secret that could bring you Ryland boys to your knees."

Chapter Twelve

Dade felt numb and in shock. Yeah, it was stupid to put faith in anything Brennan said, but Dade couldn't shake the feeling that in this one instance, Brennan had told the truth.

It's a secret that could bring you Ryland boys to your knees.

Did that gun have something to do with his grandfather's murder? Maybe. And if so, Flynn might have handed them the evidence to solve a two-decades-old crime.

Darcy Burkhart cleared her throat. She didn't groan exactly, but she looked as if that's what she wanted to do. Dade could understand why. Brennan had just said way more than he should have.

"I need to speak privately with my client." Ms. Burkhart glanced at the mirror. *"Privately,"* she emphasized. She stood and motioned for Brennan to do the same. "Is there another room we can use?"

Nate and Mason exchanged glances, and it was Nate who escorted them in the direction of the other interrogation room down the hall.

"I've got calls to return," Mason mumbled and headed out.

Dade took a deep breath so he could go back to the observation room with Kayla, but she came to him. She caught onto him when he stepped in the doorway and hugged him. It seemed natural, and it was far more comforting that it should have been.

"Charles likes to play mind games," Kayla reminded him.

Dade didn't doubt that, but maybe this wasn't a game. "The gun might be connected to my grandfather's murder. We never found the killer or the murder weapon. But there's a bullet that was taken from his body. We can do ballistics to see if this gun killed him."

"When will you know?" she asked.

He shook his head. "I asked that the test be run ASAP. Nate can give them a shove, so we might know something…soon."

And Dade hoped they could live with the consequences of the truth. Oh, man. This could hurt bad. "In the back of mind, I always wondered if my father had something to do with that murder."

There. He'd said it aloud. A first. Probably all of his brothers had thought it, but it seemed too sick to put into words.

"I'm so sorry, Dade." Like her hug, it was the right thing. It soothed him as much as anything could have. It also reminded him how deep the pain was from the loss of his father and grandfather.

It was a pain he didn't want to feel. But damn, that gun had brought it all back to the surface.

"My father left just days after my grandfather was killed," he heard himself say. "And he and my grandfather weren't the best of friends. Both of them could be hard men, and they clashed."

She eased back. Her eyes met his. "But what motive could your father have had for killing him? And then how would Flynn have gotten the gun?"

"I don't know." He scrubbed his hand over his face. "I just know that our grandfather's death left a big hole in the family."

Kayla just stood there. Listening. Waiting for him to continue. She was offering him a chance to talk this through, and Dade was surprised, shocked even, that he wanted her to hear it.

"It'll always hurt," Dade explained. "It was like being ripped apart, and then Grayson had to put us all back together again." Dade paused because he had no choice. "Grayson's the father that our real dad should have been. He raised us all. Mason, too. He helped raise us while he built the ranch into one of the best in the state."

"You helped with that," Kayla told him.

Dade shook his head and turned away from her. "I helped with roundups and picking up breed stock. Mason is the reason people respect the ranch. Grayson is the reason they respect the law and the family."

"You're a deputy sheriff," she pointed out.

"Right." Man, this hurt, too, but he thought he'd buried it deep enough. Apparently not. "Nate's a cop superstar at SAPD. And Kade, the youngest, he's made a good name for himself in the FBI. Gage did the same in the CIA before he was killed in the line of duty. Like I said, I'm ordinary, but that's okay. I've learned to live with that."

Kayla closed the door. Well, actually she slammed it. Then, she caught onto his arm and whirled him around to face her. Dade saw it then. The anger in her eyes.

"You are not ordinary," she insisted. "You saved my life. My son's life. You've bucked up against your family to protect me."

The anger faded, and there was a moment. One scalding moment where Dade thought he was going to kiss her again. Kayla must have felt it, too. That pull deep within her. Because she shook her head and gave a reluctant smile.

"Besides, you're too hot to be ordinary," she said. "Want to hear a schoolgirl-like confession? You're hands-down the hottest guy I've ever kissed. When you walk into a room, Dade, I have to remind myself to breathe."

Dade had to mentally replay that three times before it sank in. He waited for the punch line, waited for Kayla to say she was just kidding. But she didn't. She leaned in and brushed her mouth against his.

When her eyelids fluttered up, and he saw those baby blues, he knew this was no joke. Kayla thought he was hot. So, he kissed her, hard, just the way he'd dreamed of kissing her.

The rap on the door got rid of the cocky smile that Dade was sure was on his face.

The door flew open, and he spotted his brothers.

Nate looked hurt and confused. Mason looked ready to rip off their heads, especially Dade's.

"Before you have another, uh, private conversation, you might want to check the recording system. It's on." Nate pointed to the camera and microphone mounted just behind the two-way mirror. The very camera that Dade himself had turned back on before the picture confrontation.

Hell.

Kayla's face turned flame red, and she shifted her position so that her back was to his brothers.

Dade wished he could dig a hole for both of them, but he knew that groveling and looking embarrassed wasn't the way to go.

"Yeah, I kissed her," Dade admitted. "Either of you got a problem with that?"

Nate dodged his gaze, shook his head and walked away. Which meant he did have a problem with it, but he respected Dade too much to say anything.

Mason's mouth tightened as he pushed himself away from the doorjamb he was leaning against. "When you screw up, you don't do it half-assed, do you, little brother?"

No, he tended to go full-blown with it. And in this case, it was a screw-up that he knew he couldn't avoid. Kayla was under his skin, and Dade thought maybe that's exactly what he wanted.

"By the way, three of our suspects were just brought in," Mason let him know. "Winston, Alan and Carrie. Let's just say, they aren't so happy to be here, and because Grayson's not back to ask the questions, that means one of us draws the short straw."

"I'll do it," Dade volunteered. He wanted to do it because each question, and answer, could help get Kayla and Robbie out of danger.

"When is Grayson expected back?" Kayla asked, her voice wavering a little. Yeah, Mason could be intimidating as hell, but Grayson's return meant she could see Robbie.

"Not for a while," Mason told her. "Once the Rangers are in place, Grayson said he still needs to pick up some supplies. Plus, it's getting late, and it won't be a direct drive out to the safe house. That's a long-winded way of saying it might be morning before we can get you out there."

Kayla sighed, obviously disappointed. She was beyond anxious to see her baby, and once Dade finished the interrogations, he needed to call Grayson and see if he could hurry things along. Besides, Dade wanted Kayla at the safe house, too, so she wouldn't be under the same roof with Brennan and the other suspects.

"I'll bring the three in here," Dade told her. "So you can watch and listen. We already know the sound system is working," he grumbled. But he added a smile to that and landed a kiss on her cheek.

"It's SAPD again," Mel said, coming up the hall. She handed Dade the phone. "He says it's important."

Dade took the phone and also took a deep breath. Important could be code-speak for bad news. "Deputy Dade Ryland," he answered.

"This is Captain Shaw Tolbert, SAPD. I'm Nate's boss. We got an immediate match on that spent shell casing retrieved from Flynn's safe."

Oh, man. He was right, code-speak for bad news. "That means the casing must have already been in the system." Which meant it had been used in a crime.

"Yes." And that's all the captain said for several moments. "And your informant, Flynn, was right. Salvetti's prints were on the weapon. I figured it'd be best if I told you, and then you could break the news to Nate."

"Nate?" Dade questioned.

The captain mumbled another "yes." Then, he paused again. "The bullet is a perfect match to the one that killed Nate's wife."

TO KAYLA IT FELT AS IF everything was moving in slow motion and spinning out of control at the same time.

She'd watched from the hall as Dade told his brothers about the bullet. She saw the pain register on their faces—an old wound opened up again—and she felt that same pain deep within her.

The Rylands had suspected all along that Charles had been behind Ellie's murder, and they'd apparently been right.

Well, maybe.

"Only Salvetti's prints were on the gun," Dade explained, relaying what the captain had told him just minutes earlier during their phone conversation. "And there's nothing to indicate it's been tampered with. The prints are clean, in places they should be on a gun, so they haven't been planted. This gun is the real deal."

No one said anything right away. All stood there, obviously trying to absorb the horrible news they'd just learned. "The gun can't be linked to Brennan," Mason concluded, and he punctuated that with some raw profanity.

"Not directly," Dade agreed. "But we all know that Ellie's last assignment as a cop was to investigate one of Brennan's drug-pushing henchmen. And she was killed carrying out that investigation. Captain Tolbert said he was personally going to take another look at the case and see if he can make a strong enough connection between Salvetti and Brennan."

Because Salvetti was dead, that might be harder to do, but there was a bottom line here: Salvetti had been the one to kill Nate's wife, and the man had almost certainly been taking orders from Charles. Now, Nate had the gun that might eventually point to Charles, but Kayla didn't think it was going to make it easier for him to accept his wife's murder.

As if he knew what she was thinking, Nate looked up, snared her attention. "I'm sorry," Kayla said because she didn't know what else to say.

He nodded, mumbled something under his breath, and much to Kayla's surprise, Nate walked toward her. He closed his eyes a moment, but when he opened them, his attention was focused fully on her.

"I know Brennan is making it hard for you to testify, but please don't back down," Nate told her. "You might be the only person who can get him to pay for what he's done."

"I won't back down," Kayla promised. She repeated it so the others would hear. "One way or another, I'm putting Charles Brennan behind bars. Or better yet, in the grave. I want him on death row."

Mason nodded. So did Nate. Dade lowered his head, shook it, and mumbled something she couldn't hear.

Nate glanced back at his brothers. "We'll keep your son safe, no matter what. You have my word on that." When his eyes started to water, Nate quickly turned and moved away. "I have to get out of here for a while."

No one questioned that, and Kayla totally understood. She hated being this close to Charles, but now she had just one more reason to hate him—he'd hurt Dade and his family by taking the life of one of their own.

Dade glanced around as if trying to figure out where to start. He finally hitched his thumb toward the interrogation room. "I'll start with Winston and Alan," he told Mason. "I'll talk to them together. Why don't you deal with Carrie?"

"I'd rather deal with a PMS-ing diamondback." Mason's mumble was drenched in sarcasm. "What about Brennan?"

"Let him and his lawyer stew for a while." Dade caught onto Kayla's arm. "You can watch from the observation room while I chat with Winston and Alan."

"Remember to breathe, Kayla," Mason said when she walked past him.

She whirled in his direction, expecting to see

Mason's usual scary glare, but the corner of his mouth hitched. It wasn't full-fledged, but it was a smile. He gave a half shrug as if he didn't want to expend too much energy for either gesture.

"I should probably tell you that you could do better than my little brother," Mason added. "But it sounds as if this is out of your control."

It was. She had already fallen hard for Dade, and nothing was going to change that. Unfortunately. That meant there were hard times ahead for her because this relationship with Dade wasn't just complicated. It was a potential powder keg.

Kayla brushed her hand against Mason's arm to thank him. She figured the subtle approach was better with this particular Ryland. He made a sound that could have meant anything and strolled away.

"Let's get something straight," Dade said to her on the trek to the observation room. "You won't take any unnecessary chances when it comes to Brennan. We'll get him behind bars."

"And my testimony will do that," she reminded him.

Dade had the same reaction as he'd had in the hall. A head shake and an under-the-breath mumble. "Just don't do anything stupid."

That didn't sound like his first choice of words for a warning, but Kayla couldn't ask for clarification. That's because Carrie came out of the reception area and walked directly toward them.

"Mason will interview you," Dade let her know.

Of course that earned Kayla a glare. She was tired of this woman's reaction and decided to go petty.

Kayla leaned over, brushed a kiss on Dade's mouth. "I'll watch from here." Something he already knew of course, and she stepped into the observation room.

"Do I have to remind you that Brennan and she are family?" Carrie said to Dade.

"No, you don't have to remind me."

And much to Kayla shock, Dade leaned into the observation room and kissed her right back. He added a delicious little smile that Carrie couldn't see because his back was to the woman. Then, he turned, caught onto Carrie's arm and ushered her down the hall where Mason was waiting for her. However, Dade didn't even make it back to the interrogation room before Darcy Burkhart rounded the corner.

"You have a problem," Darcy announced, zooming in on Dade. She glanced in the room at Winston and Alan. Winston was seated, reading something on his phone. Alan was pacing.

"What now?" Dade asked, sounding as frustrated as Kayla felt.

"I'm requesting a trial delay because there's a conflict of interest." She slapped some papers in Dade's hand. "That's the statement I just took from my client. I've already called the judge and the county D.A. I suggest you bring in the Rangers or some other impartial agency to handle the investigation."

Oh, mercy. Had something truly gone wrong, or was this another legal ploy?

Kayla stepped out in the hall to see if she could get a glimpse of the paper that Dade was reading. But he lifted his finger in a wait-a-minute gesture.

"What the hell is this?" Dade demanded, though he'd only had time to skim the page.

"Ask *him*." Ms. Burkhart pointed directly at Alan.

Alan sank down in the chair, head dropped into his hands, and he groaned. "I'm sorry," he said.

"Sorry?" Dade demanded. "Is it true? Tell me the hell it's not true." Dade was practically shouting by the time he got to the last word.

"It's true," Alan admitted.

"What's true?" Winston asked, getting to his feet.

Dade handed him the paper, and Kayla held her breath as the D.A.'s eyes skirted across the lines.

The color drained from Winston's face. "Oh, God."

Kayla repeated that and was about to ask what the heck was going on, but Winston glanced at her, then Dade.

"Does Kayla know?" Winston asked.

"No." And Dade said that with too much regret for this not to be really bad news.

"What is it? What don't I know?" she managed to ask.

But Dade didn't answer. He motioned for Mason who was still in the hall with Carrie. "I need to get Kayla away from this and upstairs. It's late, and she's been through more than enough today."

Mason nodded. "What do you need me to do?"

"Have Mel interview Carrie," Dade instructed. "You need to take Alan's statement. After that, he'll resign as the A.D.A., and then you can arrest him and have both Alan and Brennan moved to the jail. I want both in lockup for the night. Call Nate. He can help with that."

"Arrest Alan?" Kayla repeated, but she was the only one of the four who seemed surprised with Dade's order. "Did he do anything to Robbie? Did he hurt my baby?"

"Nothing like that," Dade assured her.

That didn't ease the knot in her stomach.

"We have to talk," Dade said to her. No longer a shout. Practically a whisper.

He caught onto her hand and started walking.

Chapter Thirteen

Kayla didn't ask Dade what he'd just learned, which meant she no doubt knew this was not going to be news she wanted to hear.

Still, Dade would tell her.

It just wouldn't happen in front of Alan or any of the others. She'd had her heart bared enough today without having to go through a semipublic ordeal of hearing Brennan's latest. And there was no mistaking it.

This would be an ordeal.

With his hand still holding hers, Dade led her up the back stairs to the studio-style apartment. Once it'd been part of the jail, but when a new facility had been built five years ago, Grayson had converted it to a place where they could crash when the workload was too much for them to go home to the ranch. Basically, it was one massive area with a kitchen, sitting space, desk, bed and bathroom, but for tonight, it would be a safe haven where Kayla could hopefully get some rest.

Well, after she fell apart, that is.

Dade led her inside, locked the door and had her sit on the well-worn leather sofa that had once belonged to his grandfather. In fact, pretty much everything in the room was a family hand-me-down moved from the attic at the ranch.

"Tell me," Kayla said, and there was pure dread in her voice.

First, Dade poured her a shot of whiskey from the stash Mason kept in one of the cabinets. He handed it to her and motioned for her to drink.

She did. Kayla took it in one gulp. "Tell me," she repeated. "Was Alan working for Charles?"

"Not exactly." Dade took a deep breath and sat on the coffee table in front of her so they'd be eye to eye. "Alan committed a crime and covered it up, but Brennan found out what he'd done. Brennan insists he hasn't been blackmailing Alan, but it might take a while to prove if that's true or false."

Kayla swallowed hard. "And the crime? Alan's too young to have murdered your grandfather." She paused. Her eyes widened. "He didn't have something to do with Ellie's death?"

Because she was going to need it, Dade inched closer and pulled her deep into his arms. "According to Brennan, a little over a year ago Alan was drunk, and he was involved in a car accident. He hit and killed your husband, and then he fled the scene."

She pulled in her breath and didn't release it. Kayla held it so long that Dade eased back to make sure she wasn't about to pass out. "Alan killed Preston?"

"Afraid so." He waited for her to cry, but the tears didn't come. "Preston had a security camera in his car that activated during the crash, but when Brennan came upon the scene just minutes after it happened, he took the camera before the cops got there."

"So he knew all along how Preston died." Still no tears. She shook her head. "Honestly, I thought Charles had murdered him. They clashed more often than not, and I figured Charles got fed up and killed him or had him killed. This sounds horrible, but Preston's death was a relief to me. As far as I was concerned, he was no longer my husband. No longer anything to me."

He touched her cheek. "Are you okay?"

"Yes." But then just like that, something flashed through her eyes. "Oh, God. Charles will try to use this to throw out the case against him. That's why he told his attorney about it after all these months."

Dade wished he could disagree with that, but she was right. "Mason and Nate will be all over this. The Texas Rangers, too. Brennan will go to trial."

Now the tears came. "He can't get away with this. He can't."

Dade pulled her back in his arms. "He won't. It's true—the only reason he spilled all of this now was to call Alan's integrity into question."

"And it will," she insisted.

"It might. But I read through the case against Brennan, and I don't remember Alan's name appearing anywhere in the motion documents. This is Winston's case."

And while Dade might have some suspicions about the D.A., he wouldn't borrow trouble. Eventually Brennan had to run out of luck and dirty little secrets that had so far kept him from doing any serious jail time.

Plus, there was something else. "Brennan implicated himself today when he gave that statement to his attorney about Alan. Brennan obstructed justice by removing that camera from his son's car. That's another charge we can tack on to the others, and we can use that to revoke his bond and put his sorry butt back in jail. Well, for tonight anyway."

Kayla groaned softly. "That's something, I guess." She eased back a few inches and faced him again. "You've been good to me through all of this. I won't forget it."

Dade stared at her. "That sounds like some kind of goodbye."

She looked ready to say yes, it was. But Dade wasn't about to accept a goodbye. So, he kissed her. Yeah, it wasn't fair. It was ill-timed. But it was also what he needed. Hopefully it was what Kayla needed, too.

"Remember," he said against her mouth, "I'm the guy that makes you forget to breathe." He meant to make it sound light, but it sure didn't come out that way.

Her eyes came to his again, but there was no humor, no teasing. "That's true. And if you don't think that scares me, think again."

He brushed his mouth against hers. "Fear is the last thing I want you to feel when it comes to me."

"Too late." Her words ended in a kiss. A kiss that melted right through him.

Dade returned the favor. "Funny, you don't sound afraid." She sounded aroused, and looked it, too, with her heavy eyelids and flushed cheeks.

He felt her muscles go slack, and she slipped her hands around the back of his neck. "I'm afraid you might stop," she whispered.

Oh, man.

That did it. He was a goner. He hadn't brought Kayla up here to have sex with her, but that was an invitation he couldn't resist.

Dade could think of at least a dozen reasons to quit doing this. Damn good reasons, too. But he couldn't come up with any reason that was stronger than the simple truth. He was burning alive, and Kayla wasn't just the source of the fire, she was the cure.

"Dade," she said, her voice mostly breath, barely a whisper.

But he heard her loud and clear. "Kayla," he managed to say, even though it seemed too much to have the sound of her name leave his mouth.

"Your arm," she reminded him and eased back a little. "Be careful."

Careful and his arm were the last things on his mind right now. Dade didn't think he could keep this together very long. He'd never been a patient, gentle lover. Never had a partner who was interested in anything but hard and fast. He didn't think that was true of Kayla, though.

Restraint, he reminded himself in the same motion that he reached for her.

His hand slid around the back of her neck, and he dragged her to him. His mouth went straight to hers, and in that one touch, that one breath, he took in her scent and taste.

So much for restraint.

"Sorry," he said, taking her mouth the way he wanted to take the rest of her.

"Sorry for what?" she snapped back and stared at him. Her mouth was already swollen from their kisses. Her face was flushed. And her heavy breathing pushed her breasts against his chest.

The sight of her melted him. "Sorry for not giving you an out, for not seducing you the old-fashioned way."

Dade kissed her again. Too hard. And yet it wasn't hard enough. He pressed against her, snaring her in his arms, and dragging her even tighter against him.

"I don't want an out," she mumbled through the kiss. "Old-fashioned is overrated. And I just want you."

He didn't have much breath left, but that pretty much robbed him of the little bit in his lungs. So did the maneuver she made by brushing her sex against his.

Hell.

The bed wasn't far, just a few yards away, but the desk was closer. Grappling for position, they landed against it, the edge ramming into Dade's lower back.

The kisses got crazy hot. Dade couldn't figure out where he wanted to kiss her most, so he settled for any part of her he could reach. Which wasn't easy. Kayla was doing some crazy kisses, too, and she was trying to rid him of his shirt. Dade helped. He ripped it open.

She made a sound of relief and lowered her head to plant some kisses on his chest. It was torture. Her hot, wet mouth moving over his body as if she knew exactly what turned him on.

And she obviously did.

Because she made it all the way to his stomach. And lower. Especially *lower*. When she dropped one of those fire kisses on the front of his jeans, Dade figured this was about to get crazier.

He caught onto her, dragging her back up and turning her so that she was pinned against the desk.

"I want you naked now," he guttered out.

Kayla apparently agreed because she started to do battle with her top. Dade did more than battle. He jerked it over her head and discovered a woman with a flimsy lacy bra. It was barely there, but he removed it anyway.

Kayla was beautiful everywhere. Certain that his theory was correct, he shoved down her pants and pulled them off her. Then, her panties.

Yeah. Beautiful everywhere.

He leaned in, slowly, and touched his mouth to the pink heart tattoo on her breast. She sucked in her breath and froze. She had that deer-caught-in-the-headlights look. She was waiting. And Dade made sure the wait was worth it.

He kissed his way down her stomach. Her skin was like silk. And that scent. Not that he needed it, but it pulled him right in. Dade caught onto her right leg and lifted it over his shoulder so he could kiss her exactly the way he wanted. The way she apparently wanted, too, because she gasped. Moaned. And then cursed.

Dade was positive it was a good sign.

So was the fact that she thrust her hips forward and shoved her hand into his hair.

He would have finished her off then and there, with

the taste of her burning like fire through him. But Kayla obviously didn't want things to play out this way.

She jerked her leg off his shoulder, and with her hand still in his hair, she yanked him back up. Not gently, either. Nor was she gentle with his zipper. Kayla was a woman on a mission, and she batted Dade's hand away when he tried to help. She got his zipper down and shoved her hands into his shorts. Dade could have sworn a freight train rammed through his head.

Restraint, he reminded himself again.

It was as useless as the last reminder. Kayla freed him from his shorts and wrapped her legs around his waist.

Dade did try to ease into her, but that didn't work, either. She was tight, wet and hot. And she used those long legs to push him deep inside her.

She made a sound. Not a gasp or moan this time. Her breath shuddered, and the sound came from deep within her throat. Dade recognized it. It was something beyond pleasure. It was a sound he would have made himself if he could have figured out how to breathe.

The moment seemed to freeze. They were there, their bodies fused together. Their gazes locked. And maybe it was because of that intimate position, Dade knew exactly what she was thinking.

This felt good.

No. Not just *good.* It felt *way too good.* He'd figured sex with Kayla would be extraordinary, but this was a million steps beyond that.

"We're so screwed," he managed to say.

"Oh, yes," she managed to say right back.

They didn't take the time to weigh the consequences of this beyond-sex moment. The moment unfroze. The heat roared through them.

And they dived at each other.

Dade caught onto her hips. Kayla caught onto his back and his neck, digging her fingers into his skin and completing the thrusts inside her.

He felt her closing in around him. She was so near climax. This was usually the part when he buried his face in his partner's neck and went to that dark primal place where the only thing that mattered was finishing what he'd started. First her, so he could rid his body of this fire that was consuming him.

But he didn't do that this time.

Dade never took his eyes off her, even though his vision was blurred. He knew this would be over too quickly, and he wanted to see every moment. Record every touch, every sensation.

He wasn't disappointed.

And he wondered how many times in life reality lived up to a man's fantasy.

Kayla sure did.

She met each of his thrusts, but her grip went gentle on his neck. Her fingers stilled but not her body. The climax wracked through her and she reached for him, pulling him closer. So he was careful.

Gentle.

And it was that gentle coaxing and that look in her eyes that ended it all for him. Dade thrust into her one last time and let himself fall.

Right into Kayla's waiting arms.

Chapter Fourteen

If Dade hadn't kept a grip on her, Kayla was certain she would have slid right to the floor.

All in all, that might not be such a bad thing because Dade and she were half-naked, but with the climax high already starting to fade, Kayla knew that sooner or later they would have to talk.

Best not to be naked on the floor when that happened.

She was out of breath again. Felt as if her bones had dissolved to dust, but Dade obviously had a burst of energy. He scooped her up, deposited her on the bed that was only about twenty feet away. He had the good sense to fix his jeans so that at least one of them would be semipresentable if someone knocked on the door.

Kayla got a good look at him while he was dressing. Mercy. No man deserved a body like that. Lanky but with just enough muscles to make him interesting. And then there were the tattoos. A small dragon on his left shoulder blade and a badge on his hip. Appropriate because he was a lawman to the core.

"I know," he mumbled, sounding disgusted with

himself. He dropped down on his side next to her. "I'm sorry."

Well, that took care of any shreds of a sexual buzz. Kayla just stared at him until Dade cursed.

"Hell, I'm not sorry for *that*," Dade amended. But that didn't clarify anything until he leaned down and kissed her. "I'm sorry I didn't use a condom."

Oh. Kayla might have cursed too if her throat hadn't snapped shut.

"I'm not on the pill," she was finally able to let him know. Mainly because it'd been a year and half since she'd had sex. "But I think we'll be okay. It's the wrong time of the month."

She didn't want to get into a discussion about her irregular cycle. Nor did she want to think about this one-time sex with Dade making her pregnant. Good grief. She wasn't a kid, and even though this need for Dade had consumed her, she still should have remembered to take the simple precaution of using a condom.

He got on the bed with her, slid his arm beneath her neck and drew her closer. Just like that, her thoughts about the unsafe sex faded, and Dade—and his incredible body—took control of her mind.

"For the record, you're not as delicate as you look," he whispered.

"Delicate?" Again, she wasn't sure how to take that. "I hope that didn't disappoint you."

"Nothing about you disappointed me." And yes, there was some frustration in his voice. She understood that. Kayla was frustrated at the strength of all of this. "Besides, I wouldn't be a good fit with delicate. You're more my match."

He dropped a kiss on the top of her breast. Right on her tattoo. He might as well have poured warm wax over her because the heat went through her entire body. A slow hunger that was still there despite what had happened just minutes earlier.

"Why a tattoo?" he asked, kissing her breast again. This time, he used his tongue on her nipple.

It took a moment to form words, and her fingers found their way into his hair. "A way of rebelling."

"With a pink heart?" he mocked.

She dredged up a smile. "My rebellion has a feminine side. I wanted something pretty." And it was impossible to concentrate with his hand trailing down her back. The slow hunger suddenly wasn't so slow.

"You've got *pretty* nailed down." His breath was hot when he blew it over her nipple that he had wet with his mouth.

Kayla's breath broke, and that hunger suddenly became hot, slick and all-consuming. "What are you doing to me?" she begged.

"Post-sex foreplay." He flashed a grin that could have seduced her all by itself. But that wasn't necessary because Dade had other lethal weapons in his arsenal.

Kayla knew this would lead straight to a broken heart, but she pulled him to her anyway. She wanted his mouth. His body. She wanted all of him, all over again.

At first, she thought the buzzing was in her head,

but then Dade cursed and snatched up the phone on the table next to the bed.

"Dade," he snarled.

Kayla, too, wanted to curse at the interruption, but then she forced herself to remember that one floor beneath them in the sheriff's office there was a major investigation going on. One that was a matter of life and death—*hers*.

Dade put his hand over the receiver. "It's Misty. And she says that she has to talk to you now."

Kayla didn't even try to choke back a huff. She wanted to hear from her sister, was worried about her, but Misty's timing wasn't good. Kayla got up, sandwiched the phone between her shoulder and ear so she could dress while she talked.

Dade lifted an eyebrow at that, but he, too, put his shirt back on. Bedtime was over, much too soon, and it hurt to think this might be the one and only time she would get to have Dade.

"I'm here," Kayla said to her sister.

"I've been trying to reach you," Misty fired at her. "When you didn't answer your cell, I called the sheriff's office, and some woman said she'd connect me. Are you really at the sheriff's office?"

"I'm here." And Kayla decided to get straight to business. "Where are you and why did you take all that money from your bank account?"

Misty made a sound. Maybe surprise. Maybe outrage. It was hard to tell. "Someone's following me. I'm afraid Charles or someone is after me."

Kayla was worried for her sister, but she wished she

had more energy to deal with this. "Why would Charles have someone follow you?" She reached over and put the call on speaker so Dade could hear the answer.

"I don't know!" Misty practically yelled. "Why does Charles do anything?"

"I could say the same about you," Kayla countered. "Explain why you took the money from your account and the gun from your roommate."

Her sister made another of those sounds. "Because I'm scared. Didn't you hear what I said? Someone's following me. I need to see you. *Now.* And I don't want any of the cops around. I want us to be alone, so we can talk."

Dade shook his head.

Kayla knew he was right. The last thing she needed was to be out and about to meet with Misty. "We can talk at the Silver Creek sheriff's office," Kayla pointed out.

"No, we can't. The cops think I've done something wrong, and I haven't. Well, not intentionally anyway."

Kayla groaned and sank onto the edge of the bed. She was a hundred-percent certain she wasn't going to like this. "What did you do?" she demanded.

"Nothing!" Misty hesitated after that outburst. "I didn't know it was Charles who bought that painting, okay? I didn't know."

Kayla didn't even bother to choke back a groan. This was not what she wanted to hear.

"When did you find out Charles was the buyer?" Dade asked.

Misty made another sound. This one was definitely

from outrage. "He's listening to us? Why would you do that, Kayla? Why would you let him hear a private conversation?"

"Because there's too much at stake for this to be private," Kayla explained. "Now answer Dade's question—when did you learn Charles had bought the painting?"

Her sister took her time answering. "I figured it out a few days ago. Someone called, a man who didn't identify himself. He said he'd bought the painting as a favor and he wanted me to tell him where you were. I didn't know, but when I told him that, he didn't believe me."

Kayla could only shake her head. "The man who called was likely Danny Flynn, who's in custody for attempted murder. Or maybe it was Raymond Salvetti, who's dead."

"Like I said, I don't know because he didn't give me his name," her sister insisted.

"Did you specifically see someone following you?" Dade pressed.

"No, but I can feel it!" Misty snapped. "And I'm done talking to you. Kayla, I have to see you now."

Kayla took a moment, not because she was debating her response—she wasn't—but she wanted to word this as clearly as possible. Even though any wording would cause Misty to pitch a fit. "It's too dangerous for me to meet with you anywhere but here."

Her sister used some raw profanity. "I can't believe you're choosing that cop over me."

Kayla was about to explain this had nothing to do

with Dade, or choices, but Misty slammed down the phone.

Dade pulled in a hard breath, took the phone from Kayla and tapped the receiver. "Mel," he said to the deputy who apparently answered, "did you get a trace on Misty Wallace's location?"

Kayla couldn't hear the answer, but she saw the frustrated look on Dade's face. "All right. Thanks."

"Where is she?" Kayla asked.

"In town. The call came from the hotel at the end of Main Street."

Oh, mercy. Why hadn't Misty just told her that? Maybe because her sister was genuinely worried that Charles or someone else would find her location?

Or maybe Misty had sinister reasons?

"Don't go there yet," Dade said in that I-know-what-you're-thinking tone. He slid his arm around her. "Focus on the good."

The good. Well, she certainly had some of that. Her son was at the top of that list. The fact that he was safe with Dade's brother was another *good.* And then there was Dade. A *good* of a different kind.

The question came to her, and Kayla didn't even try to stop it. "What will happen when this is all over?"

He tipped his head to the bed. Smiled. "More of that, I hope."

Kayla didn't want to smile. But she did. "Your brothers won't approve."

"They're coming around." He brushed his mouth over hers. Instant heat.

"And in the meantime?" Kayla kissed him back.

"We just remember to breathe when one of us walks into a room."

She laughed. Couldn't help herself. "You're never going to let me forget that, are you?"

"Never," he promised.

Kayla felt herself floating and realized Dade was easing her back onto the bed. She would have gone willingly, but the phone buzzed again.

"Misty," she snapped.

Dade growled something much worse but answered the call. "This better be important," he warned the caller.

But it must have been important because Dade went still. He just listened for what had to be a full minute and then finally said. "No. I'll escort Kayla there."

That brought her off the bed. "You're not taking me to see Misty," she challenged.

Dade shook his head. "Brennan's request for another trial delay was denied. The judge wants you at the courthouse in the morning so you can testify."

MORNING HAD COME way too soon for Dade. The night had flown by despite neither Kayla nor him getting much sleep. Both of them had tossed and turned.

And ached.

Well, he'd ached anyway, and he was pretty sure Kayla had done the same.

Despite the great sex they'd had on the desk, his body had kept on burning for her even after Misty's call and the news that Kayla would be testifying soon. But Dade had finally managed to show a little restraint.

There were no condoms in the apartment, and he hadn't wanted to leave her alone to go get any. Besides, she had needed rest.

Not sex.

Except somewhere in the night, sex had felt like a need more than sleep. More than common sense. More than anything. Thankfully, Dade had kept his hands off her so they wouldn't have a repeat round of amazing but unsafe sex.

Kayla had started her morning with a breakfast sandwich and coffee that Mason had delivered and a phone call to Robbie. Despite the gloomy cloud of the trial hanging over her, talking to the baby had helped her mood. It'd helped Dade, too, though he felt a little guilty for stealing some of her parenthood pleasure.

Now, Dade finished up some emails and made some calls while Kayla showered and dressed in the bathroom. They had plenty of time to get to the courthouse, almost an hour, and it was just up the street. Still, Dade knew he would breathe easier once he had Kayla in the witness room where she would remain until she testified against Brennan.

"And then what?" he mumbled to himself.

With luck, the trial would end soon. Brennan would be behind bars. And the reason Kayla was in his protective custody would end, as well.

Dade refused to dwell on that. He had to focus on getting Kayla to the courthouse and up on that witness stand. After that, well, he'd deal with all of that later. However, he couldn't dismiss that he had complicated the heck out of their situation by sleeping with her. Not just sex.

But making love to her.

Cuddling with her in bed was not a good way to sort out his feelings for her. It was just another complication.

She stepped out from the bathroom, and there was complication number three. She looked amazing. So beautiful. And it wasn't the clothes. The gray top and skirt that had been picked up from her estate was pretty much nondescript. The kind of outfit someone would wear to court. It was the woman wearing the clothes that made them look amazing.

Dade mentally cursed.

All this *amazing* junk had to stop. He had to clear his head so he could concentrate on getting Kayla through her testimony. He was doing a decent job with his concentration until she crossed the room and dropped a kiss on his mouth.

"You look like a cop," she muttered.

Dade glanced down at his usual black shirt and jeans with the badge clipped to his belt.

"That's a compliment," Kayla assured him.

Oh. Suddenly he felt *amazing* again, so he gave in to it and kissed her. Not a peck, either. Dade made this one long and hard. When he finally let go of her, they both were smiling big goofy smiles.

Oh, yeah.

This concentration stuff was working well.

"It'll be okay," she assured him. But then Kayla

blinked. "It will be okay, right? You didn't get any bad news when you were on the phone?"

"Nothing bad," he assured her. "In fact, some of it is actually good news. Flynn was transported to the county jail last night, and he begged Winston for a deal. Flynn will testify against Brennan in exchange for a reduced sentence."

Her smile wasn't so goofy now. Her nerves were showing. "Because Flynn tried to kill me, I hope it's not a too short sentence."

"It won't be," he promised. And he would make sure of it. "Winston told Brennan's attorney about the deal with Flynn. Let's just say Brennan is not a happy camper."

She blew out a breath of relief, then stared at him. "You're right, that is good news. But does that mean there's bad news, too?"

He made a so-so motion with his hand. "Alan is out of jail on bond," he continued. "But a deputy from a neighboring town is keeping tabs on him."

Her eyes widened. "You think Alan will try to run or something?"

The *or something* hiked up her nerves. "No, Mason said Alan was ready to take his punishment. He'll be charged with intoxicated manslaughter which is a second-degree felony, and we'll also tack on leaving the scene of a crime. There's no way around it. He'll see some jail time, and he'll lose his law license."

Kayla nodded. "I'm betting Charles planned to use Alan to help him get out of this trial."

"No doubt, but it didn't work." He ran his hand down her arm, hoping it would help soothe her.

"And Misty?" she asked. "Any word from her?"

Dade had to shake his head. This fell into the bad news category. "No other calls from Misty. The Rangers traced her call to the hotel, but she wasn't there when they arrived just minutes after she finished talking to us."

Another hitch in the nerves department for Kayla. Her mouth trembled a little. "Once I've testified, I'll see if I can get in touch with her."

Dade didn't try to talk her out of that. He wouldn't have succeeded anyway because, for better or worse, Misty would always be her sister.

Kayla moved away from him and picked up the pants she'd worn the previous day. The ones that Dade had practically ripped off her. She reached into the pocket and retrieved something.

His silver concho.

"For luck," she said, and she slipped it into her bra, probably because she had no pockets in the outfit she was wearing.

Dade couldn't imagine the concho being lucky, but he wasn't about to argue with her. Whatever got her through this morning was fine with him. He only hoped it didn't set off the metal detector in the courthouse. His brothers would have a field day with his trying to explain why Kayla had his concho in her lacy pink bra.

"Ready?" he asked, checking his watch. "Mason should be waiting for us."

"Mason?" she questioned.

"I wanted two of us to escort you to the courthouse." He tried to toss that out there casually, as if going outside a single block was no big deal. But her safety was the biggest deal of all to him, and Dade wanted to take every precaution.

"Thank you," she whispered as they walked out.

They went down the stairs where Mason was waiting for them. He had his shoulder propped against the wall while he read something on his phone.

"A problem?" Dade asked.

"Just ranch business."

Yeah, the ranch ate up a major part of Mason's time, and Dade didn't want to think of how many hours they'd all spend playing catch-up when this was done.

The building was quiet for a change. Grayson was on his way back from the safe house with Robbie and Connie. Mel was at the jail with Brennan and his attorney. That left the other deputy, Luis Lopez, and the dispatcher, Tina Fox, to man the sheriff's office. But hopefully nothing else would go wrong before they had their full staff back in place.

"It's only a block away," Dade let her know. "But we're driving." With Misty unaccounted for and Alan out on bond, he wanted to be careful.

Mason and Dade put her between them and hurried to the cruiser that Mason already had waiting. They didn't waste any time, and as soon as the three of them were inside the vehicle, Dade drove away.

It took him longer to get out of the parking lot and onto Main Street than it did to drive the block. Dade didn't let down his guard, and in fact his guard sky-rocketed when he pulled up next to the courthouse and spotted Brennan.

"Charles," Kayla mumbled, obviously spotting him as well.

Brennan was in handcuffs, and Mel was heading to the side entrance of the courthouse. Probably to avoid the photographers and news crew out front.

Dade and Mason got out first, positioning Kayla behind them. Out of Brennan's line of sight. Or rather that was the plan. But Brennan saw her anyway because he came to a dead stop. No smirk or smile today.

Brennan shot them an ice-cold glare.

"Happy with yourself, Kayla?" he called out.

She didn't answer, but Dade hated that she had to be this close to the devil himself. Dade looked back to reassure her, but then he heard Mason.

"Hell," his brother growled, and from the corner of his eye, he saw Mason reach for his gun.

Dade automatically did the same. He drew his gun and took aim.

But it was already too late.

Despite the cuffs, Brennan rammed his elbow into the deputy's stomach. His motion was seamless. And fast. Too fast for Dade to get off a clean shot.

Brennan grabbed the Glock from Mel's holster and put it to the deputy's head.

Chapter Fifteen

Kayla was too stunned to move and could only stand there and watch in horror at the nightmare happening right in front of her. Charles had finally lost it, and he looked ready to kill the deputy on the spot.

"If anyone moves, she dies!" Charles shouted.

Mel froze, and Dade and Mason stood there with their guns trained on him.

"Stay behind me," Dade whispered to Kayla.

She did, but she hated that once again Dade and his brother and now Mel were taking the ultimate risk to keep her alive.

Charles kept the gun pressed to Mel's head, and he inched back until he was right against the brick exterior wall. He probably did that so no one could sneak up on him and grab the gun, but he had to realize that he couldn't escape.

Or maybe not.

Kayla got a sickening feeling. Was this some kind of calculated escape plan? Maybe he had someone nearby ready to assist.

Kayla's gaze darted around the crowd of people

who, like her, had come to a dead stop. No one looked ready to spring to Charles's aid, but that didn't mean he hadn't managed to pay off one or more of them to help him escape.

Or even kill her.

The crowd and the buildings on each side of them essentially meant they were trapped, literally in the parking lot between the two-story courthouse and the town's mortuary. They weren't close enough to either building just to duck inside. Of course, there was the cruiser and a few other vehicles they could take cover behind if it became necessary.

"Drop the gun, Brennan!" Dade ordered.

Now Charles smiled. "Not on your life. Or I should say, not on Kayla's life, because we both know she's the one I want." He dug his gun into the deputy's head. "The cop here is just a poor substitute."

Oh, God. Was he going to try to trade Mel for her? Kayla didn't want the woman hurt, but if she traded positions with the deputy, Kayla figured it would be like signing her own death warrant.

"Mr. Brennan?" his attorney, Darcy Burkhart, called out. She was in the crowd but was making her way toward them. "Stop this, please. And put down the gun."

"Stay back," Mason warned the lawyer, and thankfully she froze. Kayla didn't want Charles to have any excuse to go on a shooting spree.

"What now?" Mason tossed out to Charles. "We just all wait outside until we freeze to death or your hand gets tired?"

The corner of Charles's mouth lifted again. "I like your bedside manner, Deputy. No, we don't wait. Kayla will walk toward me, and I'll let the good cop here go."

Kayla felt everything inside her turn to ice. She couldn't stand there and let Mel die.

"You're not going anywhere," Dade warned Kayla when she took a step forward.

Mason and Dade closed ranks, stepping closer to each other so that it created a barrier between Charles and her.

"But Mel…" Kayla protested.

"He's not going to kill her," Dade whispered to her from over his shoulder. "Right now, Mel is the only thing stopping him from dying."

Even though the blood was rushing through her, causing her pulse to pound in her head, Kayla forced herself to think that through. Dade was right. Charles was too narcissistic to commit suicide, and that's exactly what he would be doing if he killed Mel.

"Well?" Charles challenged.

"There is no *well,*" Dade challenged right back. "You can't escape. The only thing you can do is give Deputy Garza back her gun and then go into the courthouse so we can get on with this trial."

"It's not a trial," Charles argued. "It's a lynch mob. I know what you did—talking that idiot Flynn into telling his lies so he could get a lighter sentence. You should have offered the deal to me, Deputy Ryland, because Flynn has blood on his hands."

Kayla shuddered. Even though she knew Flynn was

a criminal, she couldn't imagine anyone dirtier than Charles.

"Thirty seconds," Charles added. "That's all the time you boys have. If Kayla isn't over here by then, I'll start shooting."

That caused a ripple of chatter through the crowd, and even though Kayla didn't want to risk looking back, she heard some of them running. Good, because she was afraid this could turn ugly very fast.

"No deal," Dade answered. "Kayla stays put."

Charles lifted his shoulder. "Then in twenty seconds, I'll kill someone, and I'll keep killing until I have Kayla."

"Get ready to jump behind the cruiser," Dade warned her in a whisper.

But Kayla didn't get ready. She stared at Charles from over Dade's and Mason's shoulders. She had only one thing that she could use to reason with Charles, and it turned her stomach to have to do it.

"Charles, think this through," Kayla called out to him. "Preston is dead, and if you kill me, then Robbie will be an orphan. You'll never get to know him because you'll be on death row. Is that what you want for your only grandchild?"

"Robbie," Charles repeated, and there seemed to be some regret in his voice. "It's unfortunate but necessary. Besides, I have good lawyers, and that death penalty might not even happen. You'd be surprised how many legal loopholes gobs of money can find. In fact, I think I feel an insanity plea coming on."

Kayla's heart dropped. She'd held out a shred of

hope that she could reason with him if she used Robbie, but Charles was too far gone to listen to any reason.

"Jump behind the cruiser," Dade ordered her.

"You and Mason, too," she insisted.

But the words had hardly left her mouth when the sounds cracked through the air.

Oh, God.

Charles fired the gun.

DADE TURNED, HOOKED his arm around Kayla's waist and dragged her behind the cruiser. Mason went the other direction and ducked behind an SUV.

"Get down!" Dade shouted to the crowd who all thankfully seemed to be scrambling for cover.

He couldn't tell if the bullet had actually hit anyone. There were shouts, screams and the sounds of all hell breaking loose.

Brennan's lawyer was still begging for him to surrender, but Dade was pretty sure that wasn't going to happen. Her client had just attempted murder in front of dozens of witnesses, and Brennan seemed to be in the mode of last resort.

Unfortunately, *last resort* could get someone killed.

Dade peered around the cruiser. Brennan now had his handcuffed wrists looped around Mel's neck, and the gun was aimed outward, toward the dispersing crowd.

And toward Kayla.

Mel looked pale and shaky. Rightfully so. She'd been a deputy for twenty years now and had never faced anything like this.

Behind him, Kayla wasn't looking steady, either. Her mouth was trembling, teeth chattering, breath gusting, and she was praying.

"Grayson can't come driving into this with Robbie and Connie," she mumbled.

"He won't. By now he's already gotten a half-dozen calls and is arranging for backup."

Dade was sure of that, but what they needed was a hostage negotiator. Nate, preferably. This was one of his areas of expertise, and Dade hoped like the devil Nate was nearby or on his way.

"Kayla?" Brennan yelled. And he shouted her name several times in that same mocking tone.

Each shout made her tremble harder, and Dade wished he could slam his fist right into the man's face to shut him up. He was sick of the games Brennan was playing and even sicker of the effect it was having on Kayla.

"You planning to die today, Brennan?" Dade yelled back. He didn't figure for one minute that would put any fear in the man, but he needed to do something, anything, to rattle this SOB.

"Not me. No plans to die," Brennan assured him. "The deputy here probably didn't have plans, either, but that's exactly what will happen if Kayla doesn't get over here. Now!" he shouted at the top of his lungs.

"Oh, God," Kayla mumbled. She inched closer to Dade. "I have to go out there. I can't let him kill Mel."

Dade had to get his jaw unclenched before he could speak. "This isn't up for discussion. You aren't going out there because Brennan will gun you down before you make it to him. Then, he'll use Mel as a human shield to escape. If he manages that, he'll kill her, too, and anyone else he can take out in the process."

Dade glanced at her to make sure that had sunk in. It had. She nodded. And Kayla got a new look in her eyes. "I have to do something."

"Brennan will make a mistake," he assured her. "And when he does, Mason will have him."

Dade tipped his head to his brother who was about ten yards away. Mason wasn't looking back at the crowd. He had his attention nailed to Brennan, and his gun was ready. Thank God Mason had a steady hand and a deadly aim.

"Kayla!" Brennan shouted again. But this time, it wasn't just a shout. Brennan fired another shot, and this one slammed into the cruiser.

Dade cursed and pulled Kayla lower to the ground, but he wasn't sure that was any safer because a bullet could go underneath the car and hit her.

"How many bullets does he have?" Kayla asked.

Too many. Mel's gun was a full-sized 9 mm Glock, and it held seventeen rounds. That meant Brennan had fifteen more chances to try to kill as many of them as possible. But Dade kept that to himself.

"Mason, if you get a shot, take it," Dade shouted, although that order was just for Brennan's benefit. To remind him that any second now he could have bullets flying at him. Mason certainly didn't need permission to take out a would-be killer.

"How many bullets does he have left?" Kayla pressed.

Dade huffed. "Fifteen."

She huffed, too. "We have to do something to make him use up those rounds."

Yeah. Dade's mind was already trying to work that out. He could maybe move Kayla to another vehicle for cover and put the cruiser in gear and send it Brennan's way. Of course, that was a long shot because Brennan might realize the cruiser was driverless and not fire. Then, there was the danger of moving Kayla. He needed her out of this parking lot.

And then Dade saw a possible game changer.

Nate.

His brother was at the end of the morgue and was peering around the corner of the building. Nate wasn't exactly concealed, and Brennan would no doubt be able to see him if he looked in that direction.

Hell.

He hoped Nate didn't do anything stupid, especially considering his state of mind. After all, it had been only hours since Nate had learned that Brennan was almost certainly the man behind Ellie's murder.

Dade glanced at Mason who was motioning for Nate to get back. Brennan couldn't have seen Mason, either, but something must have alerted him because he turned his head in Nate's direction.

"No!" Kayla shouted, obviously aware of what was happening.

Dade couldn't risk firing a warning shot because it could ricochet and hit someone. But he had to do something before Nate stepped out and offered himself in exchange for Mel. Brennan would only kill him.

"Give me the concho," Dade said to Kayla.

Kayla's eyes widened, but she took it from her bra. The moment that Dade had it in his hand, he tossed it straight toward Brennan.

It worked.

Brennan's attention snapped in the direction of the silver concho when it plinked onto the concrete parking lot. He fired at it.

And then everything went crazy.

Mel must have realized this was her chance to get away because she dropped to the ground, and since Brennan's handcuffed wrists were looped around her neck, she pulled him down with her.

"Stay here. I mean it," Dade warned Kayla, and he rushed out to help Mel.

Nate and Mason did the same, all three of them converging on what was now a fight to save Mel. The deputy had her hands fisted around Brennan's wrist so that he couldn't aim the gun at her.

But that meant the gun was aimed pretty much everywhere else.

Dade ran toward the scuffle and kept his own weapon ready. Mason and Dade did the same. They could only watch as Brennan kicked Mel, trying to wrench her hands off his wrist.

A kick to her stomach did the trick.

Mel fell back, gasping for air, and her hands dropped from Brennan's. However, she wasn't completely out of Dade's and Mason's line of fire.

Brennan grabbed at Mel, no doubt to use her again as a human shield, but he blindly fired the gun in Dade and Mason's direction. The bullet went into the air, missing them, but Dade knew once Brennan had control of Mel that the next bullet would almost certainly find a target.

Hopefully not Kayla.

Dade prayed she was still behind the car where he'd told her to stay.

Brennan latched onto Mel's hair, and Dade cursed when he realized he still didn't have a clean shot. He was so focused on finding a solid shot that it stunned him when he heard the sound.

The familiar thick blast.

A bullet.

The shot slammed into the side of Brennan's chest, but it didn't bring him down. Brennan stopped, and his attention zoomed to his left.

To Nate, the man who'd just shot him.

But it was too late for Brennan to duck and take cover. Nate fired a second shot directly into Brennan.

Brennan mumbled something.

Then he dropped to the ground.

Chapter Sixteen

Kayla held her breath and prayed those shots hadn't hit Dade.

She'd obeyed Dade's order to stay put, but she couldn't stay down. Kayla peeked over the cruiser to make sure Dade and everyone else was all right.

So far, so good.

Thank God. Dade, Mason and Nate were all still standing. Mel, too.

But she couldn't say the same for Charles.

He was on the grassy strip by the exterior courthouse wall, and Kayla watched as Mason went to him and put his fingers against Charles's throat. Mason shook his head.

"Is he dead?" Kayla asked, but there wasn't enough sound in her voice for it to carry.

Still, Dade must have heard her because he said something to Mason, turned and hurried toward her. He holstered his gun and pulled her into his arms.

"It's all right," he whispered. "Charles is dead."

"Dead," she repeated. Despite Dade's grip on

her, she started to walk toward the body. She had to make sure.

"He's dead, Kayla," Dade tried again.

But Kayla kept going. Of course Dade was plenty strong enough to stop her, but he must have sensed that this was something she needed to do.

As she approached the body, Mason stepped away to go to Nate. Nate didn't look any steadier than Kayla felt. Probably because he'd just had to kill a man. Kayla leaned down and as Mason had done, she put her hand against his neck to feel for a pulse.

Nothing.

But when she drew back her hand, she saw the blood, Charles's blood, on her fingers.

She stared at the blood and braced herself for whatever emotions were about to slam through her. But Kayla was surprised that she felt nothing but relief. Maybe that made her a sick person, but for the first time in years, she felt free, and she could give her son a safe and happy life.

Some of the crowd came forward, as well. Charles's attorney was at the front of the pack and kept mumbling how sorry she was to Nate and Mason. Winston was there, too. But Kayla picked through the people and caught Nate's gaze.

"Thank you," she mouthed.

He nodded, but this had to be a bitter relief for him. He'd finally gotten his wife's killer. However, that wouldn't give him back his wife.

"You don't need to be here," Dade told her, and he

would have ushered her out of there that very moment if Kayla hadn't held her ground.

Kayla walked closer to Mel. The deputy was bruised and scraped up, but her physical injuries didn't look serious. "What did Charles say right before he died?"

Mel glanced at Dade as if seeking his permission, but Kayla stepped between them and looked Mel straight in the eyes. "Tell me, please."

For several moments, Kayla didn't think the deputy would do it, but Mel finally lifted her shoulders. "He said, 'Tell Kayla it's not over.'"

Both Dade and Mason cursed, but it was Dade who got Kayla moving. This time digging in her heels didn't help because Dade scooped her up and carried her to the police cruiser. The moment they were inside, he drove away, leaving the chaos of a crime scene behind them.

"Brennan said that to get in one last jab," Dade insisted.

No doubt, but it made her sick to think that he hated her so much that he wanted her to be tormented even after his death.

"Grayson will be back soon with Robbie and Connie," Dade reminded her.

She nodded, thankful that soon she would be able to hold her baby. But even now, just minutes after Charles's death, she was already thinking, what was next?

Where would she go, and what would she do?

There would be no trial, so there was no need for her to stay in town. Or Silver Creek for that matter. She cringed at the idea of going to her estate because there was probably still blood and shot-out windows from the attack where Salvetti and Flynn had tried to kill her.

Besides, there were no good memories there.

But where?

It surprised her to realize her best memories were those with Robbie and Dade. The oatmeal breakfast in the kitchen at the ranch safe house. The phone conversation Dade had had with Robbie after Grayson had gotten her son to safety. How had her life, and her heart, become so tangled with Dade's that it was hard for her to imagine a future without him?

"Are you okay?" Dade asked her.

"Yes." But they both knew it was a lie. The adrenaline was roaring through her, and the thoughts and images were firing through her head.

Especially the images.

She didn't want to close her eyes and see Charles, or his blood on her hands, but she did, and Kayla wondered when this part of the nightmare would finally go away.

Dade parked behind the sheriff's building and ushered her in. Judging from the deputy and dispatcher's somber faces, they'd already heard the news.

"Grayson needs to talk to you," Tina, the dispatcher, relayed to Dade. "Nothing's wrong with your baby," she quickly assured Kayla. "He just needs to go over some police business with Dade."

Dade reached for his cell, but then stopped. He glanced down at her hands. "Why don't you go upstairs and wash up? Once Robbie is here, I can take all of you out to the ranch."

Kayla blinked. "The ranch?"

"For some downtime," Dade clarified. "The town will be buzzing with reporters and gawkers for the next couple of days."

Of course. Because this would be big news. It was possible the entire thing had been caught on film by a camera crew and would be replayed over and over on the news channels.

Dade nudged her in the direction of the stairs, and Kayla forced one foot ahead of the other. Each step seemed to take way too much energy, probably because she was in shock, but she would get this blood off her hands.

The apartment was just as Dade and she had left it, and her attention went straight to the bed with the rumpled covers. The place where Dade had made love to her. Or maybe it had just been sex for him. Later, she would sort all of that out, but for now she needed her son. Once she had Robbie in her arms, she didn't intend to let go for a long time.

She made her way to the bathroom and turned the water on full blast in the sink. Kayla grabbed the bar of soap and started to scrub.

The tears came.

They sprang to her eyes so quickly that she didn't have time to try to blink them back. She hated Charles for what he'd done, but she couldn't completely dismiss the waste of a human life. Robbie's blood kin. His grandfather. A man her son would never know.

Kayla stared into the sink as the blood-tinged water and soap suds spiraled down the drain. She reached to turn off the faucet, but she saw something out of the corner of her eye.

A gun.

She got just a glimpse of it before the arm curved around her neck, and the barrel of the gun jammed against her back.

"Like Charles said, it's not over, Kayla," the person growled in her ear.

"Tina said we needed to talk," Dade greeted Grayson when his brother answered.

"You okay?" Grayson immediately asked.

"Yeah." And that was mostly true. Kayla and he had come out of a dangerous situation without a scratch, and that was nothing short of a miracle. Still, it would be a while before he wouldn't think of how close Kayla had come to dying—again.

"How's Kayla?" Grayson continued.

"Shaken up more than she'll admit. Seeing Robbie will help. How long before you get here?"

"About fifteen minutes. I kept Robbie and Connie at the sheriff's house down in Floresville."

No wonder it was taking Grayson so long to get here. Floresville was an hour and a half away from Silver Creek. But it was smart for his brother to take them that far away. As bad as the ordeal with Brennan had been, it would have been much worse if Robbie had been put in danger, too.

"What are you going to do about Kayla?" Grayson wanted to know.

Good question, but Dade didn't have an answer that his brother would like. "I want to keep seeing her," Dade confessed. "Do you have a problem with that?"

"No, and neither will anyone else in the family," Grayson said as gospel. And it would be. Even though they were all adults now, Grayson was still head of the Rylands, and what he said was pretty much a go.

"Thank you," Dade mumbled.

"Don't thank me yet. We've all got some long hours ahead of us to tie up this Brennan mess."

Yeah. And the mess that Alan had left them. "I'll let Kayla know that Robbie will be here soon."

Dade ended the call and hurried toward the stairs. Despite the fact he'd just witnessed a man's death, he was feeling darn good. The green light from Grayson was no doubt responsible for that and so was the woman waiting for him in the apartment. Dade only hoped that Kayla wasn't standing up there trying to figure out how to tell him that it was over between them, that she couldn't stay in Silver Creek any longer.

His good mood faded a bit.

And then it vanished completely when he opened the apartment door and saw Kayla's expression. She was in the doorway of the bathroom, and her face was paper-white.

"What's wrong?" Dade asked, and he went to her so he could pull her into his arms.

But he froze when he saw the gun.

His stomach crashed to the floor, and every muscle

in his body went into fight mode. He reached for his weapon.

"Don't!" someone warned. It was the person on the other end of that gun.

It was a woman's voice, and one that Dade instantly recognized.

"Carrie," he spat out. "What the hell do you think you're doing?"

"Tying up loose ends," Carrie calmly answered. "I thought I'd be finished doing that before you got here. Guess not. I really hadn't planned on killing you, too, but you got here a little sooner than I figured. Now, take out your gun using only two fingers and toss it onto the counter. Do anything stupid, and I'll kill her where she stands."

Dade believed her. He didn't know why Carrie was doing this, but there was no hesitation in her voice.

"Your gun," Carrie repeated. "Put it on the counter. Now."

Dade hated to surrender his weapon, but he had no other choice. He couldn't stand there and watch Carrie kill Kayla. So Dade did as this nutjob asked and laid his gun on the counter.

Carrie inched Kayla forward but not too far. Carrie's back stayed to the bathroom where there were no windows and therefore no way for anyone to sneak up on her. That meant Dade was going to have to figure out how to disarm both Carrie and this situation.

"Brennan is dead," Dade told Carrie.

"Yeah, I saw it happen. When I realized he'd been killed, I sneaked in the back. Tina was busy on the phone and didn't see me so I came up here and waited. I knew you'd have Kayla wash the blood from her hands."

Even though her every word was critical, Dade listened to make sure no one was coming up the stairs. Grayson would be arriving soon, and Dade didn't want Robbie coming into this.

Dade looked past Kayla. Or rather, tried. Hard to do with that look of stark fear on her face. God, she didn't need to go through anything else. But Dade pushed that aside and snagged Carrie's gaze.

"Is this about me? About us?" he asked. "Because if it is, then this isn't the way to win me back."

Carrie laughed, a quick burst of air, but there was no humor in it. "No, it's not about you. Well, maybe just a little. Let's just say I probably wouldn't have taken the job if you hadn't dumped me for her." She gave Kayla a hard jam to the back.

Hell.

"We broke up months ago," Dade reminded her, although he doubted she would listen to reason. After all, Carrie was holding Kayla at gunpoint. "And if this isn't about me, what is it about?"

"Money," Carrie volunteered.

"Charles is paying her off," Kayla provided. She still had some fear in her expression, but now there was anger, too.

"Hard to pay someone off if he's dead." Dade kept his attention fastened to Carrie. Especially her trigger finger. If it tensed, then he was going to have to dive at the women and pray for the best.

"Charles set it up before Nate killed him. One of his offshore lawyers is holding the money for me. All he has to see is Kayla's death certificate, and the cash is mine." Unlike Kayla, there wasn't a shred of emotion in Carrie's voice. All ice. "He sent instructions through one of his employees for me to help him. First, I took Kayla's phone from her car and made it look as if she'd been in touch with Salvetti."

Well, that was one mystery solved, and it probably had been easy because Carrie had come to the estate in her official role as a paramedic.

"And then Brennan told you to do this?" Dade tipped his head to her gun.

"Yes," Carrie answered. "He said I was to tie up loose ends if he could no longer do it."

"I'm a loose end," Kayla added. Her gaze drifted to the door, and Dade knew she was thinking about Grayson's arrival. This had to end before his brother came up the stairs with Robbie and Connie.

"So Brennan paid you to kill Kayla?" Dade asked. "Why would you agree to do that? Is this really just about the money?"

"The money...and her." Carrie glared at Kayla. "I was in love with Preston, and she took him from me. She didn't care that she broke my heart. Heck, I'll bet she didn't even love him. She just didn't want me to have him."

"I didn't know about you," Kayla insisted. "Preston never even mentioned you."

"Liar!" Carrie practically shouted. "He loved me,

and he would have kept loving me if you hadn't gotten in the way. I should have been the one married to him."

"I wish you had been," Kayla mumbled.

Dade remembered the photos of Kayla's battered face and knew that was true. Carrie clearly had no idea of Preston's true nature.

"So, you're going to kill Kayla because Preston dumped you?" Dade pushed. He wasn't sure he'd get a sane answer, but he wanted to hear it anyway.

"Damn right," Carrie spat out. "I should have been Preston's wife, living with him in a fancy house. I should have had all that Brennan money. Not her. Well, now I'll have some of it, and I'll rid the world of this man-stealing witch who got in my way."

Dade couldn't believe the rage he was seeing and hearing, but he had to keep his own rage in check and get Kayla out of this. "How much did Brennan agree to pay you?" Dade asked Carrie. "Because I can match it."

"A million dollars." Now, Carrie smiled. "Is she worth that much to you, Dade?"

"Yes." And in that moment he knew that was completely true. Kayla was worth that and more.

She was worth everything.

And that included dying for her.

Even if he had to trade his life for hers, he was not going to leave Robbie an orphan.

"Yes?" Carrie challenged.

"Yes," Dade repeated. "I'll make the call and have the money sent anywhere you want. Better yet, I'll double Brennan's offer."

Carrie hesitated, and Dade said another prayer that she would jump at the chance for blood money. But then something flashed through her eyes.

Not just anger.

This was one step beyond that.

"You barely know her," Carrie spat out. "And you're willing to give up so much for her? The witch has brainwashed you. Just like she did Preston. Can't you see that?" She cursed, not waiting for his answer. "You've changed, Dade, and not for the better."

Dade disagreed with that. He had changed. He no longer felt like the bad boy of the Ryland clan. He was the man who was going to save Kayla's life.

"The money?" Dade reminded Carrie. "I'm offering you two million dollars." And he adjusted his feet so he would be able to move better.

"No deal," Carrie told him. "I'd rather have Charles's money."

"You mean you'd rather kill Kayla," Dade fired back.

"That, too."

When Carrie smiled, Dade knew he couldn't change her sick mind. Maybe if she thought she had Kayla out of the way, she would stand a chance with him. And maybe she just wanted him to suffer because things hadn't worked out between them.

Dade glanced at Kayla and gave her a look that he hoped she could interpret—brace yourself.

He lowered his head and launched himself forward.

KAYLA DIDN'T HAVE TIME to react.

One moment she was standing with Carrie's gun

jammed to her back, and the next moment Dade dived right into them.

All three of them went crashing to the floor.

Something rammed hard into Kayla, maybe it was Carrie's gun, but whatever it was, it knocked the breath right out of her. Not a good time for that to happen because she needed to help Dade get that gun. It wouldn't be long, maybe just seconds, before Grayson walked in with Robbie.

Gasping for air, Kayla managed to roll to the side, and she got a better look at the life-and-death struggle. The three of them were wound together, and her right arm was hooked between Dade and Carrie.

Thankfully, Dade had managed to get his hands on Carrie's arm, and he had a death grip on her. That was the only thing that prevented the woman from aiming the gun. Unfortunately, Carrie's finger was still on the trigger, and she made use of that.

She fired.

The blast echoed through the room and through Kayla.

It was deafening, probably because the gun was so close to her ear. Certainly someone downstairs had heard it and would come up to investigate. Kayla didn't know if that would be good or bad because it would be impossible for anyone to get off a clean shot.

Kayla tried to move away, to untangle herself, but Carrie must have noticed what was going on because the woman kicked Kayla right in the chest. Her breath was already in shreds, and that didn't help. But it did rile her to the core.

She couldn't let Carrie get away with this.

Kayla rammed her elbow into Carrie and used the leverage to force herself out of the mix. But Dade was there in it, his hands still locked around Carrie's wrist.

Another shot slammed into the ceiling.

Even though it didn't come close to Dade or her, Kayla couldn't risk a shot ricocheting off something and hitting Dade.

Frantically, she looked around the room for anything she could use as a weapon. The first thing she spotted was a heavy silver-framed photo of Dade and his brothers. Kayla snatched it from the counter and brought it down, hard, on Carrie's head.

Carrie made a sound of outrage and tried to turn the gun on Kayla.

Dade cursed and held on despite Carrie kicking any and every part of his body that she could reach. She also managed to get off another shot.

"What's going on in there?" Deputy Lopez yelled from the other side of the door.

"It's Carrie," Kayla shouted. She didn't know whether to tell the deputy to come in or stay put.

"To hell with this," Dade snarled, and he rammed his elbow across Carrie's chin.

The woman's head flopped back, but she didn't stop fighting.

Kayla could only watch in horror as Carrie managed to maneuver her body, twisting it, until she broke free of Dade's grip. For just a second. In that second, Dade grabbed at Carrie again, but Carrie's attention was focused only on Kayla.

"You're a dead woman," Carrie threatened. And she brought up the gun.

Just as Dade latched onto it and Carrie's hand.

He bashed both against the floor. But not in time. Carrie pulled the trigger again.

Kayla immediately knew something was wrong. The sound was different this time. Not so much of a blast but a deadly sounding thud. And she knew.

Someone had been shot.

"Dade!" Kayla yelled. She grabbed him by the shoulder and dragged him away from Carrie.

She saw the blood then.

So much blood.

And Kayla felt her heart stop. God, had she lost him? Had Carrie managed to kill Dade?

The timing was horrible, but the only thing that kept going through Kayla's head was that she hadn't gotten the chance to tell him that she loved him.

"Dade," Kayla said through a sob.

He turned his head and caught her gaze. "I'm okay," he assured her.

But Kayla shook her head and stared at the blood.

Dade climbed off Carrie, and in the same motion, he hooked his arm around Kayla to move her away from Carrie. But Kayla still saw the woman.

Lifeless, the front of her green scrubs soaked in blood.

Carrie still had a grip on the gun that she'd fired.

And when she fired that last bullet, she'd accidentally shot herself.

"It's over," she heard Dade say.

And he pulled Kayla into his arms.

Chapter Seventeen

"Are you sure this is okay?" Kayla asked—again.

Dade tried to give her a reassuring nod—again. It had only been two hours since Carrie had tried to kill them, and he figured Kayla would need a lot of reassuring until it was nothing but a bad memory. He took Robbie from the infant seat in the back of the cruiser. Robbie flashed Dade a big sloppy grin and babbled some sounds. Happy sounds. Unlike his mom, Robbie had no apprehensions about coming to the Ryland ranch.

"Da da da," Robbie babbled.

Dade knew he was just trying to say his name, but it melted his heart anyway.

"The ranch is big," Kayla commented as she stepped from the front passenger's seat. She looked up at the sprawling two-story redbrick house.

Dade took a moment to try to see the place through Kayla's eyes. Yeah, it was big and getting bigger. Three thousand acres, but Mason was constantly in "buy" mode when it came to adjoining land. And the house, well, it had gone through changes over the years, too.

"Grayson and Eve are having a new wing put on so they'll have more room for their baby," he let them know. He tipped his head to the addition that had already been framed. "Nate and Kimmie live in the left wing with Kimmie's nanny, Grace. I already called and talked to Grace, and she said she'd help out taking care of Robbie."

"That's kind of her," Kayla said softly.

Yeah, and it might become a necessity because Connie had decided that she needed a break. Dade couldn't blame the woman because she'd spent the last couple of days in danger, in hiding and on the run. Before that, she'd been in hiding with Kayla. Hardly the best employment situation.

Kayla's gaze went from the left wing to the porch that extended across the entire front of the main house. Unlike her estate, the ranch was homespun and didn't have a high-end decorator's touch.

"It's really beautiful," Kayla said, looking back at him. She smiled both at Dade and Robbie, but her smile couldn't hide her nerves. "But I probably should have gotten a room at the hotel while my place is being repaired. Especially because I don't think I'll be going back to the estate."

Dade stopped. This was the first he'd heard of this, and Kayla and he had spent the last couple of hours talking.

"Too many bad memories," she added.

He didn't doubt that, but he didn't like that Kayla was making plans that she hadn't talked about. Of course Dade had done the same.

Her attention drifted to the other vehicles in the drive. Mason's truck. Nate's Lexus. Grayson's SUV. "Your brothers are here."

"Yeah." Dade had made certain of that. It was part of the *plan*.

And that led him to his next thought.

This might be a mistake. A huge one. But sooner or later he wanted his family to meet Kayla and Robbie— *really* meet them—not with bullets flying or while neck-deep in an investigation. That investigation was over now. The danger, too. And it was time Kayla faced his brothers under normal circumstances.

Normal.

Finally.

It wasn't perfect, but they were getting there. No more threats to Kayla's life. No more Brennan. No more Carrie. Heck, Kayla had even managed to reconcile with her sister. Over the phone anyway. In a day or two Dade would see about getting them together face-to-face for a little mending time because they now knew that Misty hadn't had a hand in the attempts on Kayla's life.

"Kade, my youngest brother, is at work at the FBI office in San Antonio, but he'll be here later tonight," Dade let her know. "They won't bite," he whispered and nudged her onto the porch.

"Even Mason?" Kayla questioned.

Dade shrugged. "He'll behave." He hoped. With Mason you were never quite sure what you were going to get.

The front door flew open, and a silver-haired woman

came rushing out onto the porch. Kayla would have taken a step back if Dade hadn't caught onto her arm to anchor her in place.

"Kayla, Robbie, this is Bessie Watkins, the woman who takes care of us."

"I do at that. I cook, clean and give 'em you-know-what when they need it." Smiling from ear to ear, Bessie went straight to Robbie. "Now here's a handsome little angel."

Robbie approved of the compliment and gave her a grin.

Bessie scooped the baby right out of Dade's arms, kissed him on each cheek and then hugged Kayla. "Welcome to the Double R Ranch."

"Thank you," Kayla managed, but she still didn't sound comfortable.

"The others already had lunch," Bessie let them know. "But if you're hungry, there's plenty of roast beef and pecan pie left. And I'm fixing a big pot of chili for dinner."

Yeah, and Dade could smell it. Walking into the house was always like coming home for Christmas, and he would never take that for granted.

With Robbie cuddled in her arm, Bessie ushered them inside, past the foyer and into the massive family room. Again, no fancy stuff here. Hardwood floors, leather furniture and a floor-to-ceiling limestone fireplace with some log simmering in the hearth. The only artwork was family portraits and paintings of some of the ranch's prize-winning livestock.

To Kayla it must have been like walking into the lion's den.

There was a basketball game on TV, volume blaring, and Mason, with a beer in his hand, had claimed one of the oversize recliners. Nate was stretched out on the floor while Kimmie, his daughter, arranged little plastic horses on his stomach and chest. Grayson and Eve were on the sofa making out.

Well, kissing anyway.

"Newlyweds," Dade whispered to Kayla, and he cleared his throat so it would get their attention. It did. Everyone stopped, even Kimmie, and stared at Dade and their visitors.

For one bad moment, Dade thought this had been a mistake to spring Kayla on them and vice versa, but then Eve leaped off the sofa and hurried to them. Like Bessie, she gave Kayla a hug. Dade, too.

"Thanks," Dade told Eve, returning the hug. Eve might have been only his sister-in-law, but he loved her as much as he loved his brothers.

"Kayla and this handsome little angel are staying with us a few days," Bessie let them know.

She sat Robbie on the floor next to Kimmie, and the little girl—God bless her—immediately offered Robbie one of her toy ponies. There was only two months difference in their ages, with Kimmie being slightly older, but they were almost identical in size.

"Mason will get your bags from the car," Bessie insisted. "Won't you, Mason?"

Mason stared at them. And stared. Before he finally grumbled something and climbed out of the recliner.

"I'll help," Nate said, getting off the floor.

"The bags can wait," Dade insisted, and that drew everyone's attention back to him.

He swallowed hard. It was a do-or-die moment. And everything hinged on what happened in the next few minutes.

Dade took a deep breath and turned to Kayla. "I'm in love with you," he blurted out.

Other than the TV, the room went stone-cold silent. Even Robbie and Kimmie quit babbling.

"I didn't know," Dade continued, "until I saw Carrie holding that gun on you."

"Now, that's romantic," Mason snarled.

Dade shot him a scowl. So far, this wasn't going well. He could deal with Mason's snark, but Kayla's mouth was partially open, and she was staring at him.

A dozen things went through his head, none good. She was about to run for the hills. Or laugh. Or tell him that it was the adrenaline crash talking. After all, it'd been only a couple of hours since Carrie had tried to kill her.

Kayla caught onto his arm. "Uh, we should probably talk about this in private."

Dade held his ground. "I considered that, but I figured sooner or later, preferably sooner, I wanted my family to know how I feel about you."

She nodded. Got that deer-caught-in-the-headlights look. And nodded again. "Okay." She scrubbed her hands down the sides of her dress. "I'm in love with you, too."

That hit him like a sack of bricks.

Oh, he'd wanted the words, but he hadn't expected Kayla to admit it without some prompting. He also hadn't expected to feel this way after hearing those words come from her mouth.

Yeah, it was shocker. His knees were weak. His thoughts spinning a mile a minute. But most of all, Dade was over the moon.

"It's true?" he checked.

"Yes," she verified and cast another uncertain glance at his gob-smacked siblings.

That *yes* was enough for him. Dade put his arm around Kayla's waist and hauled her to him for a kiss. And not just a peck. He wanted this to be a kiss they would remember for the rest of their lives.

He caught the sound of her surprise with his kiss, and he moved into it, letting the taste of her slide right through him. Like hot whiskey. And sex.

Especially the sex.

But he tried to put that on hold for a moment even though the kiss was a reminder that he would like to drag her off to his bed and soon.

Someone cleared their throat—Bessie, he realized. "Why don't I take the little ones to the nursery?"

"In a minute." Dade figured he might as well go for broke. He looked at Bessie, Eve, his brothers and the babies. "I'm going to ask Kayla to marry me. I just want to make sure nobody has a problem with that."

More stares.

Except for Kayla.

She made another of those happy melting sounds of surprise and launched herself into his arms. Dade realized then that her response was the only one that mattered. And Robbie's, of course, but Dade and the little guy seemed to be on the same page because Robbie clapped his hands and babbled, "Da da da."

The baby was clearly a genius.

"I love you," Dade reminded her.

Kayla kissed him. Again, not a wuss kiss. This one had Mason growling, "Get a room, all right?"

Both Kayla and Dade were smiling when they finally broke the kiss. "And your answer to that marriage proposal?" Dade reminded her.

"Yes." No hesitation whatsoever, although she did cautiously eye the rest of the clan.

There it was again. The feeling that he'd just been hit hard and loved hard all in the same moment. Dade never considered himself a gushy kind of guy, but he suddenly felt like gushing.

"Well, it's about time you got a good woman in your life," Bessie declared. She hugged them both again.

So did Eve. "Welcome to the family," she told first Kayla, then Robbie.

Nate came next, and Dade knew this was a huge concession for his twin. Nate was still reeling from the news of Ellie's killer, but that didn't stop him from pulling Kayla into his arms.

"You'll be good for Dade," Nate whispered to her.

"He'll be good for me," Kayla whispered back.

And Dade hoped like the devil he didn't disgrace himself by getting misty-eyed.

Nate pulled something from his pocket. A silver Double R concho. "I picked it up from the parking lot," Nate explained. And he took Kayla's hand so he could put it in her palm. "I would give it to Dade, but he might throw it away again."

Dade just shook his head. Throwing it away just wasn't working because this was the second time it'd turned up. "Kayla can decide what to do with it," Dade let her know.

Her hand immediately closed around it. "Then, I'll keep it."

Eve pulled her neck chain from beneath her blouse to reveal her own concho. It was a gift Dade had given her for Christmas. "It makes me feel like part of the family."

"You are family," Dade clarified.

Eve smiled, brushed a kiss on his cheek. "Soon Kayla will be family. Robbie, too."

Grayson was waiting right behind Eve, and when she stepped to the side, his big brother was there to give Kayla his own welcoming hug. This was like the Ryland version of a receiving line.

"This family can always use some more females," Grayson teased. "And apparently another wing of living quarters." But his expression turned more serious when his gaze met hers. "Welcome to the family, Kayla."

Oh, man. That put some tears in her eyes. Eve's, too. This was going much better than Dade had expected, but then, this was his family. There was a lot of love in this room.

Then, Mason stepped forward. He didn't snag Kayla in his arms. He just stared at her. And stared.

"You could do better, Kayla," Mason told her. He lifted his shoulder. "But not much."

Coming from Mason, that was a warm fuzzy welcome, and much to Dade's surprise, Kayla leaned in and kissed Mason on the cheek. Dade couldn't be sure, but he thought Mason might have actually blushed. It was hard to tell under those multiple layers of stubble.

"I'll get the bags," Mason said, strolling out. Nate was right behind him.

Eve scooped up Kimmie. Grayson took Robbie. "We'll show Robbie the nursery. It's like a toy store in there."

"And I'll check on dinner," Bessie piped in, following the others out.

Dade knew it was a ploy to give Kayla and him some alone time, and he was thankful for it. He didn't waste even a second before he pulled Kayla to him and kissed her.

"Marry me?" he said against her mouth.

"I've already said yes."

"Yeah, but I wanted to hear it again."

Kayla smiled, and he caught that smile with another kiss. "Yes," she repeated. But then she pulled back, blinked. "Are you sure about this?"

He didn't blink, but he did frown. "You're not sure?"

"No, I'm positive. I love you. I *really* love you. But I have so much baggage with a bad marriage under my belt."

"Then it's time you had a good marriage. To me," he clarified, causing her to smile. "Because I *really* love you, too."

But again, her smile faded. Because there was nothing she could say or do that would make him change his mind, Dade decided to end her doubts with another kiss.

He backed her against the wall, next to the portraits of his family, and he put his mouth to hers. Dade didn't stop there. He pressed his body against hers, until there wasn't a sliver of space between them. And he kept kissing her until he heard that sigh. That little sound of surrender and pleasure. Kayla melted against him.

"Well?" he challenged. "Got any doubts now?"

Kayla eased back, her chest pumping for air, her heart racing. "None. I love you, Dade Ryland, and more than my next breath, I want to be your wife."

Good. That's exactly what he wanted, too.

Dade smiled and pulled her back to him for another kiss. "Welcome home, Kayla."

* * * * *

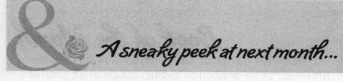

A sneaky peek at next month...

INTRIGUE...

BREATHTAKING ROMANTIC SUSPENSE

My wish list for next month's titles...

In stores from 18th January 2013:

☐ Nate – Delores Fossen

& Kade – Delores Fossen

☐ Flash of Death – Cindy Dees

& The Vanishing – Jana DeLeon

☐ Rancher's Deadly Risk – Rachel Lee

& No Escape – Meredith Fletcher

☐ Colton's Ranch Refuge – Beth Cornelison

Available at WHSmith, Tesco, Asda, Eason, Amazon and Apple

Just can't wait?

Visit us Online

You can buy our books online a month before they hit the shops! **www.millsandboon.co.uk**

0113/46

Book of the Month

MILLS & BOON

Medical Romance

SCARLET WILSON
An Inescapable
Temptation

BOOK OF THE MONTH

We love this book because...

Nurse Francesca Cruz takes a job on a cruise ship bound for the Mediterranean and finds herself trapped with gorgeous, arrogant doctor Gabriel Russo! Unable to escape temptation, the tension between these two reaches fever pitch and will have you longing for a cooling dip in the ocean!

On sale 1st February

Visit us Online

Find out more at
www.millsandboon.co.uk/BOTM

0113/BOTM

Special Offers

Every month we put together collections and longer reads written by your favourite authors.

Here are some of next month's highlights— and don't miss our fabulous discount online!

On sale 18th January

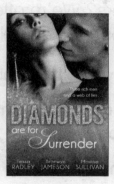

On sale 1st February

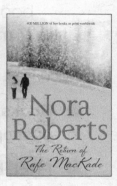

On sale 1st February

Save 20% on all Special Releases

Find out more at
www.millsandboon.co.uk/specialreleases

Visit us Online

0213/ST/MB399

2 Free Books!

Join the Mills & Boon Book Club

Want to read more **Intrigue** books? We're offering you **2 more** absolutely **FREE!**

We'll also treat you to these fabulous extras:

- 🌹 **Books up to 2 months ahead of shops**

- 🌹 **FREE home delivery**

- 🌹 **Bonus books with our special rewards scheme**

- 🌹 **Exclusive offers and much more!**

Get your free books now!

Visit us Online

Find out more at
www.millsandboon.co.uk/freebookoffer

SUBS/ONLINE/I

Mills & Boon® Online

Discover more romance at
www.millsandboon.co.uk

- 🌹 **FREE** online reads

- 🌹 **Books** up to one
  month before shops

- 🌹 **Browse our books**
  before you buy

  ...and much more!

For exclusive competitions and instant updates:

 Like us on **facebook.com/romancehq**

 Follow us on **twitter.com/millsandboonuk**

 Join us on **community.millsandboon.co.uk**

Visit us Online   Sign up for our FREE eNewsletter at
www.millsandboon.co.uk

WEB/M&B/RTL4

The World of Mills & Boon®

There's a Mills & Boon® series that's perfect for you. We publish ten series and, with new titles every month, you never have to wait long for your favourite to come along.

Blaze®
Scorching hot, sexy reads
4 new stories every month

By Request
Relive the romance with the best of the best
9 new stories every month

Cherish™
Romance to melt the heart every time
12 new stories every month

Desire™
Passionate and dramatic love stories
8 new stories every month

Visit us Online
Try something new with our Book Club offer
www.millsandboon.co.uk/freebookoffer

M&B/WORLD2

What will you treat yourself to next?

Ignite your imagination, step into the past...
6 new stories every month

INTRIGUE...

Breathtaking romantic suspense
Up to 8 new stories every month

Medical Romance

Captivating medical drama – with heart
6 new stories every month

MODERN™

International affairs, seduction & passion guaranteed
9 new stories every month

nocturne™

Deliciously wicked paranormal romance
Up to 4 new stories every month

RIVA™

Live life to the full – give in to temptation
3 new stories every month available exclusively via our Book Club

You can also buy Mills & Boon eBooks at
www.millsandboon.co.uk

Visit us Online

M&B/WORLD2